PRAISE FOR *HEART ON A LEASH*

"An effortlessly charming debut! *Heart on a Leash* gives us great comedy in the form of feuding-family shenanigans, along with swoony romance . . . and huskies. What more could you want? This is an engrossing read that will take you on a trip to small-town Alaska and make you fall in love."

—Jen DeLuca, author of *Well Played*

"*Heart on a Leash* had my heart from page one. . . . Whether you're a dog lover, cat lover, or romance lover, you're sure to fall head over heels for this book."

—Sarah Smith, author of *Simmer Down*

"With two charming leads, three irresistible pups, and a small town unlike any I've read before, *Heart on a Leash* tugged at my emotions and warmed my soul. The perfect book to snuggle up with and savor."

—Rachel Lynn Solomon, author of *The Ex Talk*

"A small-town romance that defies cliché. Complex family rivalries, swoon-worthy romance, and (of course!) adorable dogs make this a heart-melting love story."

—Michelle Hazen, author of *Breathe the Sky*

"A heartwarming contemporary romance that puts a new spin on the enemies-to-lovers trope, *Heart on a Leash* takes us on an insightful journey of falling in love without the support of family. Sexy and sensitive, the undeniable chemistry between the heroine and hero (and a pack of adorable huskies) drive the story to its charming conclusion—tail wags and HEA included."

—Samantha Vérant, author of *The Secret French Recipes of Sophie Valroux*

HEART ON A LEASH

Alanna Martin

JOVE
New York

A JOVE BOOK
Published by Berkley
An imprint of Penguin Random House LLC
penguinrandomhouse.com

ISBN: 9780593198834

First Edition: April 2021

Printed in the United States of America
1   3   5   7   9   10   8   6   4   2

Cover design by Farjana Yasmin
Book design by Alison Cnockaert

To those who dare to love when others choose to hate.

1

IN RETROSPECT, TAYLOR Lipin would consider the termite chilling on her toothbrush to be an omen. At six thirty in the morning, however, it was simply disgusting. She screamed, flung the toothbrush into the trash, and retrieved the spare she'd had the foresight to stash in her bathroom cabinet. Five minutes later, standing under the hot shower spray, she took heart in the knowledge that her day was unlikely to get any worse.

By the time she stopped at the coffee shop near her office to meet her best friend, she'd mostly put the termite out of her head. Stacy had texted to say she was running late, so Taylor ordered for both of them and stepped aside as she waited for their prework caffeine infusions to be prepared. The shop smelled wonderful, a blend of coffee, sugar, and vanilla that set Taylor up for disappointment each weekday morning. In a city filled with coffee shops, she'd yet to find one that could make her favorite drink as well as the place in her hometown. Likely it had nothing to do with the quality of the beans or the baristas and everything to do with nostalgia, but that was life.

A new text arrived before either Stacy or the coffee, and Taylor read it, expecting a second update from her friend. Instead it was from her sister, and that was when Taylor recalled both the termite and that old saying about what happens when you make assumptions.

Emergency. About Mom. Call me soon.

The chaotic chatter of dozens of voices, the hiss of the espresso machine, the barely audible beat from whatever song was being pumped through the shop's speakers—it all dissolved beneath the thudding of Taylor's heart as she read the message a second time. Cool, unflappable Lydia was not prone to hysterics.

Was it a heart attack? Cancer? A bad fall?

"Taylor L.?" The barista calling her name snapped her out of the endless stream of morose questions.

Taylor took a deep, steadying breath. If her mother was in imminent danger, surely Lydia would have called. That would be sensible, and her older sister was nothing if not sensible and dutiful. Therefore, Taylor wouldn't panic, and she'd take a sip of her coffee before calling. God knew, she'd probably need the caffeine.

Since there was still no sign of Stacy, Taylor carried the drinks over to a slightly quieter corner near the entrance and dialed Lydia.

Her sister picked up on the second ring, leaving the caffeine with no time to work its magic. "Taylor?"

For someone who'd sent a text declaring an emergency only a minute ago, her sister seemed awfully surprised to hear from her. But Taylor was too concerned to point that out. "What happened?"

"You actually called. I was hoping to catch you before work, but I didn't expect that."

Lydia's incredulity required her to take another sip of her drink. "You said it's an emergency. Of course I called. What's wrong?"

Lydia seemed to collect herself, and her voice returned to normal. "Mom took off."

"What do you mean *took off*? That's not a euphemism, is it?"

"What? No. She got in the car and drove. To Anchorage, I think. They're getting divorced."

For a second, Taylor thought she must have heard her sister incorrectly. Mom and Dad divorced—no, it didn't make sense. Then her sister's words sank in, and confusion warred with relief. So her mother was fine, but her mother was also clearly not fine because a fine mother wouldn't be asking for a divorce. Taylor felt like the universe had slapped her. "They've been married for almost thirty-five years. This is impossible. They're so happy."

She'd thought they were anyway. Lydia's tone, hinting at her lack of calls home, wasn't entirely unwarranted, but her parents had always seemed happy when she did call or during the one or two times a year when she visited.

She wasn't the only one confused, though, which made Taylor feel better. "I know. I'm blindsided."

Taylor glanced toward the door as a fresh wave of people entered the shop, but still no Stacy. "How's Dad handling it?"

Lydia made a strangled noise. "He's acting indifferent. He's more worried about how this will affect his reelection."

That made as little sense to Taylor as any of this news did. Sure, her father was as poised and reserved as Lydia, but he should show some emotion. Worrying about his next election had to be a way to deflect the pain. Divorce hadn't been a scandalous sort of thing in decades, and everyone in her hometown knew her dad. Their opinions were unlikely to be swayed at this point. "Maybe he's in shock."

"Maybe, but this was two days ago."

"Hold on. This happened two days ago and you waited to tell me until now?"

"I wasn't sure how you'd take it." Lydia didn't sound the least bit apologetic.

"So you were concerned about my reaction, and therefore decided to send me a vague and alarming text at eight in the morning? Two days!"

That finally put her sister on the defensive. "Well, if you came home for more than just Christmas, I might assume you cared more. When Mom first left, I figured everything would eventually blow over so there was no point in worrying you. You could go on being blissfully ignorant of our lives."

"That's low." Taylor squeezed her coffee cup so hard the plastic lid popped off, and her restless fingers fumbled as she set it on the table. "I don't get a lot of vacation time."

Lydia sighed. "I'm sorry. I'm just stressed out. Can you come home for a week or two? I could use some help."

Taylor was sympathetic. Part of her wanted nothing more than to do exactly that. Run home, hug her dad, and fret over every detail with Lydia while they consumed questionable quantities of chocolate and wine. She wanted family and security, but home for her was currently Los Angeles, and the rosy haze of her childhood memories had been ripped away with this call. Changing the state she was in wouldn't change the facts.

"Remember the part about me not getting a lot of vacation time?" Taylor ran a distracted hand through her hair. "My company was bought out last week, and things are unstable at the moment. I'm not sure I could get the time off approved. I'll call Mom and Dad and offer my support, and we can talk more later."

"*They* don't need your support. They seem to be doing just fine. *I* need your support, but I need it here. To help out with the inn."

The Bay Song Inn was the boutique hotel her grandparents had opened back when their small town was first becoming a tourist destination in the late seventies. When her grandparents had decided to retire twenty years later, her parents took over the inn, but her father had mostly left running it to her mother and Lydia as he became more involved in town management.

"You expect me to abandon my job to help with yours?" She understood her sister was in a bind, and the family business was obviously important, but Lydia was being completely unreasonable. Or so Taylor's only partially caffeinated brain was telling her.

"Look, I wouldn't ask if it wasn't serious. When Mom left, I thought it was simply to find a lawyer, but it's been two days, and she's returning my calls with one-line texts telling me not to worry. As if that's possible. I checked her closet and she must have packed at least a week's worth of clothes. I can't handle the business side of the inn and the hospitality side at the same time. I don't care what kind of midlife crisis she's having; Mom's timing is awful. Tourist season has begun. We're booked solid every week through August, and with weddings most weekends."

"That's . . . wow. That's amazing. Grandmother must be thrilled."

"She is, but that's assuming everything doesn't go to hell because I can't handle the work by myself. Since *Travel and Leisure* named us one of the ten best places to get married in Alaska last year, it's been unbelievable. And I will not be the person who lets the inn get run into the ground."

That honor was almost solely due to Lydia's efforts, Taylor was certain, and she didn't doubt her sister's commitment to the business. "Can't you hire someone?"

"I would have if I'd known Mom was going to go AWOL, but like I said, tourist season has already begun. No one's available, especially no one who knows the job like you do. Even if I could beg someone I trust to help out part-time, I'd have to train them. Tay, I need you."

Taylor grimaced. Now she understood the real "emergency" from Lydia's text. She did have a pretty good idea of what the job entailed, and it was precisely what she'd never wanted to do.

Ever since she was little, Taylor had been determined that—in her six-year-old self's words—she was going to be a "business lady." Little Taylor had devoted countless hours to making her Barbie dolls into perfect "business ladies," which had mainly meant they wore stylish clothes, worked in tall buildings, and bossed people around. Her understanding had expanded as she grew older, but her desire to leave home and work someplace with tall buildings and stylish clothes had not. Taylor had taken off to Southern California for college and never turned back.

It was true that sometimes she wondered if she was still chasing an ephemeral ideal, because working in marketing had not lived up to her childhood expectations. And it was also true that sometimes, more frequently in recent years, she'd started wondering if she should have left childhood ideals in childhood and chosen a field that didn't make her feel like her soul was being crushed on a daily basis.

But it was just as true that returning home and working at the inn remained on her list of Things to Consider Only before Selling Off Internal Organs. But even then, it might depend on which organ. No one needed two kidneys.

Lydia was still speaking, and Taylor caught the end of her last sentence. ". . . to help shut down the gossip too."

"What gossip?"

"The usual. Mostly people speculating about affairs and garbage like that. All instigated by the Porters, I'm sure."

Taylor snorted. Possibly living so long in L.A. had changed her perception about such things. "Can anyone back home actually have an affair without everyone else knowing about it?"

"Dan Fidel, the high school principal, carried on with a third-grade teacher for two years before his wife found out. So yes. But that's not the point. The Porters are spreading lies, and rumor is Wallace is considering running against Dad for mayor. They've been looking for ways to cut us down since the article. We can't afford to let them see us struggle. This is about family, however fractured we currently are."

With her free hand, Taylor poked at the foam on her coffee. Sure, it was only eight in the morning, but she might need something stronger to drink if this was turning into a Lipin-Porter battle on top of a regular family disaster. Unfortunately, she could easily believe the Porters would try to take advantage of her family's situation. After the Bay Song's write-up, they'd started a whisper campaign that the hotel had only gotten such a glowing recommendation because her family had bribed the writer. Or, depending on which Porter was talking, because Lydia had slept with the guy.

It was easy for Taylor to roll her eyes from the California coast, but back home, the nastiness was something her family had to deal with on a daily basis. It was also another reason Taylor had been eager to leave.

The coffee shop's door opened, and this time Stacy entered, along with a whiff of exhaust from the delivery truck idling outside. Her friend waved and began worming her way through the crowd.

"We can talk more about this later," Taylor said. "I need to go."

"Fine. Will you think about what I said? Please."

"Promise." It was an easy one to make. Taylor doubted she could do anything else.

"Are you all right?" Stacy asked. "Sorry I was late. My alarm didn't go off, but you look more stressed than I feel."

"My parents are getting divorced." Taylor filled Stacy in, leaving out the part about her sister's gossip worries, her father's election concerns, and why the Porters would make everything worse. Explaining the ridiculous century-old feud would take more energy than she had.

As soon as they stepped outside, Taylor regretted not getting an iced coffee. On a day when the temperature threatened to hit the nineties, there was a lot she missed about living three thousand miles to the north, not that she would ever admit it.

Her hometown was hardly the frozen wasteland conjured up by most people's visions of Alaska, but even though temperatures could creep into the seventies in the summer, it rarely got as hot as L.A. was half the time, and there was always a salty breeze blowing off the bay. On days like these, she missed that scent, which had been replaced by the stench of exhaust and smoldering concrete. She also missed the harbor and watching the boats as they bobbed on the water, and she missed looking out her window and stretching her neck to see to the tops of mountain peaks that seemed to vanish into the sky. She didn't miss tourist season, when the town swelled to bursting like an overripe grape, but L.A. was a tourist town year-round. The city had its own charms, and palm trees were pretty, but it was a world away from Helen, Alaska.

"You should go home and help her," Stacy said. "Even if it's only for the emotional support. Family is family. Lizzy Fernandez worked remotely when she had to go to Phoenix for her grandmother's funeral. You should ask. I mean, assuming you can work from Alaska as easily as here. Can you?"

Desperate for the air-conditioning, Taylor breezed past her to head inside. "Depends on what exactly my sister expects me to do."

"I just meant, like, will you have an internet connection?"

Taylor blinked at her and then, despite everything, burst out laughing. "Um, yes. We have the internet in Helen. It's not as speedy as it is here, but it's sufficient. We also have this newfangled electricity stuff and running water. It's pretty civilized. Even the bears sometimes wander into town to check their voice mail."

Stacy's cheeks turned pink, and she laughed too. "Shut up! I wasn't sure. But wait, do bears really wander into town a lot?" Her eyes grew as round as cartoon orbs.

Yes, bears did occasionally wander into town, but not as often as Stacy seemed to be thinking. Since her friend's reaction amused her, and goodness knew she needed the laugh, Taylor opted to merely smile and let Stacy wonder.

She wondered too—about whether working remotely was feasible. Trying to balance her regular job with helping out Lydia sounded like hell. More to the point, since the merger, she wasn't sure that would be an option, but she supposed she could look into it.

Taylor's smile lasted approximately ten minutes longer, at which point the ominous termite on her toothbrush and her phone call with her sister collided in a perfect storm that would have had her laughing hysterically if panic hadn't seemed like the smarter choice.

The storm arrived in two emails. The first came from the large, impersonal management corporation that had bought out her apartment building last year. They'd been making tons of updates to the building since, and while that was nice in theory, Taylor often felt like she was living in a construction zone with all the resultant noise. But the email did not contain a notice about more repairs. Rather, this was a notice that the builders had found massive termite damage. An exterminator had been contacted, and they'd be fumigating soon. She had to leave for a minimum of three days.

Super. That seemed like a good reason to ask about working remotely. But then the second email arrived, this one from her boss, who was calling a division-wide, mandatory meeting. Taylor knew that couldn't bode well, and sure enough, when she left the meeting twenty minutes later, working remotely was an issue she no longer needed to worry about.

The company's new owners had just laid off her entire division.

Taylor walked out of the meeting, clutching the coffee

that was a poor imitation of her hometown's finest, and sat on the edge of her desk. She was dazed from one too many blows in a short period, concerned about her bank account, and really ruing her morning optimism about the termite on her toothbrush.

"As an upside, I guess you can go help your sister," Stacy said, smiling glumly.

"I suppose so." She raised her coffee cup. "To unemployment."

Stacy tapped Taylor's cup with her own. "To days hunting for jobs while lying on the beach."

That sounded a whole lot better than what Taylor anticipated. Lydia would be thrilled, but no matter what she tried telling herself about nicer weather, sisterly bonding, or her favorite coffee, Taylor couldn't help but feel like she was planning to leave behind a perfect storm for a category five hometown hurricane.

2

JOSHUA KRANE WAS an hour late leaving work, and Jay, Pepper, and Bella were displeased. The huskies paced in the hospital's accounting office behind Elise's chair as though they'd been neglected all day.

"Drama queens. The lot of you." He knew for a fact the medical billing specialist had taken all three on an extra walk this afternoon.

"Yes, they are," Elise confirmed. "You'd think they weren't getting showered with attention all day. Like anyone can resist those faces."

Belatedly, Josh realized he was still wearing his stethoscope, and he stuffed it into his backpack rather than return to his office and make the dogs wait any longer. As was true for Elise, he also had a hard time resisting those faces and the way Jay's tail in particular wagged with such enthusiasm.

"Yes, I'm sorry it was a long day." He scratched each dog's head, being sure not to show favoritism as he attached their leashes. As the eldest, Bella was laid back, but Jay and Pepper had been locked in a struggle for attention since they'd come into Josh's life. If Pepper was getting pets, Jay demanded them too. If Jay had curled up next to him, Pepper would jump on her brother and try pushing him out of the way. It would have been funnier if they each didn't weigh over forty pounds. "Has it calmed down out there?"

"For the moment, so you should probably leave before someone else tries to blow himself up."

Although Elise wasn't wrong. If someone did try it, he'd get hauled back to deal with it since he was on call overnight. He'd been about to leave earlier, when two emergencies tumbled through the hospital's door at the same time. First was Tommy, a local ten-year-old who'd hit a rock while riding his bike and was brought in bleeding and likely with several broken bones. Then came a tourist who'd done something untoward while hooking up a propane tank and had proceeded to set his right arm on fire. Hence Elise's comment.

Josh's specialty was internal medicine, not emergency medicine, but like with so many rural hospitals, Helen Regional Hospital couldn't attract enough specialists to keep the ER open twenty-four hours a day without assistance. When he'd agreed to the job here, he'd agreed to extra training as well so he could spend one ER shift per week patching people back together. Today wasn't supposed to have been one of those days, but life—and emergencies—happened, so Josh had handled the tourist while the regular emergency doctor helped Tommy. Lucky for the tourist, the burns had only been second degree, and after bandaging him, Josh had sent the man back to his RV with the suggestion that he stick to real charcoal for his grilling needs. The food tasted better that way too.

After ten hours spent mostly cooped up inside the

clinic, he was as eager as the dogs were to leave and get some exercise. It was funny how exercise seemed to beget the need for more exercise. A few years ago, Josh would have laughed at the idea that after a long shift he'd want to go for a walk, but then he'd moved to Helen and his cousin had given him dogs. Three highly energetic dogs, to be exact.

Jay—given name Jewel, which Josh refused to call him because it was an awful name for a dog—had been one of Kelsey's adoptees. Or intended adoptees. While she was acerbic when it came to humans, Kelsey had a weakness for adopting rescues, particularly older ones who were less likely to be wanted. It was something of a family tradition, aided and abetted by their grandmother who volunteered for a husky rescue organization.

Kelsey currently had three huskies, too, all from the same litter, and had intended to add Jay to her family. But one of her dogs—appropriately named Romeo—had attachment issues, and he hadn't taken well to the four-legged addition. Kelsey had tried to integrate Jay but eventually decided it wasn't going to work.

On Josh's first day arriving in Helen, Kelsey had shown up at his door with three of the prettiest dogs Josh had ever seen. "I brought you a welcome present. It was only supposed to be two, but today's your lucky day. Adopt two dogs, get one free."

"Now that I have a house, I was going to adopt a dog, Kels. But adopt *a* dog, as in one."

She'd snorted. "Like Grandpa always said, you can't have too many dogs or too much whiskey."

"Grandpa died from liver failure when he was fifty-nine. His advice should be considered suspect at best."

"Fine. Skip the whiskey, keep the dogs."

Josh had wanted to be annoyed, but Jay, Pepper, and

Bella had sniffed him a few times, circled the boxes waiting to be unpacked in his living room, and gazed up at him adoringly like they now owned the place, and Josh knew he wasn't going to hand his cousin back the leashes.

"What am I supposed to do with three dogs while I'm at work?" he'd asked, utterly bewildered. "I was going to ask if you could dog-sit for me, but I guess that's not possible if Romeo doesn't get along with them. Don't huskies need lots of exercise?"

"And companionship." Kelsey nodded, knowing she'd won this battle of wits. "Take them with you."

"It's a medical clinic. I can't have a dog there, never mind three." Except, apparently, he could. He was no longer in a big-city hospital, but a small one where the back-office staff were only too happy to dog-sit while Josh was with patients. The huskies got several walks a day from them and all the pets a dog could hope for.

As for Josh, not only did he suddenly have three canine personal trainers to keep him in shape, he had an instant way to meet people. Although, to be fair, he would have had that anyway. His uncle's family, which included Kelsey, was well-established in Helen. While Josh didn't immediately benefit from having Porter as a surname, once his relationship to them was understood, he was considered almost as good as a local. As an air force brat, Josh had lived in his share of places growing up, and he knew how unwelcoming small towns could sometimes be to outsiders, so that was no small benefit. In fact, it had become a bit of a joke that his older patients had only transferred their care to him so they could check in on his mother.

Josh never told them that his mother thought her family was absurd, or that she'd warned him about taking the job in Helen and the risk of getting caught up in the Porter family feud. He'd assumed his mother was exaggerating. After all, he'd been here for fourteen months, and he hadn't seen anything to raise his eyebrows. Sure, Porter and Lipin kids played pranks on each other, and there were Lipin-owned restaurants and shops that he'd been told by his family to avoid. But Josh had seen nothing like the stories his mother had told him from her childhood, where even elementary school PTA meetings were an excuse for fistfights.

That was for the best, especially as he was only in his second year of a five-year loan forgiveness program for working in a rural hospital, and he was counting on that debt being wiped out. Medical school was expensive, living in Alaska was expensive, and rural doctors did not make the same sort of money big-city specialists did. The program alone hadn't been what had enticed Josh to move to Helen, but it had certainly made the decision easier.

It was a perfect day for the last week of May, lightly overcast and in the upper fifties, and the park Josh headed toward was packed with locals and tourists alike, walking dogs, eating ice cream from the stand at the western edge, or simply gazing at the boats coming and going from the harbor. One medium-size cruise ship had arrived this morning, and Josh could see people in the distance swarming around the docks. In another week or two, the town's population would grow by a third, and the dock district, filled with the majority of the town's restaurants and hotels, as well as the galleries and artisan shops, would be impossible to navigate a car through without cursing.

If anything, it was days like this that had truly sold Josh on Helen. With the bay on one side, and the mountains surrounding it from another, it felt like the earth enveloped the town in a glorious hug. As a bonus, the water insulated the inhabitants from the worst of winter. It still got cold enough for winter sports—it was Alaska, after all—but for a guy who disliked the heat and loved the outdoors, Helen was basically geographic perfection.

Above, a flag whipped about in the wind, and at Josh's feet, the huskies struggled against their leashes. They'd seen Kelsey making her way over with Romeo, Juliet, and the littlest one, Puck. They frequently met after Josh's shift ended. Kelsey did freelancing and ghostwriting, and she often bemoaned the lack of human contact. Josh, having the distinct honor of being one of the few humans she could tolerate, had become her outlet. Before him, it had been her twin brother, Kevin, but he had started dating someone, which meant he saw his sister less. A circumstance that Josh suspected bothered Kelsey, though she tried to hide it.

"We're getting a brewery," Kelsey said by way of greeting. "Or a brewpub. One or the other, or maybe both. Is there a difference actually?"

"Where?"

"That old building on the western end of town." They started down the flower-lined path leading toward the bay. As petite as Kelsey was, the huskies appeared to be dragging her along, but Josh knew she had them well under control. "That's what's been going on over there since spring. And get this, the guy who's opening it? He's from Florida."

"That might explain why no one's seen him much. He probably locked himself inside and is refusing to come out." The extreme south was just one of the many locations Josh had lived growing up. While he'd liked exploring new towns, he missed the snow and sledding, and the one time he'd found a bug the size of his hand crawling on his pillow in South Carolina was rather traumatic.

Kelsey shook her head. "It's mad, and this town is being overrun by outsiders."

Josh declined to point out that he was an outsider who'd contributed to the town's growth by moving here recently. "This town only survives because people like to come here and spend money. Besides, maybe the beer will be good."

She grunted. "I don't like beer."

"Also, isn't your father the one who sold that building?"

Kelsey narrowed her big blue eyes, which, combined with her blond ringlets, made her look like a seriously pissed-off cherub. But only fools who didn't know better mistook Kelsey for angelic. Even his aunt claimed the twins had been born fighting like a couple of hellhounds. "Yes, my father would sell off the town to the Lipins if he thought it would make him a profit. We don't see eye to eye on that, for sure."

In a way, it was ironic. Kelsey's parents were extremely well off thanks to her maternal grandparents, who'd made a fortune in the oil business. His aunt and uncle had been using some of the money they'd been gifted to buy up pieces of Helen and sell them off at huge profits. The case for and against additional development was a looming political battle, with the town evenly divided.

"It kills me to secretly be siding with Greg Lipin on this," Kelsey said, "but we do not need to keep expanding."

"Has the mayor formally come out against more development?"

"Depends on who you ask, but it's shaping up to be an

issue for the next election if my dad decides to run. He's got an opening now. You heard about what happened?"

They fell silent for a minute as a couple of kids ran up and asked if they could pet the dogs. Kelsey knelt and held the slightly twitchy Romeo while the other huskies basked in the adoration. The breeze blew hair in Josh's face, and a couple walked by talking about the salmon they wanted to bring home. His stomach rumbled. Both he and his four-legged children needed their dinner soon.

"So what happened?" Josh asked as they started their walk again.

"Oh, right." Kelsey perked up. "The Lipins are getting divorced. Apparently she just up and left for Anchorage the other day. Dumped his ass."

There was no need to ask which Lipins, although there were several in town. If Kelsey had meant anyone other than the most prominent family members, she'd have specified.

Josh winced. "That's awful."

"Right?" Kelsey sounded positively gleeful. "But the question is why? My dad's betting that it's because Greg was having an affair, but I'm personally hoping Denise was having the affair and left to be with her lover. Either way, it should be fun to watch the drama unfold."

His mother's distaste for the Porter-Lipin feud came back to Josh with a twist of his stomach. Kelsey seemed to be courting the drama, even relishing it. Josh didn't understand, but then, he didn't understand any of it. The two families had been arguing since long before he was born.

Although he was no amateur historian, from what Josh could tell, the feud had started in 1909 when William Porter accused Anton Lipin of stealing one of his dogs. Lipin had denied it, a brawl broke out, and what happened after that was hazy given the lack of good public records. The law had certainly gotten involved, and it apparently had rendered a verdict neither side was happy with. After that, depending on whom Josh listened to, the Lipins had retaliated by either cheating his family out of land or cursing a generation of Porter women to barrenness. What was never in dispute was that, to this day, the Lipins were liars, thieves, and quite possibly witches.

Josh had to wonder if his family's habit of collecting dogs had something to do with the feud. A way of rubbing an old wound in the Lipins' collective face perhaps. Previously he would have assumed people who loved dogs couldn't be willing to do terrible things to other humans, but the PTA fistfight rumor had proven true enough. Good old Grandma Porter had taken a swing at some Lipin woman while arguing about a bake sale.

Josh supposed he shouldn't have been surprised. Kelsey must have inherited her bloodthirsty streak from someone.

"I don't see what's fun about watching people be hurt," he said.

Kelsey sighed. "It's the Lipins. I realize you're a doctor, but come on, Josh. They're cat people. What else do you need to know?"

Josh considered this news in light of his recent theory about his family's dog obsession. "Shouldn't animal lovers stick together?"

"Cat people are aloof and snobbish, exactly like the Lipins. It's their nature. We dog people are open, generous, and friendly. So no."

Josh couldn't help but laugh. "If I called you open and friendly, you'd punch me. Don't deny it. Anyway, it's absurd. Leave me out of the gossip."

After a childhood of upheaval, all he wanted was peace. It was yet another benefit of taking a job here after his last relationship disintegrated. Helen was a comparably small town. He could treat small problems.

It was the opposite of what his ex had wanted, which was to move somewhere she deemed exciting. She'd called him risk averse like it was an insult, but Josh didn't see it that way. He saw it as wise. So he wasn't a risk taker, or perhaps he'd never found anything in life worth risking a lot for. Aside from the constant moving around as a kid, he'd had to live with the anxiety of knowing his father might one day leave and never return. He would take stability over daring any day, please and thank you.

All of which was a long way of saying there was no way he was getting sucked into a family feud.

"You're a part of the family," Kelsey said ominously. "Don't think you're going to be able to avoid it."

At first, Josh thought she was talking about the feud in general. Then he realized she meant the gossip.

At least, he hoped she just meant the gossip.

3

◇━━━━━━━━━◇

KELSEY TOOK OFF a few minutes later, leaving Josh with a definite sense of unease. He knew she and her brother could be vicious when provoked, and his family had spoken derisively of the Lipins and their luxury hotel for as long as he could remember. Although the fact that his other uncle owned a B and B probably had something to do with that professional rivalry. But aside from snide comments, no one had said or done much to penetrate his consciousness on the topic. He'd laughed off his mother's long-suffering tales of family wars as nothing more than embellished memories, a product of the way children overly dramatize everything around them.

Now, he wondered.

When his uncle's B and B had suffered a fire a few years ago that destroyed an outbuilding, his family had blamed the Lipins, despite the fire inspector never being able to officially conclude it was arson, and there had been accusations of sabotage to fishing and cruising vessels on both sides going back decades. Josh also knew a town the size of Helen didn't need two weekly newspapers, but it had them. Not because there were enough local happenings to fill even one, but because the Lipins had started their own as way to fight back against the so-called libel printed in the one Josh's great-aunt had started. And although he didn't entirely trust his family historians, it was true that mysterious deaths had plagued both families in the early 1910s after the dog-stealing accusation, fists, and denials had flown. As a doctor, however, Josh wasn't about to rule out perfectly natural medical reasons for any of them, particularly when the official records were so spotty.

He had half a mind to call his mother and ask questions when he got home, but likely he was the one doing the overdramatizing this time. It had been a long day, he was hungry, and he was reading more malice into Kelsey's tone than existed. She was just enjoying gossip the way most of the world enjoyed gossip, particularly about people they didn't like. Even if his uncle did decide to challenge Gregory Lipin in the mayoral race, it wasn't like Josh would have to get involved. As a physician with a duty to treat everyone who needed care, he had good reason to claim neutrality.

"All right, guy and girls," Josh said, tucking away his phone after checking the time. "What do we do for dinner?"

Jay, most unhelpfully, barked with excitement. All the dogs recognized the D word and wanted some too.

"Was that pizza? Yeah, I agree. Best not to cook tonight. I'm too tired." Honestly, it was a good thing Kelsey had gifted him dogs. It kept him from scaring people away when he talked to himself.

Jay barked happily again along with support from his sisters, leaving Josh to question whether they all understood *pizza* as well. Josh wouldn't put it past them to have made the association. They were pretty damn smart, and pizza crusts were one of their favorite foods, Jay's in particular. Apparently the husky had been found enjoying a pizzeria's discarded pies after he escaped his original owners.

Leaving the path, Josh cut across the park. There were two pizza places in town, the best of which had a wood-fired oven and was tucked into the quieter side, surrounded by B and Bs and not far from the clinic. Josh could walk there, then take his slices back to his Jeep and drive home.

As he neared the main road, a group of men and women who sounded like they'd had too much to drink rambled past. Josh followed them with his eyes as they continued up the sidewalk. They were clearly tourists and, given their trajectory, were probably heading to the Bay Song Inn. He could just make out the hotel's red roof as the road sloped slightly upward.

The Lipins' hotel sat at the far eastern edge of town overlooking the water on one side, the mountains on another, and a large courtyard and manicured gardens on the remaining two. Obviously, Josh had never gone inside, but he'd walked by it on many occasions, and even from the road, every view clearly screamed opulence. He didn't have to go inside to know each one came with a price tag to reflect that. There were easily a dozen hotels and motels in Helen of varying quality, and a dozen more bed-and-breakfasts to choose from. Staying at the Bay Song was a mark of prestige not intended for the budget vacationer.

His thoughts once more distracted by family matters, Josh crossed the street and forgot to pay attention to the uneven curb. His foot banged painfully against it, and he tumbled forward. Automatically, his hands shot out to steady himself, and Jay's leash slipped from his fingers.

Josh swore. Jay, who was normally well behaved but who loved people even more than pizza, had darted ahead and run straight into a woman emerging from a side street. She shrieked and stumbled backward. For a terrible second, Josh was afraid she was going to fall over. She caught her balance, but enough damage had already been done.

"Jay. Here now." Josh snapped his fingers, and the husky trotted to his side, trying and failing to look innocent. Embarrassed by his clumsiness and that his dog had gotten away, he cast an apologetic glance in the woman's direction.

To his relief, she was grinning. "Aw, it's okay. He startled me, that's all. What a pretty boy you are."

Presumably she was talking to his dog.

She crouched down to pet Jay again, and Josh swallowed. Speaking of pretty—one glance at her and every exhausted nerve snapped to life. Her brown hair was pulled back in a ponytail, and her cheeks were flushed from heat or exertion. She was dressed like she'd gone for a run. Friendly brown eyes framed with thick lashes took him in as she rubbed the husky's head. Amid a sea of strange and temporary faces in town, she stood out, bright as the sun.

He changed his opinion. She wasn't pretty after all. She was absolutely gorgeous.

As a rule, Josh tended to stay away from tourists. Most of the people flowing through town during the summer tended to be around for only a couple of days anyway. They came off cruise ships or came to get on cruise ships, and they hung around to do some shopping or take boat tours of the bay. The ones who stayed longer were mostly outdoorsy types who were here to hike and kayak and fish. Either way, the town tended to attract crowds of older couples or families. Occasionally, rowdy groups of younger people, probably like the ones he'd recently seen heading toward the Bay Song, came for weddings. But overall, Josh didn't see these transient people often unless they banged themselves up on their adventures and arrived at the ER for repair.

He did have friends who sought out the latter type of traveler for one- or two-night stands, but he didn't have much interest in that kind of thing himself. Stability and quiet were the opposite of sex with virtual strangers, to his mind anyway. His reticence had led to a bit of a dry spell over the past year, and possibly that was why this woman was making him reconsider his hands-off approach.

It also could have been her adorable yet somehow sexy-as-hell smile.

"Wow, your eyes are amazing," she was saying to Jay.

Jay's heterochromia always drew attention, and it really was striking. The pale sapphire blue of his left eye was what had earned him the name Jewel, or so Josh had been told. Whatever the story, his dog was beaming as if he knew he was being complimented. Not that Josh could blame him under the circumstances. Pepper and Bella, on the other hand, were not having it with Jay getting all of the pets, and Josh let them beg for their fair share.

"I sense jealousy." Smiling, the woman doled out attention to the newcomers as well.

"Very much jealousy," Josh said, feeling a little himself. He wouldn't mind this woman's hands all over him. "They'll let you continue to pet them forever. Just a warning."

"They must be used to the attention."

"Oh, yes. And they love people, which is kind of amazing since this one in particular"—he pointed toward Jay—"had a rough childhood. His readiness to forgive and move on makes him a better person than most humans." He was, unsurprisingly, thinking of his family and their unwillingness to let go of some purported hundred-year-old theft.

The woman stood, brushing dog hair off her running pants, and sneezed. "They usually are." The weariness in her voice suggested she had her own group of people in mind.

A minute ago, Josh's most pressing need was for pizza, but his empty stomach had become an afterthought. Something about this stranger had diverted his attention and kept his feet planted in place. "How are you finding Helen?"

He couldn't be 100 percent positive she was a tourist, but given the way she'd drawn his eye, odds were he'd have noticed her around before if she was a local. So her answer surprised him.

"Bigger." She laughed, a contagious sound that made his own face break into a smile and stirred his blood. The breeze coming off the bay was cool, but he was suddenly growing warm.

The woman tucked stray hair behind her ears. "It seems every time I come back, there's something new. I saw more houses being built over here, and I was informed a brewery is opening up soon." She paused and a flicker of uncertainty passed over her face. "I'm assuming you live here, based on the way you asked that question."

Josh grinned in spite of his confusion. "Recent transplant, but yeah. I just learned about the brewery myself, so you're as well informed as a local."

"I have a sister who apprised me of all the news once she heard I was coming to visit."

"Ah. How long are you staying?" Did that sound too interested or eager? Josh imagined himself resembling Jay, tail wagging with excitement, and he cringed internally.

"A couple weeks, maybe longer."

A couple of weeks? He could work with that. A couple of weeks was long enough to have some fun without any worries of getting seriously attached since that would obviously not be smart if she was in town only temporarily. Besides, he wasn't eager to rush into more inevitable breakup pain. Fun, on the other hand, was something he'd been lacking lately and something he was definitely eager for. Actually, fun was something he'd been lacking for a while, if he was being honest. Medical school hadn't provided much time for it, and residency had worn him to the bone. Josh had nourished great hopes of more fun and relaxation when he'd moved to Helen, but aside from taking the dogs hiking, that hadn't manifested. At last he had an excuse.

So yeah, he was absolutely following Jay's overeager example. But damn. He was interested in this woman like he hadn't been interested in anybody for a long time. He hadn't dated since his breakup, and clearly the past year and a half was catching up to him all at once in a sunny smile that hit like a blizzard.

Any feelings of unease left behind by his walk with Kelsey stood zero chance of resisting its force.

SPEAKING OF TIME," Taylor continued reluctantly, "I'm starving and was on my way to pick up some pizza for dinner. Were you heading that way?"

Was that subtle? Did she care? A seriously hot stranger was smiling at her in a way that made her pulse speed up more than it had while she'd been running. She didn't want to break off the conversation, but Lydia was going to be exhausted by the time she wrapped up for the day, and Taylor had promised food would be waiting for her.

Taylor thought she should be exhausted, too, but instead she buzzed like a live wire. She'd had to be up before dawn to catch her flight, which had arrived in Anchorage in the early afternoon. When she'd landed, all she'd wanted was a nap. The whole trip had been hastily planned, and she hadn't been able sleep much the night before. But somewhere on the drive to Helen, she'd started waking up. The closer she got to home and all its baggage, the more alert she'd grown. Her body had reacted as though it were bracing for danger.

Her father had been perfectly—alarmingly—cheerful when she talked to him last, and he'd avoided her attempts to talk about Mom. Her mother had returned her voice mail with only a few texts, assuring Taylor that she shouldn't worry and that she loved her. As far as Taylor could tell, her sister was the only person acting at all rational about the situation. Taylor had almost called her favorite aunt and uncle to see what they had to say, but ultimately, she had decided that could wait until she was in town.

Josh motioned down the street. "Actually, I was going to get pizza myself."

The way he said it made Taylor wonder if that was true, but she wasn't about to worry. She wanted a reason not to dislike being back home, and he would do. With his dark hair and blue eyes and the trace of stubble around his jaw, he would do very well. If he and his adorable dogs wanted to walk her to Basil's, she wouldn't challenge fate.

"Two weeks?" he asked. "You must love your sister or get a lot of time off."

She couldn't suppress a groan. "Lots of time off at the moment. I got laid off a few days ago. Conveniently, I got a call the same day asking if I could come up and help with some things, so here I am. It worked out for one of us."

"Sorry about the job."

"I'll find something." She barely wanted to admit it to herself, never mind a stranger, but in the hours after she got the news, she'd actually felt less stressed than she had in a long time, and her ex-boss's impromptu party that afternoon, though a nice distraction, hadn't had anything to do with it. It was as if a mild pain in the back of her neck, so subtle it had become part of the background, had suddenly vanished. Taylor didn't think she'd hated her job, but at some imperceptible level she must have regarded it more negatively than she'd realized. For the moment, she had freedom. Freedom to choose what to do next.

Alas, freedom didn't pay the bills. She was going to have to devote a couple of hours each day to updating her résumé and job searching.

And maybe another hour to figuring out who the hot guy with the dogs was so she could bump into him again. Or hell, she could simply ask. He had been eyeing her up, after all. In L.A., everyone seemed to be taller, thinner, and overall more put together than she was. Usually blonder too. If they weren't, they were looking for someone who was. It was nice not being overlooked for an aspiring actress for once.

"So what did you move here for?" In Taylor's experience, everyone who chose to live in Helen, as opposed to being born there, did so for one of two reasons: either they were in the tourism industry, or they were outdoorsy people themselves. Often both. In this guy's case, she suspected the second. His athletic build was evident beneath the shirt he was wearing, a broad chest tapering to a narrow waist. She'd bet the arm muscles hidden beneath his sleeves were nicely corded and that he had the calves of a hard-core hiker.

Wow, she was seriously in need of some dating excitement if she was imagining a stranger's forearms.

"I'm a doctor. There was an opening here, and it seemed like a good place to move to."

Doctor. That was unexpected. She wondered if the hospital had needed to expand with the growing population. "You sound like you might be regretting that decision."

He shook his head. "Nah, just a long day. And what do you do when you're employed?"

"I work in marketing." She sneezed again, which was what she got for petting this guy's dogs. If only they weren't so cute, and huskies too.

One childhood trip to cheer on mushers and meet their sled dogs was all it had taken to make nine-year-old Taylor stop longing for a pony and start begging for a dog. But her parents had refused, supposedly because of her allergy. As she got older and discovered there were actual medications people could take for allergies, she began to suspect the real reason she couldn't have a dog was because having dogs was something the Porters did. In fact, it was fair to say the Porters had an obsession with dogs. Among the lot of them, they probably owned enough huskies to put together more than one Iditarod sled team.

"Not many jobs like that around here," the cute dog-walker said, bringing her back to the present.

Taylor shook her head. No, there weren't, which was

as big an inducement as any to find a position similar to her old one and get out of Dodge fast. "I'll be heading back to L.A. when I'm done here."

"In about two weeks." He seemed to be mulling this over.

They turned the corner, closing in on Basil's Brick Oven Pizza, and Taylor realized she still didn't know this guy's name. Usually when she was visiting, it was around Christmas and her entire visit was focused on family. The only people she saw whom she wasn't related to were old family friends. It felt strange to introduce herself to someone in Helen, which made little sense. She was constantly meeting people in L.A., whether for work or because they were friends of friends. But meeting someone here felt momentous. Not in a great or grand way, but in a way that hinted at there being more going on than she could see.

Probably, it was nothing more than the serendipity of meeting a very cute guy on her first day back. Her steps were lighter than they should be given how long she'd been up, and what other explanation could there be?

"I'm Taylor, by the way." The words came out rushed, but she managed to stop herself before including her last name. Even though this guy was relatively new to town, that name came dragging a lot of baggage. There was a chance he'd recognize it, and that was a chance she didn't feel like taking. Growing up, she'd rarely been anonymous. If she was going to see this guy again, and she hoped she would, it would be nice to talk to someone who didn't immediately make assumptions about her based on her family.

"I'm Josh, and of course you've already been introduced to Jay, Pepper, and Bella." He pointed to each dog

in turn, and the huskies' ears perked up at the sound of
their names.

Jay was easy enough to identify with his dual-colored
eyes, but Taylor found herself making a mental note that
Pepper was indeed a mottled—peppery—gray, and
Bella was white and tan. Apparently an optimistic part
of her was already planning to see the dogs and their
owner again.

The pizzeria's doors were propped open, and both
warmth and the wonderful scents of baking bread and
garlic spilled onto the sidewalk. About half the tables
inside appeared to be taken, and more people sat outside.
They were either true locals who considered the day's
temperature to be balmy, or tourists who hadn't wanted
to leave their dogs behind when they went to dinner.

Taylor went in and didn't notice Josh wasn't with her
until she got in line to order. He caught up a moment
later, minus the dogs, whose leashes were now attached
to the metal fence by the outdoor seating area. The
woman sitting next to them either knew them or had already been won over because she was feeding them bits
of pizza crust.

"You wouldn't by chance want to grab a table with
me?" Josh asked. His smile was all charm, but she could
detect a slight uncertainty in his voice, as though he
wasn't at all used to asking random women to join him
for dinner.

That was kind of sweet, and would have helped his
case if she hadn't already been inclined to say yes. "I'd
love to."

"But . . ." He chuckled at her surprise. "I could hear
the hesitation."

Blood rushed to her cheeks even though her excuse

was real. "I promised my sister I'd be returning with our pizza after my run, and she's not going to be happy if I make her wait while I eat mine. Another time? To my knowledge, my calendar is wide open after six every day."

"Tomorrow then?"

She let out a breath she hoped was unnoticeable. He didn't think she was pushing him away. "Tomorrow then."

She and Josh exchanged numbers, she pet each dog goodbye and sneezed a third time, and then Taylor had to fight down a stupid smile that kept wanting to spread across her face the entire way back to the inn. She was still dreading having a face-to-face conversation with her father, but maybe, just maybe, this unexpected trip home wasn't going to be as awful as she'd feared.

4

BY THE TIME Taylor reached the family hotel, she was realizing she should have driven into town. Going for a run was one thing, but she couldn't run while also carrying a pizza, and the Bay Song was situated far enough outside the town proper that the pizza was going to be cold by the time she walked it into Lydia's apartment.

The road curved slightly through a copse of evergreens, and Taylor passed the Tavern—the inn's restaurant that was open to the public—before heading toward the main building. Aside from the restaurant, the inn itself comprised two main buildings. The first held the reception area, the kitchen, a small dining room, and the function room. A handful of guest rooms were on the second, and an apartment was on the third. The second building, which contained the majority of the guest rooms, was connected to it via an open-air walkway that passed through a courtyard where weddings and events could be held outside, weather permitting.

Lydia had taken over the third-floor apartment several years ago, after their grandfather's health had declined to the point where multiple trips up and down the stairs each day were no longer feasible. The private staircase ran along the side of the building, sporting a fresh coat of gray paint. Due to the rain, snow, and salt water, it was easy for buildings in Helen to show their age, but Lydia was fastidious about maintaining the inn, and given that business was booming, apparently she could afford to be.

Taylor nudged the apartment door open with her hip, half expecting her sister to still be working, but Lydia was in the living room, pulling open the sofa bed where Taylor would be sleeping for the foreseeable future. Usually when she visited, she stayed with her parents, but Taylor had rationalized that since she'd be working at the inn, she ought to stay there.

That it was likely to be uncomfortable staying with her father when her mother might return home anytime surely had nothing to do with her decision.

Surely.

"Oh, good." Her sister inhaled deeply and tossed a pillow onto the blankets she'd laid out. "Tell me there's sausage and mushrooms on that. I'm starving."

"As you requested, but it's going to need reheating." Taylor dumped the box on the kitchen counter.

Perhaps it was the way her sister set out the wineglasses, but Taylor had to marvel that, even changed into a pair of yoga pants and a T-shirt, Lydia looked far more put together and elegant than Taylor ever could.

On the surface, they didn't appear so different. Her sister's eyes and hair were a darker brown, and Lydia kept her hair long, whereas Taylor got irritated when it crept below her shoulders. Their builds and features were similar, too, although Lydia was a couple of inches taller and generally more slender. With her perfectly oval-shaped face, she also managed to look far more like their mother than Taylor did.

But that was as deep as the similarities went. Taylor preferred beer to wine, dogs to cats, and she defied the family genes by being the first Lipin in generations to get seasick. No doubt she was also the first Lipin ever to run away to Southern California too.

There was some irony in that since, with the right clothes, Lydia would likely look far more at home in L.A. than Taylor ever had. But what passed for fashion in Helen versus in Los Angeles was as far apart as the towns were geographically. Taylor had had a hell of a time packing clothes for this visit since she owned very few things these days that wouldn't make her stand out like a poorly prepared tourist.

"I don't suppose you have any beer?" Taylor asked.

Lydia wrinkled her delicate nose. "Sorry. Dad had some in the fridge, but they're all gone."

Taylor tsked. "I expect you to be a better hostess than that."

"Like it or not, you're family and don't count as a guest." She sighed heavily and her shoulder drooped. "And honestly, I'm not really entertaining anyone else these days. So wine?"

Taylor nodded. She was an uncomfortable mix of twitchy and giddy. Although wine wasn't her first choice, it might help take the edge off so she could sleep. "Social life around here is that exciting, huh?"

"Precisely." Lydia helped herself to a slice of pizza and took a bite without bothering to reheat it. "Grandmother keeps trying to set me up with people she's met one way or another, and each is worse than the last."

"How so?" Unwilling to indulge in cold pizza, Taylor stuck her slice in the microwave.

"The last guy was very rich."

"And that was bad?"

"I think he was a junior executive at some oil company."

Taylor grunted. Guys who wore suits to work were not her thing, but she would have thought they might be Lydia's thing. Clearly, she needed to catch up with her sister more often.

"And his name was Chad." Lydia punctuated her displeasure by plopping onto a chair at the small kitchen table.

Taylor coughed as she poorly swallowed her wine, and she joined her sister. "I see the problem. Who wants to scream out 'Oh, Chad' while they're in bed?"

Lydia giggled. "Right? I mean, I'm sure he was fine, but he also sounded like the kind of guy who'd expect me to give up my life here to go be his perfect housewife or something. Long story short, our grandmother thinks my ovaries are drying up and I'm going to end up a lonely old cat lady, which is ridiculous. But the truth is, my social life is nonexistent outside a few friends, and even they've become more scarce as they've started families."

"You could move to L.A. Lots of men around there, and none of whom you remember from before they went through puberty." She grinned at the immediate and sardonic expression on her sister's face.

"Pass. How's your dating life?"

Taylor bided her time, chewing her pizza. She'd been ready to gush to Lydia about the cute dog walker and find out if her sister knew who he was, but it no longer seemed like a great idea given that it was impossible to tell how Lydia really felt about her social life. Lydia knew how to present a perfect face to the world, no matter what she was feeling. Making jokes was no guarantee she wasn't truly lonely, and Taylor didn't want to rub her good fortune in her sister's face.

"Dating in L.A. is about what you'd expect dating in L.A. to be like," Taylor said, reaching for another slice of pizza.

Truthfully, Taylor knew this was partially her own fault. Since high school, her dating history was littered with guys who couldn't hold down perfectly respectable, if not exactly prestigious, jobs. As much as she'd like to pretend it was a coincidence, Taylor also knew it was a not entirely subconscious way of defying her family. Unfortunately, men like that tended to make lousy relationship material. Also unfortunately, she couldn't seem to break the cycle. Bad tattoos and poor work ethics had become her dating habit. If she hung around Helen long enough, she'd probably find out why Josh was entirely unsuitable too.

"Tell me what you need me to do," Taylor said, eager to change the topic of conversation for both their sakes.

"Mom was the hospitality manager. Basically, she oversaw the kitchen staff and guest services and was a part-time wedding coordinator."

Lydia filled her in while they ate the rest of their dinner and until their father stopped by about a half hour later. He was tall and broad-shouldered, and though his untrimmed beard had turned a mix of auburn and white since Taylor had seen him last, he looked as hearty and unconcerned as he'd sounded on the phone, despite everything.

Lydia raised an eyebrow in Taylor's direction as if to say *I told you so* while Gregory Lipin enveloped Taylor in bear hug.

"It's good to have you back," he said, helping himself to one of the remaining slices of pizza. "I love seeing both of my girls together."

"How are you?" Taylor asked slowly, like maybe he could comprehend her better if he had time to think on each word.

Her father waved off both her and the chair Lydia offered him. "I'm fine. Don't let your sister worry you. Everyone's fine."

Lydia snorted, and scooped up her cat, Merlot, who'd finally wandered out of the bedroom.

"Really?" Taylor drained her wine. Running for mayor of Helen wasn't exactly like running for mayor of a major city, but her father still knew how to put on a good face. Lydia had come by her talent honestly, which made it impossible to fully trust either of them when it came to anything emotional.

"Swear." He rubbed Merlot's head and made ridiculous cooing noises at the cat, who seemed to enjoy it immensely. "I was afraid you girls would react this way, but I'm fine and your mother's fine. The only things that worry me are keeping this place running smoothly and whether Wallace is going to challenge me in the next election. Damn Porters are acting like this is their big break."

"Vultures," Lydia said. "But you've held the position for years, and you've been serving on town committees and doing volunteer work for as long as I can remember. What have the Porters done—donate money occasionally and buy up land? People will remember the difference."

"We have to hope. Honestly, I'd turn the job over to most anyone who wanted it, but not Wallace. He'd turn this town into a strip mall if he could make a buck from it."

Taylor stared forlornly into her empty glass, not entirely able to disagree but not wanting to get involved either, especially as her father's complaints about Wallace turned into a more general update about all the awful things the Porters had said or done since the last time she'd been home.

"So, daughter the younger?" Her father grinned, having finished a tale about how a couple of Porters had allegedly tried to cheat so their children could win the big prizes at the town's Easter egg hunt. "How long will you be sticking around this time?"

"I planned for about two weeks." She moved her plate to the dishwasher while her father lobbed questions at her about her job, or lack thereof, for the next ten minutes.

Once he left, Lydia shook her head. "See what I mean? It's like it's nothing."

"Maybe he knew it was coming?" It wasn't a happy thought to assume her parents had been hiding difficulties from her and Lydia for a while, but it was just as hard to believe her mother's leaving came entirely out of nowhere. Taylor had foreseen every one of her relationships ending, but then, she'd almost always been the one doing the dumping.

Lydia just sighed at that and held up the wine bottle. "More?"

"Pass. I think I've had enough. What I really want is ice cream from the Dairy Dock, but I'm too lazy to head back downtown." The Dairy Dock claimed to have been serving up homemade ice cream since before Taylor was born. When she was a child, trips to the Dairy Dock had been a rare treat because their mother was annoyingly strict about sugar. Now, that she was an adult, they were still rare because the creamery—like many of the town's tourist-facing businesses—was only open during the summer, and Taylor's visits tended to occur only around Christmas.

"I don't think I've had ice cream from there in years. We'll have to do it while you're here." Lydia grabbed Taylor's arm. "It's nice to have you back for more than a couple days, Tay. Even if you hate us."

Taylor rolled her eyes. "Stop being melodramatic. I don't hate you. I just wanted something different. It's not like it's easy to drop by for casual visits, and it's not like you guys visit me on the regular either."

Lydia scowled with defeat. "Fine, fair point. But it's not like I don't want to. It's just . . . L.A. is so far away."

It was. That had been part of its allure.

Taylor stretched, and all the exhaustion she should have been feeling previously seemed to catch up to her at once. The wine might have been too good at its job, or it might have been guilt landing on her shoulders with a thud.

The thing she could never tell Lydia was that she hadn't wanted to visit much, even though she'd missed her family. She'd been busy. Busy trying to create a new life and a new identity for herself.

Perhaps on some subconscious level she'd also worried that if she came home for too long, Helen would begin to dig its hooks into her. Somehow she'd been able to escape once, but if she wasn't careful, the town would refuse to let her leave a second time. It made sense because now that she was here, she found it difficult to remember why being here was something she'd tried so hard to avoid. The evening air hummed in her veins, the sun shone brightly through the windows, and the rustling

of leaves and chirping insects sounded like home. Even
the breeze smelled right; not simply better, although
that, too, but familiar. Her jog earlier had made her remember how much she'd missed the way the mountains
towered over the buildings, as if standing sentry around
the town, and the colorful but weathered paint on the
storefronts.

Years of living among steel buildings and being surrounded by Spanish-style architecture had given her a
new way of viewing Helen. The mix of kitsch, Old West,
and Native influences blended into something that re-
sembled a picture postcard at every turn. It was either
beautiful or tacky or a bit of both, but it was always
worth framing.

Taylor hadn't exactly forgotten any of this, but she'd
been able to dull the memories so they affected her less.
They were faded like old photographs, making it impossible for her to recall the vivid details that would otherwise have driven her home more often.

Well, driven her home more often if she'd had the
time and money to make it happen. The distance between Helen and L.A. was both an allure and a detri-
ment.

Taylor yawned. "Is it too early for me to sleep?"

"No, go ahead. I need you up bright and early tomorrow morning." Lydia's smile was pure malicious sisterly
amusement.

While Taylor texted her mother to let her know she'd
arrived safely at her sister's, Lydia finished the cleanup
and then retreated to her bedroom. Taylor plopped herself down on the sofa bed. It wasn't terrible, but it definitely wasn't as comfortable as the guest bed in her
parents' house.

Merlot had been resting in the middle of the bed's

faded comforter, and he watched her warily. Although she preferred dogs, Taylor had great affection for her sister's cat, possibly because he was more like a cat-dog— super affectionate and always searching for pets. So it was weird that when she reached over to him, he turned his back on her and jumped off the bed.

Taylor narrowed her eyes at him. "Fine, be like that. We'll see if I bring you new toys at Christmas."

In typical cat fashion, he didn't seem impressed by her threat, but in her bedroom Lydia laughed.

At least she'd had good luck with some dogs today.

With that thought, Taylor got out her phone and brought up the website for the hospital. She found a short bio for a Dr. Joshua Krane and a photograph that didn't do him justice. His eyes were much prettier in person. On the plus side, nothing about him screamed he was secretly a serial killer, but he had to have some fatal flaw. Now that she was coming down from her stress-induced high, a cute doctor with dogs sounded too good to be true.

Possibly, that flaw would be that he didn't actually text her tomorrow. But if he did? She'd simply tell Lydia she was meeting a friend for dinner. That seemed like the kindest option given her sister's grumbling.

Taylor plugged her phone in to charge, closed the blinds, and fell asleep almost as soon as her head hit the pillow.

5

⤜━━━━━⤛

JOSH WAS RELIEVED to be meeting up with Kelsey after work, because he needed advice. Not that his surly cousin was the best person to ask about the help he required, but she'd lived in Helen her whole life. Presumably, at some point, she must have done something sociable.

If he'd had a moment, he would have texted her earlier, but Josh had seen patients back-to-back all day and still fell behind schedule because his nine o'clock had been complaining about worrying symptoms. In order to not get stuck late two days in a row, he'd needed to economize on his break—walking his dogs with one hand, eating a sandwich with his other, and using the voice assistant on his phone to text Taylor between bites. Honestly, he was pretty damn proud of his multitasking, and he'd gotten his schedule back on track so his afternoon patients didn't have unreasonable waits. But it had made consulting with Kelsey impossible.

"I have news!" His cousin practically skipped over to him as they met at their normal spot by the park. Even her huskies seemed more excited than usual as the six dogs mingled about their legs, tails wagging and leashes twisting.

"I have questions."

"Hold them. My news might answer them."

Josh rather doubted it unless his cousin had been spying on him. "You look like you'll burst if I do anything else, so please. I don't enjoy fixing those kinds of injuries."

Kelsey made a sound that sounded disturbingly like a cackle. "Get this. The Lipin situation must be worse than it appears. Greg Lipin's younger daughter—"

"No."

His cousin's words slurred off, and her expression made Josh fear her brain had melted down with his refusal to hear her out. "What?"

Josh held up his free hand. "I don't want to know. I don't want to be part of it."

"Oh, come on. When did a large stick get inserted up your ass?"

He glared at her, and she shrugged innocently. "I want to maintain my distance from all of this. One day a week I have my shift in the ER. Anyone could end up in there with a life-threatening issue, so the last thing I need is to develop negative associations with an entire family of people I've never met. The less I know, the more capable I am of doing my job objectively."

He hoped he could do that regardless, even if the guy who'd almost hit Pepper on his bike the other day came through the doors, but Josh saw no reason to unnecessarily test himself. And honestly, that wasn't the point. His real reason for relying on the professionalism excuse was that he figured Kelsey would have an easier time accepting it. Saying he hated conflict was only likely to egg her on.

Kelsey groaned in an exaggerated fashion. "You're no fun sometimes." She leaned down and ruffled Puck's fur. "Uncle Josh is no fun, is he?"

The husky quit inspecting whatever it was that had fascinated him in the grass, and barked once in Josh's direction.

"Uncle Josh is a lot of fun," Josh corrected her. "In fact, Uncle Josh has a date tonight."

Kelsey almost tripped over her dogs. "You have a what?"

"A date. It's a thing where people who are interested in other people go out and spend time together."

"Uncle Josh thinks he's a comedian." Kelsey squinted at him as the early evening sun peeked through the cloud cover and then disappeared again. "With anyone I know?"

"Doubt it. Just someone I met yesterday after Jay almost knocked her over."

"That's an interesting tactic for meeting women. Seems like they'd be just as inclined to flip you off as to agree to a date."

"I got lucky this time."

"Got lucky or are hoping to get lucky?"

Josh decided to use the opening to flip Kelsey off.

Two German shepherds being walked down the other side of the path caught the huskies' attention, and after a struggle to keep all the dogs happy, Josh turned back to his cousin. "I need your help. We're meeting at the Espresso Express in . . ." He checked the time. "An hour. But she doesn't live around here, so I need to have some suggestions. Where would you take a date for dinner?"

"I don't date. When hounded, I meet the men my family sets me up with at the Espresso Express, drink coffee, and leave expediently."

"I realize you're a misanthropic recluse, and I respect that. But you've lived here your whole life. Surely you know people who have dated, or have overheard tales of good places to go should you want to socialize in that fashion."

His cousin laughed. "You're really trying. It's cute."

"I haven't gone on a date since I moved here. It's been a while." That was probably part of the reason he was making a big deal out of it. Another part was Taylor's smile. When he closed his eyes, Josh could see it clearly, and it had the same effect on him as it had yesterday. It made him want to smile too. To touch her lips and see if she tasted as warm and inviting as she looked. He'd been too busy to dwell on that memory much, but every time he'd stolen a precious second today, he grew more excited to see her again. Excitement meant he was feeling pressure.

Helen sported dozens of restaurants—at least during the summer when everything was open—but most ranged in atmosphere from beer-and-burgers casual to food-served-wrapped-in-wax-paper casual. Over the past year, Josh had tried most of them, and regardless of presentation, the food was generally good. But none of them screamed that they were an obvious choice for a date.

Ironically, there was an obvious date choice—the Tavern at the Bay Song. It was the most upscale spot in town—relatively speaking—and had a reputation for excellent food. Since it was technically part of the Lipins' hotel, however, stepping into it would be like entering enemy territory. He might not want to be dragged into the feud, but he wasn't about to purposely stir that century-old pot. And who knew? If half the stories his family told were accurate, his meal would probably be poisoned.

"Fine." Kelsey blew a curl out of her face. "Do you know anything about this woman? What kind of food she likes?"

"Pizza. We were both getting that for dinner last night, though, so I need something different."

"So helpful. Okay, here's a suggestion—ask her what she likes and let her choose the type of food."

Josh frowned. "Shouldn't I have some ideas?"

"Sure, but let her make the first call. If she doesn't know the restaurants, let her tell you what she likes to eat, then make suggestions based on that. Women like to know their opinions matter."

"Doesn't everyone?"

"Probably, but your gender has a terrible habit of trying to push your preferences on everyone else." She raised a hand. "Not saying you do this, but there are trends."

"You know, when you're not plotting the demise of an entire family, you show some hidden depths, Kels."

Kelsey snorted. "All my depths are hidden because it's a rare person who deserves to see them."

FORTY MINUTES LATER, Josh parked his Jeep outside the Espresso Express and wondered when he'd gotten so rusty at dating. True, it had been a long time since his last first date, but a childhood of moving from school to school had honed his social skills. By the time he'd gone to college, meeting and befriending new people was as mundane an event as tying his shoes. He therefore had no excuse for stressing out over conversation topics, especially since Taylor had been plenty easy to talk to yesterday.

Still, he'd come prepared with a mental list of ideas, all of which vanished from his brain when he got out of the SUV and saw her sipping a cup of something by the shop entrance.

The short, swingy dress she was wearing was probably fine in L.A. but completely incompatible with Helen's breezy weather. It kept trying to crawl up her legs, and she looked so damn sexy doing her best to hold it down while stray strands of hair blew across her face. Despite her efforts, some sort of mark was visible as the edge of the fabric lifted. At first Josh thought it was a bruise, then he realized it was part of a tattoo. His grip tightened around the door handle as he fought down the desire to slide her skirt up higher and run his finger up that smooth skin until he could see the whole design.

Taylor headed over before he could drag his thoughts out of the gutter. "Hi."

"Hi." He should have rehearsed a greeting in addition to thinking of conversation topics, because he suddenly couldn't remember additional words. His vocabulary had been reduced to concepts—*skin, thigh, lick. Want.* "That smells good."

Well, those were words, and the aroma coming off her cup was strong, but they did not seem like the best words, for sure. Josh cringed. Still, that had to be better than blurting out the images running through his head.

"Double espresso with extra foam and cinnamon. It's my favorite, and for some reason, no other place makes it as good as they do here. My sister worked me hard today. I needed the caffeine boost." She smiled, and once again he felt like he was being hit by a lead weight. Also, the phrase *worked me hard* seemed to activate the nerves in his groin. "Do you mind if we get somewhere out of the wind? As much fun as my Marilyn Monroe impression can be, it's getting tiresome."

"Right, yes." Josh shook himself and opened the passenger door for her. "Sorry. Your Marilyn impression is A-plus though."

Taylor slid onto the seat and immediately sneezed. "We can pretend it was on purpose and not because I forgot how the wind picks up in the evening. I'm not sure why I bothered packing a dress, but I did, so this seemed like a good time to wear it."

There wasn't a single restaurant in Helen that would turn someone away for wearing jeans, but Josh wasn't complaining about seeing more of her legs or the way the dress's bodice accentuated her breasts. The clingy fabric aside, he was thrilled she'd dressed up too—if you could count his khaki pants as dressing up. Josh did since it was the sort of thing he'd wear to work, but he wondered if someone used to L.A. fashion would think he hadn't put in any effort.

"So I guess that means any restaurants with outdoor seating are out." He grinned at the way Taylor winced, and was glad he'd decided to take Kelsey's advice and not plan too much. "What do you like?"

"Oh, I'll eat almost anything. At least anything that doesn't involve sushi or avocados."

Taylor crossed her legs, once more flashing a tease of that tattoo, and Josh made the Herculean effort to keep his eyes on her face. He couldn't afford another trip to fantasyland while driving. "You live in California and don't eat avocados? Is that allowed?"

She laughed. "It's goddamn nightmare. They're on everything, ruining all my favorite foods with their slimy green goo."

"I can promise you're unlikely to find avocados here unless they're in guacamole." Josh didn't particularly mind guacamole, or sushi, either, but Taylor's vehemence was far more entertaining than his ambivalence. "We have lots of seafood instead."

"We do have seafood in L.A. We are on a coast, if you recall."

Josh shook his head. "But it's not the same. Ours is better."

"True—I'm unlikely to find avocados on it here." She sighed happily. "Didn't you say you moved here only recently? You're already sounding like a native—*We have the best seafood in the world.*"

Her eyes twinkled, and Josh's smile turned sheepish. "Don't they say converts are the most zealous believers? I've been converted. I do love it here."

Taylor's face seemed to lose its sunniness, but the moment passed so quickly Josh wasn't sure if he'd imagined it. "Helen has its charms."

Something about the way she said it convinced him he hadn't misread her split-second expression. Josh decided not to press, but he grew more curious about what had driven her from Helen to L.A. "So seafood?"

"Someplace with seafood is fine, although I imagine that's every place. Honestly, I'd love a burger and a beer. Somewhere with a good draft list would get my vote."

"Burgers and beers?" She was gorgeous and funny, and had excellent taste; the more time he spent around Taylor, the more he liked this woman. He'd have to give Jay an extra treat for running into her.

"What can I say?" Taylor shrugged. "I'm a woman with a simple, unsophisticated palate. Or so my friends tell me."

"As they all eat avocado toast?"

"With their sushi."

Laughing, Josh started the Jeep. "Welcome home then. I know the best spot for burgers and beers."

Taylor leaned back in her seat and fastened her belt. "Excellent. I knew meeting you on my first day in town was going to lead to good things."

6

◦———◦

ENSCONCED IN THE restaurant's far corner with a flight of beer samples for sharing, Taylor was strangely content, or as close as she could be while in her hometown. Possibly it was because Josh was a relative newcomer, so she didn't associate him with Helen, or maybe it was simply the lack of formality in their surroundings when she was used to flashier dates. But whatever the reason, being here felt right somehow. Natural.

It didn't hurt that her date was nicer to look at than any setting could be. The blue shirt Josh wore heightened the brilliant color of his eyes, and the bit of stubble he'd sported yesterday was gone. But even without it, her memory had not done him justice. She suspected he'd look good no matter how he was dressed.

Her stomach fluttered. She suspected he'd look even better without any clothes, which was really not a great thought to start off the evening. How was she supposed to remember how to hold a conversation when she was picturing him naked?

Taylor spun the silver bangle she wore on her left

wrist in circles, trying desperately to banish the images
that were running through her mind. The bracelet had
been a gift from her parents when she graduated from
college, and since her parents were currently getting divorced, the reminder ought to have distracted her.

It did not.

She had to get a grip. Just because she hadn't been
with anyone in a while was no excuse for her body to get
ahead of her better judgment. Assuming she had such a
thing.

Across the table, Josh leaned against the back of the
booth, and the way his gaze roamed over her did not
make banishing her dirtier thoughts any easier. She got
the distinct sense he was imagining the same things, and
faint shivers of anticipation trickled down her back.

"I'm glad you're not horrified by my taste in restaurants," Taylor said, absently grabbing one of the beer
samples.

"Beer and burgers? What's there to be horrified
about?"

She smirked and tried the mystery beer. Luckily, their
server had left a list of what they'd ordered, because she
hadn't been paying attention. She'd been too busy noticing how the cords of muscles in Josh's forearms flexed
now that he'd pushed up his shirtsleeves. Apparently she
was really developing a thing for arm muscles, and the
nice thing about arm muscles was that they were attached to shoulder muscles that were attached to chest
muscles. Josh's shoulders were broad but not bulky, and
his chest tapered to a slim waist, convincing her that
those muscles would be lovely as well.

And she was back to picturing him naked.

Taylor cleared her throat. "Well, if you were one of
my friends, there would be lots to be horrified about.

Half of them are vegetarian, and almost another half don't eat beef. Plus, at any one time, someone is doing low carb and someone else is going gluten-free, and so even the fries I intend to eat would be questioned."

"L.A. sounds rough."

"Oh, L.A. is wonderful." She overemphasized the *wonderful* as though trying to convince herself of it, which was odd. She did love it there. Truly. She supposed it was just that she was comfortable at the moment. Being in Helen was like reveling in a pair of warm slippers after strutting about in an L.A. designer heel. Experience told Taylor that the comfort phase would pass and soon she'd be longing for sun and style. "Have you ever been?"

"Strangely enough, I've never made it to Southern California, although I feel like I've been almost everywhere else."

Taylor spent the next several minutes tasting beers while Josh regaled her with all the places he'd lived growing up. She was equal parts fascinated and jealous, and for the first time, she thought it was odd that her family owned an inn but never traveled far themselves. Since she'd lived in only two places and had never made it east of the Rockies, she badgered him with questions about his travels, which he didn't seem to mind.

They hadn't glanced at the food menu by the time their server returned to collect their orders.

"How is it that you lived so many places?" Taylor asked once the server had left.

"My father was in the air force."

"That must have been rough—the constant moving around." How very much the opposite of her childhood, where the children she'd known since preschool had moved through the grades with her until graduation.

She'd had familiarity and stability, but no surprises or excitement.

"I got used to it, but yeah, there were times that weren't fun. But that was mostly when my father was deployed. It wasn't the moving around that was rough as much as the alone time."

"Alone time?"

Josh spun one of the beer samples around on the table, once more drawing Taylor's attention to his arms. "My mother's a nurse, and she couldn't always get shifts that matched my school schedule. Let's just say I learned to cook at a young age."

A man who could cook? This did nothing to lessen Taylor's interest. "Cooking is a useful skill."

"No doubt. Now ask me if I like it." Josh laughed, seeing the way her face fell. "Sorry. Maybe if I'd learned some other way, but I will forever associate cooking with being thirteen years old and having to follow the dinner instructions my mom left for me when I'd rather be outside playing with friends."

"Aw, but you did it. You were a good kid."

"I was a good kid." He lowered his head, still laughing, and his cheeks reddened. "I had to be when my mom tried so hard. When she wasn't working, she went to every one of my soccer games, and when I was real young, she made a point to go to the local synagogue and learn how to say Hebrew prayers so I could celebrate Hanukkah while my dad was gone. Starting a pot roast for her was the least I could do. But I still hate cooking."

That was fair. And sweet. A little surprising too. "You're Jewish?"

"More or less. My father's family is, but neither of my parents are religious. We celebrated Christmas and Hanukkah in our house only because they didn't want me to feel left out. But as far as I was concerned, Halloween was the best holiday."

"Halloween is the best holiday. You can't beat dressing up and free chocolate."

"And carving pumpkins."

"And carving pumpkins, yes. So you've lived basically everywhere," Taylor concluded. All the beer sampling enabled her to ignore the thing about living everywhere but Southern California. "Yet somehow you ended up choosing to live in Helen. Got to say, I don't understand that decision."

Josh finished the last of the taster glasses, and Taylor realized he'd been smiling throughout the entire conversation so far. So had she. Was it the beer, or was it her fascination with the company that was keeping her cheeks from aching?

"I like snow."

She shook her head. "Lots of places get snow. We don't even get as much snow as most of Alaska."

"I'll rephrase—I like snow in moderation. I also like hiking and kayaking. I liked the idea of working at a small hospital versus a big one, and I liked that there are loan forgiveness programs for working at rural hospitals. And I have family here."

"Ah." Taylor recalled there being one Jewish family in Helen when she'd been in school, and she wondered if that was whom Josh was referring to.

She also supposed she understood his motivations better. One of the few things she didn't like about living in L.A. was being so far away from her own family. It was the family drama—mostly the feud—that she didn't miss.

On that thought, she dragged her gaze away from Josh long enough to sweep the restaurant for familiar faces. It was a newer place—it must have opened after she'd moved away—and Taylor wasn't sure whether the owners leaned Lipin or Porter, or if they'd managed the rare feat of maintaining an uncomfortable neutrality. She hadn't recognized anyone when they arrived, but it was inevitable that she'd run into someone soon, and she hoped it wouldn't be a Porter making snide remarks about her parents' divorce.

"So what about you?" Josh asked. "What made you run off to L.A.?"

"Oh, you know the cliché. Small-town girl, big-city dreams." She rolled her eyes, but only because she didn't have a more logical explanation. It was better to laugh at herself than admit that maybe those dreams hadn't been such a great idea.

"Acting dreams?"

Taylor had reached for the full-size beer their server had brought over, and was glad she hadn't had a chance to sip it yet or she'd have choked. "Oh, no."

"Seemed like a possibility. You do manage an excellent Marilyn impersonation."

"That was my dress more than me."

"True. But even Marilyn would have to be jealous of your smile."

Heat crept up Taylor's neck. Back in L.A. that kind of line would have had her rolling her eyes, but given the way Josh looked at her, she got the impression he honestly thought it. "You don't have to flatter me."

"Is it flattery if it's true?"

She wagged a finger at him. "I have to admit you're very good at it."

Josh grinned. "Well, I can't do any impersonations of my own, so I do need a different talent."

Oh, God. She'd giggled. Since when did she do that? Beer sloshed over the sides of the glass as Taylor's hand shook with her laughter. Swearing to herself, she set it down and grabbed a napkin to clean up her mess.

Josh reached for his, too, and their hands collided as they each wiped up the spill. Sparks shot up Taylor's arm from his fingers, and they danced around in her stomach. Some kind of self-preservation instinct warned her she should move her hand before it got too familiar with Josh's touch, but her muscles refused to obey. She liked his hand close, liked the feel of his skin, and she wanted more of it.

Josh glided his thumb slightly to the left so he touched her again, and though it was subtle, she didn't doubt that he'd done it on purpose. It was as if he sensed her temptation to pull away and was trying to convince her not to. He seemed to read her all too well, which was both unnerving her and daring her to discover if he could continue that trend.

Their server returned at that moment, saving Taylor from suggesting they abandon dinner for someplace more private. And also saving her from abandoning her senses entirely.

By necessity, Josh let go of her, and they fell back into conversation after finally ordering food. Although she couldn't help being disappointed, she was also relieved. This date was becoming a whole lot more intense than she'd bargained for. Josh was too easy to talk to and too nice to touch, and everything was going too perfectly. It couldn't last. Every guy she'd dated had shown what a mistake he was, usually sooner rather than later. Josh's deal-breaking flaw would make itself known eventually.

IT DID NOT do so, however, over dinner, and the absence of a flaw or simply anything bad went straight to Taylor's head. The more she was around Josh, the more she wanted to be around him until she'd reached the point where she didn't have the will to leave. Dinner was over, and she knew she should return to Lydia's because she had an early start tomorrow morning, but she was too drunk on Josh's company to care. She was searching for excuses to prolong things, and God help her, if Josh suggested she go back to his place, she wasn't sure she had it in her to refuse. Her time in town was limited; she should live it up while she could.

Josh appeared to be doing his best to keep his hands off her since that one encounter with the beer spill, but as they made their way toward his Jeep, he linked a tentative finger around one of hers. In answer, she locked it firmly in place, her senses once more going on high alert with his touch. Luckily, that seemed to be the response Josh was waiting for, because he replaced his one-finger grip on her with his whole hand.

"So." He paused by the side of the Jeep, but didn't let go of her.

"So." When Josh stood this close, when she could detect the faint lemongrass soap scent on his skin, she definitely didn't trust herself to make a smart decision. Her heart pounded, which was kind of absurd. L.A. was overstuffed with hot guys, but she hadn't reacted like this to a touch since she was a hormone-crazed teenager.

Josh looked torn, and Taylor suspected he was debating similar thoughts. Then an idea must have struck him, because his face lit up and he flashed a mischievous smile. "Want to go check out the new brewery?"

Their server had talked about it over dinner, so it wasn't only Lydia who was intrigued. No one had met the guy who bought the building or knew when the brewery was opening or exactly what it was going to contain. Since she didn't live in Helen, Taylor's curiosity was minimal, but she saw Josh's suggestion for what it was—an attempt to prolong the date without outright inviting her over, at least not yet. He'd been cautious with her yesterday and cautious tonight. With every step forward, he gave her an opportunity to step back, and she was as appreciative of it as she was charmed.

"Let's do it." She was reluctant to let go of Josh's hand to get in the car, but he gave her a light squeeze before walking her around to the passenger side.

Taylor sneezed twice on the drive to the far-eastern edge of town, and her eyes itched but she didn't dare rub them lest she smear her mascara. If she intended to see Josh again, and she damn well intended to do that, she had to do something about her allergies. Those adorable dogs of his had clearly made many trips in his car.

Josh parked along the edge of the lot, but even though it was plenty light out, there wasn't much to see. A large trash container sat with its lid partially ajar, stuffed with construction debris, but the old building's exterior didn't appear much different. There was no sign, and nothing but blackness showed through the windows. An unmarked pickup truck and an electrician's van were parked out front, and another pickup truck was visible around the side of the building.

Taylor climbed out of the SUV along with Josh, feeling silly. This was private property, so technically they were trespassing, but the building was at the end of a long road and there wasn't a lot else nearby. Just the slight trip inland meant less wind, but she continued to hold down her dress with her right hand. Her left one clung to Josh's as they crossed the parking lot.

"Not opening anytime soon, I'm guessing," Taylor said.

"No, but someone's here." Josh pointed toward the closest window. "There are lights on inside."

She let him lead her closer to the window. At this distance, it became apparent someone had taped paper over them from the inside, but Josh was correct. A sliver of light peeked around one of the edges at the top where the paper had been cut. "Contractors working?"

"The van would suggest it, but it's surprisingly late on a Friday."

The gap in the paper was over Taylor's head, but Josh strained on his toes for a better view. She didn't like that he'd had to let go of her to do it, but watching him was entertaining. His dark hair flopped over his ears as he bounced on the balls of his feet, and he must have known he looked silly, because he laughed at himself.

"Anything?" she asked, clasping a hand over her mouth.

"I can't see a thing, and stop laughing. I'm sure there are dozens of breweries by you, but this is the second most exciting thing to happen around here since I moved in."

Taylor started to ask what the first most exciting thing was, but a door creaked behind them, and male voices drifted into the lot.

It had to be the beer at dinner, but the idea that they might actually get in trouble for trespassing struck Taylor as both hilarious and terrifying, and she wasn't alone. Josh stifled a swear and grabbed her hand, yanking her toward the corner. They ducked around the side of the building just in time as two men, probably the electrical contractors, judging by their conversation, ambled down the front steps.

Too late, Taylor realized they'd been forced to run around the side of the building that was closest to the vehicles. The contractors were heading toward the van and the pickup out front.

"This way." Josh nudged her lower, and they crept around the second unmarked truck, ducking out of sight. Gravel shifted beneath Taylor's feet, and Josh caught her before she slipped. "Just stay low."

Suppressing a fresh fit of giggles, Taylor allowed herself to sink into Josh's touch. The warmth of his body spread across her back, and her blood heated. She knew they were being ridiculous, but she hadn't had this much fun in forever. It was like being back in high school, trying to hide from chaperones at a dance so she could make out with her boyfriend.

The van's engine started, followed shortly by the pickup's, but neither Taylor nor Josh moved. She couldn't guess what he was thinking, but she was quite content to stay crouched where they were, Josh's body pressing into hers. Then the two vehicles started to back away, and Taylor and Josh were scrambling again to change position so they wouldn't be seen as the contractors circled the lot to the exit.

"Come on." Josh tugged her by the hand until they stood against the side of the building once more.

"You're good at that," Taylor said, keeping her voice low. "Any kind of criminal history you're not telling me about?"

Her cardigan had slipped from her shoulders in all that sneaking, and Josh pulled it back into place. His fingers lingered on her for a moment longer than strictly necessary, and some of Taylor's giddiness receded under a wave of new emotions.

"I did spend a lot of time playing jailbreak when I was younger. Pretty sure my friends and I terrorized the neighborhood, sneaking around in people's yards after dark. But actual criminal history? No. Do you frequently go on dates with criminals?"

Taylor coughed into her hand. "Once. No wait, I guess twice. Maybe."

Josh had clearly not been expecting that answer, but her dating history was littered with prizes. It's why she kept waiting for his fatal flaw to drop. "Really?"

"Oh, well, you know. Not like violent criminals, but this musician I dated a few times had a couple drug arrests in his past. He was in drug counseling when I met him."

"That's not exactly what I intended when I said 'criminals.' Good for him for getting help."

"Yeah, but . . ." She cringed. "I did have to dump him when he got busted for selling to middle school kids, so it wasn't as *good for him* a situation as I thought."

"Fair point. You said it happened twice though?" Josh gave her a curious look.

She had said that, hadn't she? Obviously she'd said too much, letting all this silliness carry her away. Taylor felt her cheeks flush. "You're going to think I'm an idiot."

"Nothing so far has led me to think you're an idiot."

"That's because you're too nice to let on. But since I did bring it up, I bartended a bit to pay my way through college. At one point, I was dating the guy I worked for, and so he used to let me drink."

"On the job?" Josh's brow pinched in confusion.

"Sometimes, but the bigger point is that I was underage. But neither of us ever got caught, so maybe that shouldn't count as criminal?"

Josh rubbed his chin. "Hmm. I'm not sure getting away with it should be where we draw the line on whether something's criminal. However, I'm willing to overlook these youthful indiscretions since you've developed better taste as you've matured."

"Are you sure about that?"

"I don't have a criminal record."

"Neither did my bartender ex." Taylor raised her finger in an *aha* gesture. "And I'd like to point out that we're currently trespassing—your idea. And, by your own admission, you used to do that all the time as a kid."

"Well, damn. You're right; I am kind of shady. No wonder you agreed to go out with me."

Taylor laughed, some of her embarrassment slipping away even as she wondered what in the world had gotten into her. Not only was she talking about her disastrous dating history on a first date, she was confessing to some of the stupidest stuff she'd gotten up to in her oh-so-rebellious youth. Yet she couldn't stop the flow of words. Something about Josh made him so easy to talk to. Apparently too easy.

For his part, Josh seemed to be taking her confession in stride. He just looked highly amused, which was way better than horrified. Considering it sounded like he'd been a model child—trampling through neighbors' yards aside—this conversation could have gone a lot worse.

"So, since we're trespassing, as you pointed out . . ." Josh grabbed her hand again, and Taylor clamped her free hand over her mouth to cover a scream of surprise as he began dragging her to the front of the building. "No sense breaking the law if we don't get anything out of it."

Taylor stumbled to a halt, crashing into him. Not get anything out of it? She'd beg to differ. She was getting quite a bit out of it, and the gleam in Josh's eyes suggested she wasn't the only one. "Do you have a plan, or do you just like yanking me around?"

Josh made an indecisive gesture. "Both? How about I lift you up and you spy for me?"

"You want to pick me up?" The excuse to have his

arms wrapped around her, and her body pressed against his was too good to forgo. Taylor released the hem of her dress, which she'd been holding down, and held out her arms. "Okay then. Grab me."

A wave of heat flashed over Josh's face as he stepped closer, and he raised an eyebrow. "You should watch your phrasing."

"What makes you think I didn't?"

He didn't seem to know how to respond to that, but he swallowed audibly and gave her one of those stares that suggested he was thinking dangerous thoughts. Instead of acting on any of them, though, Josh wrapped his arms under her ass. "Hold on."

Taylor was so busy trying not to react to where his hands or face were that she cried out when he suddenly hoisted her into the air. She reached out for purchase, and her arms landed around his neck. She'd thought her blood was pumping hard before, but that was nothing compared to now. Her dress's skirt had ridden up when he lifted her, and cool air bathed her legs, but she barely noticed.

Josh wasn't making any unwelcome moves—if that was even possible—but she was acutely aware of how tightly their bodies were pressed together, and especially that his face was only inches away from her chest. If they'd been lying in bed together, they could have been in far-less-intimate positions. Her whole body felt flushed.

With the boost, she was a couple of inches taller than he was, and Josh held her up toward the window. "See anything?"

Taylor blinked hard and attempted to concentrate on the request, but her imagination had fixated on the idea of being in bed with him. Preferably with a lot less clothing.

Craning her neck, she peered into the crack of light. "Lots of wood. Some partially installed track lighting, I think. Nothing exciting. Looks like the place is undergoing a remodel."

"No beer?"

"No beer in sight."

"Bummer." Josh adjusted his grip on her. "Ready to go down then?"

Taylor gave him her best sardonic expression. "Now who's got to watch their phrasing?"

His retort involved releasing her for just a second so that she shrieked, but catching her before her feet touched the ground. And then he didn't let go. His arms draped around her waist, her dress bunched up between them.

"That should have been disappointing," Josh said, his voice low, "but under the circumstances, I don't feel very disappointed."

Belatedly, Taylor remembered her hands remained on his neck, but rather than remove them like she should have, she left them there. Compared to some of the places she was considering placing them, his neck was safe. "These circumstances, you mean? Definitely not disappointing."

Josh bent his face closer to hers. "So are you going to remove your arms?"

"Depends. What will you do if I don't?" His chest rose and fell, pressing against her breasts. Each time he inhaled, the fabric rubbing across her nipples sent shock waves down to her groin.

"I might have to kiss you."

"That would be tragic." Taylor paused and pulled herself closer, and she could feel Josh's body react against hers. "Completely tragic to move my arms."

"Completely." He raised one hand to cup her cheek, and then Taylor's brain melted down as his lips touched hers.

The kiss was sweet and slow, and left her burning up under her skin—a thousand nerve endings consumed in fire that spread from her face down to her fingertips and to her toes, curling in her shoes. After all the lusty thoughts she'd been entertaining about Josh this evening, she craved something wilder. Harder. She suspected he did too. Instead, the way he toyed with her mouth was agonizing in the best possible way, and she knew she'd been right about his ability to read her. He wouldn't make this easy for her, and she'd thank him in the end as she melted in a pool of liquid heat.

How Josh could stand to kiss her like this was a mystery. The man must have far better self-control than she did, or so Taylor thought until the hand that had been around her waist dropped to her leg and Josh lifted her dress a couple of inches.

7

WAS THAT A tattoo I saw?"

Josh didn't want to stop kissing her, but if he didn't come up for air, he was going to lose his mind. Focusing on Taylor's leg might not have been the wisest decision, but it was too late. His eager hand gathered her dress and slid the fabric up a little higher. Just an inch. Just slowly enough to let her protest. But she didn't. Of course not. She inhaled sharply, and her smile dared him to lift it higher.

It was a terrible idea. He had half a mind to push the dress to her waist and go down on her in the middle of the parking lot. Her lips were soft and tasted lightly of beer, and he was dying to know what the rest of her skin tasted like. He'd start with kissing that tattoo, work his way up the tender areas of her inner thigh, push aside whatever she was wearing underneath . . .

This wasn't him. He didn't like to rush things, which was one of the big reasons—aside from stress—he didn't pursue casual dating or sex in the first place. The more the anticipation, the longer the buildup, the sweeter the release. That had made the two weeks Taylor would be in town seem like the perfect timing. It was long enough to not rush things, short enough to keep their relationship casual. But from the very beginning tonight, his plan had started falling apart.

He'd wanted her something fierce as soon as he saw her holding her dress down earlier, but the way she'd made him laugh all evening, even the cute way she scowled when she sneezed—that did something worrisome to him, something that only made him want her more. Before, she was gorgeous. Now, she was becoming irresistible. Josh wasn't sure how to handle that, and it was testing his willpower.

Taylor tucked her hair behind her ear. "You're going to have to ask nicely if you want to see the rest of it."

"Nicely, huh?" He should absolutely not kiss her again. Or slide his hand farther up her thigh. They were in a parking lot, for goodness' sake. A deserted parking lot to be sure, but a parking lot nonetheless. In theory, any of his patients could walk by and see him, and he'd never be able to look them in the eye again, especially not if any of his mother's old friends saw him making out with a woman in public.

Yet he was kissing her again anyway. Pulling her closer so the softness of her breasts pooled against his chest, and the planes of her stomach pressed against his growing erection. Even still, despite the temptation of her five-foot-whatever body, he fought to touch her lips lightly, gently. If he gave in to the need coursing through him, it was all over. He might never be able to stop, so he had to hang on to some semblance of control.

Taylor moaned and the sound almost broke him. Perhaps that was why he didn't hear anything else until a door thudded shut nearby.

The sound succeeded where his willpower was failing. Startled, Josh pulled away and let Taylor's dress fall back into place. The way her cheeks flushed alerted him that the person responsible for the noise was closer than expected even before he heard the scuff of feet on the brewery's front steps.

Busted, and after they'd had so much fun evading the electricians too. Amazing how distracting a pair of soft lips and a tattoo could be.

Taylor waved awkwardly, and Josh turned around to see a strange guy standing a few feet away return the gesture with the same embarrassed expression. Maybe Taylor knew him, but Josh was simply thankful it wasn't one of his patients. He absolutely had to revive the self-control Taylor had killed, before he was caught in a truly compromising position.

"Um." The guy scratched his neck, and Josh admired the man's ability to not run back inside the building, which was something Josh probably would have done if their positions were reversed.

"Sorry." The word came out strangled through his embarrassment. "We were just hoping for a peek inside."

Right, because peeking inside was exactly what they'd looked like they were doing a moment ago.

The stranger had clearly seen enough not to buy it, but he mostly held his smirk in check. He appeared to be in his late twenties or early thirties and wore a sweatshirt over a pair of paint-stained jeans. "Not much to see inside yet," he said. "I was hoping to open this summer, but I had a few delays."

"Oh, are you the owner?" Taylor flashed him one of her sunny smiles, and damn if it didn't burn up the worst of the awkward tension.

"Uh, yeah, I am." He held out a hand. "I'm Ian."

They all shook, and Josh and Taylor shared their first names. "Everyone is excited to see what you do with the place," Josh added.

Ian winced. "Don't tell me that—the pressure. It was nice meeting you, but I've got to run to the hardware store before they close."

Taylor tugged on Josh's hand as Ian got into his truck. "We should go too. Before I lose any more blood to the mosquitoes."

Mosquitoes, like tourists, were an unrelenting force in the summer, but Josh had barely noticed them all evening. His attention had been focused on Taylor.

"Good idea." Mosquitoes aside, meeting Ian was a clear reminder about the perils of public kissing. Of course, if public kissing was over, Josh had to think about how to navigate what happened next. His body was begging him to invite Taylor over. His brain was warning him to slow down.

"What you said to Ian reminded me of something," Taylor said, interrupting his indecision. "You said earlier that the brewery was the second most exciting thing to happen around here in a long time. What's the first?"

Josh groaned, and a second wave of embarrassment crashed over him. "You were supposed to ask that question when I said it, not wait until the moment's fled. The first is obviously you showing up."

"Ah. You're very funny."

"I was going for charming, but I'll take it."

"Charm is overrated in humans. Leave that to your dogs." She paused by the passenger door long enough for Josh to trap her against it with his body. Odds seemed to be against his brain winning the to-invite-or-not-to-invite argument, especially when Taylor toyed with his shirt. "I have to admit, I was hoping you'd have the dogs with you so I could play with them again."

"So that's why you agreed to see me—for the dogs. Story of my life. Sorry, since I didn't know where we were going, I thought they'd be happier left at home."

The last word hung heavy in the air. Josh had intended it to simply be a factual answer, but as his voice died away, he became acutely aware that it was also an opening.

Taylor's brown eyes searched his face, and he could tell she was aware of it too. Given he was likely to choose poorly, he'd let her decide what to do about it, and he opened the door for her.

Taylor sneezed and followed it with her adorable cringe. "I need to pick up some allergy meds."

"I was wondering about that sneezing habit of yours. Would you like to stop by Safeway?"

"That would be great."

Okay then. They were both putting off the next decision for a bit longer. He could live with that. In fact, a trip to the store wasn't a bad idea regardless. Josh was 90 percent sure he didn't have any condoms, and that seemed like the sort of thing he should remedy just in case. It had never occurred to him to do so beforehand, since even contemplating inviting a woman home on a first date was an entirely new experience.

Luckily, the family planning section turned out to be an aisle over from the allergy and cold medicine section, so Taylor didn't have to witness him being presumptuous. He'd just turned the corner when an unfamiliar voice called out her name.

"Mrs. Miller, how are you?" Taylor asked. It might have been because he was feeling possessive of her attention, but Josh would have sworn Taylor didn't sound happy about being sucked into a conversation.

"Oh, I'm fine. I had no idea you were in town." The Mrs. Miller woman lowered her voice, but the store was dead and it carried easily. "Is this because of your parents?"

Taylor attempted to respond, but the other woman talked right over her. "A damn shame is what it is, and those Porters spreading gossip about it. Saying your parents were having affairs?" She clucked her tongue in disgust. "No one with any sense believes that. I don't understand why your father can't do something about it, what with being the mayor and all."

Those Porters? Taylor's father was the mayor— Gregory Lipin?

The woman kept right on with her rambling, but Josh didn't catch another word. His head was spinning. After the time he'd spent telling Kelsey to leave him out of the feud this afternoon, he'd gone and stepped into a giant pile of it. Why hadn't he ever bothered to ask Taylor what her last name was? How, for that matter, had he reached a point where he'd been considering inviting her over, sleeping with her, without knowing such a thing? It wasn't as though he, personally, cared that she was a Lipin, but it sure did show him how reckless he was acting.

Josh took a deep breath. He had to slow down. Regardless of what he thought about the feud, he had no idea what Taylor thought. For all he knew, once she learned he was a Porter, in blood if not in name, she might run home and wash her mouth out with soap.

Abandoning the condoms, he headed over to the exit to wait impatiently for Taylor to extricate herself from the chatty Mrs. Miller. She emerged from the store a few minutes later, clutching a bottle of generics, and tossed Josh an exhausted expression.

"Sorry about that. She's one of those people who can talk without stopping to breathe."

"Not a problem." Honestly, he ought to thank the woman, though he wasn't feeling particularly grateful. "You're Gregory Lipin's daughter?"

A string of emotions flashed over Taylor's face in succession—surprise, wariness, and finally resignation. "You heard that? Yup. I take it you know who my father is."

"Your father's the mayor. I think everyone knows who he is, and who the Lipins are."

"A name that lives in infamy." She yanked open the car door before Josh could open it for her. "It was nice being anonymous for a bit. Now you know another reason I ran off to L.A."

Josh's eyebrows shot up in surprise. He'd suspected there was more to it than the answer she'd given him at dinner, but he hadn't expected this to be it. "To get away from your family?"

"To get away from the family baggage." She flopped against the seat. "I mean, you're new to town, and it sounds like you still know about my family drama. You have no idea what it was like growing up here."

He had a better idea than she realized, and he needed to explain that quickly before she found out and thought he'd purposely hidden his situation from her. Josh ran his fingers through his hair, bracing himself for her reaction. "My family makes knowing your family drama inevitable. Before she married and left Helen, my mother was a Porter. When I said I had family in town, that's who I meant."

Taylor's eyes opened wide. He was standing beside

the open passenger door, and she lunged past him and grabbed the handle. "Get in." Her voice had filled with dread. "Mrs. Miller might come out any second, and if there's a chance she recognizes you, we shouldn't be seen talking."

Before Josh could protest that they'd already been seen together by lots of people at dinner, not to mention Ian at the brewery, Taylor pulled on the door, and he had to skirt out of the way to avoid being hit as she closed it.

Josh blinked. Well, she hadn't jumped out of the car and run away, so he'd take that as a positive sign.

Warily, he climbed back into the Jeep and pointed out the dinner problem. "Are you sure it makes a difference at this point?" Despite his skepticism, Taylor's paranoia was contagious, and he kept one eye on the Safeway doors.

"I didn't recognize anyone at dinner," Taylor said, slipping her sunglasses in place. "That doesn't mean no one recognized me, but we might have gotten lucky. Chances are over half the people in the restaurant weren't locals. And it's unlikely Ian will remember us beyond those weirdos making out in public."

Taking his cue from her, Josh put on his own sunglasses. "I'm not local enough to believe anything other than that the feud is stupid, in case you're wondering."

A smile flickered across Taylor's lips and disappeared. "I was actually. I'm glad you didn't drive off and leave me stranded in the parking lot."

"Not my style." Josh tentatively picked up her hand. "I'm glad you didn't jump out of the car and run away screaming."

"The girl who took off to California?" Taylor laughed sharply. "I'm the family rebel. I hate the feud. I hate the drama. I hate that I'm supposed to fall in line and that no matter what I do, as long as I'm here, I'll never be anything other than a soldier in a war I didn't start."

Josh tightened his grip on her hand, entwining their fingers. Far from resisting, Taylor did the same. That seemed to settle matters, and some of the tension drained from his shoulders. "So if we're in agreement, can we plan to do this again?"

Part of him was definitely going to go to bed disappointed that he hadn't invited her over, but Josh was no longer certain she'd have said yes if he did. And logically, he knew ending the night early was for the best.

Taylor was biting her lip and obviously agitated, but she let out a slow breath as she turned to him. "Yes, I want to do this again. Just maybe not this exactly. We'll need to be careful. Going out together would be seen as a serious breach of family loyalty."

"I don't know about your family, but I'm an adult. No one in my family better expect me to listen if they lecture me on who I date."

"If you think all they'd do is lecture you . . ." Taylor shook her head. "How well do you know your family, Josh?"

Her tone suggested she thought he was being naive, and he couldn't help but bristle. "My mother told me stories, and I know some of them are true. But this is different. My grandmother was in the middle of an argument when she took a swing at one of your aunts. There's no arguing here, no fighting. No provocation."

"Talking pleasantly to me might be seen as provocation. Kissing me? That's like dropping a nuclear bomb." Taylor cut him off as he tried to protest. "It doesn't matter what we say about it. Our families are not rational. Trust me. I don't want them to dictate how I spend my time while I'm here, but if we want to do this again, we need to do it on the sly."

He wanted to believe Taylor was being overly dramatic, but he couldn't bring himself to commit to the idea. She had to be though. Even with everything he knew and the way his cousin was reacting to the current Lipin drama, a nuclear-bomb kiss sounded absurd to his ears.

But Josh's gut twisted in worry, in no small part due to the shadow that had settled over Taylor's face. There was, after all, nothing wrong with being cautious. In fact, it was the smart play. Taylor would be around for only a couple of weeks, so if there was a chance of avoiding family conflict, he might as well agree with her wishes.

It would make seeing her more challenging, but he liked a good challenge, and if it slowed down the pace of their relationship, tonight proved that might not be such a bad outcome. It was time to ditch plan B—act reckless—and return to plan A—get to know Taylor better and prolong the anticipation.

8

AT HER INSISTENCE, Josh dropped Taylor off at the end of the driveway leading to the Bay Song. She got the sense that he remained skeptical about how their families would react if anyone found out about the date, but Taylor knew in her bones she was right. Whether Josh believed she was paranoid or not, she was doing this for him. In two weeks she'd be gone, and the feud could fade away from her conscious thoughts until it was once more a nonissue. He would have to live with the consequences on a daily basis.

One date when neither of them knew who the other was could be accepted as a mistake if word got around. But two—absolutely not. So as much as she would have liked to go back to Josh's after they left Safeway, part of her had been relieved he hadn't asked. She didn't know how good a liar he was, but she was out of practice. If they'd been spotted by someone with a vested interest in tattling, she would have a much easier time shrugging the date off as a mistake and claiming nothing exciting happened if it were true.

As things stood, it was only mostly true. She'd had lots of fun talking to Josh, and her body still hummed from the charge everywhere he'd touched her. He would have been perfect if not for his fatal flaw, but she'd known there would be one. There always was, and maybe she should be thankful Josh was a Porter. If things continued to go as well between them the next time they saw each other, she'd be at risk of getting more attached than she wanted to be. Being a Porter, however, meant there was a giant "Beware!" sign on his forehead, one she couldn't forget. It would make it easier for her to leave him behind.

Laughter rang out from the deck at the back of the Tavern—a rehearsal dinner winding down. Even if Josh didn't change his mind, she couldn't see him tomorrow because Lydia had already roped her into helping with the wedding.

Helping Lydia—that was what she should be focusing on. Taylor did her best to clamp down on her post-date adrenaline so she didn't appear too suspicious, but her restless fingers tapped with tension against her palms.

"Have fun?" Her sister was doing dishes, and she paused wiping down a pot.

"Yup." Too late, Taylor realized she should have checked her hair and the state of her dress. Hopefully, if Lydia noticed anything, Taylor could blame a disheveled appearance on the wind. Quickly, she kicked off her shoes, praying that might be the only question if she could escape fast enough, but she wasn't that lucky.

"Who were you out with again?"

With her back to her sister, Taylor swore silently. She'd never actually given Lydia a name because doing so was risky, but it looked like she didn't have a choice. "Clara Jeffries," she said, settling on the name of a friend from high school whom Lydia hadn't known well.

Like most of her friends from school, Taylor had drifted apart from Clara during college, but they remained lightly connected thanks to social media. From that, she knew Clara was married, expecting a baby over the winter, and teaching sixth-grade math at Helen Regional Middle School. Those details would give Taylor something to talk about if Lydia asked after her.

In fact, she should reach out to Clara for real since she was in town for so long. Normally, her trips home didn't leave much time for that sort of socializing, but two weeks was twice the usual.

"How is she?" Lydia asked, hanging the pot on a rack over the stove.

"Good." Facebook made it seem that way, at least, so Taylor told herself it wasn't a lie.

She reached around Lydia to fill a glass of water and hurried into the bathroom to take an allergy pill. Her eyes were still itchy, but she also hoped her quick escape meant her sister wouldn't have the chance to ask more questions. Lying to her parents when she was a kid was one thing; lying to her sister these days was another.

Unfortunately, Taylor had no reason to believe that Lydia wouldn't flip out if she discovered the truth. Her sister was pretty much a pacifist but she was also dutiful, and she'd never said much to convince Taylor that she thought the feud was absurd. Lydia's reaction was a coin flip that could go either way. Since that was the case, it was best to play it safe, as she'd told Josh. She just wished playing it safe didn't make her feel like a jerk.

Coming out of the bathroom, Taylor knelt down to pet Merlot, but Lydia's cat flicked his tail at her and darted away. Great. Even the cat thought she was being a jerk.

This was why she couldn't stay in Helen. The town ruined everything, including the good mood she'd been in. The complacency—the comfort—she'd felt while hanging out with Josh was gone. And faster than she'd expected.

Tomorrow then. Tomorrow she'd have a couple of hours to devote to job hunting, and no matter how much she wanted to turn her nose up at the job listings she found, Taylor vowed she'd apply for a minimum of three. It wasn't a lot, but it was a start.

IF THE DOGS hadn't woken Josh up with their barking, the pounding on his door would have. Groaning, he glanced at the time. Usually the dogs let him sleep in for another half hour on his days off, but the distinct racket below made that irrelevant. His huskies rarely barked and never at strangers, so whoever had the audacity to stop by at seven in the morning on a Saturday had to be someone they were super excited to see.

Only one person fit that description, so Josh wasn't surprised to discover his cousin outside when he rambled down the stairs a minute later. "What are you doing here so early?"

Kelsey removed her sunglasses, revealing a pair of matching dark circles under her eyes. "We have a problem."

"We do?" In spite of the lack of coffee in his system, Josh's thoughts immediately jumped to Taylor, and his pulse spiked.

He'd gone to bed last night with his brain puzzling through their family dilemma and the taste of their final kiss on his lips. Both had kept him awake, and when he'd finally fallen asleep, an odd mix of anxiety and lust had fueled his dreams. He wasn't entirely over either this morning, but thanks to Kelsey's unexpected arrival, the anxiety was predominating.

"You would think, in this day and age," Kelsey said, ignoring his question, "that people would be allowed to live their lives and love their loves, and it would be no big deal. But no, not in our family. Everything in our family needs to be hard. There is no 'love is love' here."

Josh swallowed and kept his back to her as he opened the sliding door onto his deck and fenced-in backyard so the dogs could go out and do their business. His bold declaration to Taylor—that no one in his family had better lecture him about his relationships—had come back to haunt him already. He should have known Kelsey would be the one.

Josh didn't like to argue under the best of conditions, and before his first cup of coffee was far from it. "Kels, can I just—"

"Nope, you need to let me finish. I had to listen to my father rant last night, so now you have to listen to me rant. It's only fair. Someday you'll get to rant, and when you do, I promise I'll listen. But for now, it's me." She pointed her thumb at her chest.

"I can explain." Wait, what was he doing? He didn't owe her or anyone else an explanation. Screw that. This was why he needed caffeine before he socialized. Josh pushed by her into the kitchen in search of the magic liquid.

"What do you have to explain?"

Her response caught him off guard, and he banged his hand on the cabinet. Was this not about him and Taylor? Had he been about to blab all without reason?

Josh made an attempt to clear what felt like a guilty expression off his face before glancing over his shoulder. "Um . . . I don't know? Coffee?" He held out the bag.

"Please. Actually, do you have anything for breakfast around here? I'm starving and haven't eaten yet."

"There's bread for toast." He had to go food shopping.

"Oh, you buy the good bread." She stuck four slices in his toaster. Presumably a couple were for him. "We need to do something for Kevin."

"What happened to Kevin?" Josh pressed start on the coffeepot and headed into the dining room to let the dogs gathered at the door back in.

Kelsey let out a cry of frustration. "Haven't you been listening to anything I've said?"

"You haven't said a whole lot yet."

Yawning, his cousin got on the floor and helped him wipe mud off the dogs' feet. "Kevin got engaged yesterday, and my dad lost his shit."

Josh frowned. "I thought your dad liked Peter."

"My dad claims he likes Peter. Just not as a son-in-law. Do you see where this is going?" She patted Pepper on the butt, and the husky wandered into the kitchen, Kelsey's presence no longer as attention grabbing as Pepper's empty food dish.

"Yeah, yeah," Josh muttered as three faces beseeched him for breakfast. He turned to Kelsey as he got out the dog food. "Go on."

She crossed her arms as she leaned against a counter. "Apparently my dad was fine with my brother dating guys as long as Kevin didn't decide to marry one of them. Apparently, my dad assumed my brother was going through a phase since he'd also dated girls in the past. And apparently, my dad does not understand the definition of bisexual and just assumed Kevin would settle on a woman when he got serious about things—his words, not mine."

Josh swore. Poor Kevin. Now he felt guilty again and with a good reason—he was relieved to not be the one drawing his uncle's wrath. Josh rubbed his head and willed the coffeepot to brew faster. The aroma was lovely, but the fumes didn't do much for his wakefulness. "What did your mother say?"

Kelsey snorted. "She says very little when my dad loses his temper, not that it's easy to get a word in for any of us. Kevin texted me when the news broke, so I went over to their place to provide backup, although I don't think I accomplished much. Luckily, Peter wasn't there to see my family acting like assholes, but he'll find out soon enough."

Kelsey collapsed into a chair as the toaster finished, and Josh set two slices of bread and the butter in front of her. He didn't have the heart to tell Kelsey that her father's behavior didn't surprise him in the slightest. *Old-fashioned* was the euphemistic way to describe his uncle's views on certain subjects. The man's initial acceptance of Kevin's relationship had surprised Josh, but he supposed he'd been provided an explanation for that.

Again, his thoughts drifted to Taylor's warning last night. His uncle would almost certainly explode if he found out Josh was dating a Lipin, but would he really do more than yell?

Shaking his head, Josh poured them each a mug of coffee. This wasn't a time to worry about his relationships. Kelsey had come over because she had to vent, and he needed to support her brother.

"You should have heard him," his cousin was saying. "Going on about the dumbest things, like who's going to carry on the family name and what about grandkids?"

"What does Nate think? Does he know?" Kelsey and Kevin's older brother was a firefighter for the US Forest Service and currently stationed in Washington state. Since Nate and Josh were closer in age than he was to Kelsey, Nate had been the cousin Josh used to be closest to. But they'd lost touch as they'd grown older, and Nate only made it to Helen a few times a year during the off-season.

"Kevin said Nate sent him a congratulatory text and demanded to be his best man, so I'm sure he's happy. Nate's like you; he prefers to keep it low drama. My dad's not going to rope him in unless he's positive Nate will side with him since he's the kid my dad's the most proud of. He wouldn't want Mr. Hotshot Firefighter to argue with him."

"What can I do?" Josh asked. "Besides the obvious and wishing Kevin and Peter congratulations."

Kelsey stirred an unhealthy amount of sugar into her coffee and sipped it before answering. "I want to throw them an engagement party. Someone has to step up to the plate, and honestly, you're the only one I can count on."

"Of course I'm in. Sounds like a good plan." Briefly, he wondered if Taylor would be in town by the time they pulled it off, but then he remembered she wouldn't be allowed anywhere near it even if she'd wanted to go. Which he was positive she wouldn't.

Josh grimaced into his coffee.

Kelsey slapped the table without warning, and he jumped along with he dogs. Jay shot her a decidedly displeased look from over his food dish. "Okay, I'm done. Give me happy thoughts. Since I'm here, tell me about your date."

Josh stuffed a large bite of toast in his mouth.

"Come on. Where'd you end up going?"

Swallowing, he told her. "After dinner, we went to the brewery and met the guy who owns it. His name's Ian."

Kelsey narrowed her eyes. "What were you doing at the unopened brewery?"

Since there was no way he was telling her most of what they'd been doing, Josh shrugged and took another bite of food.

"You're being awfully cagey," Kelsey said. "Did it not go well? Oh—or did it go very well? Is she here?" His cousin swiveled around in her seat as though she could see through the walls and up the stairs.

"No, she's not here. Damn, Kels."

"I don't judge."

"Yes, you do. Constantly. About everything." He got up to refill his coffee and offered her the pot, too, but she shook her head.

"Okay, you're right. I do." She pointed a finger at him. "But in fairness, so does everybody. I'm just willing to admit it. And seriously, I really don't care who sleeps with who or when or how often they do it. I'm not that kind of person."

Josh believed that, but he also believed it was a statement made in reaction to her father's attitude about Kevin and Peter. "Unless it's a Lipin?"

He knew better than to ask a question he didn't want an answer to, but it was too late to take back the words. They'd bubbled up from some hidden defensiveness and not-so-hidden anxiety.

"Well, obviously," Kelsey said, licking butter from her fingers. "We have to have some standards."

Josh forced a smile and, no longer in the mood to eat, tossed the rest of his toast to the dogs.

9

BITTERSWEET CHOCOLATE BROKE over Taylor's tongue, and she moaned with delight even as the hot cookie burned her mouth.

"It's good that I don't have access to your baking year-round or it would do terrible things to my health," she told Marie.

The inn's head cook chuckled at her from across the kitchen island. Marie stood just shy of five feet, and with her dark eyes and thick hair that fell in waves to her waist, she'd always reminded Taylor of a fairy. That hair was now white as freshly fallen snow, and the contrast it provided against her warm brown skin only heightened the effect. She'd been working in the inn's kitchen for as long as Taylor could remember. On paper, supervising the kitchen might have been her mother's—and currently Taylor's—job, but there was no question who was really in charge.

The Sugpiaq woman patted Taylor on the cheek. "I miss having you in my kitchen year-round. You were always my favorite assistant."

"Your favorite nuisance, maybe," Taylor said, and Marie scoffed.

When Taylor was younger, weekend mornings in the kitchen with Marie had been her favorite times, even though they had meant she couldn't sleep in. The Bay Song provided a breakfast of daily made quiches and pastries to guests, and Marie and her assistants arrived around five in the morning to prepare everything. Little Taylor had been there whenever she could, undoubtedly getting underfoot. But rather than kick her out, the head cook had put her to work—beating eggs, measuring ingredients, and sprinkling nuts and sugar. Taylor credited Marie with her interest in cooking that had persisted to this day. Goodness knew she hadn't gotten it from either of her parents, both of whom had always been indifferent to the idea of freshly prepared hot meals.

"You were never a nuisance." Marie set the final tray of chocolate chip cookies on a rack to cool, and slipped on a Stanford University sweatshirt as she got ready to leave. Her granddaughter would be attending the school in the fall, and Marie was both proud and terrified of her going so far away. She'd been peppering Taylor with questions about California since Saturday, and Taylor's explanations that L.A. and Palo Alto were not right next to each other and she didn't know much about the latter made no difference.

Like many people in Helen, to Marie, everything in "the south" was presumed to be mere minutes away from each other. It was the local equivalent to Stacy's assuming there was no internet in Alaska.

"I am sorry your mother took off the way she did," Marie said, "but I'm glad to have you back. You know, you could consider staying if you don't like the jobs down there." She nudged Taylor in the ribs.

"You're all ganging up on me." Lydia had been casually suggesting that Taylor might want to extend her stint as the inn's hospitality manager since she'd overheard Taylor complaining while she searched through job listings a couple of days ago.

Marie clasped a hand over her heart and feigned innocence. "Never. Now, don't eat all the cookies before you put them out for the guests. Got it?"

"Hey, if you don't want me eating them, then stop making them taste so good." Taylor waved her pencil at the older woman, and Marie rolled her eyes.

"You were always a chocolate fiend."

The cook slipped out the kitchen door, and Taylor glanced down at the wine inventory list she'd been working on. Marie's assistant had left for the day once the kitchen cleaning was done and the coffee service was set up. In a half hour, Taylor would brew the coffee and set it and the cookies out in the lounge area. Until then, she had time to figure out what her mother had been doing with the wine purchasing, which was a task that might have been easier if her mother had kept electronic records. As it was, Taylor had to squint and turn the notebook left and right to decipher her mother's handwriting.

So far, this was turning out to be the toughest part of the job. Taylor hoped that if—no, when—her mother returned, she'd appreciate the time her daughter was taking to enter all her bookkeeping into Excel. On the bright side, having to go back through months' worth of lists and invoices was giving her a crash course on this part of the job. While Taylor had been familiar with the big picture of her mother's responsibilities, the minutiae were new. Taylor had finally talked to her mother the other day, and Denise had gone over the job with her. But the conversation had been unsatisfactory in many ways—starting with the fact that her mother hadn't indicated any plans to return soon, and ending with her apparent obliviousness to the mess she'd left Lydia. Luckily, just as Marie had the kitchen under control, the head of housekeeping was also a veteran at the job and had been able to fill Taylor in on those details as well.

She snatched another cookie—her last, she promised herself—and got back to work, ignoring the voice in the back of her head that whispered what a boring job this was. That voice had been nagging her for a few days at this point, and Taylor recognized it for what it was—a lie. A lie she'd concocted in her determination to go to L.A. and do something ostensibly exciting with her life.

The truth was that she was enjoying herself. So far, the work had made good use of her organizational and presentation skills, particularly with the wedding she'd assisted with. For once, she wasn't trying to sell people items they didn't need, but selling them on the ones they'd already purchased, whether it was the inn's complimentary evening wine and cheese or a wedding's custom cocktail. There was satisfaction in making people happy.

"I can do that back in L.A. too," Taylor muttered to herself. Which was true. She liked hosting her friends for dinner, cooking new foods, and making fancy drinks. It just wasn't easy given how small her apartment was, and she had to admit that there was something nice about being paid for her effort.

A text arrived, and Josh's name flashed over her phone screen. Now there was an experience she couldn't replicate back in L.A.

In her haste to read the message, she dropped the pencil and it rolled to the floor. Taylor forced her lips to stop smiling and squared her shoulders. Just because she felt stupidly giddy whenever Josh texted her didn't mean she had to act stupidly giddy.

Her mouth remained neutral only for as long as it took her to read the message. Want to have dinner later?

Yes, of course she did, but Taylor's good mood took a hit as she considered their situation. They'd gotten together once since their first date and the unfortunate discovery that they were on opposite sides of the world's most pitiful war. They'd met in the park, each with their own cup of coffee. Each wearing sunglasses. Josh had also worn a baseball cap, and Taylor had worn a sweatshirt that read "Alaska" across the chest, something she'd borrowed from the inn's lost and found. She'd figured it made her look like a tourist. They'd talked, which was nice, and she'd gotten to play with his dogs, which was fun. But as far as dates went, it had frankly sucked. There had been no comfortable conversation like on their first date and certainly no touching. Given how much time she'd spent thinking about touching him, that might have been the worst part of it. The gap between them had been torturous when she could recall the taste of his tongue on hers and the sensation of his hand on her leg.

She'd been annoyed and frustrated by the experience, despite that she liked seeing Josh, and Taylor knew he felt the same. They'd been texting extensively over the past couple of days. But if Josh thought the so-called date had changed her mind about hiding their time together, he was wrong.

Taylor was about to remind him of that when a second text arrived. My place is available. No pressure, but not doing that coffee farce again.

Taylor grinned. Combining dinner with going to his place—there might yet be an upside to this whole clandestine dating problem.

* * *

IN, QUICKLY." JOSH hustled Taylor through the side door that led into his kitchen. Once she was safely hidden from view, he carried her bike around to the backyard and concealed it in his shed.

Glancing over the fence into his neighbors' yards, he assured himself no one had been watching. Then he swore. He was living in a spy movie. A bad one, seeing as no self-respecting secret agent would waste time in Helen.

Taylor had removed her shoes and was receiving an abundance of husky kisses when he entered his house through the sliding doors. Whether she was enjoying them with her allergies, he was less certain. She acted like she was, and to his surprise, she'd remembered his dogs' names.

And Kelsey claimed all Lipins were cat people.

His cousin—no, his family—had been getting inside his head. He was not about to start dividing the world into cat people and dog people, Lipins and Porters. He and Taylor got along great, which just proved the rest of the world had hang-ups.

"Hey, hey." Josh dragged an excited Jay and Pepper off Taylor. As usual, the two siblings were locked in a dire competition for attention. "Down. Let her be."

If he couldn't slobber all over her, it seemed unfair that they could. The most he'd gotten to do was give her a quick peck on the cheek before practically shoving her into his house.

"It's okay." Taylor rubbed Jay's head and stood. "Better than okay. It's good. I needed that. It's been a long afternoon."

"What happened?" She hadn't mentioned anything was amiss when he'd texted her earlier.

Taylor winced. "It's . . . nothing. Don't worry about it."

He touched her arm. "Is it the job search? The divorce? Anything I can help with?"

His help preference would be, say, a naked massage, but he'd do whatever she needed.

She sighed. "Some of your family members were posting nasty things about my father and the divorce on the town's Facebook group. They were taken down quickly, obviously, but it's . . ."

Obnoxious? Frustrating? Exhausting? He'd have guessed some combination of the three from her expression, and guilt by association took a bite of Josh's insides. "I'm sorry. My family has issues."

Taylor kissed his cheek. "It's not just your family that has issues, and it's not your fault."

"No, but this time it's my family spreading malicious rumors, from the sound of it. I could try talking to them." It wouldn't work, and it wouldn't be as fun as a naked massage, but he could attempt it.

But Taylor heard the futility in his voice or, more likely, had a better understanding of it than he did. "You aren't responsible for them."

No, he wasn't, and yet he couldn't shake the feeling that he ought to try for her sake.

Josh pulled her close and wrapped his arms around her. Taylor hesitated for half a second, then melted into his body. It was so perverse that their families were at war, and yet she felt so right next to him.

He kissed her forehead and threaded his fingers through her hair, and his body stirred. It would be all too easy to keep kissing her, to nibble his way down her face to her lips and to work his hands under the fabric of her shirt. He'd spent hours thinking about it and so much more since last Friday. But he'd promised himself that wasn't the goal when he'd invited her over for dinner. Her presence here was because it was the best they could do for a date, not because he wanted or expected her in his bed.

Taylor's fingers dug into his back. Knowing she desired the same thing he did made it all the more difficult for him to release her, but damn it, they were going to have dinner before things went any further. He'd had a plan, and it did not involve letting his dick dictate the evening.

"It's a wonder we turned out as normal as we did," Josh said, taking a step back.

"Are we though?" Taylor finger combed the hair he'd mussed. "Tell me your eccentricities."

"None. I have none." Josh opened the bag sitting on his kitchen counter and removed the food he'd bought for dinner. "Since we couldn't go out, I brought dinner to us. You said you liked Indian."

Taylor inspected one of the containers. "I do. Salmon curry—you know, you don't see that too often anywhere else. Is there nothing we can't stick salmon in around here?"

"Is there nothing Californians can't stick avocado in?"

"Good point." She finished unpacking the food while Josh got out plates. "I'd have cooked, you know."

"This is a date. Just because we can't have it in public doesn't change that. You shouldn't have to cook."

"I like cooking."

Josh grinned. "That's your eccentricity then."

"No, my eccentricity is that I can cook six different types of macaroni and cheese, depending on my mood. Just cooking itself isn't that weird."

"Six different types?" He let that sink in a moment before silently agreeing that she was correct. It was weird. "Isn't macaroni and cheese just macaroni and cheese?"

"Philistine. Not my macaroni and cheese. Be nice and maybe I'll let you try a batch before I leave."

Before I leave. Of course she was leaving, probably in just over a week. He'd known it and counted on it, but the words were a kick to the stomach anyway.

"I'd like that. And in return, I'll share my talents with you, which are, um . . ." He searched the room for something he could offer, and his gaze landed on his backpack, visible in the living room. "I can patch you up if you burn yourself on the stove, or sew you up if you slice open a finger?"

Taylor laughed. "Come on. I'm sure you have talents besides that."

"Oh, I do. Maybe I'll share those with you later." He'd intended the words to come out light and flirtatious, but instead they were heavy and heated.

Taylor's smile flickered for an instant and turned devious. "I'm counting on you not to be overselling yourself."

Josh swallowed. "You'll have to be the judge of that." He opened the fridge, desperate to change the topic as once again they danced near the edge of his restraint. "Beer?"

Taylor seemingly understood or shared his dilemma, as the heat lifted from her face. "Sounds good. So, back to your abnormalities. Do you have six toes on each foot, or like pickles with your omelets? Oh, I know—do you perform *Hamilton* while you're in the shower?"

"Since when is singing anything from *Hamilton* abnormal? And pickles and eggs are delicious."

Rice fell from the spoon Taylor was using to scoop it onto her plate. "That was a joke about the pickles, right?"

"Yes. Omelets require mustard if you're going to include pickles."

Taylor made a gagging noise and shoved the rice container at him. "If I feel sick to my stomach, this date ends early."

"In that case, absolutely no more food jokes." Josh raised his beer bottle in her direction. "To us, the lone Porters and Lipins without bizarre hang-ups."

Taylor tapped her bottle against his.

"I have a rock collection," Josh said after they'd been digging into the food for a few minutes.

The sudden reversion in topic seemed to catch Taylor off guard, and she shook her head. "A rock collection?"

"I collected rocks when I was a kid, one from every place I lived." He smiled sheepishly. "I thought I wanted to be a geologist when I was younger."

"That's not so strange. But you still have them?"

Josh nodded. "That's why it's my eccentricity, right? They've moved with me from town to town, to college, to med school, to here. They're currently in a box in the attic."

Taylor seemed to consider this as she sipped her beer. "Touché. That is a perfectly nondisgusting quirk."

"Thank you. I tried."

She stared at him for a moment, and then something like surprise spread over her face. "Aha. All your other quirks are gross, aren't they? That's why it took you so long to think of one you could share."

"Like I'd tell you. But I am male, so it's safe to assume."

Taylor laughed and missed her mouth with her forkful of food, and Josh bit his tongue. Objectively, that sort of behavior was funny, not hot. Except, where Taylor was concerned, it was a total turn-on for reasons that remained elusive.

Everything about her turned him on.

"You could have just said you collect dogs," she said, her gaze sweeping over to the three in the kitchen doorway. Pepper and Jay were gnawing on their antlers, but Bella—older and wiser—was watching the floor like a hawk, waiting for crumbs to drop.

Josh rewarded her for her patience by tearing off a piece of naan and holding it out. The husky snatched it in a flash. "Yeah, but my whole family collects dogs. That doesn't seem abnormal to me. Speaking of which, you seem to be sneezing a lot less."

"I sneezed before you came back inside, but luckily the medication appears to be helping. I'd hate to have wanted to run away as soon as dinner was over." She said it casually, but there was a devious light in her eyes that was impossible to miss.

He had half a mind to declare dinner over right now, but Josh once again told his body to behave. Patience was the game plan for tonight, so he just smiled back. "I'd have hated for that too."

10

⤝———⤞

JOSH HADN'T NEEDED to worry that Taylor would be in a hurry to leave. Once dinner was over, she drained the last of her beer and spun in a circle around his kitchen. His place wasn't large, and from her vantage point, she could see the entire downstairs, including the living room and the cluttered so-called dining room table that was his makeshift desk.

Josh assumed she was searching for the dogs, who were dozing lazily in the corner, but she put her hands on her hips. "This is a surprisingly well-furnished and decorated bachelor pad. I'm impressed."

He laughed and shut the dishwasher. "I'd like to take more credit, but the real touches came from my paternal grandparents. My parents inherited almost everything from them, and they passed most of the furniture and paintings on to me since I was a poor med school student at the time."

"Oh, I'm sorry."

He waved off her condolences. "I didn't know them

that well. Hazard of a childhood moving around while they stayed in Alaska."

Taylor nodded thoughtfully. "It does make visiting from anywhere else a challenge. My family seems to believe I deliberately snub them, but I don't think they realize the time it takes to get here."

"To be fair to your family, I'd be upset, too, if I didn't see you often."

She narrowed her eyes at him. "There you go again, trying to be charming. What did I tell you about that?"

"I'm naturally charming because I have cute dogs?"

She elbowed him in the ribs. "Okay, that's kind of true, but not what I told you."

"But good enough, right?" Josh caught her elbow and pulled her closer.

Now, his body screamed, *You've had dinner. We can move on to other things.*

It seemed pointless to argue. Taylor's hair smelled faintly of peaches, and it didn't make a difference that he knew it was her shampoo. He wanted to taste her, to run his mouth over every inch of her skin. She clutched a fistful of his shirt to steady herself, and Josh's breath hitched.

Taylor didn't let go immediately, and when her other hand slid around his waistband, any hope he had of suggesting they watch a movie or do something remotely platonic died away. Josh was no longer even sure what those things were. All his brain could focus on were her hands. Her lips.

"Taylor?"

"Yes."

"Can I—"

"I said yes."

His brain was so completely befuddled it took him a second to understand. "Damn it. Don't confuse me."

She reached up and kissed him.

It cleared up any confusion.

She tasted good, so good that his memories of kissing her last week hadn't done the deed justice. If they had, he wouldn't have been able to put off doing it again for this long. Blind, hungry need threatened to overtake him. It had been so long since he'd kissed anyone or touched anyone like this, and no one had ever so easily or quickly aroused him this way.

Breathing hard, Josh pulled apart from Taylor, but he didn't let go of her, and his hands slid under her shirt, heedless of what his brain was ordering them to do. "We need to take this slowly."

She looked up at him, lips red and pupils dilated. He must have tried running his fingers through her hair and didn't even realize it. It framed her face in a cloud. "I already said yes. What's wrong?"

Nothing was wrong. Well, other than that they couldn't be seen in public together because their families were absurd. But otherwise nothing. Everything was perfect, too much so. "I want to savor this. To know I didn't rush it."

Taylor arched an eyebrow, and her hand sank lower, cupping the bulge in his pants. "Just slow?"

Josh sucked in air, painfully. It wasn't only his cock that was throbbing anymore. Every nerve in his body was a live wire, vibrating with tension. "Slowly but surely."

Biting her lip, Taylor released him, and the same hand worked its way under his shirt until it rested flat against his stomach. "You are kind of charming actually."

Great. Apparently he merely had to torture them both for her to admit it.

"Also frustrating as hell." She narrowed her eyes, and

her fingers clenched as she did, digging lightly into his skin.

"That's fair." She knew he was frustrating the hell out of himself, too, right?

He bent down and slowly kissed her again, leaving his hands where they remained around her waist until the bare skin of her back seared his palms. Taylor seemed to be taking her cues from him and did the same. She was either testing her own willpower or trying to return the torture. But when she made a whimpering noise in the back of her throat, he couldn't take it any longer.

Josh pushed the hem of her shirt up. "Take this off."

"Just this?"

"Yes." *No.*

Her devious expression clearly communicated that she was considering defying his request, but then she pulled the material over her head and let the shirt drop to the floor.

Oh, fuck him. This was a terrible idea. How was he ever going to follow through on his plan? Did he even have a plan? His brain was short-circuiting.

Taylor reached to undo her bra clasp, and that struck him out of his daze.

"Not yet." He grabbed her hands, and held them out to the sides, using the moment to stare at her longer. The blue lace of her bra barely contained her breasts, and when he finally couldn't hold himself back any longer, he let her arms go and cupped them. Taylor's eyes closed as he drew his thumbs over her hard nipples.

This was why he needed to go slowly. He had to acclimate himself to her, inch by inch. Explore her, inch by inch. Too much at once and he'd explode.

"Josh." She fisted his hair as he peeled back the lace of her bra and sucked one nipple, then the other. "You're killing me."

That made two of them. He answered her by undoing the button on her pants and watching her shove them down as quickly as she'd discarded her shirt.

"Better?" He couldn't take his hands off her perfect breasts even though there was now so much more to explore.

"Not entirely." Taylor used his waistband to pull him closer again. "But I am glad I wore the right underwear tonight."

"There's wrong underwear?" He raked his gaze over her, trying to memorize the curve of her hips, the scrap of blue that disappeared between her thighs. He had a hard time believing anything on her could look wrong.

"They're not all fancy, you know. And they don't always match."

"I did not expect to learn anything about women's underwear tonight, but thanks for the lesson."

Taylor leaned into him and pressed her mouth against his. It was an invitation he was helpless to resist, even though he suspected correctly that it was a ploy. While she distracted him with her tongue, her fingers undid the button on his pants. He was lost in a haze until he heard himself moaning as she wrapped a hand around his cock.

"Shit." He snagged her wrist and held it in place before she could do anything else to torment him.

Taylor was laughing, having gotten what she'd wanted, and she didn't let go. "That's a secret I just told you, by the way. Most men don't take the time to appreciate the effort we women go to, but now you know."

"Your underwear?" With her hands squeezing his shaft, his already addled brain was struggling to follow her line of thought.

"Yes."

"You know you'd look fucking gorgeous in anything, right?" He couldn't take it any longer, and he grabbed her around the ass, walked her over to the sofa, and helped her lie down.

Josh tossed the extra cushions to the floor, giving her more room to spread out, and not wanting anything to impede his view. The tattoo he'd noticed on their first date was visible at last, and it wasn't one image but several. A flock of bluebirds flew up her thigh.

"When are you . . ." Taylor lunged for him again, and he easily dodged her.

"Soon." He was going to lose the choice and come in his pants if it wasn't. "But I haven't finished yet."

Taylor gasped as he bent over her and nibbled the soft skin on her stomach, taking his time to suckle every delightful inch on his journey down. Beneath him, Taylor squirmed and whimpered, and he couldn't get enough of that either.

"You're infuriating. Just like I'd expect a Porter to be. Are you ever going to give me a turn?"

He grinned in spite of his raging lust and tugged down the lace of her panties. "Stop complaining like a Lipin and maybe."

He thought she cursed him, but he couldn't be sure through her moans.

He pulled the lace down farther, seeking to taste more of her, and Taylor cried out as he flicked his tongue over her clit. Josh nearly lost it himself at the sound. "What was that?"

"I want you inside me."

"Please?"

"Please."

He slipped one finger into her. Enjoying the way her hips bucked was the only thing keeping him from yanking his own pants off.

Taylor wet her lips. "Damn you, Porter."

Josh laughed unsteadily and added a second finger to the first. "Technically, I'm a Krane."

"Technically, if you don't strip and put your cock into me soon, I'm going to have to finish this myself."

"That's . . ." He swallowed. "Not as much a threat as you think it is as long as I can watch."

"Josh."

There was a hint of a direct order in her voice, and he couldn't hold back any longer. Looking at her, touching her, was hot. Her pleading and moaning was hot. Her demanding was an irresistible force of nature that his body couldn't ignore.

He hadn't planned to fuck her on the sofa. No, the plan—if there had been one at all—was to keep teasing her, moving slowly, and working their way upstairs. So much for that.

Josh darted into the bathroom and returned with a condom faster than she could ask where he was going. Taylor hadn't moved, and she stared at him as he tossed off his clothes, her lips slightly parted, eyes wide. He removed her bra as he hovered over her, and Taylor's hands pulled his face closer. Her mouth sought his.

He had so many things he wanted to say—how much he liked her, how much he wanted her, how beautiful she was. But the words dissolved as he entered her, and there was nothing left but the sensation of her body.

Taylor wrapped her legs around him, pressing him deeper. Slow was no longer an option. She rubbed herself against him, and he kissed her throat, chasing the breathy moans that cranked his arousal up to unbearable levels. He'd pushed himself to the brink, and holding out wasn't going to be possible for long.

"This?" Josh worked a hand between them, fingers seeking her wetness.

"Oh, God. Yes." She cried out a moment later, her body thrashing around him. He followed almost instantly, pleasure so strong it felt like it was ripped out of him, leaving him in shreds.

Boneless bliss followed, one perfect moment of peace.

It was soon replaced by the vague realization they were both sliding off the sofa.

Swearing, Josh reached out with an arm to brace them, which only sort of worked, and Taylor cracked up. The arms she'd wrapped around his neck tightened, and she shook with silent laughter. Adjusting his position, Josh held her closer, his face buried in her hair while they both let the excess emotion work its way out.

One minute he was collapsing in the best orgasm of his life. The next he was rolling around on the floor with laughter. Without a doubt, it was the strangest post-sex moment of his life. But far from feeling awkward, it felt nice.

No, better than nice. It felt perfect.

There couldn't have been a clearer sign that he was in deep trouble.

11

◇————————◇

IT HAD BEEN two days since Taylor had fallen off a sofa with her naked body wrapped around Josh's. Two days and she still couldn't get him out of her head. How good his mouth had tasted. How he'd felt even better entering her. How tempting he looked, standing over her, all trim muscles and hard lines. She was perpetually wet and bothered when she thought she ought to be embarrassed by the whole sofa deal. But even that had been funny, and it hadn't slowed them down for long.

She was going to miss that kind of sex when she left, the kind that was hot and mind-blowing but also fun and somehow real at the same time. Real as in she didn't need to perform because Josh took care of her, and she didn't need to hide because being with him was never awkward. That sort of sex was as elusive as a blizzard in L.A.

She had to face it—she'd gotten more than she bargained for when she'd hoped he would give her a reason not to hate being in Helen. And she was going to miss all of him when she left, not just the sex but the jokes and conversation too.

Then again, who was she kidding? She'd been on the job hunt for a week and hadn't heard a peep. Extending her stay in Helen might not be the worst idea, as long as Lydia was willing to pay her a meager salary. If there was another upside—say, a certain doctor who could use his hands with the precision of a surgeon—that simply made her lucky.

And yeah, seeing more of her family was an upside, too, of course.

On that thought, it couldn't hurt to arrange another secret date with Josh. She hadn't seen him since the night of the great Sex So Amazing You Fall off a Couch fete, although it hadn't been for lack of trying. Unfortunately they both had other obligations that precluded additional physical contact, and phones could only do so much to make up for that, particularly when she didn't have much privacy.

A text arrived as Taylor picked up her phone, but it was from Stacy. They'd been texting back and forth all morning in what had started out as job search commiseration but had evolved into Taylor spilling all about her Josh situation. She needed an outlet, and certainly no one in town would do.

You fell off a sofa? Stacy followed up with a long string of laughing emojis. I'd have died. Did he cushion your fall like the gentleman he obviously WASN'T if you were going at it that hard?

Luckily there were a bunch of pillows on the floor so it wasn't a far fall.

Taylor neglected to mention the part about how hitting the floor had finally woken up Josh's dogs, who'd come over to investigate, but the memory made her laugh. Especially since Josh had not been as amused at the time.

The inn lacked office space, so she'd taken over a small room off the dining area that her mother had used. Framed photos of herself and Lydia as kids watched over her from the walls, and she had half a mind to flip them around so their prepubescent selves wouldn't be shocked by her behavior. Behind her, the heavy wooden door was propped open, and a screen door let in a light breeze to counteract the heat emanating from the kitchen.

I did tell you he's a doctor, right? Taylor asked. I'm sure he could have patched me up if real damage was done.

Yes, a doctor and your mortal enemy. I find it hilarious that you finally date a respectable guy and you still can't bring him home to your family.

She'd never thought about it that way, but Stacy had a point. Hilarious isn't the word I'd use.

Taylor turned her gaze to her laptop to get back to work and almost flew out of her skin when someone tapped on the screen door. No one should be back there since the door was largely invisible to anyone but inn staff. It opened onto a closed-off section by the kitchen delivery area.

Banging her knee on the table, Taylor twisted around, expecting to find a too-curious guest. Instead she discovered someone who had even less business being in the vicinity.

She barely managed to hold in a curse as she hustled Josh inside. "What are you doing here?"

He lowered his hood and kissed her. "Why did you think I asked where you were at the inn?" He kept his voice low like she had, showing he had some common sense even if it wasn't enough to keep him away.

"What if it wasn't me in here?"

Josh shot her a sardonic expression. "I peered through the screen and saw you."

"Yeah, well. Stop it with your logic."

The door to the dining room was open a crack, but breakfast was mostly over. Only an older couple remained, and they were getting up to leave. To be safe, Taylor shut it anyway and turned the lock on the doorknob. Then she closed the back door behind Josh.

He held out the to-go cup of coffee he was carrying. "I also brought you a treat. One double espresso with extra foam and light cinnamon."

If she hadn't already forgiven him for taking such a risk, that would have done the trick.

The window next to the door had no curtain, so Taylor did the best she could—she lightly shoved Josh against the back door so he couldn't be seen easily through the window. Then she stood on her toes and kissed him.

It had been only two days, but kissing him was like discovering she'd been dehydrated and he was her first glass of water. Every cell felt more alive. Every nerve woke up. She inhaled deeply, breathing in the scent of his skin and soap, amazed how it sent ripples straight to her groin.

Once her thirst had been slaked, Taylor took a slight step back. "Thank you, but this was a terrible idea."

"Oh, I don't know." Josh grinned. "I was afraid I might get struck by lightning when I stepped onto the property, but I'm not dead yet, so I'd say it worked out okay."

She poked him in the stomach. "You could be caught."

"A situation best avoided. Don't worry, I'm convinced. That's why I was careful." He caressed her cheek, and Taylor's eyes closed involuntarily. "Tell me you're sorry I stopped by and I won't do it again."

Warm fingers traced the outlines of her lips, and she had the overwhelming urge to take one in her mouth and suck. Instead she bit him lightly because he'd won the argument and she hated losing. "Damn you."

"Thought you'd see it my way."

"You're a smug bastard."

"A charming bastard."

"That's only when you have the dogs around." Taylor frowned. "Where are they?"

Josh motioned to the door. "In the Jeep, waiting for me some distance away. I didn't intend this to be a long visit. My shift starts in thirty minutes." He had one of his ER shifts ahead of him, which was why she couldn't see him later. "I just didn't want to go another day without kissing you."

Taylor sighed heavily to cover up the way her heart giddily skipped a beat. "You're really trying for that charming label, aren't you?"

"Is it working?"

She shrugged. "Maybe a little."

More like a lot, but he could figure that out himself.

Josh's smug grin suggested he had, and he grabbed her hands. "So when can I see you again for real?"

Taking time off was a strange concept, but her family had always set aside Sundays and Mondays as nonwork days unless there was an emergency. Taylor rationalized that she shouldn't feel bad about following their schedule, and she filled Josh in.

"I'll see you tomorrow then," he said. "How long can I have you for?"

"What did you have in mind?"

"Not sure yet." He swung her arms lightly while his expression turned thoughtful. "I have to be at work Monday morning, but I'm sure I can come up with something else besides ravishing you on my living room floor."

"I have no problem repeating that plan."

"Good to know."

"In fact." She removed her hands from his and undid his pants button. "I owe you payback."

Josh inhaled sharply. "You don't owe me anything."

His mouth might be saying that, but the heat in his eyes suggested his body wasn't opposed, and Taylor took her cue from it. Josh had taken a risk coming here, but that risk added an undeniable extra thrill.

Her phone buzzed with a new text, and Taylor ignored it. Her mind was made up. Josh's *you don't owe me* was not the same as *don't do this*, and she suspected he wasn't going to launch another halfhearted protest. She wet her lips and curled her fingers around his increasingly hard shaft.

Someone knocked on the inn door.

Panic swept over Josh's face, and Taylor froze. Her mouth, which a second ago had been salivating with the urge to taste him, went dry. "Yeah?"

"It's me." Lydia's voice was followed by her sister trying the locked doorknob. "Tay?"

That was the problem with taking risks. Sure, the possibility of being caught was a turn-on, but actually being caught was terrifying. "Um, one second."

Pulse racing, Taylor spun around, trying to figure out what to do. Somehow Josh managed to keep a cooler head. He buttoned his pants, pulled her close for a quick kiss, and vanished out the back door before she could even whisper goodbye.

Her mouth still tingled with anticipation, and Taylor gingerly latched the screen after Josh, praying her sister couldn't hear any noise.

Fear gave way to the irritation of unfulfilled desire, and Taylor opened the door for Lydia. "What's up?"

If she hadn't been so caught up in her own roller

coaster of emotions, she might have noticed the turmoil on Lydia's face sooner. "Mom's back."

SITTING AT HER parents' kitchen table, Taylor wrapped her hands around the cup of coffee in front of her. She was already a jittery mess and didn't need more caffeine, but she also wasn't about to let that stop her. Her parents' house felt sharp and brittle, as though one wrong word could crack the walls and send the building crumbling down on them. A little alcohol would smooth over her own sharp edges, but it was early to drink, so the coffee would do. The steam was soothing and reminded her of all the best parts about being in town.

Which, at the moment, was a reminder she desperately needed.

This cozy kitchen, where the family gathered to drink hot chocolate and play board games every winter when she was home, had turned as weird as the rest of the town. Familiar yet not. Welcoming yet uncomfortable.

"You just left me to run the inn all by myself," Lydia was saying to their mother. She wasn't sitting but pacing, arms crossed, by the oven. "You didn't even tell me when you would be back."

"You should have had help." Their mother cast a knowing glance toward their father, who was sitting at the table across from Taylor. He said nothing and sipped his own coffee.

Taylor had seen where her mother's gaze darted to, but Lydia misinterpreted the direction. "I was lucky that Taylor was able to come up. She has her own job."

Taylor followed her father's example and drank more coffee.

"I wasn't referring to Taylor, although it was very sweet of her to come home and help." Denise Lipin tucked some of her hair behind her ears and rested her hands on the back of Taylor's chair. She'd cut her hair and added highlights not all that dissimilar to the sort Taylor put in her own hair, but seeing anything like that on her mother was odd. The phrase *midlife crisis* came to mind, but regardless of the reason, Taylor couldn't deny that the lighter streaks took a good decade or so off her mother's already stubbornly youthful face.

Besides, *midlife crisis* seemed like too benign a description. It's what she and Lydia had teased their father about a couple of years ago when he'd traded in his sensibly sized truck for a beastly-sized one. "All the better for carting around the snow machines and all the plants your grandmother's installing around town" was how he'd justified it. He'd taken their knowing smirks good-naturedly. Life had been normal then.

Scowling, Taylor focused on her mother's words. *Sweet* had nothing to do with her return. Obligation and unhappiness, more like. She had a feeling she was being dragged into a bigger argument, but didn't see what it was or how to remove herself from it without taking a swing at those brittle walls, and she did not want to be responsible for an additional disaster.

When no one said anything, her mother sighed. "I had to get away. Taylor understands, and anyway it's all worked out."

More silence followed that. Against the distant ticking of the grandmother clock in the next room, Taylor slowly realized that whatever her mother meant, to the contrary, she was the only one who actually didn't understand. Great. She'd been left no choice but to go in swinging.

Never mind alcohol. She needed chocolate.

Taking a deep breath, Taylor pushed her cup away. "No, Taylor doesn't understand."

Her mother smiled sadly at her. "I just meant that you ran away too. You know what it's like to have to leave."

Taylor closed her eyes in frustration. "I didn't run away without warning. I didn't leave anyone hanging or ditch my responsibilities." She should have stopped after the first sentence, but she resented being dragged into the argument. This day had turned sour amazingly fast.

"Leave without warning, no," her father said, speaking up for the first time. "But we were all counting on you returning after college. To help at the inn. To be a part of the family."

Her mother nodded, and her sister wasn't rushing to defend her. Taylor was going from uncomfortable to resentful to seriously pissed off with each tick of the second hand. Especially since she understood what *be a part of the family* was code for—do your duty in fighting the Porters. It wasn't enough to inherit her mother's eyes or her father's stubbornness. No, she had to inherit their asinine war too. She'd thought moving to California would get her out of that one, but it was becoming clear that she could no more easily shake off the role of soldier than she could change her bone structure.

Her hands clenched as she stood. "This isn't about me. This is about the two of you failing to work out your shit and it getting dumped on us."

"No one said it was about you, Tay. Calm down." Her mother's gentle tone only further infuriated her. "We're not upset that you left. Or I'm not. I'm glad you did what you needed to."

"Swell. Everybody's happy." Taylor raised her arms in despair and cast a glance at Lydia. Her sister was staring at the tile floor, looking closer to their mother's age than Taylor had ever seen her. Every line of her face was strained. "No, wait. No one's happy, because the family is breaking apart."

"The family is not breaking apart," her father said with such unexpected force that for a wild second Taylor's hope rose to untenable heights before crashing to the floor. "You will still have a mother and a father, and we will still have you."

Her mother absently played with the sugar bowl sitting on the counter. "I didn't expect the two of you would take this so hard."

Taylor didn't know what to say to that, so she grabbed her cup and drained the last, bitter sips of coffee from it. Why did Josh have to be working such long hours today? She needed to curl up in someone's lap, and some more naked time wouldn't be a bad distraction either. She'd take playing with his dogs, but the dogs had gone with him. That left her with no one else to snuggle with, seeing as Lydia's cat continued to shun her.

"Thank you both for stopping over." Her mother gave Lydia a tiny shake on the arms, but pulled Taylor into a full-body hug. "I hate that you only make it up here once a year normally, and I wish we could talk more today. But now your father and I have some things we need to discuss. We'd just as soon work this out on our own rather than pay lawyers."

Lydia's mouth tightened even further, and Taylor's gut shriveled. Apparently both of them had been harboring the same secret hope that this divorce idea was a temporary fit of insanity.

"What happens to the inn?" Lydia asked.

Their father rubbed his head. "That's one of the items we need to discuss."

Taylor knew a dismissal when she heard it, and she'd been waiting impatiently for this one. Torn between wanting to yell and cry, she'd managed to do neither, but this reunion had not gone how she'd anticipated, and she felt as bitter as her coffee dregs. "Fine. Mom, try not to leave town again without saying bye. I'm heading back to L.A. soon."

That was to say, she was allegedly heading back soon, seeing as she hadn't bought a plane ticket yet and had just been thinking this morning about extending her stay. Still, if her mother had been trying to make her feel guilty about going to California, she could play the same childish game.

"Of course. I'll be here through Monday," her mother said. "My art class doesn't start until Tuesday, so there's plenty of time."

Her mother had signed up for a painting class in Anchorage, which proved how delusional Taylor had been to hope this situation was temporary. Since when did her mother paint? She'd always loved art and had decorated the house with knickknacks and paintings she'd picked up over the years. But she'd never shown an interest in doing it herself.

Hands in her pockets, Taylor clomped along behind Lydia back to her sister's car. "I need chocolate."

"How about we go get that ice cream?" Lydia suggested.

Her sister must be glum, too, if Lydia wanted sugar, and Taylor nodded. The Dairy Dock would do. It wasn't like she could get her favorite organic, fair-trade super-dark chocolate at the local grocery store. She'd looked.

Ten minutes later, ice cream had been obtained and they returned to the inn to eat it and get back to work. With chocolate caramel fudge melting on her tongue,

Taylor found it in herself to ask the question that had been bugging her since the scene in her parents' kitchen.

"Have you been upset with me all this time for leaving?"

She followed her sister toward her office behind the reception desk. Early afternoon, the lobby was empty, and the gas fireplace that was more for show than heat was off. It would be switched on in the evening when Taylor put out the wine and cheese. The lobby was a rustic sort of room that looked grander than it was because of the richly colored furnishings yet smaller than it was because of the dark paneled walls.

Her question seemed to derail Lydia, and her sister veered away from the desk and dropped into one of the cushy wingback chairs by the fireplace. "You know, it's funny you ask. Once I was kind of resentful."

Ice cream dripped off Taylor's spoon while she waited for Lydia to finish both her thought and her spoonful of pistachio. "Really?"

She'd never considered that a possibility, nor had she considered the idea that her parents had expected her to return home. She knew they hadn't wanted her to leave in the first place. She'd been expected to follow in the family footsteps, to conform to their expectations, to be a good little Lipin and show up those who'd cheer if her family failed. Taylor had hated all of it, and once she'd won the battle to go, she assumed they'd given up on her.

"Once," Lydia said again. "But then it dawned on me that there had been nothing keeping me from leaving too. The family would have thrown a stink like they did when you announced you wanted to leave, but they couldn't have stopped me."

"Why didn't you then?"

Lydia smiled ruefully. "Because I'm not you. I'm a wimp."

"You are not a wimp. Lipin girls aren't allowed to be wimps. We have to be fighters for the good of the family." Taylor could taste her own bitterness through the sweetness of the ice cream.

"I am a wimp, and I never got into a fight. The most I ever did was key Wallace Porter's car once on a dare when I was drunk, and it was a small mark, too, because I was terrified of being caught." Lydia waved her spoon around as she punctuated the thought. "Seriously, leaving for college in Anchorage almost did me in, and the only reason I managed it was because I knew you'd make fun of me if I showed fear. But that was enough adventure for me."

Taylor couldn't stop the smirk that crept over her lips. "I would not have."

Lydia stretched out her leg and lightly kicked Taylor in the shin. "You're not even trying to lie, but whatever. Back to my original point—this is home for me. Are there things about living here that make me want to scream? Totally. But I chose to deal with them because this is where I belong."

"Whereas I chose to run away?" Taylor's amusement was fleeting, and she swirled her spoon around her mostly empty dish. The ice cream wasn't making her feel better after all.

"Only you know if you ran away or ran toward something. Either way, don't let Mom and Dad make you think I'm angry at you. I'm not. I'm just glad you're back for a bit. I'm sure you're usually off having too much fun doing whatever people do in L.A. to miss us, but around here, one absent person is noticeable. We like having you around. I like having you around, even if my living room currently looks like a tornado hit it."

Lydia's reassurance made her feel better, so Taylor

stuck out her tongue in an effort to lighten the mood. "I'm trying to keep my stuff compact, but it's not like it's a large apartment."

"Merlot and I were managing fine."

"Merlot weighs about eight pounds and doesn't require a suitcase. And speaking of your cat, he's decided he hates me."

Lydia wrinkled her nose and scraped the bottom of her dish. "I've noticed. What did you do?"

"Nothing." Unless she counted hanging out with a Porter, but surely Lydia's cat couldn't sense that.

Although couldn't animals sense things humans could not, like earthquakes? Lipins and Porters sleeping together was a bit of an earthquake, metaphorically speaking.

Possibly it was a damn good thing cats couldn't talk.

Her sister pursed her lips in disbelief, and Taylor put on her most innocent face. "Maybe you smell like L.A.," Lydia said, getting up.

"Maybe your cat's developing a bad attitude in his old age."

"Don't be mean to my little fluffypants."

"Fluffypants? Oh, my God. You do need to go on more dates. Your hormones are out of control."

Lydia whimpered, leading the way into her office. "Don't you start sounding like Grandmother. If I hear more talk about the state of my thirty-year-old ovaries, there's going to be a new feud in town, and I don't think any of us can handle that."

"You going to sic the vicious Mr. Fluffypants on me?"

"A brilliant idea." Lydia tossed her ice cream cup in the trash. "You're full of them."

"Ha ha." Taylor tossed away her container, too, and turned to head toward the kitchen. It was almost time to set out the afternoon coffee and cookies. Marie had the day off so someone else would be baking them. That made them less of a temptation.

"I actually mean that," Lydia called after her. "I've been appreciating your input."

Surprised, Taylor paused. "You seem to have this place well under control without me and my horrifyingly radical suggestions, as I believe they've been called."

Lydia acknowledged the compliment with a shrug. "I've made some tweaks and modernized a bit, but big, sweeping ideas are your strength, not mine. Not all of them are bad, and it helps me to hear them."

"Not all of them are bad." Taylor laughed. "Thanks. So you want me to keep nagging you?"

"If I can't convince you to come work for me, then yes. By all means, keep helping out for free." This time Lydia stuck her tongue out.

Taylor laughed again and hurried to the kitchen as though she was running away, this time from a not-so-subtle hint.

12

⊸━━━━━⊷

THANKS TO HELEN'S booming tourism industry, the summer months were filled with free outdoor concerts—an unexpected perk that Josh had grown to love. By the time he finished work and got Jay, Pepper, and Bella ready to go, a good-size crowd had already gathered at the park for the evening's event. This week's band was playing a mix of folk-pop covers.

Josh shortened the huskies' leashes so they couldn't stray far and bother the people spread out on blankets, and he scanned the area. Taylor had also planned on stopping by, and Josh intended to casually bump into her amid the crowd since it was the best they could do to enjoy the concert together.

Before he could find her, however, a friendly voice called out his name, and Josh temporarily abandoned his search. Adrian worked at the hospital as well, in the emergency department, and he'd been instrumental in helping Josh become more comfortable working his weekly ER shift. Adrian and his wife also loved dogs, knew the best ski trails in the area, and had basically given him a life in Helen beyond the people his family had introduced him to. But Adrian had a family of his own, as did most of the people Josh had met, and he frequently felt like a third wheel when everyone got together since he had no spouse and no kids.

Chatting with Adrian and Christine at the park, while nice, also had another drawback. It drove home the unfortunate state of his current predicament. What he wouldn't give to be like normal people, the couples sitting on the grass, eating a picnic dinner and listening to the music. But there would almost certainly be other Lipins here, and he knew for a fact that Kelsey would be as well.

Taylor had been right to not want to make trouble, a fact confirmed by Josh's mother when he'd finally called to ask about the feud. Her response had been filled expletives and anecdotes, but it amounted to a single piece of advice: stay out of it. No kidding. He'd refrained from mentioning it might be too late.

As it turned out, Josh wasn't the first to spot Taylor weaving her way along the park perimeter. That honor went to Jay, who barked with happiness, his tail wagging and whacking Josh in the leg. His dogs loved everyone, but they especially loved Taylor. Josh wasn't sure if they'd picked up on his cues, or if they just had exceptionally good taste in humans. Though, to be fair, the way Taylor showered them with attention when she was over at his house likely had something to do with it too.

The sky was overcast and threatening rain, but Taylor wore sunglasses regardless, a look Josh suspected had more to do with providing them some extra cover. While the huskies tugged at their leashes, frustrated they couldn't rush her, she moved along casually, trying to make it look like she wasn't purposely heading their way.

"Calm down, guys," Josh said under his breath. He understood their frustration all too well, but it was bad enough the dogs drew lots of attention for simply existing. He hoped no one noticed their attention was aimed at a certain woman.

Taylor reached them at last and turned her dazzling smile away from Josh to the dogs. "Hey there."

It was a contest among the three huskies to see who could ensnare her favor first, and Taylor laughed as she was set upon by doggie kisses.

"I think they like you," Josh said. Translation: *I like you. I miss you.* He hadn't seen her since they'd gotten together on Sunday.

Taylor rubbed Jay's head. "I think I like them too."

Josh decided to interpret her comment as referring to all of them. *Stop making me jealous, dog*, he thought as Jay buried his muzzle in her chest.

Taylor shifted position to better keep her balance. "Getting a little personal there, Ja . . ." Her words trailed off as she glanced up, and the laughter died on her face. "Just give me a second to stand up."

Josh chuckled at her attempt to recover from saying Jay's name until he heard someone speaking behind him. Then he froze.

A second later, new huskies darted in front of him, and Kelsey stood at his side. Positive the expression on his face gave their ruse away, Josh forced the world's most awkward smile. "Hi, Kels."

Just as Taylor clearly recognized his cousin, Kelsey clearly recognized Taylor. Her lips pressed into a firm, unforgiving line, even as her dogs begged for Taylor's attention.

Taylor made a show of petting Juliet and Puck, then took a step back. "Cute dogs."

If she was feeling the same sort of panic he was, she was doing a decent job of hiding it. His own instincts were telling him to flee like he'd done when Taylor's sister almost caught them over the weekend.

Kelsey looked between them with a strange expression, and for a moment Josh thought she was going to tell Taylor to never touch her dogs again. Then she nodded curtly. Apparently she could contain her hostility for a Lipin if said Lipin was willing to compliment her dogs.

Without another word, Taylor turned away. It was the only wise move, but Josh's stomach sank.

An uncomfortable silence engulfed Josh while he waited for what Kelsey was going to say. Before she could speak, though, or accuse him of anything, another familiar face appeared through the crowd.

Ian's face lit up when he saw Taylor, and a spark of jealousy ignited in Josh's gut. He couldn't hear their conversation, but he saw the way Ian gestured toward him and the confusion on the other man's face. That meant Kelsey likely noticed it too.

Josh had no idea what Taylor was telling him, but whatever it was, it didn't appear to have persuaded Ian. Maybe he could cut Ian off before he said something incriminating in front of Kelsey?

Luckily, the universe answered his prayers before Josh could make a move. Taylor disappeared, and Ian glanced back at Josh. But unlike most people who took the dogs as an invitation to come closer, Ian only held up a hand in greeting. Josh waved back and tried not to let out an audible sigh of relief as the other man walked away.

"You know that guy?" Kelsey asked.

He needed to sit and breathe. Kelsey focusing on Ian rather than Taylor was another lucky break, and the release of his stress left Josh's body crashing like he'd just finished strenuous hike.

"Yeah." Josh guided the dogs in the opposite direction from Taylor. "Remember I told you I met the guy opening the brewery? That's him."

Kelsey made a disgruntled noise.

"You can't dislike someone you've never met."

"Sure I can. Did he come over and say hi to you? No. Did he want to pet my dogs? Also no. It was rude."

No, it was a goddamn miracle. That said, Josh could see how Kelsey might think Ian's behavior was unusual, especially in a town like Helen. "He could have been in a hurry to go somewhere, or maybe he doesn't like dogs."

Kelsey gaped at him. "Well that's a good reason to dislike him. Hell, even Taylor Lipin stopped to pet your dogs. Come to think of it, that was weird, but she was always the weird Lipin."

"Who's the weird Lipin?" Kelsey's brother and his fiancé sneaked up on them from behind, apparently having caught the end of their conversation and sparing Josh from admitting to something he shouldn't.

Twins didn't necessarily have to look much alike, but no one had told his cousins that. They were like an artist's rendering of the same person—one drawn with feminine features, the other with masculine. They were even dressed similarly today, both in light blue jackets and jeans.

As for Kevin's fiancé, Josh had met Peter Chung only a handful of times, but he liked him and the fact that he was much more laid back than either of his cousins. Sometimes it was good to have another calming influence around.

Conversation paused while Kelsey and then Kevin announced they wanted ice cream. He hadn't eaten dinner yet, but Josh decided why not and joined the others. The close call with Taylor and Ian had unsettled his stomach.

"Back to the weird Lipin," Kevin said after Kelsey had decided to pay for everyone's dessert. "I need information."

Peter caught Josh's gaze and made a face that Josh could only describe as *Oh God, not this again.* Apparently, Peter had heard plenty about the Lipins already.

"Taylor," Kelsey said. "Remember her?"

Kevin's face was puzzled. "She was weird? I thought she was the troublemaker."

Kelsey sucked ice cream from her spoon while she pondered this. "She's weird now. I caught her petting Josh's dogs."

"Petting dogs is weird?" Peter asked.

"Not for normal people, no," Josh explained, somehow keeping a straight face. "But it is for Lipins."

"Exactly." Kelsey either chose to ignore his sarcasm or couldn't hear it over her own dislike.

Peter twirled his spoon thoughtfully. "I thought Lipins didn't go anywhere near your family and vice versa."

"I suppose Taylor wouldn't know who Josh was," Kevin said. "Did you know who she was?"

Josh quickly shook his head, telling himself that nonverbal responses weren't the same as outright lies, which was, of course, ridiculous. He was splitting hairs so thin not even a scalpel would suffice for that cut.

"I don't know who she is either," Peter said.

Kelsey lowered her voice dramatically. "She's the Lipins' prodigal daughter. The mayor's child who left town."

Peter cast his eyes at Josh as if to question whether he was missing something.

Josh opted to shrug. "You know, the Lipins having a

prodigal child makes them sound cooler than us. Why don't we have one?"

"Excuse me, I tried to take the hit for our team," Kevin said as he stole a spoonful of Peter's ice cream. "But apparently being a queer college dropout doesn't have the same panache around these parts as it used to."

Peter's eyebrows shot into his hairline. "Really? Because if your father's reaction to our engagement was lacking in panache, I'd hate to see what would happen if he wasn't boring."

Kevin laughed without much humor. "Listen up then. Have I never told you the story of the time he took Kelsey and me fishing, and she hit another boat?"

Kelsey snapped her fingers at her twin. "Hello? I bought you that ice cream because I was trying to be nice. You could return the favor and not tell embarrassing stories about me."

Josh grinned, trying to ignore the many pairs of eyes staring up hopefully at his ice cream dish. "I wasn't aware you were familiar with the concept of nice."

"I'm familiar; I just find it painful to implement. All the more reason you should eat your fucking ice cream and listen to me."

Josh ate some of his fucking ice cream. "Go on then. The Lipins have a prodigal daughter, and she's returned. Why do we care?" He knew why he cared, but there was a certain morbid curiosity in hearing what his cousin would have to say.

"It obviously has to do with the divorce. So our spies tell us."

"You have spies?" Peter cast another questioning glance around the group, leaving Josh to wonder what kind of conversation Kevin was going to have with his fiancé later.

"Of course." Kelsey tugged on Puck's leash as the husky attempted to investigate the closest trash bin. "You think the Lipins don't spy on us? Even friendly nations spy on each other, and we are not friendly nations."

Ice cream curdled in Josh's stomach. Kelsey was likely right about the Lipins. If his family was spying, they probably were too. He added it to a list of questions to ask Taylor, although he doubted she could answer.

While the conversation drifted to the engagement party Kelsey was determined to throw for Kevin and Peter, Josh took out his phone and sent Taylor a text. He'd been meaning to ask her over after the concert but hadn't had the chance, and Kelsey's comments were getting under his skin.

Sneaking around had amused him for a bit, but he was getting awfully sick of it.

SINCE SHE COULDN'T enjoy the concert with Josh, Taylor strolled through the park, hoping to find people she could hang out with in public. It was an irksome situation, but she tried her best to see the bright side. Maybe she'd run into friends she hadn't seen in years.

She was feeling the lack of friendly faces at the moment. In her group chat, Stacy and a couple of her other L.A.-based friends were sharing photos they'd taken of each other at a party over the weekend. They mostly looked silly and drunk, but also like they were having a good time, and their wish-you'd-been-here messages did nothing to improve Taylor's mood. As much as she wanted to spend time with Josh and was learning to enjoy hanging out with Lydia, it wasn't the same as a friend group cultivated over years.

Running into some Helen-based friends might have

improved her spirits, but, as nothing in Helen worked out the way it was supposed to, it wasn't friends she bumped into, but family. Her uncle Dex was her dad's youngest brother, and he and his wife, Marissa, had always been the "cool" aunt and uncle when she was growing up. They were still some of the most fun members of her family, but they were chatting with Taylor's grandmother, who was most definitely not.

If Dex and Marissa were easy to talk to, her grandmother's designation was "harder than a diamond." It wasn't so much a generation gap as a personality one. Taylor had always been too wild, too talkative, and too unruly for her grandmother's taste. She protested as loudly as anyone else when Taylor had taken off for California, but Taylor had always been convinced her grandmother was secretly relieved to see her go. It was probably also why she didn't bug Taylor as much about her love life as she did Lydia. Lydia's genes were the preferable ones for passing down.

Small favors.

True to form, her aunt and uncle hugged her in greeting, but her grandmother just solemnly nodded her head. They spent the next several minutes talking about the concert and what Taylor was doing at the inn, and Taylor asked after her cousins who were still in high school and therefore not about to be seen in public with their parents.

"Did you do the gardens by the town hall this year?" Taylor asked her grandmother. She wasn't sure why she bothered making the effort when the troublemaker brand was likely hers to keep forever, but she felt she ought to try. Especially given her length of stay in town.

Her grandmother's steel-gray eyebrows shot up, an expression more of curiosity than surprise. As though she didn't trust Taylor's interest. "I did, with help of course."

Her grandmother chaired the town beautification committee. Gardening had always been her passion.

"It's really lovely. The color scheme pops." She should say something more about it, but her grandmother would expect her to know the names of all the flowers, and, well, she didn't. There was a time when her grandmother had tried teaching her and Lydia everything she knew about gardening, but Taylor had never been interested, although she'd faked it for a bit to make her grandmother happy. Revealing her ignorance now would have the opposite effect.

"Your grandmother does an amazing job every year," her aunt said. "It's too bad you don't usually get here during the prettiest season to see it."

Taylor had already reached the same conclusion. Seeing the town when it wasn't covered in snow and slush was much nicer. Unfortunate, because it made her prone to wanting to stay longer.

"Speaking of which," her grandmother interjected before Taylor could reply, "I understand you'll be staying a couple more weeks to help out Lydia?"

News traveled fast, but she'd always known that. "I might as well since she needs it."

"That's excellent. I'm glad to hear it." For once, her grandmother sounded like she actually meant it. Taylor had to bite down the urge to ask her to repeat herself for posterity. "It's what you were always meant to do. Your grandfather and I had high hopes that one day you and your sister would carry on the business."

And there was the punch line.

Taylor's stomach sank, and the smile on her face twitched in a way she hoped wasn't noticeable. Of course her grandmother was finally happy with her. She was being a good little Lipin and living up to family expectations. It didn't matter that she actually liked working with Lydia. The idea that she'd been expected to do it regardless rankled and made her not want to like it.

In her calmer moments, Taylor realized that was silly. But was it really any sillier than being told which hairdressers were off-limits to Lipins when she mentioned wanting a trim the other day?

Taylor had never intended to rebel. She'd just wanted to be her own person, but as a Lipin living in Helen, that was not a simple thing—if it was even an option at all.

13

TAYLOR HID HER bike in the shed in Josh's backyard like he showed her the first time she'd come over. It had only been a little over a week, but in many ways it felt much longer. Her resistance to working at the inn had softened, and she'd grown closer to her sister. There was an easy rhythm to her days here, like the waves' regular lapping against the shore.

But that predictable rhythm extended to the bad as well as the good. As it had been the first time Taylor sneaked into Josh's house, her mood was grim. Seeing him would improve it since just the thought of him made her happy, but it stunk that this was becoming part of her pattern.

Determined not to drag him down with her unhappy thoughts, Taylor squared her shoulders and slipped in through the sliding doors as she'd been instructed. Immediately, three furry tornadoes charged her, doing as good a job to chase away her bad mood as their owner could have. It was impossible to feel down in the face of so much enthusiastic affection.

"You distracted them from their dinner," Josh said as Taylor got up. "I didn't think that was possible. Maybe the stories about your family are correct—you're a witch."

"Is that what your kind say about us? We're witches? And I thought you didn't like us."

Josh kissed her, and Taylor burrowed into his arms until his touch blocked out the remnants of her mood. "Not all of us. Some of us like you very much."

"Hmm. Prove it." She reached up to press her mouth to his again, and Josh obliged. She suspected it wasn't a hardship for him, but he took each kiss so seriously it was as though she were kissing him for the first time, every time. There was a thoughtfulness and a purpose in his lips that said he hadn't started taking his time with her for granted. Quite the opposite actually. Each moment was an opportunity to win her over. The experience was wholly unlike the careless kisses she'd grown used to from past boyfriends, and it made her blood sing and her toes positively curl with pleasure.

If the dogs hadn't chased off her unhappy mood, that sort of kiss would have vanquished it entirely. But something must have given her gloom away because Josh cupped her cheek. "What's wrong?"

Taylor started to deny it, but he looked at her with such concern that it was impossible to contain her burdens. "Just the usual."

"Family?"

She dropped onto his sofa. Pepper's rope was on the cushion next to her, and Taylor picked it up. In her eagerness to play tug-of-war, the husky skidded over the wood floor and grabbed the other end. "What else?"

"Beer?"

"Chocolate?" Taylor started sliding off the sofa as

Pepper gave a good pull, and a tennis ball was dropped at Taylor's feet by a jealous Jay. She grabbed it with her free hand and tossed it.

Josh scrunched up his face and then wordlessly started ransacking his cabinets. Taylor was about to call him off when he let out a triumphant cry and returned to the living room with a box of cookies. "Will that do?"

She was normally too much of a food snob to eat store-bought cookies, but she kissed him on the cheek for making the effort. "Thank you."

"So what now?" He motioned for Bella to scoot aside so he could sit next to Taylor and opened the box.

"I changed my plane ticket today." She took a bite of the cookie Josh held out for her and was surprised it tasted better than she'd have expected. Maybe that was because he was feeding her.

Maybe it was also because of the way Josh's face lit up with the news. Taylor's heartbeat skipped a dizzying rhythm in her chest. She should not be so happy to see that he was excited. This wasn't how the two weeks between them were supposed to have worked out.

Josh seemed to get a grip on whatever he was feeling and tucked her hair behind her ear. "That's a bad thing?"

"No. I mean, it's not great that I haven't found a new job yet, but I realize I was being overly optimistic." She took another bite of cookie while she searched for the words to explain her issue. "My family is thrilled that I'm staying longer, and even though I'm choosing to stay and there are things I like about being here"—she poked him in the chest—"I feel like a failure."

"Because you haven't found a job in only two weeks? That's not a long time to be looking."

"No, I mean I'm a failure because my family is happy." She cringed. "That sounds awful, but the longer

I'm here, the more they get to think they were right and I shouldn't have left in the first place."

She was making it sound like her pride was wounded, that she had to show them all. But that wasn't right either. Maybe she couldn't explain herself properly to Josh because she wasn't making sense, period.

Josh nudged her closer, and Taylor gratefully took the opening to practically climb onto his lap. Cookies and chocolate were nice, but they were nothing compared to what a pair of strong arms wrapped around her waist could do.

"You said you left because you hated the feud and didn't like being infamous," Josh said. "Whatever you might feel today or tomorrow or ten years from now, you couldn't have been wrong to leave if that's what you were feeling at the time."

Taylor locked her arm around his and smiled in spite of everything. Josh would understand that part, but she'd never explained the entire reason she left. "I also wanted to get out of Helen. I wanted to be in a big city and work in some industry that seemed glamorous. But jobs that require you to wear heels are not all my younger self thought they would be."

"Ah." He rested his chin on top of her head. "So the job search is making you have second thoughts about your career, but if you admit that to your family, they'll get an I-told-you-so moment."

"So it's my pride." She frowned, still unconvinced.

"I didn't say that. Do you think it's your pride that's hurt?"

She shook her head and tried to articulate her jumbled emotions once more. "I think I had to get away and do something new to figure out who I was. You're a Porter— Krane, whatever—but you didn't grow up here, so you don't know what the pressure to fall in line is like. It's a noxious cloud that smothers you, and there's no escape from it because everyone knows who you are and has certain expectations, for good or bad. Even when I tried to rebel, I was just conforming to someone's expectations of what a Lipin would do."

Josh was silent a moment, his fingers stroking her hair. "So leaving was the ultimate act of rebellion because no one on either side expected that."

Taylor had never thought of it that way, but Josh made sense. Lipins and Porters didn't typically leave. They staked their claim on the town and fought to protect their own and hold their territory. By leaving, she'd flipped the bird to everyone and showed them how petty she thought their war was.

"Staying around longer," Josh continued, "bothers you because you see it as an act of surrender to your family's expectations."

Mouth agape, Taylor twisted around in his arms. "I think you just explained what I've been trying to put my finger on for days. Are you sure your specialty isn't psychiatry?"

He planted a kiss on her nose. "Positive. I have no business mucking about with other people's brains. But I've heard my mother caused a stir when she left town to marry my dad, and let's just say I've been thinking a lot about family and expectations lately myself."

TAYLOR'S EXPRESSION WAS knowing—the feud. He didn't have to say it out loud for her to understand.

Tonight's experience at the park had cemented Josh's disgust. Taylor needing to run away before they'd had a chance to talk had merely been the first in a double-header of feud-related irritation. Not long after everyone had gotten ice cream, Kelsey and Kevin's parents had made their presence known. In an effort to buy Kevin and Peter time to disappear into the crowd, Josh had gotten stuck to talking to them, and as a result, was forced to listen to his uncle gripe about how some Lipin had swooped in and taken the parking spot he'd been heading toward at the bank. Josh had gotten the sense his uncle Wallace had also wanted to complain about Kevin's engagement but knew better than to do it in front of him, so his spleen had vented extra bitterness on what he assumed was a safe topic.

Little had he known. Josh played with the dogs to keep from blurting out things his uncle wouldn't want to hear. He should have said something, but he'd been mentally bracing for Taylor to return to L.A. and wanted to respect their decision to lie low. With the end so close, causing trouble now would be stupid.

But Taylor wasn't leaving, and while not needing to say goodbye was the best news he'd gotten in a long time, it added a new complication. How did they plan for more time together when all their plans were constrained by their families?

Josh relayed the story, leaving out the part about Kevin and Peter. "Family expectations. No one asks me if I hate your family, which of course I don't. Why would I? No one even asks me if I care about the feud, which of course I do, but not for the reasons they'd assume. They carry all this hate around and expect me to haul some of it for them. I understand exactly why you left. It's not fair."

He sounded like a petulant child—*it's not fair*. But it

wasn't. That he had to sneak around to see Taylor was not fair. That his cousin and Peter were going to get married without his uncle's blessing wasn't fair either.

"No, it's not." Taylor shifted on his lap, turning to face him, and her knee brushed his groin. Heat flooded Josh's bloodstream. He was torn in two. Two desires. Two frustrations. He wanted to hold her and find comfort in their shared burden. And he wanted to carry her up to his bed and unleash his emotions in a less verbal manner.

There were pros to both options, and since he couldn't decide, he tugged her closer and kissed her fiercely. Her body fit so well against his, soft and round in all the best places. She comforted him as much as she turned him on.

"It's not fair." Taylor's fingers splayed over his chest. "There's so much here that makes me happy, but the pressure to fall in line—it's like a rope. It ties me up and drags me down, and makes everything impossible."

Even through his heavy cotton shirt, he could feel each of Taylor's fingers like erotic pinpricks. "My mother warned me. I thought it wouldn't affect me, and maybe it wouldn't have so much if it weren't for you."

"My fault, huh?"

"My best bad decision ever. Jay's been rewarded mightily for his part in entrapping you."

The dogs had calmed down from playing with Taylor, but at the sound of his name, Jay's ears perked up. He trotted over to the sofa and rested his head next to Taylor's legs.

Taylor scratched him behind the ears. "Good puppy. See the trouble you've caused?"

Jay looked up at her with adoring eyes, and Josh laughed. "That's why dogs are better than people. No unrealistic expectations. Just unconditional love."

"That's a pretty convincing argument, but can dogs do this?" She leaned forward and kissed him, threading her fingers through the hair curling around the nape of his neck. The mild arousal simmering in the back of his brain grew unrelentingly stronger. He nudged Taylor's legs wider so she was more comfortably straddling him, and she sank lower onto his body.

"That is a point in your favor," he admitted. His cock pressed painfully into his jeans, but his hands unbuttoned hers instead and peeled back the fabric as best he could until he caught a glimpse of white lace.

The cuddle-and-commiserate portion of the evening appeared to be over. He was ready to move on, and the way Taylor wet her lips made it clear she was too.

"Upstairs." He didn't relish the possibility of falling off the sofa again, nor did he particularly need a canine audience.

Their clothes left a trail behind them on the steps. Josh had imagined dragging Taylor to his bed in a rush, but their progress was slow, impeded by his inability to keep his hands and mouth off her and the fact that every time she stroked him, the blood rushed from his head, leaving him temporarily immobile with need.

Taylor wrangled him onto the bed first this time, situating herself on top of him. He had his own frustration to work off, but so did she, and he couldn't complain. There was so much pleasure in letting her sweat off the tension for both of them. She was truly the most beautiful thing he'd ever seen.

Her mouth crashed into his, and Josh slid his fingers— already slick with her wetness from their trip up the stairs—between them. She came with a strangled gasp, pushing herself higher above him again, luxuriating in sensation as he felt her body convulse. Josh waited as long as he could after her breathing steadied and gave himself over.

Taylor nuzzled her face against his neck, and he wrapped his arms around her, warm contentment spreading through his muscles. "I hope you feel better because it's my turn next."

He could feel her grin, but she didn't raise her head to speak. "Do your worst."

"Never. Only my best for you." He just needed a few minutes to recover because every nerve ending had been blown out.

Later, as Taylor was curled up next to him, his alarm set for an ungodly early hour so she could sneak back to the inn, Josh finally followed up on the news he'd been meaning to ask about. "So how much longer are you staying?"

"Not sure yet." Taylor's eyes were closed and her words slurred together. "Can't be too long. I'm wearing my winter clothes and it's summer here."

Josh chuckled. It had become clear that, when it came to clothes, Taylor had wholeheartedly embraced the Southern California spirit. She'd admitted to wearing the same couple of pairs of jeans and sweatshirts over and over, and lamented not having a reason or opportunity to show off her favorite outfits. He teased her about her love of heels and sparkles—so out of place in Helen—but he'd buy her a whole new wardrobe if it meant she'd stay through the fall.

In the relative darkness of the room, the smile on his face faltered. That was not the sort of thing he should be thinking. Two weeks with Taylor had been the ideal length of time. But their two weeks were about up, and her future duration in town was unknown. That was dangerous. It foretold of eventual heartache when she left.

Except did he really believe he was fooling himself? The thought of her leaving had filled him with dread since their first date. None of this had gone how he'd planned. He'd liked her way too much from the very beginning to be okay with an end. All he could do was hold on tight and prepare for the worst.

But it also meant the damnable feud was a bigger problem than anticipated. He was so tired of sneaking around, and he'd never gotten to ask Taylor about family spies. What the hell were they going to do about that? It wasn't as though he hated hosting her at his place each time they wanted to see each other, but it was limiting. Sharing meals was nice, and the sex was fucking amazing, but there was so much more he wanted to do with her.

And they couldn't. They couldn't risk it.

Unfair. The word bounced around in his mind like a mosquito he couldn't swat. It was unfair that their families made being together so hard, and it was unfair that their families were going to drive Taylor to leave again.

So, for the moment, Josh held her tighter and listened to the sound of her breathing as he stared at the ceiling, trying not to dwell on the inevitable.

14

THERE ARE THOSE two boxes in the corner." Taylor's dad pointed at the ones in question. "They're mostly clothes and some other knickknacks your mom doesn't want, so she wants you to go through them before we donate anything."

Nostalgia rippled through Taylor in a wave that felt reminiscent of nausea. They were standing in her parents' office, the room that had once been her bedroom. It hadn't looked like her old bedroom in years, but today it was especially wrong. Her mother's belongings had been packed up, ready to be driven to Anchorage. Another nail in the coffin of hope. She had to accept it was well and truly dead.

When her father had invited her and Lydia for dinner and to "go over some things," she hadn't expected this was what he'd meant. She could have been having dinner with Josh. Instead she was watching her childhood decay before her eyes as she picked over the discarded bones of her mother's life.

First her mother had cut and dyed her hair. Now this?

"Why is Mom getting rid of so much stuff?" Taylor asked.

"I wouldn't call it 'so much.' Those are mostly old clothes or ones that don't fit her anymore that have been hanging around. She's got her own space now and is trying to simplify, she says. She got some book about decluttering." He chuckled. "I'll be honest—this I've got to see. Your mom is a collector, not a simplifier."

Taylor was in no laughing mood, but she understood the sentiment. It was difficult to imagine her mother, who liked to overdecorate, decluttering, but it was just as hard to imagine her cutting her hair. So what did Taylor know anymore?

Taylor's gaze fell on some large, cloth-wrapped objects leaning against a wall that looked nothing like clothes, and definitely like nothing that she associated with her mother.

Lydia must have been questioning the same items. Her sister pulled back a cloth that appeared to be an old bedsheet. "What's this?"

"Oh, those were your mom's old paintings."

The way he phrased it made Taylor do a double take. "Paintings *she* painted?"

"Yup. They've been in the attic." Her dad stuffed his hands in his pockets. "I thought she might like them to decorate her place, so I wanted to take them to her with the rest of the boxes."

Taylor attempted to imagine her mother, she of the atrocious handwriting, meticulously working a paintbrush, and failed. Yes, her mother was taking an art class, but the idea that her mother had painted in the past was an alien concept. Again, Taylor felt like there was a whole secret world out there that she'd missed.

"She stopped around the time you were born," her

dad was saying. "Figured she got bored with it or had too much to do, taking care of two kids plus the inn."

The offhand way he said it made Taylor want to scream, *And where were you while she was taking care of two kids plus the inn?*

She knew the answer to that question. Her father had been pursuing his interest in town governance. Eventually, the inn was entirely under her mother's control.

It seemed like a stretch to say the feud had destroyed her parents' marriage, but Taylor was beginning to suspect that it hadn't helped. As far back as she could remember, her father had kept busy doing volunteer work that had finally culminated in running for office. But becoming mayor hadn't just been his answering the selfless call of public service. Like so many decisions, it had been driven by the feud. It was a way to make the Lipin power in town official.

The only surprise at the time was that the Porters hadn't immediately run someone against him, but it became clear that they'd chosen a more subtle, economic strategy to fight back.

Taylor pressed her lips together and opted to say nothing of these thoughts. But for the first time since Lydia had called to say her mother had run off, Taylor's anger toward her absent parent cooled. Maybe her mother really had grown bored, or maybe her father had not been a very supportive partner.

And now her father was packing her paintings up and driving her belongings to Anchorage? Was he being thoughtful, or was he trying to cleanse the memories of her from the house? Taylor hoped for the former, but she wouldn't want to place bets at this point. Both her parents were acting strangely, which was why it was so hard not to believe this was some kind of phase for them.

"How's pizza sound for dinner?" her father asked. "I'll stop by the restaurant when I pick up your grandmother."

"Sounds fine," Lydia said.

Pizza twice in two weeks was a bit much for Taylor's preference, but she simply shrugged, too lost in her thoughts to care.

Her father's heavy footsteps drifted away while she examined her mother's painting. Judging artwork was far outside her skill set, but from her purely ignorant perspective, Taylor thought it looked impressive. Certainly it was way better than anything she could have done and nothing she'd have been ashamed to have hanging on her walls.

Lydia sat back on her heels. "That's the barn where Nana and Papa keep their plane."

Taylor recognized it as soon as her sister said the words. Nana and Papa were her mother's parents, who lived five hundred miles north in Fairbanks, and that was indeed the red barn in their backyard. The scene was captured during winter, the snow drifting high against the old red-painted wood and piled thick on the brown roof. In the distance, evergreens sank under its weight. The oil paints captured the winter well enough that Taylor felt cool.

Of course, imagining Fairbanks in the winter generally had that effect. Stacy and her L.A. friends might think Helen was cold, but Helen's winters were downright toasty compared to what places in the Interior, like Fairbanks, contended with.

Taylor unwrapped the hoodie she had tied around her waist and put it on. "Mom wasn't bad. Guess I now know where you got your talent from."

"Me?" Lydia shot her a bewildered look.

"Your sketching." Did her sister still do that? Strange that she didn't know. Sad too. She remembered Lydia had won a couple of prizes for her drawings in high school, but aside from watching her sister doodle on the mail, Taylor realized she hadn't seen any evidence that Lydia still picked up a pen and a sketch pad.

"Oh." Her sister tucked her hair behind her ears. "I guess I haven't really felt inspired to do that in years. I was never great at it anyway. It was just for my own entertainment."

"Please. You were very good. I was jealous."

"Please yourself. You could have done it too. It just takes practice, but you were always too busy getting into trouble."

Taylor fought down a smirk. Lydia was right about one thing—she'd lacked the patience to learn. Whether practice would have helped was another story. Taylor assumed talent had to count for something, and she suspected her mother's had skipped right over her.

"Let's peek at the rest of the paintings," she said.

There were seven canvases in all, none of them framed. Two appeared to be landscapes of places around Helen, one more was identifiable by their grandparents' house, and the others were unknowns.

"Do you remember Mom painting?" Taylor asked her sister.

Lydia shook her head. "If she quit when you were a baby, I'd be too young. I didn't even know these were in the attic. I'm surprised they're in as good a condition as they are."

"I'm not sure I can handle any more surprises."

Lydia made a strange face but said nothing as they rewrapped the paintings.

"Should we check the boxes?" Taylor sat on the car-

pet and pulled the first of the two donation boxes closer.
Who knew what they'd find next? She hadn't been kidding about being tired of the unexpected.

"Sure." Lydia drew out the word as she sat next to her.
"So, speaking of surprises, you'll never guess who I ran
into yesterday at the concert while you were hanging out
with Clara."

Sensing not just a surprise, but a bad surprise, Taylor
quit opening the box. "Who?"

"Clara."

Well, damn. She'd never even gotten around to meeting up with Clara—at the concert or elsewhere—because
she'd been spending time with Josh. Although it wouldn't
have made a difference if she had, Taylor felt like she
was doubly busted. "Ah."

"That's all you're going to say?"

It was all she could say at the moment. Her words and
excuses had fizzled away, and Taylor was left with nothing. Nothing but the truth, anyway. And the truth was
problematic.

Lydia sighed. "Come on. Tell me about the guy you're
seeing."

Taylor considered whether the box in front of her was
big enough to crawl into and disappear. "What makes
you think I'm seeing anyone?"

"Honestly, Tay. Because I'm your sister. I was suspicious of the whole Clara thing from the start."

Taylor wondered about that last bit, but it hardly mattered. Yeah, Lydia was her sister, and Taylor didn't like
keeping things from her, but confessing to Lydia that
she'd gone out with Josh was a can of worms she feared
opening. Not matter how sick she was of hiding it.

"Does being my sister give you psychic powers?" De-
flection wasn't the same as lying, was it? And lies of

omission weren't the same as lying right to her sister's face, were they? Taylor wasn't sure, but this sort of behavior didn't sit right with her. Then again, she'd been lying about Clara all along. What right did she have to make excuses for herself because she'd been caught?

Lydia didn't deign to play along with her coyness. "In the past two weeks, you've spent more time allegedly hanging out with friends than you ever did when we were in school. That might fool our parents, but not me. Also, you get these giddy smiles on your face when you read your text messages. It must be a guy. So who is he?"

Taylor took her time by removing the top item from her mother's box—a lightweight jacket. Unfortunately, it was obvious from the way Lydia tapped her fingers on the cardboard that all her stalling was simply increasing her sister's determination to uncover the dirt. "He's no one you know."

"Does *no one I know* have a name? Where did you meet him?"

"His name is Josh." Saying that much was a gamble, but it was a common enough name that Lydia shouldn't associate it with anyone in particular. "I met him my first day back in town when I was picking up the pizza. Honestly, I didn't mention it because you seemed down on your social life and it felt rude." Taylor winced in apology.

That, at least, was honest. She hadn't known then whom Josh was related to.

Her sister seemed to chew over this, and Taylor hoped she'd said enough to make her drop it. But then Lydia shook her head. "I do believe that. But I don't understand why you're being so evasive. Josh who? I might know him."

If there was anyone Taylor felt safe confiding in, it was her sister. But as she'd already decided, Lydia was a coin flip. Taylor had no idea which side—hers or the feud's—her sister would land on.

She also wasn't sure she had a choice other than to confess. If she outright refused to say more, Lydia would rightly grow suspicious and inevitably jump to bad conclusions. If she lied, she might get away with it for a while, but eventually Lydia would casually say something around her father or other family. That would also be bad since, among them, they likely knew every Josh in town. Either way, soon everyone would be party to the war crime she was committing, and Taylor would be in deep shit. No, the best course of action was to come clean and pray her sister would protect her secret even if she disapproved.

"Josh Krane." Taylor swallowed. "He's a doctor."

If only she could stop there. Given Lydia's expression, that name meant nothing to her. But if Lydia didn't know to keep quiet, she wouldn't. Taylor had to follow through.

"A doctor? Isn't that a step up from the guys you usually date?"

Under other circumstances Taylor would have made a snide retort. In this case, the truth was all the snark she needed and then some. "You tell me. He's Wallace Porter's nephew."

The shirt Lydia had been unfolding slipped from her fingers. "A Porter?"

Taylor hushed her even though there was no one else currently in the house besides her parents' cats. "In my defense, I didn't know that when we went out the first time. He was just a hot guy with cute dogs."

"But you've known since. Tay!"

"I just . . ." She flailed, waving her hands around uselessly. "He's not from around here originally. He wasn't raised on a steady diet of feud bullshit the way we were. I like him."

Groaning, Lydia covered her face with her hands. "It's not bullshit. It might be stupid, but it's something that all of us who live here have to contend with on a daily basis. That means him too."

"He hates it."

"Good. He's sensible; that's a good quality in a doctor. But it doesn't change anything. Did he know who you were when he asked you out?"

"No."

Lydia leaned closer, her voice thick with suspicion. "Are you sure?"

"Yes! As soon as he learned, he told me who his family was."

"Just making sure he wasn't sent to spy on us."

"Right. Of course." Taylor rolled her eyes. "You know this isn't how normal people behave, right?"

"I've heard tales." Lydia's tone was heavy with sarcasm to match her own. "You always have to go for the worst possible men. If they're not dealing drugs, they're wannabe musicians who can't hold down steady jobs. And oh, didn't you date some guy who was part of the Russian mob at one point?"

Taylor waved her finger in front of Lydia's face. "I'm ninety-nine percent sure that last one was an undercover cop."

"Uh-huh. And I bet you're one hundred percent sure Josh is a good Porter. You're not going to stop seeing him, are you?"

"I told you. I like him. A lot."

Lydia's face clouded over, but it also filled with something that looked annoyingly like pity. "It can't go anywhere. You know that."

Of course she knew that, but Lydia's words slammed into Taylor's brain like a block of concrete. Her mind rebelled.

Stupid. She was so stupid, but it was too late do anything about it. Yes, she liked Josh a lot. It was going to hurt like hell when she left. But not leaving, well, that wasn't going to happen. And even if some freak circumstance forced her to stay—say, an earthquake toppling California into the ocean—a relationship between them couldn't go anywhere because of the feud.

Or could it? Lydia's response was more sympathetic than what Taylor had expected. Maybe she ought to hope for better among her family instead of writing them off as mindless soldiers.

These were dangerous ideas.

"Of course. I'll be leaving for L.A. again eventually. Please, can we keep this between us? I don't want to be the one to ignite the next great battle."

Lydia pressed her lips thin, but finally she nodded. "No, no need to toss gasoline on a gently burning fire. But, Tay, be careful. And be alert. Even if Josh is a totally wonderful guy, the people around him aren't."

"Trust me. We're being careful."

"That's not the same thing as what I said, but okay. The collective you should be careful too." Lydia picked up the shirt again and then threw it back down as though she couldn't concentrate on anything else. "No wonder Merlot doesn't like you anymore. You probably smell like Porter dog all the time."

Taylor frowned. Could the cat's shunning of her have been that simple? Damn. Even the family pets had sides. "Technically, he's a Krane."

Lydia held up a hand. "Don't even with me when I'm doing you a huge favor."

"Noted."

The sound of a car pulling into the driveway alerted them that their father was back. Taylor took a couple of calming breaths, just noticing now how her pulse had sped up with anxiety while talking to Lydia. She had to text Josh and let him know their secret was out, but not here.

The way Lydia had taken the news gave her hope, but her dad had brought reinforcements in the form of her grandmother. She wasn't going to risk anything with them around, but maybe she could lay the groundwork for a reveal, just in case another one happened without her consent.

15

⚬⎯⎯⎯⎯⎯⎯⎯⚬

JOSH DOUBLE-CHECKED THAT the last of the tent stakes was firmly in place before covering up his yawn. Even for someone accustomed to long ER shifts, it had been an exhausting day. And it wasn't over.

Taylor's sister knew about their relationship. Josh wasn't entirely comfortable with that, but it had its upsides. Lydia had arranged for Taylor to take two days off that coincided with his own days off, and that had allowed them time to finally get out from the smothering confines of Helen. They'd left town early this morning for Chugach State Park and hiked about ten miles round-trip before settling down at the campsite Josh had snagged at the last minute.

On one hand, being away from home and their families, the source of so much frustration, was a gift. The air smelled better, thick with the calming scent of evergreens. The water he'd packed tasted cleaner. And the sky looked bluer as the usually hidden sun peeked out through breaks in the clouds. On the other hand, his feet and legs hurt in new and exciting places.

While the hike Josh had chosen had an elevation gain of not even a thousand feet, the distance over rough terrain had more than made up for it. Naturally the huskies hadn't seemed to care, and the views of the lake at the end rendered it all worthwhile—even the flies and mosquitoes. Pepper and Bella had immediately dived into the chilly water, with Jay following warily behind. They'd splashed around for a bit, and then he and Taylor had taken turns tossing sticks into the lake and letting the dogs chase after them. Josh had never seen the huskies so happy before, and he silently promised to take them on more long hikes although his muscles wailed in protest.

Afterward, he, Taylor, and the dogs had relaxed on the grassy banks and eaten a late lunch while six-thousand-foot, snow-covered peaks towered over them. Fortified, they'd looped around the lake, scrambling over boulders and searching for beavers—partly for fun, and partly because beavers and dogs did not get along.

Back at camp, all the excitement was catching up with everyone. Even Jay, Pepper, and Bella had finally flopped down exhausted by the campfire ring, too tired to chase another squirrel. Josh wasn't sure how Taylor was managing to stay upright as she cooked macaroni and cheese over the camp stove. It had to be sheer stubbornness. One thing he'd come to admire about her was that she was determined to live her life the way she intended, whether that was running off to California or making the dinner she wanted to cook.

Glad her back was to him so she couldn't see him wince, Josh stood, and stuck the hammer back in his Jeep. The aroma of salmon drifting off the camp stove was heavenly, and he pulled a couple of beers from the cooler.

Coming up on Taylor from behind, he wrapped his arms around her waist and kissed her neck. He'd discovered she was ticklish there, and she didn't disappoint with the way she wiggled in his arms.

"You shouldn't do that. I'm sure I stink."

He pressed his nose closer to her skin and inhaled. "I love the way you smell." He licked her neck, too, and she squirmed again. "And the way you taste. A little salty with sweat."

"You are so charming."

"See? I knew you'd come around."

She pretended to smack him with the spoon before scooping cheese sauce over the cooked pasta. "This should really go in a pan and get baked in an oven."

"Even if it doesn't taste half as good as you do, it's going to be delicious."

"Will you stop that?" Taylor spun around to face him and glared. "Dinner is ready and you're making me want to jump you."

"That's a bad thing?"

"I'm not sure I have the energy for it until I refuel."

"Oh, well then, let's get you fed." As if he had the energy for it at the moment.

Taylor didn't need to know that he was one breath away from collapsing where he stood. Nope, he was a total manly Alaskan outdoorsman who could hike ten miles, catch and prep some salmon for dinner, pitch a tent, and still have energy left over to make his girlfriend see stars later.

Totally.

Maybe he should stop taking leisurely walks for exercise and start hitting a treadmill.

Taylor placed thick cuts of grilled salmon over each bowl of pasta, and Josh carried them to the picnic table, where the beer was waiting. By the fire ring, one of the dogs—mostly likely Jay—started snoring. They'd been fed already, and it was a testament to how wiped out they were that none of them were begging for their share of the salmon.

"What variation of your mac and cheese is this?" Josh asked as Taylor sat across from him.

"Number three."

She removed the bandanna she'd been using to keep her hair controlled, and strands fell out of her ponytail. Frowning, Taylor pulled it back, revealing a smidge of dirt by her left ear. Josh couldn't decide whether to wipe it up for her or leave it because it was adorable.

She was adorable, dressed in borrowed, mud-stained pants and one of his fleece pullovers that was several sizes too large. He just wanted to curl up next to her, which he would. But later. First there was food to eat and topics to discuss.

"It comes down to the cheese blend," Taylor said, "the seasoning, and of course the salmon."

"You're a culinary genius."

"I know."

Josh fought to keep his second bite in his mouth as he laughed. "I was expecting more humility."

Taylor grinned, flaking off some of her salmon. "I always win our mac and cheese competitions back home."

"You have mac and cheese competitions?"

"What can I say? My friends and I party hard."

"If this is how you party, I like it." Honestly, he liked the way she did everything. It was why it was so good to be away with her. To be able to relax. To breathe. To simply exist as the two of them without also being Porters and Lipins.

An eagle circled along an updraft over the trees, and

clouds once more obscured the sun. The temperature seemed to drop as it hid, although this time of year the light would never truly disappear. Through the woods on either side of them, faint voices drifted by from other campsites. Josh would have preferred a more secluded area, but getting any on a whim had been sheer luck. Besides, the more human noise, the less likely they were to encounter any predators.

After they cleaned up from dinner, Josh started a fire, and Taylor got out the ingredients for s'mores. He didn't think he could eat another bite, but was a camping trip really a camping trip without toasting marshmallows?

They had to talk about Taylor's sister and what their secret being out meant, and with the fire warming his toes, the time had probably arrived. Josh hesitated, though, enjoying the crackling and popping and the scent of the burning wood. Enjoying the warmth of Taylor's body next to his, a warmth more potent than any the fire gave off.

"I didn't tell you yet, but the day Lydia found out about us, I also learned that my mother used to paint." Taylor stuck a marshmallow on the end of her toasting fork.

Josh wasn't sure why she was telling him that, but he assumed she had a point, so he accepted a marshmallow in silence and let her explain.

"My dad thinks she gave it up because she didn't care enough, but that's not what I think. I think she felt like she had to give it up, and I think it ate at her. I think she resented it, and that resentment built over time because she didn't tell him what she felt. She hid things, and your heart can only take on so many burdens before your chest aches with them." Taylor sighed, the marshmallow fork hanging loosely between her fingers. "I'm sure that makes no sense medically, but what I'm trying to say is—I know I'm the one who urged you to keep us a secret, but I'm not sure that's the best choice anymore. I'm staying longer. Hiding was a fine short-term solution when we were a short-term fling. But we matter more than that to each other now, don't we?"

"Yes." He wanted to say more, but his voice was too heavy with the emotion behind that one syllable. She—they—did matter. A great deal more than he'd intended.

Taylor nodded. "So, I've been thinking over the last few days, maybe secrets are part of the bigger problem. Maybe someone has to come forward and just say how much the situation sucks and how ridiculous it is. My sister is okay with it. I can't imagine she'd be the only one. But if no one is willing to take a stand, then nothing changes."

Josh wanted to laugh, but it was funny only in the worst sort of way. Family circumstances had made Taylor change her mind, but his family had made him change his mind too.

Sighing, Josh raised his marshmallow to the flames. "My uncle can't handle my cousin's engagement. He's not going to be able to handle me dating a Lipin."

"I know some people, maybe most, will lose their shit. But we just need a few."

A few was what—three, four? They had one, and from the sound of it, Lydia had agreed to keep quiet. That was a far cry from being okay with it. "My cousins, the people I'm closest to, have already confirmed to me that anything between consenting adults is acceptable unless one of those adults is a Lipin."

Taylor dropped her stick farther until the marshmallow hit the dirt. "You think they'd be the ones most open to it?"

"Possibly not, but they're the ones I know best. The ones who'd have the most loyalty to me and so would be the least likely to do anything stupid." He plucked Taylor's fallen marshmallow from the ground and tossed it toward Pepper, who gobbled it up eagerly—the perk of being the last of her siblings to fall asleep.

"I do love that you want to rebel more," Josh added.

"You like that I'm reckless?" Taylor raised an eyebrow as she stabbed a new marshmallow onto her fork, and Josh took her hand.

Her skin was cool, despite the fire, and soft, and he traced his thumb across hers protectively. "I love that you're adventurous and daring. That you're not content with letting things that are bad stay bad." And yet he couldn't convince himself it was wise to follow her example in this situation.

But why not? This wasn't like the disagreements he'd gotten into with his ex, who didn't understand why he hadn't chosen a more exciting medical specialty or why he didn't want to live in a major city. Those were just personal preferences, a mismatch of ideas for their lives. She'd thought the life he wanted was boring. He thought the one she'd wanted was stressful.

This time, he and Taylor wanted the same thing to be with each other, to live their lives as they liked. Surely, that carried weight.

It was odd feeling so much turmoil while surrounded by so much peace. For a few minutes, there was only the crackling campfire and the sounds of distant birdcalls and chirping insects. The trees and mountains surrounding the site were tall, and the sky was wide. It all conspired to make the problem at hand feel small and manageable.

Josh inspected his marshmallow and frowned. There was an art to toasting a marshmallow to perfection. Too close to the flame, and it blackened or, worse, caught fire and turned to sugary ash. Too far away, and it barely got warm. In order to avoid marshmallow flambé, he had a tendency to eat tepid marshmallows. Taylor, he noted, just shoved her marshmallow into the fire.

And that there was their problem condensed down to a single campfire. She was a rebel. He was a chronic conflict avoider. They weren't trying to change each other like he and his ex had. They simply had to work together like they were now—holding hands while they each toasted a marshmallow their own way.

As if reading his thoughts, Taylor made a sad face at his marshmallow and held out her stick with her perfectly browned one. "Do you need to trade?"

"Never." He defiantly stuck his into the flames. "If we're going to do this, we need to think about how. It needs to be planned and purposeful."

"Are you referring to the marshmallow or going public with our relationship?"

"Going public." His marshmallow caught fire, and Josh yanked it out and blew on it. It was slightly black in spots, but perfectly browned in others. He'd take that as a good omen.

Taylor nodded. "I absolutely agree."

"Okay then." He bumped her marshmallow with his like a toast, although he wasn't sure if it made sense to toast what was likely to be a disaster.

GETTING AWAY FROM home and their families had been the best gift Taylor had never asked for. She owed her sister big-time. But while she felt mentally refreshed, her sore legs and the blisters on her feet were another story.

With her day officially over, she stretched out her calves on Lydia's sofa bed and booted up her laptop. Her sister was finishing up work, so Taylor had time to check her email and job search progress. Neither was particularly high on her list of things she wanted to do. In her first two weeks, she'd sent out dozens of applications, and nothing had happened.

Part of her reeled at the idea that she hadn't merited an additional look from any of the companies, but another part was secretly relieved that she had an excuse to extend her time with Josh. Only today, her excuse was looking like it might run out. One of the marketing firms she'd applied to had gotten back to her and wanted to set up an interview. Taylor knew she ought to be elated—it was one of the more promising options—but her stomach clenched.

"Be happy," she whispered to herself, and her brain promised her she was.

Her body continued to suggest otherwise.

Determined to ignore her uncooperative gut, Taylor read the email a second time and checked the dates and times the company had offered. She could either fly back to L.A. later this week, or take the company up on their offer to do the interview via video call. Taylor suspected that in person would be in her favor, but it would be so much easier and cheaper to do the interview from Helen.

Not to mention she wouldn't have to leave Josh.

On the other hand, if she traveled to L.A., she'd get to see Stacy.

Speaking of her friend, it had been a couple days since she'd checked in because of the impromptu camping trip, so Taylor sent Stacy a text with the interview update. They'd been comparing notes since, unfortunately, they were often competing for the same positions.

Stacy's response came back in seconds. Does this mean you'll be coming back? Followed soon by: Jerks. I applied there too and haven't gotten an interview.

Considering that Stacy had gotten a couple of interviews she hadn't, Taylor didn't feel bad about laughing at the second message. But the first one was something she had to take seriously. I'm looking into it. I miss you!

I miss you too! Tales of your hot doctor will be more fun if you tell them to me over margaritas. Just saying.

That was true, and she did want to see Stacy again regardless. She just dreaded the long, expensive flight that would go with it.

Still, there was no point debating the issue before she checked flight times and cost. Why sweat her reasons if the universe took the choice out of her hands? That would be ideal.

Her phone buzzed with another text, and absently Taylor reached for it, assuming was Stacy again.

Instead it was her grandmother. I'm downstairs. Come see me.

That was odd. Taylor couldn't imagine why she'd be stopping by the inn or texting her specifically. Briefly, she considered pretending she was busy somewhere other than Lydia's apartment, but she discarded the idea. Lydia might have told her grandmother she was upstairs, and it would not help their rocky relationship to put off what was surely inevitable.

Given the time, the inn's main building was quiet. Taylor found her grandmother in the dining area, arranging a vase of freshly cut flowers. She racked her brain for their names in case she was forced to comment and came up with gaillardias and dahlias, but there were some other yellow blooms that were a mystery.

"Where were you this weekend?" her grandmother asked by way of greeting. "Don't lie."

Taylor's eyebrows shot up. Sometimes she had a hard time believing her usually jovial father was related to his mother. "I went camping."

"Yes, but with whom?" There was steel in her voice to match the color of her closely cropped hair. Taylor suspected if someone sliced her grandmother open, they'd find steel for her bones too.

"A friend."

"A Porter friend?" Theresa Lipin stopped fussing with flower stems and stared Taylor down with her cool eyes. "Are you going to tell me you didn't know he was a Porter?"

Overwhelmed with confusion, Taylor blinked. Had Lydia blabbed after all? She couldn't believe it of her sister. She didn't want to. But how else could her grandmother have found out?

Taylor opened her mouth and said nothing, unsure what to ask first. As it turned out, she didn't have to ask anything. Her grandmother tapped a few times on her phone and held it out for Taylor to see. Someone had caught a photo of her and Josh when he'd picked her up to leave for the trip. It had been so early in the morning that they hadn't been worried about being super stealthy, and obviously that had been a mistake.

So that was one question answered, and it led to a hundred more. Such as, had her grandmother been spying on her? Taylor felt sick.

Worse, she also felt defensive. Old instincts, the kind that had made a habit of getting her into trouble when she was younger, flared to life. "Technically, he's a Krane."

Her grandmother snatched the phone away with such

force that the pair of reading glasses she wore on a chain bounced against her chest. "A friend of mine saw you, and when she realized you were there with that Porter, she thought I should know."

Shit. During their entire trip, as they'd delighted in not needing to hide, they'd only been enjoying a delusion. And what about Josh? Had her grandmother informed his family? It struck Taylor as unlikely, but she needed to protect him.

"You're very quiet. You'd better not be wasting your time coming up with excuses. There are none." Her grandmother set the phone on the table, but she didn't return to her flowers. She crossed her arms, daring Taylor to wilt.

"I'm not thinking of excuses. I'll own my actions. I just hope you aren't planning on telling Josh's family yet because—"

"Telling his family?" Her grandmother grabbed her by the arm and marched her into the lobby. The lone desk clerk took one glance at Theresa and found a reason to busy himself elsewhere. "Do you see this? Your family's legacy?"

There was nothing to do but go with the flow. Protesting would get her nowhere, and storming back to Lydia's apartment would provide no refuge. Taylor gritted her teeth. "Yes."

"That is where you belong. These are the people I talk to. You are the one speaking with Porters and, presumably, doing more than speaking, if you spent a night with one."

Okay, she really didn't need the conversation to go there. Not with her grandmother of all people. "Good. Is that all then?"

"There is nothing good about this. Your parents are

going through a difficult time, your father's position as mayor might be in jeopardy, and that man's family is conspiring to make their lives worse. They are grave dancers delighting in our weakness. You should be here supporting your parents and sister. Instead you're sleeping with the enemy. It's disgraceful on so many levels, Taylor Anne."

"I am supporting everyone. The whole reason I came here was to help Lydia. Spending time with Josh doesn't interfere with that."

"No, it interferes with everything. Have you forgotten what it means to be a member of this family? Is that what living so far from home has done to you?"

Taylor was tempted to bang her head into the fireplace stones. This was ridiculous. Her grandmother wasn't even a Lipin by birth, but she could somehow out-Lipin her granddaughter.

How long had it taken for her grandmother to be assimilated? Or had she already shown a predilection for that sort of behavior and attitude, and was that why she'd been invited into the family in the first place? Among Taylor's various relatives, of which there were many since her grandfather had been one of nine children, spouses had bought into the Lipin clan with varying degrees of enthusiasm. The ones who couldn't fit in at all tended not to last long.

Then there was Taylor. She'd been born in and had run away from it.

"Has living so far from home made me see how silly this feud with the Porters is? Yes. The answer is yes. Josh isn't a bad person."

Her grandmother snorted, but it was a most ladylike snort. "Bad is in their blood. They've repeatedly tried to ruin various family enterprises. One of them is threatening to run against your father for mayor. They started a smear campaign against your sister because they're jealous of her success. And I haven't even touched on their history of assaults and vandalism and God knows what else. They're all descended from the worst sort of people—thieves and cutthroats. Mercenaries."

Yes, and according to Josh, the Porters believed her family were witches. This was getting to be too much. "You can't actually believe that."

"Can't I? I've seen what they can do. They accused your ancestors of stealing dogs. They framed them. And why? So they could steal our land when we were found guilty. It was a giant con that luckily they were too clumsy to pull off or our family would have been driven out of town. And they're still mad about it. That's why Wallace Porter is carrying on their shady tradition by trying to buy up every property in the area. I'm telling you these things for your own protection. You are my flesh and blood, and I will not stand by and allow that family to hurt you. When I was your age, there were repercussions for a Porter man who laid a hand on a Lipin woman."

That wasn't hard to imagine. When her grandmother was Taylor's age, the origins of the feud would have been only a generation or two removed, and Taylor couldn't stop herself from pointing that out. "It would be nice to think that in the ensuing decades we've become more civilized and let go of old grudges. Are you sure our family isn't the one who's descended from cutthroats?"

Her grandmother's eyes opened wide, and color rose to her tanned cheeks. "You cannot treat barbarians with civility. They don't understand the concept."

Taylor raised her arms in exasperation. "Then what do you want me to do? I'm not apologizing for liking

Josh." *Liking.* She chose the word carefully. It wasn't wrong. She did like him, and it was easier than . . . telling the truth? What was the truth?

Taylor pushed the worrying question aside. While staring down her disapproving grandmother was not the time to contemplate her feelings.

"I expect you'll end things with the Porter immediately."

"That's not going to happen." Taylor crossed her arms, mimicking her grandmother's stance. After suggesting to Josh recently that they needed to put an end to the secrecy on their own terms, she wasn't about to back down. Although she hated discovering it was harder than she'd expected. She might play at being the rebel, but apparently some part of her didn't like disappointing her family.

"I'm not asking you, Taylor."

Then this conversation was over. Taylor turned and started toward the door. She should have known this was how it would end. She'd expected lectures and could deal with them, tune them out. She didn't take ultimatums.

Before leaving, however, she paused as a new thought struck her. "Do my parents know?" It was always good to be prepared.

Her grandmother was spry and easily caught up to her. "Not yet. I just received the information this afternoon. But if you believe they'll think differently, you'd better wipe that notion from your head."

No, they wouldn't think differently. Even in her most optimistic moods she wasn't naive enough to believe that. She merely hoped they would know better than to issue an ultimatum, like her grandmother had. She'd found it was easy enough to live with people's disappointment as long as they were quiet about it.

As for Lydia, Taylor wasn't about to let on that her sister had been keeping her secret, but she'd have to give Lydia a warning so she could decide how to handle it. The only question that remained then was whether her father would throw her out for refusing to break things off with Josh. Lydia might run the place these days, but her parents owned the inn, and that included the apartment where her sister lived.

Refusing to allow her to stay there would be unfair to Lydia, though, and Taylor crossed her fingers that her father wouldn't pressure her sister for that reason. Lydia needed her—that was a fact no one could argue with.

That said, Taylor marched back up to the apartment with fury burning through her veins. She didn't want to leave Lydia without help, and she didn't want to deal with a flight back to L.A. And God knew she didn't want to leave Josh. But maybe getting out of Helen for a few days while she did the interview was not such a terrible idea. Josh was a breath of sweet air, but this town and everything about it was suffocating her again.

16

⚬―――――⚬

THE CAKE HAD been cut, the toast had been offered, and the boat swayed beneath Josh's feet. Nearly thirty people milled about the deck, champagne flutes or plates of cake in their hands. Most were friends with Kevin or Peter, and the rest were family—but certainly not as many of them as there should have been.

Kelsey and Kevin's parents might not hold official titles as heads of the Porter family, but their wealth gave them that role unofficially. Never mind that most of the money had come from a non-Porter source in the form of Aunt Catherine's parents. If Uncle Wallace wasn't supporting Kevin's engagement, a whole lot of Porters were going to be cowards and keep their heads down. Or such was Josh's opinion.

He supposed he didn't have much right to call other people cowards, though, seeing as he'd so far declined to raise the issue of his own relationship.

Poking at his cake, Josh wandered as far away as he could get from the noisy crowd, which wasn't far on a boat of this size even though it was the largest in his cousin's sightseeing fleet. Kevin might joke about the shame of being a college dropout, but Josh wasn't sure why he'd bothered attending college in the first place. Being on a boat had always been Kevin's first love, and taking people on tours of the bay and the nearby glaciers was a job he'd been born for.

Case in point: it was on such a tour that Kevin had met Peter when he had just arrived in Helen to begin his doctoral work—something to do with studying the effects of climate change on salmon populations.

Thinking of his cousin's happiness brought Josh back to his own less-than-happy dilemma. Since Taylor had warned him that her entire immediate family knew about their relationship, he'd been waiting for word to reach the Porters. Although it was unlikely that the Lipins would spread the news to his family, he wouldn't have put it past them. If there was one thing Lipins and Porters might agree on, it was that they shouldn't mix.. But no one had said anything to him, and no one appeared to know his secret. Still, the threat of it getting out hung over Josh's head like a thundercloud.

Worrying that he'd be struck by lightning was his own fault at this point. Taylor had convinced him on their camping trip that they should stop hiding, that what they had together deserved better. How they should do it and whom they should confess to—that was the part they'd never figured out. But given their precarious situation with the Lipins, Josh had promised Taylor he would break the news to his family, since clearly anyone finding out by accident was the worst-case scenario. It seemed wisest for him to do it while she was in L.A. for her job interview and wouldn't be around to deal with any fallout. But he hadn't figured out how, at least not without getting electrocuted.

The right moment, the right person to talk to first—someone who would be open-minded and understanding—that was what he told himself he was waiting for. The truth was, though, he was stalling. There was no perfect person, and the right moment was never going to present itself. He simply had to do it and deal with the mess.

Maybe tonight. Watching the careless way Kevin had an arm draped around Peter, the way Peter leaned over and kissed Kevin's alcohol-flushed cheek—it stirred the courage in his veins. He wanted to be able to do that with Taylor. Hell, he simply wanted to be able to bring her here, like any other girlfriend or boyfriend. If she'd been around, maybe that's how he should have done it. Just brought her along. Screw subtlety. There would be nothing subtle about his family's reaction, after all.

But that wasn't courage stirring in his veins; it was probably champagne. Damn convenient champagne, too, since bringing Taylor hadn't been an option.

Besides, if Taylor were in town, bringing her tonight would have ruined the celebration. It wouldn't have been fair.

Excuses. He had more of them than his family had dogs.

Josh cast a wary glance at the sky, half expecting an ominous cloud to have physically manifested above him.

"You look gloomy, man. More booze?" A hand thrust a champagne glass toward him.

Josh snapped out of his reverie and turned his attention away from Kevin and Peter. The hand holding the glass belonged to Parker Ivanson, one of Kevin's friends who also worked for the sightseeing company.

Josh pushed the glass away with his plate. "No more booze for me, thanks."

"Ah, well. Your loss." Parker downed most of the

glass at once and checked out the crowd of partiers. "Was it too much to ask that one of Peter's friends be hot and, you know, female? It's a Saturday night, and the only reasonably attractive woman around is Kelsey, and I think she's as likely to tear off a man's dick as appreciate what it could do for her."

"You think? Should we ask her?" Josh raised his fork to signal his cousin's attention, and Parker shoved him against the railing.

"You trying to get me killed?"

Josh just grinned. Parker wasn't completely terrible, but he too often came close, and it always got on Josh's nerves. He couldn't figure out why Kevin was friends with him other than that Parker's father and Josh's uncle were also friends.

"She wouldn't murder you." Not literally anyway. "Besides, I know who's working the ER tonight, and I can vouch that you'd be patched up almost as good as new."

Parker swore at him with more creativity than Josh would have expected. "Sometimes I don't see the family resemblance in you, but then you do shit like that. It's vicious."

"It's not vicious. It's loyalty." It was also the best way to call Parker out for being an ass. Kelsey wouldn't have wanted him to fight her battles for her.

"Yeah, yeah." Parker waved away his rebuttal. "Family loyalty. I get it."

Under the circumstances, being considered loyal to his family was hilarious. Josh scraped a large blob of frosting off his cake and ate another bite. His family would call him a traitor. He'd called them ridiculous. Telling them about Taylor was going to be anything but funny.

The evening sun passed behind a cloud, turning the water black and dropping the temperature. Josh continued to pick at the overly sweet cake, one ear tuned to Parker's rhapsodized description of the hot tourists he'd taken sightseeing earlier today and one on the soothing sound of the waves breaking against the hull. Parker could talk and talk and talk some more. He only paused when Kelsey finally came bouncing over.

"Just look at the two of them. Aren't they adorable together?" The most un-Kelsey-like grin she wore as she gazed at her brother and Peter fell as she turned her attention to Josh's plate. "Why don't you eat the frosting on your cake, you freak?"

Josh handed her the plate. "For a second there, you almost sounded like you didn't despise all of humanity, Kels. I was worried."

Kelsey sneered at him as she scooped up his uneaten frosting with her finger.

"Yeah, so when are you ever going to do something normal, like date?" Parker asked. They way he watched Kelsey suck the icing from her finger made it clear it was not a wholly disinterested question, and Josh hid his smirk.

Kelsey popped the finger from her mouth in an oblivious fashion. "Who says I don't? Just not you. But since we're asking personal questions, Josh, what ever happened to that woman you went out with?"

"She left." Sadly, at the moment, it was true. He wondered how Taylor was spending her Saturday night in L.A.—out with friends at the sort of fashionable bars and restaurants that didn't exist in Helen? Were strangers hitting on her? Dumb question. Who wouldn't want to do that?

Josh decided to assume she was relaxing at home by

herself until it was proven otherwise when he called later.

"That's the best kind of woman," Parker said. "Tourists. You don't have to toss them out of bed, because they show themselves out."

Kelsey wrinkled her nose. "You're such a sleazebag."

"What? If it's what both people want, what's the issue?" Parker demanded.

"The issue is the way you frame it. You make it sound like women are tissues. We're not something you blow a wad into, then toss."

Josh guffawed into his sleeve. Parker had no idea how deep a hole he was digging as he continued to argue with Kelsey, but it was the perfect distraction from his Taylor problem.

"True or false—you would sleep with anything that was willing and female." Kelsey pointed a finger at Parker.

Parker cocked his head from side to side, considering. "Willing, female, and hot. Sure. I mean, with a few exceptions. For example, I'd never sleep with Lydia Lipin, even though you have to admit she's smoking." He nudged Josh on the arm in a don't-you-agree kind of way.

Josh glanced down at his hand, wishing he hadn't refused the offer of champagne. "I'm not sure I'd recognize Lydia Lipin if she walked into my office."

Kelsey grunted. "Well that's one redeeming quality of yours. That's the tactic I'm taking with my father—at least Kevin isn't engaged to a Lipin. Honestly, it's absurd I have to do this."

Yup, he should have taken that champagne. Kelsey was the one person who might at least hear him out about dating Taylor. Which meant there was no hope for his family. Which meant another day was going to go by and he'd have to admit to Taylor that he hadn't said a word.

THE INTERVIEW HAD gone well, or so Taylor thought. She'd spoken to a lot of people, been asked smart questions, and had asked smart questions in turn. The preparation she'd spent most of yesterday doing had paid off. She should have been excited and cautiously hopeful about the end to her unemployment. Instead she felt a whole lot of whatever.

She was, she realized with chagrin, anxious to return to Helen. After Taylor had spent nearly three weeks up north, slipping back into those L.A. designer heels wasn't as great as she'd anticipated. Her feet, like the rest of her, had not grown bored with her hometown's comfort yet. In fact, her hometown's comfort was very much on her mind as the Southern California temperatures edged toward triple digits.

Well, her feet—and every other part—would get their comfort back soon. She'd gotten in late Friday, had spent the weekend prepping, and would be flying out tomorrow morning. And between now and then, she had the one plan she'd most looked forward to—drinks and dinner with Stacy. She'd dearly missed their regular get-togethers while she was gone.

After changing out of her interview clothes, Taylor popped into the post office right before it closed to collect her mail since she'd forgotten to get it on Saturday. That, apparently, was a mistake. She hadn't expected much since all her bills were handled online, but the pile of junk mail the clerk handed over was absurd.

Taylor flipped through stacks of paper she had no interest in and no intention of carrying to the restaurant. "Is there a recycle bin?"

"Over there." The clerk pointed to her left. "And there's one more thing. Hold on."

One more thing? Another bundle of catalogs she hadn't signed up for and offers for credit cards she didn't want?

The clerk set a package down on the counter. "You want the hold order to continue?"

"Yes, thanks." Distracted by a package she hadn't ordered, Taylor checked the sender information, but all it provided was the name of a major online retailer.

Had she ordered something before she'd left and forgotten about it? Who knew anymore. Her last days home had been a blur.

After disposing of the junk mail, Taylor tucked the package under her arm and continued on to the restaurant. Stacy had already grabbed a table, and amid much hugging and catching up, Taylor brightened with a new realization.

"Mexican food." She let out a happy sigh into the extensive margarita menu.

"What about it?" Stacy asked. "Did you want to go someplace else?"

This restaurant had always been one of their favorites, and Taylor shook her head. "No. I'm reminding myself that one of the things I missed about being here was the Mexican food. So that's another thing on my list."

"You made a list?"

"A mental one. I've been recounting to myself everything I missed."

"I see." Stacy made a curious face. "What else made the list?"

"You."

"I'd better have. What else?"

"Oh, well, you know. Having a place to myself. My own bed. All the shopping options. My extensive collection of sundresses that just aren't needed in Helen." Taylor counted off on her fingers. "Not paying exorbitant prices for basic groceries."

Stacy rested her chin on her hands when Taylor paused. "And?"

"That was about as far as I got until I recalled Mexican food."

"I see." She said it again with the same tone.

Taylor raised the menu to cover her face. So what? So she'd missed absolutely nothing of substance, except for her friends. Okay, and her L.A.-appropriate wardrobe. But pretending she missed the attractions that drove so many people to L.A., like the beaches or the nightlife, would be disingenuous. She'd rarely ever taken advantage of them, unless friends like Stacy had initiated it. She was more of a hiking, kayaking, and snowshoeing kind of woman.

Contrast that pitiful list with, say, the list of things she missed about Helen, and . . . nope, she wasn't going there.

Thankfully the server arrived then to take their drink orders. A margarita was exactly what Taylor needed to keep her thoughts in line.

"So what's in the package?" Stacy asked, grabbing a tortilla chip.

"No idea. I don't remember ordering anything." Taylor picked it up and gave the box a good shake. Something inside shuffled.

Stacy pulled a utility knife from her purse and offered it over. "My father taught me to always carry one with me. I'm surprised you don't always carry one, given the bears roaming through your streets back home."

Taylor laughed and cut into box. "Bear spray works far better. If you're close enough to use a two-inch blade, it's already too late."

Stacy shuddered.

"Please. I'll take the risk of a bear sighting over a guarantee of rush-hour traffic on the 405 any day." Taylor tore open the packaging the rest of the way and pulled out an item she definitely had not ordered—a husky plushie. "Oh, my God."

Her fingers shook as she read the slip of paper she found on the bottom of the box.

In case you missed my dogs. Hope this arrives in time. Wishing you lots of luck at the interview!

—Josh, Jay, Pepper, and Bella

"Is that a stuffed animal?" Stacy reached across the table and picked up the plushie. "Oh, how cute! Wait, doesn't your enemy boyfriend have dogs? Is this from him?"

"Him and his dogs." She let the paper fall from her fingers, feeling like someone had punched her in the gut, but in a good way.

This is what she should have felt like after her interview. Like she couldn't stop grinning. Like her head was spinning. Like the world was shifting under her feet.

It was only a toy, a sweet, thoughtful gesture. It wasn't anything that should shake her up this way. But oh, she was shook.

"Damn, Tay." Stacy handed back the husky. "You've got it bad."

"What?" She was absolutely not going to rub the plushie's fur against her cheek and pretend it was Josh. Not in public.

No, she'd save that for later when she was alone and free to think about how she was going to show him how much she'd missed him. Naked and in multiple positions. God knew she'd tried to tease him about that over text last night, but she'd felt more silly than turned on. It had to have been interview nerves, as she'd become quite creative with the sexy texts she'd sent from Lydia's apartment in the weeks before she'd left.

Tonight, she'd have to try again. Perhaps with video. Her hands could never compete with his, and her imagination could never replicate the way his skin smelled when she buried her face against him, but his voice could work magic. She loved that gravelly quality it took on when he became aroused. Just hearing it did all sorts of things to her own body.

"It seems like he might deserve your affection." Stacy snapped her out of her increasingly restaurant-inappropriate thoughts. "That was sweet of him."

"He's thoughtful."

Stacy's chin returned to her hands. "Mmm. And we've already established he's cute, smart, good in bed, and has adorable dogs. No wonder you're smitten."

Ignoring the smitten comment, Taylor tucked the husky back into the box before she did something stupid. "I do miss his dogs."

"But not him?"

"I miss him."

"A lot." Stacy raised her eyebrows.

She started to protest, but it seemed pointless. "Maybe."

Their server returned with their drinks, and Taylor took a long sip of hers. Alcohol rarely provided clarity, but that was fine. She didn't need clarity. She needed confusion. Denial.

"Do you even want the job you interviewed for?" Stacy asked.

Her friend was not going to let her have either confusion or denial. "I don't know."

Except she kind of did, and the answer was no. It was the inevitable conclusion of her trip and her inability to come up with a meaningful list of things she missed. Far from hating working at the inn like she'd expected, she enjoyed it. And she also enjoyed spending more time with Lydia. She'd hoped this intermission would help her cope with her family's reaction to her dating Josh, and perhaps it had too well. She was ready to return.

And she was more than ready to see Josh again. She was eager. Just the anticipation of it made her smile through the mess she was making of her life. It made her smile even though returning to him meant going back to dealing with the feud and the fallout from her family's discovery. If he could have that effect on her, it suggested some pretty scary ideas about her feelings for him. They were a lot stronger than she'd ever intended them to get. She could play the denial game all she wanted—hell, she could pretend she only missed his dogs—but she was falling for him. Hard.

What in the world was she supposed to do about that?

17

BLEARILY, JOSH GRIMACED at his reflection in the passenger-side mirror. His forehead was going to bruise, and the butterfly bandage over his eyebrow wasn't so hot either. More concerning were the dizziness and nausea, which was why he was currently being escorted home by one of Helen's finest while the woman's partner followed in their squad car. Josh appreciated the gesture, but not the downturn his day had taken.

Everything had been going so well too. Taylor had texted to say she'd gotten the gift he'd sent her, which was a relief. He hadn't wanted to tell her to check her mail, but it had been starting to look like she might not do it before she left. He knew it was silly to send her a care package when she was gone for only four days, but from his perspective, it had been a long four days. Sure, he might not have seen her every day if she had been in town, but it was different knowing she was around. California might as well be the moon. Thankfully, she'd be back tomorrow.

Of course, he still hadn't confessed their relationship

to his family like he'd promised himself he'd do before she returned, and he was in no condition to do it now.

Until an hour ago, he'd been in the middle of his weekly ER shift and everything was quiet. Then a drunk driver had been brought in. A belligerent drunk driver. The EMTs had been going over his injuries, and Josh had been ordering a tox screen when the guy suddenly and violently lashed out. In the effort to restrain him, he'd gotten in a couple of good blows. One had knocked the wind out of a nurse, and another had sent Josh flying backward until his face had rather forcefully met the corner of a cabinet. He'd blacked out for only a second, but a second was long enough. Blood had dripped into his eyes, dizziness had set in, and the nurses had practically carried him out of the room with strict admonitions to heal thyself. Adrian had been called in to take over for the rest of his shift.

"It's this one." Josh pointed to his house, and the officer pulled the Jeep into his driveway. "Thanks for the lift. Did you need anything else?"

The cops had already added his statement to their report, and the officer shook her head. "We should have everything, but if not, we'll give you a call. Take care, Doc."

"Thanks, Laura." Josh made sure he was steady on his feet, then opened the back door for his dogs to climb out. They were unusually subdued, apparently sensing his state of being. "Come on, guys."

Walking slowly so as not to set the world spinning again, Josh herded the dogs to the house. He heard the cop car pull away as he unlocked the door and made his way inside. With a yawn, he dropped off his keys, removed his jacket, and contemplated what to do next.

He wanted to sleep, but it was too early for that, which

meant it was the head wound talking. If he went to bed now, he'd have to get up in a couple of hours to let the dogs out one more time, so he might as well plop in front of the TV and enjoy the unexpected evening off. Taylor was out with her friend so he shouldn't bug her, which was unfortunate.

Mind made up, Josh grabbed a glass for water and took a good look at his kitchen. Perhaps it was his head, but something seemed off. It was messier than he'd left it. The dogs' bowls were . . . missing?

He set the glass down, blinked a few times, and turned his attention to the rest of the house. No, it was not his head, and it was not only the kitchen. He'd swear he could feel the moment his blood pressure spiked because his head started to throb.

Someone had trashed the place. The food bowls, with whatever had remained of the huskies' breakfast, had been tossed into the living and dining rooms, scattering bits of food over the floor and furniture. The glass in every picture frame had been broken, and his personal laptop that was sitting on the dining room table looked like someone had taken a hammer to the screen. Sofa cushions were tossed around and drawers pulled open, spilling their contents onto the floor. By some miracle, the television remained untouched, but it was the only thing in either of those rooms that hadn't been.

Belatedly, Josh realized Jay, Pepper, and Bella were acting strangely too. They weren't barking but whimpering, circling around his feet in agitation. Whoever had done this had invaded their space as well.

"Stay," he told them as he crept toward the dining room. The kitchen floor seemed safe, but it was impossible to tell from his vantage point how much glass might be on the dining room or living room floors.

He thought he should be worried, but if the intruder hadn't left, surely the dogs would have picked up on it. Mostly he felt bewildered, dizzy in a way that wasn't the result of a blow to the head but that was likely not helped by it either. There was also a bitter irony in that the cops had just dropped him off, and he'd need to call them back.

Swearing quietly, Josh shuffled into the dining room, half expecting to discover that the intruder had smashed the glass on the sliding doors to get in, but they'd seemed fine. Whoever had done this must have picked a lock.

He was about to go check the upstairs and see if anything had been stolen, when he saw the note lying under one of the broken picture frames on the table.

Leave Taylor alone or the next thing that breaks around here will be a lot more personal.

So that's what this was about. The fucking feud.

Understanding that actually made him feel better. This wasn't a random crime, but a logical sequence of cause and effect. That was less frightening and more enraging. Forcing his hand to unclench, Josh set the crumpled paper back on the table and read it again. The idea of ending up as another anecdote in the Porter-Lipin feud was infuriating, but he wasn't going to be threatened into leaving Taylor either.

The next thing that breaks will be a lot more personal. Part of him wondered what exactly they had in mind, but he didn't doubt the Lipins were capable of carrying out their threats. This break-in had likely been orchestrated to prove it.

Damn the Lipins. And his family too. It took two to go to war, after all. But if they thought he was going to cower, they would learn their mistake. The only person who got to tell him to leave Taylor alone was Taylor. All threatening him did was make him want to hold on to her more tightly.

He closed his eyes briefly, imagining her scent, her touch on his stinging skin. Imagining pressing himself against her, and the way her ass curved under his hands as he held her.

Although he was trying to calm down, these thoughts were having the opposite effect. It must have been the adrenaline because he was getting hard, craving her body. It was good she wasn't around to provide temptation. Not with his head as it was.

After a brief debate about whether he should hold on to the note, Josh stuck it in his junk drawer—a reminder to be more alert. He'd learned enough to know that calling the police was something that was not done when it came to the feud. He'd thought that was absurd, but standing in the middle of the debris field that was his kitchen, he realized it was also wise. Calling the cops would alert both families to what had happened. It would escalate the situation because his family would want to retaliate, and he couldn't let that happen. It might put Taylor at risk.

A more thorough inspection of rooms showed little glass on the floor, and Josh swept it up first since the dogs were getting restless in the kitchen. As he tackled the rest of the cleanup, his phone rang. Without bothering to see who it was, he answered.

His uncle. Just what he needed. "Josh, you have to come over this minute."

Annoyed, he collapsed onto a chair. It was after eight o'clock, and he'd had enough family drama for one day. Hell, he'd had enough for a lifetime. "Can it wait?"

Even as he said it, the oddness of his uncle's request penetrated his foggy brain, as did the urgency in his voice. Something was up. It didn't seem impossible that his uncle's call and the break-in were related.

"There will never be a good time," his uncle said, which was as good a confirmation as any that the fan was still flinging shit. "Get here as soon as you can."

Groaning, Josh let his hand drop. His head continued to ache, and he doubted he was okay to drive. But mostly he wondered what else the Lipins had done.

KELSEY GRUMBLED ABOUT Josh asking for a ride, but twenty minutes later she'd picked him up and was pulling into her parents' driveway. Josh had hoped to keep her out of his house when she'd arrived, but he was too slow. Luckily, any questions she might have asked about why all his picture frames were smashed had vanished the moment she saw his head.

"I shouldn't be taking you here," his cousin said, shutting off the engine. "You should be getting checked out by another doctor if you're too dizzy to drive."

Not wanting to discuss his injury any more than necessary, Josh got out of the car. "I already was. You know, beneath your ice queen exterior, you can really be a nagging mother hen."

"Say that again and I'll make your left eyebrow match your right."

Conveniently, Josh's aunt and uncle were both waiting for him in the living room. Nothing appeared amiss, but his uncle's expression was grim. He stood in front of the window, gripping the life out of a day-old copy of the *Anchorage Daily News*.

With a mix of trepidation and relief, Josh took a seat

near his aunt. The dizziness hadn't returned yet, but he didn't trust himself to remain standing for long.

He started to ask what was wrong, but his aunt cut him off. "Sweetheart, what happened to you?"

"It's nothing. We had a violent drunk in the ER."

His uncle snorted, but Josh's aunt released her tea mug and reached for his forehead. "If that's why Kelsey drove here, you need to see a doctor. Are you dizzy, nauseous? What about vision problems?"

"I'll be fine." Flinching, Josh inched away from her probing fingers. "I'm the doctor, remember? Tell me why I had to get here so urgently. I'd still have been working if it wasn't for my head."

The lines of concern on his aunt's face deepened, and she turned to his uncle. Josh did the same. Since no one appeared to be in immediate danger from the Lipins, the throbbing in his head was making his patience short.

"Something came to my attention last night thanks to Dennis." His uncle tossed the newspaper aside. "I'd like to give you the chance to explain yourself."

Kelsey appeared in the doorway, clutching a plate of what appeared to be cobbler. His aunt was always baking, and always foisting her latest sweets on whoever stopped by the house. Belatedly, Josh realized he hadn't been offered anything, and that was another bad sign.

He rubbed his forehead. Why hadn't those painkillers kicked in yet? Did he need to take more?

"Dennis Ivanson?" That was Parker's father. Josh had no idea what Dennis might have said that would have his uncle riled up. The only thing that came to mind was his relationship with Taylor. While it was unlikely that Dennis would have discovered them, it wasn't impossible.

This could be bad, and he wasn't in the best state for dealing with the fallout at the moment. Plus, when he considered what the Lipins had done when they'd learned, Josh no longer had any illusions as to how bad the situation could get. That said, he wasn't about to jump to conclusions. He'd almost told Kelsey everything once by assuming she knew more than she did.

"Yes, that Dennis," his uncle said. His tone was like a whip, the words snapping at Josh's sore brain. "Surely you're aware that our family has loyalists keeping an eye on the Lipins."

Loyalists—fancy name for Kelsey's fabled spies, if he had to guess. Josh held in a sarcastic laugh. "Yes."

"This person overheard a conversation between some of the Lipins. A conversation about you." Josh's uncle paused and stared expectantly at him. With his close-cropped gray hair, he could have been a drill sergeant on the prowl if it weren't for the bit of middle-aged paunch at his waist.

Even with his pounding head, Josh could figure out the rest of this story. The overheard conversation had to have been about his relationship with Taylor, and his uncle was waiting for him to fill in the missing details. No jumping was necessary to reach that conclusion.

Josh buried his face in his hands. This was what his procrastination bought him. If he'd owned up to everything over the weekend, he could have had this conversation on his terms. It didn't matter that his paranoia had been validated. Now he had a throbbing head, a possible concussion, and two pissed-off families to deal with at the worst time.

"Well?" his uncle demanded.

Sighing, Josh lifted his face. Hadn't he had a conversation with Taylor about the fact that he was a grown man and there was no way he was letting anyone in his family lecture him about whom he dated? It seemed like a lifetime ago. "Yes, I've been seeing Taylor Lipin. That's what you want me to admit, right? Not that it's any of your business."

"What?" That squeak came from Kelsey, and a bite of cobbler fell off her fork.

Grasping at whatever steadiness he had left, Josh got to his feet. The news was out, and that was that. In his current state, he had less interest than usual in what would follow, so it was time to leave. "If that's all you wanted confirmation of, you could have asked over the phone. I have to get home. The dogs need to be let out."

More like he had to get home and protect his dogs before Kelsey decided to kidnap them. He wouldn't put it past her to declare he no longer deserved them.

"We're not done yet," his uncle said.

Josh turned to Kelsey, his ride, but she stared at him with wide eyes. If he'd thought he could make an easy escape, he was wrong. His cousin was not going to be any help. He was on his own.

"Actually, we *are* done." It was exhausting, but he strove for his most reasonable voice. Calm, authoritative, adult. All the things his uncle's furious eyes and his aunt's disappointed lips were attempting to deny him. "I realize you're unhappy about this, but I'm neither a teenager nor your child. You don't get to tell me who I can date."

"She's a Lipin, Josh." Kelsey again. "Oh, my God. Is she why you've been busy lately? Have all the times you've claimed to be working too much to go out actually been times you were with her?"

In retrospect, driving himself, dizziness and all, might have been better than having Kelsey along. "Of course I've been hiding it. I knew all of you would react like this."

His aunt murmured something Josh couldn't hear under his uncle's roaring disapproval. "Listen to your cousin. That woman's a Lipin. She can't be trusted, and you don't have a lick of sense in your head. I knew it was a mistake when my sister married that—" He slammed his lips together and spun toward the window.

"'That'?" Although Josh was in no state for any of this, his hands curled into fists, daring his uncle to finish even though part of him didn't truly want to know the missing words.

Maybe he was still jumping to conclusions, but Josh had heard sentences cut off like that before, and he knew how they tended to end. With his blue eyes and nonstereotypically Jewish last name, Josh encountered anti-Semitism mostly from people assuming he was just like them and feeling free to let their ugly side show around him. Until he confronted them, that was. As much as he despised conflict, there were some things that couldn't be left alone. After that came the mouths clamping shut in his presence. Josh had been through it before.

With family, though, that was new. His mother and his uncle had never been close, and Josh hadn't thought much of it. Not all siblings were. But now he wondered if there might have been another reason for it that no one had ever bothered to share with him.

His uncle picked up the newspaper he'd tossed, looking like he needed something to do with his hands. "That man who dragged her around the country," he finished weakly. "That made her forget her roots. She taught you nothing."

The words *nice save* danced on his tongue, but Josh merely closed his eyes and focused on his breathing. The gesture wasn't just for show. His uncle's volume and the stress were making his head pound worse. Sarcasm might feel good, but it wasn't going to get him out of here faster.

"Actually, my mother taught me a lot. Like how I should stay out of your fight. Now can we resume the yelling later when my head doesn't feel like it's going to split open?"

"Yes." His aunt's voice was softer than his uncle's but every bit as forceful. "Sweetheart, we're simply concerned for you. Even if this thing you have with the Lipin girl is a temporary fling, it's not a good idea."

"It's a damn stupid one," his uncle interrupted. "The day my flesh and blood dates a Lipin—"

"I need to go."

"I'm serious, Joshua." His uncle approached with heavy feet. "You need to break things off. I was thrilled when you moved here. I thought you wanted to be a part of this family in spite of your mother. But I cannot tolerate this. Those people have a long history of wronging our family, starting when they tried stealing your great-great-grandfather's sled dogs. As if those dogs would ever turn their backs on their real owners. But they bribed the law and almost got away with it, and when they couldn't, they came for our land and our businesses. They tried to hurt our children, and they still do to this day."

Josh's aunt laid a hand on her husband's arm. "Wallace, perhaps this is not the time."

"He has a bump on the head. It won't kill him."

No, but you all are driving me to thoughts of homicide. Josh winced, trying to scoot around his uncle to get to the door, and he glanced at Kelsey. She was frowning intently into her plate. She probably felt embarrassed by her father's comments, but Josh knew better than to assume she'd side with him. The moment his head stopped hurting, Kelsey would be on his case with the full force of her anti-Lipin attitude. Claws out and teeth bared.

It was a damn good thing Kelsey had been too distracted to notice the state of his house. She'd probably try to rip open the intruder with her bare hands. He loved her for that, but he did not need the additional complications weighing on him. It would be hard enough to convince everyone to calm down as it was.

"If we're done," Josh said, aiming for the door, "I'm leaving. Kelsey, are you going to drive me back or do I walk?"

Kelsey was silent the entire drive. Josh wanted to believe it was out of concern for his head, but most likely it was simply because she was too pissed off to talk. He didn't care. He'd take the silence gratefully.

No longer interested in TV, Josh collapsed onto his sofa when he got home. He had to warn Taylor that his family knew their secret, too, but that would be all he told her. He didn't want to lie to her about the break-in, but he didn't want to worry her more. If she noticed the broken frames and asked, he'd tell her. If she didn't, he'd keep quiet. His conscience could live with that compromise, and if he was lucky, threats from her family would be his alone to deal with.

He was strangely okay with that. After building a life around seeking stability and avoiding unnecessary risk, he was fresh and ready for this battle. He'd found Taylor, and she was a risk worth taking.

18

⊰⊱────────⊰⊱

SO THE PORTERS knew about her relationship with Josh.
Taylor had spent most of her trip back to Helen pondering
this point. According to Josh, his uncle had yelled at him
like he was a child, but that was all that had happened.
Paranoia and a long history of stories she'd been fed about
Porter aggression made Taylor wonder. Josh had sounded
stressed, which was no surprise, but he'd also been distracted during their conversation. She had a hard time
understanding that. When her grandmother had confronted her, she couldn't think about anything else.

Still, Josh had told her he had to deal with an alterca-
tion in the ER, too, so he might have just been exhausted.
Josh had gotten off easier than she would have expected,
which meant either there was more to the story than he
was telling her or the worst had yet to come. That was a
troublesome thought.

The unhappy possibilities kicked around in Taylor's
skull right until she pulled her suitcase up alongside her
sister, who was standing in front of the Bay Song, watching a landscaping crew unload a truck full of flowers. That

was when Taylor noticed that all the flower beds lining the driveway, as well as all the beds around the building itself, had been torn asunder. The larger shrubs remained in place, but it looked like someone or some animal had dug up every flowering plant and ornamental grass.

"Tired of the old color scheme?" Taylor asked, although this could not possibly have been Lydia's handiwork.

Lydia shot her an it's-not-funny glance. "We were vandalized last night."

"What?" With a closer inspection, Taylor concluded that whoever had yanked out the flowers had probably been human. They'd mostly been piled in clusters, and while it appeared haphazard at first, the plants were too perfectly preserved for it to have been an animal.

Lydia motioned for Taylor to follow her around back. "Whoever did it was thorough. It's not just the front. They destroyed everything around the patio and the breezeway too."

Taylor swore. Outwardly, her sister appeared as calm and poised as always, but after a few weeks in her company, Taylor was getting better at picking up on Lydia's more subtle cues. There was a tightness around her mouth, and her tendency to fidget with her rings reminded Taylor of her own habit of playing with her bracelet when she was stressed.

Lydia's anger was to be expected, but the low-burning fury in Taylor's veins surprised her. Then again, it was hard to ignore that this was her family's business when she was living and working here. And not only that—it felt like a little bit of hers now too. She was angry not just for her sister's sake, but for her own.

"I don't suppose anyone caught the guy?" She almost said "the Porter," because who else would it have been? That someone would vandalize the inn on the same night that Josh's family discovered their secret could not be a coincidence.

Lydia grabbed Taylor's carry-on and led the way up the stairs to the apartment. "No. Marie discovered what happened when she arrived this morning. Caleb was working the overnight shift at the desk, and he swears he didn't hear anything, which isn't surprising. He was probably in the back office most of the time."

Taylor set her suitcase down in what had become its semipermanent spot in Lydia's living room. Did she share her suspicions with her sister? Guilt urged her to do so. There was a good chance she was responsible for this in an indirect way.

But Lydia spoke again before Taylor could explain. "It's got to be the Porters. I don't know who else would do it. I just don't know what set them off this time, although I suppose they don't always need an excuse to be assholes. Sorry," she added after a pause. "Maybe your Josh is the exception to the rule."

Taylor grimaced as she retrieved her toiletry bag so she could freshen up. She was the one who should be apologizing. "I have a feeling it was me that set them off. Josh told me last night that they learned about our relationship."

"Oh, Tay."

"I'm sorry." Taylor cringed.

Lydia rubbed her temples. "It's not your fault that they did this, but I told you to be careful. How did they find out?"

"Josh didn't say. Could have been the same way Grandmother found out for all I know." She set down her makeup bag and proceeded to pull her hair out of its failing ponytail. As usual, it had been a long trip to get here, and she was looking as worn down as she felt.

Lydia could tell her it wasn't her fault, but that didn't

lessen the guilt. She'd made a choice, and the Porters had retaliated. It didn't dampen her enthusiasm for seeing Josh later, but it sucked nonetheless.

"What are you going to do?" Taylor stuck her head back into the living room as new thoughts occurred to her. "Did you call the cops?"

"What's the point? You know they refuse to get involved anymore, and Dad would be furious if he found out I tried it."

Dad was going to be furious regardless, but Taylor didn't bother saying the obvious out loud. "If Grandmother or Dad finds out, they're going to strike back."

"I'm aware, but it's not like I can hide the damage. Dad might not notice we have new flowers, but Grandmother definitely will. And I don't think she'll buy me claiming to have wanted to change things up in the middle of June."

"We have to break this cycle." Taylor's grip tightened on her hairbrush. "Someone has to."

"Yeah, good luck with that."

Merlot chose that moment to smack Taylor with his tail as he walked past, and she narrowed her eyes at the cat. Great. Even the family pet thought she was being unrealistic.

OH, MY GOD." Taylor nearly dropped the six-pack of beer she was carrying as she stared at Josh's face.

He smiled sheepishly at her and stepped aside so she could enter his house. When he'd mentioned a violent patient during his ER shift, he'd declined to reveal that his face had made the acquaintance of the guy's fist.

Putting aside her shock for the briefest of seconds, Taylor darted inside and waited while Josh scanned the street. Sure, their families both knew, but as they'd discussed after she got to Lydia's, flaunting their relationship might not be wise.

Although, at this point, Taylor was just assuming both their families had spies everywhere.

While Josh shut the door, Taylor took a moment to greet his dogs. Not that she'd had much choice. They'd all dashed in from the living room and were jumping up and circling her with excitement. Their combined enthusiasm made her feel temporarily better, but also nearly knocked her off her feet.

"Settle down so Taylor can breathe, guys," Josh said, for all the good it did. Bella calmed down, but Pepper grabbed her rope and Jay got his ball, and they demanded Taylor play with them. She indulged them briefly, but they couldn't distract her long, and finally Josh shooed them away.

Torn between horror and exasperation, Taylor set the beer on Josh's table and marched over to him. "Are you okay?" Without waiting for an answer, she flung her arms around him.

"Careful there. You almost banged my forehead." Her hair muffled his words, and Josh held her tighter.

"Someone else sure did." She could sense the tension in his muscles, every inch of him pulled taut. He needed a good massage, which was a service she'd be happy to provide later.

First, she wanted to hold him, and Taylor closed her eyes, crushing him harder and hoping the hug provided some comfort. With her face buried in the crook of his neck, she kissed him, dragging her lips over his stubble and enjoying the prickling sensation. She'd spent so much time imagining how to make their reunion memorable, but now that she was here, she doubted Josh was up for any of her more creative ideas.

Slowly, some of Josh's tension seemed to melt away, and he relaxed into her. The delicious hard planes of his body didn't become soft, but they yielded into hers. She wanted to envelop him, in more ways than one, and silently cursed his injuries.

"You feel good." Josh's breath tickled her ear.

"So do you." She could feel his growing arousal along with her own, and if she weren't so concerned about him, she'd have insisted they celebrate her return immediately.

Instead, Taylor pressed a hand to his cheek. Josh sported a bandage over his right eyebrow and a nasty bruise that ran from his cheekbone to his hairline. The whole area looked swollen and tender, and he winced as he smiled at her.

"Why didn't you tell me how badly you got hurt?"

Josh inspected the beers she'd brought. "It didn't seem relevant."

"Not relevant? You look awful." He pouted at her word choice, and she rolled her eyes. "I mean, you look slightly less hot than normal. Is that better? Purple is not your color."

"Better, but no worries. In a couple days, that part of my face will fade to green, and I've been assured that green is, in fact, my color."

Taylor poked his arm. "You downplayed the extent of it."

He had the decency to at least look guilty. "I was more concerned about filling you in on my family."

"I see." Taylor thought of the dug-up flower beds and debated whether to mention them. "I'm sorry you needed to deal with your family's freak-out without me around for comfort."

Josh held her gaze for a strangely long moment, then

he took her hands. "You're here now, so that's what counts. My plan had always been to tell them—someone anyway—about us while you were gone. I'd just have preferred they learned on my terms."

"I know it seemed like a smart idea at the time, but do you really think they would have freaked out less if they'd found out from you?"

He floundered for a second. The bit of tension she thought she'd drained from him returned, clouding his eyes. "Maybe not. Probably not. But that way I wouldn't have been made to feel like a teenager caught out after curfew."

"I think if my father believed he could ground me, he would have. Were you forbidden from seeing me too?"

"Something like that." He opened his mouth like he was about to say something more, then reached for the beer. "Did you bring me a present?"

"I did. From my favorite brewery. You can't get it here, so I smuggled it all the way back in my suitcase. And believe me, the bottles breaking on the flight and ruining my clothes was a much bigger concern for me than the news about your family."

Try as she might to reassure him about the her anxiety levels, Taylor wasn't sure if the quip landed. Josh was eerily perceptive about her moods. Normally, that was endearing.

"Thank you." He kissed her lightly, but she could tell even that caused him some pain.

Taylor pressed her fingers to his lips, wishing she could do more than offer sympathy. "Poor you."

"Yes, poor me. I've been waiting for you to nurse me back to health."

A thing she very much looked forward to doing, but with Josh wincing every time they kissed, it was definitely going to be a more subdued reunion than the ones she'd been fantasizing about over the weekend. "Don't tell me you're a doctor with a sexy nurse fetish."

"No. Can't say I've ever found people in scrubs sexy. But that reminds me—when people weren't gawking at my face at work, I heard a rumor that someone vandalized the Bay Song. Is that true?"

Taylor groaned. "Yeah, someone ripped out the flower beds. Lydia thinks it was probably someone in your family, and under the circumstances, I'd bet she's right."

"I'd bet she is too. Our families are both really going on the offensive all of a sudden."

"Our?" Taylor stepped back in alarm. "What did mine do?"

For a second time, Josh hesitated. Then he seemed to shake off whatever was going through his head with a sigh. "It would appear that last night a few dozen people launched an online campaign against me on a couple professional sites. No real reviews, just lots of one-star ratings with useful comments like 'He sucks.' My insistence on things like the importance of vaccinations does have a tendency to piss some people off, so it might not be your family, of course, but . . ."

"But it almost certainly is. They learned a trick or two from your family. The Bay Song has been the victim of targeted ratings bombs before. God, what a mess. I'm sorry."

"It does confirm for me how questionably helpful review sites are." He laughed wearily. "This mess is exhausting. What is wrong with our families?"

"That's a question likely answerable only by a highly qualified therapist. But if I had to guess—bad parenting?"

"Most definitely some of that."

"Vitamin D deficiencies?"

Josh waved his hand from side to side. "Eh. In the winter, absolutely. In the summer, probably not."

Taylor glanced around the sofa. Bella was snoozing on her doggie bed, and Jay and Pepper were gnawing their antlers. "It certainly can't be a lack of unconditional love."

"No, and my theory that people who love dogs can't be jerks has been unequivocally disproven."

"We might never know the full cause."

Taylor sneezed, and suddenly she was staring down another problem. She hadn't bothered taking allergy pills while she was gone.

Josh laughed when she pulled a bottle of pills from her purse, and he handed her a glass of water. "Tell me more about how the interview went."

So Taylor recounted what happened in more detail than she'd bothered with over text. Josh seemed to relax as she spoke, but she couldn't help but feel like there was something off. Not something about him precisely, or was it? She couldn't put her finger on it other than to think something was different. It made absolutely no sense, and Taylor did her best to push the odd feeling aside. Most likely it was anxiety due to their families gearing up for a battle. That cast a shadow over everything.

"Taylor?"

She realized she'd trailed off and was abscntly petting Pepper, who'd settled on her feet. "Sorry, long day. I was just thinking that getting hit on the head and dealing with your family all at once—it doesn't seem fair. Bad things come in threes, right? What's going to be next?"

Josh shrugged. "If I were superstitious, I'd say the ratings attacks ought to count. So by that logic, I should be safe for a while."

Despite the tension evident in his shoulders, he threw her an easy smile. Taylor tried to take relief in that, silly as it was, but she remained convinced that something was wrong.

"Especially," Josh continued, "since you're here. I don't need luck if I have you." He wrapped his arms around her from behind and pressed his lips to her neck.

Worried though she was, Taylor couldn't stop the smile that spread across her face. Being trapped in Josh's arms hadn't gotten old yet. Rather, the feeling spread delicious warmth throughout her body. Yes, she'd fallen hard. It was a dilemma in its own right since she had no intention of staying in town.

That was an even worse feeling than thinking something was off about him, and Taylor told herself to stop worrying. Maybe it was simply Josh's injury weighing on her, fooling her brain into believing the situation with their families was more dire than it was. In fact, that sounded very likely. Back-to-back revelations with their families, plus seeing Josh banged up, were guaranteed to play havoc with her nerves.

Taylor entwined her fingers with his and brought his hands to her face. The scents of lemongrass and laundry detergent were ones she'd come to associate with him. Back in L.A., she'd passed by a shop with a similar lemongrass aroma spilling out and had mentally been taken back to Josh's bed. "So you don't think it would be easier if I left for good? It would make all the drama go away."

Josh shifted behind her. "That's a joke, right? You leaving might make things simpler, but it would not make them easier. It's going to be hard as hell when it has to happen. Let's not rush it."

He squeezed her tighter, and Taylor closed her eyes. She hadn't been entirely joking. With everything weighing on her mind, she'd needed to ask. But she also wished she hadn't. The thought of leaving permanently was too unpleasant to dwell on while they were together.

"Just checking," Taylor said, careful not to smack his swollen cheek as she turned to kiss him. "I think it's time to change your luck entirely."

"I don't suppose that includes you getting naked?"

She got up and pulled on his shirt to lead him out of the kitchen. "We can start there."

19

JOSH POKED GINGERLY at his face, as if hoping it would be less tender than it had been the last time he did it. Which was maybe ten minutes ago. Unsurprisingly, he remained sore, yet he was feeling worlds better than he had yesterday. Although that might have had more to do with Taylor staying over last night than any healing.

Something had been bothering her all evening, and Josh couldn't tell if it was her concern for him or something else. He'd asked her what was wrong the few times he'd caught her staring into space, and each time she'd snapped out of it and shaken off the mood. Eventually, he'd given up. Possibly it had something to do with the vandalism at the inn, and even if not, he wouldn't have been surprised if she simply hadn't wanted to add to his troubles by sharing disturbing news. He couldn't blame her for that, seeing as he was holding back about his break-in, and he just hoped what he had told her—about the online harassment—hadn't been what bothered her. Whatever it was, though, her mood convinced him that withholding information had been the right choice.

Still, he wished she would have talked to him, though, so he could comfort and distract her. Her presence alone was plenty distracting for him. He liked having her in his bed. Liked sleeping with her limbs entwined with his and waking up in the middle of the night, hearing her breathe. And he absolutely loved falling asleep with the taste of her on his lips and the memory of her body rocking above his. He wanted her wrapped around him every night before bed. Someone could bottle that sense of euphoric contentment and make billions.

Eleven hours after Taylor had left, though, the feeling had all but worn off. Josh had finished with work, and he stared into his cabinets wondering what to do about dinner. He wished he shared Taylor's love of cooking, and more than that, he wished she were free tonight to come over. He'd cook anything she wanted if that were possible, but she was working late and besides, he supposed it was only fair that he let her spend time with her friends and family too.

Outside, a light but steady rain fell, washing away the remnants of his good mood and any hope of giving the dogs another walk. Kelsey had texted to say she'd stop by since their usual afternoon get-together hadn't happened. If he was smart, he'd use the time to brace for her arrival. Kelsey hadn't lit into him yet about Taylor, and Josh was under no illusions that her visit would be a friendly social call.

Unfortunately, he wasn't feeling particularly smart. It had been a trying day with difficult patients on top of the ongoing drama about the online ratings. Some of his patients—no doubt spurred on by his family—had launched a counteroffensive and bombarded him with glowing reviews. While he appreciated the support, he was less than appreciative of the entertainment this ordeal was providing his coworkers, and he had a bad feeling it reflected poorly on his professionalism even though he had nothing to do with it. At this point, he wanted to do nothing more than crawl under a blanket and poke his fingers in his ears until everyone's voices had grown raw from the endless commentary.

"Knock, knock!" Josh tore his gaze from his cabinets as a soggy Kelsey shut his door behind her. She pulled her jacket off, sprinkling water over the scuffed wood floor. Heedless of the mess, all three of his dogs ran over to her, barking excitedly. "I hate rain."

"I'm surprised you left the house." He'd always figured one of the advantages to working from home was not needing to step outside when the weather stank. But maybe her need to yell at him in person had been strong enough to overcome an aversion to the weather.

Kelsey let out a disgruntled noise as she petted each of the huskies in turn. "I wanted to check on you. You look worse than you did Monday. Did you put ice on that?" She reached out as if to prod his puffy face, and Josh smacked her hand away.

"Touch and die." The pain had almost entirely subsided, unless, of course, he accidentally rubbed his eye or otherwise poked at the affected area like he'd done a minute ago.

"You have some ice around here, don't you? Put more on." Kelsey flung open his freezer.

"It's fine. It's going to look worse before it gets better. Thank you for your concern, though, mother hen."

She narrowed her eyes at him but shut the door. "Fine.

This is the attitude I get when I care. Do you understand why I try not to?"

"If you cared more often, it might not be so tempting to tease you when you do."

"Jerk. No wonder someone tried to bash your face in."

He'd been about to ask Kelsey if she wanted any coffee, but Josh paused. "No one bashed my face in. I told you what happened."

"Yeah? Then why was your house trashed when I came to pick you up the other night? Why did I see a locksmith here yesterday morning?"

"I . . ." Shit. So much for hoping his face had distracted her.

Resigned, Josh got up and filled the coffeepot with water as he collected his thoughts. This was worse than Kelsey yelling about Taylor, but unlike that fiasco, there was still a chance of keeping this knowledge contained. "Who else knows about the house?"

"At the moment, no one." Kelsey tapped her fingers against his counter. "Tell me the truth this time, and maybe I'll keep it that way."

"Are you really blackmailing me?"

"That depends. How scandalous is the story?"

Very, by Porter standards. He was rather surprised Kelsey hadn't figured it out herself.

Josh kept her waiting until he had the coffee brewing. "I'm telling you the truth about my face. But the house—someone broke in while I was at work on Monday."

"Yeah, I gathered that much. Were you robbed, or was this personal?"

Say you were robbed. Kelsey had given him an excuse, but he had little confidence in his ability to pull off the lie. When he didn't answer right away, she guessed.

"It was the Lipins, wasn't it?" She raised a blond eyebrow. "They know about you and Taylor."

Josh glanced into the living room, where Jay and Bella had sprawled across the floor, unconcerned about the accusations flying twenty feet away. His dogs were not going to save him. That was the trouble with huskies. Even if they hadn't loved his cousin, they were too friendly a breed to make adequate guard dogs. "Why do you assume that?"

"Duh. Because we're not thrilled, and I'm sure they're not either. Plus, it would be like them. Wouldn't it?"

"I wouldn't know."

"Liar." Kelsey grabbed the sugar Josh had set out, and proceeded to dump a revolting amount in her mug. "Did they warn you to keep your filthy Porter hands off their precious girl?"

"Basically." He pulled the note out of the drawer and handed it to her.

Kelsey muttered something under her breath and passed it back. "Are you going to be sensible and do what everyone wants you to?"

Josh glared at her. "It's not what's wanted by the only two people whose opinions matter."

His cousin groaned. "Come on! While I understand the fun in pissing off the Lipins, have you looked in the mirror? Do you think the Lipins will do any less damage to you? There are lots of women in the world. You can find another one who gives you a hard-on."

"We are done with this conversation."

"I'm trying to protect you, Josh. You're the soft, gushy, nice one in the family. You lack the killer instinct." Kelsey spread out her arms and waved them around the kitchen in her irritation. "You heal people;

you don't destroy them. So you need to listen to those of us who are mean—we're trying to protect you."

Josh's hand shook as he poured the coffee, some combination of laughter and annoyance. Kelsey wasn't wrong. Normally, he'd do his best to avoid conflict, but the Lipins could threaten him all they wanted. He'd made up his mind and he wasn't going anywhere. "You called me gushy. Gushy? You are a damn mother hen, Kels. A vicious one, but it still counts."

Kelsey snatched her mug from him. "And you are too sweet to survive around here, not to mention too stupid. I wonder who the Lipins hired to threaten you."

"I told you—we're done with this conversation. Overdone. It's burnt."

"The Goodmans maybe?" She sipped her coffee thoughtfully. "The Lees?"

Giving up, Josh ignored her and proceeded to get out dinner for the dogs. "You're not going to tell anyone about this."

"You can't ask me that. After what the Lipins did—"

"Yes, after what the Lipins did. I'm serious, Kels. I do not want this situation to escalate. I do not want Taylor to get hurt."

"Like I said, you're gushy."

He shouldn't have made coffee. He should have cracked open a beer instead. He needed a fucking drink. "What I am is responsible. If you talk and anything happens to Taylor . . ."

He couldn't finish the threat because he didn't know what he would do. But if Kelsey thought he was too nice for violence, she might have a change of mind. Josh had been provoked to a fight only once, but he had taken his father's advice to heart—if you threw a punch, you made it count. It had taken three friends to pull him off the other boy. It would take a hell of a lot more than that to pull him off anyone who touched Taylor.

"God, you really have a thing for her, don't you?" Kelsey shook her head. "How long has this been going on?"

"A few weeks."

His cousin glared at him. "You've been lying to us, hiding this from us, for weeks? Damn, Josh. I could almost—almost—understand if you thought she was hot and wanted to do something stupid. A one-night hookup or something. But this is just being selfish."

"I'm selfish now, as well as gushy? How am I selfish?"

"Selfish because you're betraying your family. My father can be an asshole—I won't deny that—but he was right that you moving here made everyone happy. But rather than act like a member of our family, you're choosing this. Her."

Oh, yeah, he needed a drink. Kelsey was starting to piss him off big-time. "What about me doing things that make me happy? Taylor makes me happy. Taylor likes me for who I am, gushy and all. Or is Kevin the only one allowed to defy the family for his own happiness?"

Kelsey's arms fell, and her palms slapped the counter. "That's not fair."

"No?"

"Peter has done nothing to offend our family. That's why my father's being an asshole in his case."

"Neither has Taylor."

Kelsey pressed her lips together, and Josh could practically see her brain spinning as she racked her memory for some particular slight of Taylor's from childhood. She must not have come up with anything convincing because she sipped her coffee, her face strained. "I want you to be happy, but let's be real. Relationships have nothing to do with long-term happiness. Relationships are the antithesis of happiness, and my brother will figure that out for himself soon enough. So will you, and in the end, you'll realize all this misery could have been avoided and that you upset the family for no reason."

"Relationships are the antithesis of happiness?" Josh repeated. "That's cynical, even for you. What happened to you, Kels?"

A storm swept over Kelsey's face, and she drained her coffee like she was washing away a memory. Josh instantly regretted his flippant tone because perhaps something had happened to her. He'd assumed she was being melodramatic.

He started to retract his remark, but Kelsey talked over him. "We're talking about you, not me. I don't know if you're a hopeless romantic or just naive enough to believe a Porter and a Lipin can have a relationship, but let me mother hen you a bit more. Even under the best of conditions, love is a big fat lie. You're as doomed as everyone else. So please, stop setting yourself up to get hurt."

Without another word, she dumped her cup in the sink and blew out the door.

From the sofa, Jay lifted his head and whined at her back before turning to Josh as if to ask, *What was that about?*

Josh could only shrug. "I've got no idea either."

IF YOU'RE ABSOLUTELY set on the third weekend of July, we can hold the date for a week." Taylor escorted the bride-to-be and her fiancé out of the inn's function room and toward the lobby. "But next summer is filling up quickly."

To sweeten the deal—literally—she offered them some of Marie's cookies while she finished answering their questions. Maybe she should have gone into sales instead of marketing, or most likely, it was just the pride she took in the hotel that made talking it up to potential clients easy.

Lydia emerged from her office as Taylor shared the last few pleasantries with the newly engaged couple and waved them off. Taylor's smile drooped with exhaustion as soon as the inn's main door closed. Thank goodness it was time to return to her sister's apartment and kick off her shoes. Never again was she scheduling an appointment so late in the day.

Taylor frowned. What a stupid thought. Of course she wouldn't. This wasn't her real job, after all. She had, what—another week or two? What Lydia would do after that, Taylor wasn't sure. Their mother wasn't coming back anytime soon. She'd called when Taylor was in L.A. to wish her luck at her interview, and she'd let on that she'd taken on a part-time job at a hotel in Anchorage.

Thinking about both leaving and her absentee mother made Taylor antsy, so she pushed the thoughts aside and concentrated on the bottle of rosé her sister had chilling in the fridge.

"When did you pull this together?" Lydia asked, holding up the wedding information packet Taylor had created. The couple who'd just left had taken her only hard copy, so her sister must have printed another.

Taylor yawned. "I started working on it last week before I left. It's pretty rough still. I was thinking it would be great if you had prepackaged plans for different budgets. It should be professionally designed and printed in color, but then you could hand it out to people who are considering the inn. You could even send electronic copies to people who inquire online, and . . ."

She stopped at the door, realizing her sister was gaping at her. "What?"

"Nothing. Go on. And what?"

Taylor held her tongue while she dashed though the light rain and up the stairs to her sister's apartment. Kicking off her wet shoes, she recollected her thoughts. "Well, I was also thinking, what if you partnered with some of the local tour companies to offer discounted rates on excursions for the bride and groom or the whole wedding party? There are only so many weekends in the summer, so they book quickly, but people get married year-round. Alaska's never going to be a destination for winter weddings like the Caribbean, but with a package that makes cross-country skiing or snow machining part of the festivities, you could book more weekends in the colder months."

Lydia pulled the cork from the rosé and poured two glasses. "I can't believe your old firm laid you off. That's a brilliant idea."

Taylor dropped onto a chair, savoring the wine. "It's a little idea and doesn't have much to do with my old job."

"Still. You're putting that business degree to good use."

"Please. You're the one who got this place a reputation in the first place." She wiggled her sore toes. Why did they hurt so? She hadn't worn new shoes, and the pair had never hurt her in L.A.

As usual, everything was different in Helen.

"Please yourself. All I did was freshen up the buildings and improve the website. The town and scenery did the rest." Lydia sipped her wine and leaned forward. "Have you heard about the job yet?"

"My interview was only a few days ago."

"Then forget them. Come work with me permanently instead."

Taylor closed her eyes. It was so tempting. She'd been aware for weeks now that she enjoyed her responsibilities here far more than her old job. In part it was because she simply liked working with her sister and Marie, but she also liked the chance to use her organizational and presentation skills on a product that had made her proud, and lately the other responsibilities had been growing on her too. Not so much when she had to do things like assist the grumpy guests whose in-room heater had died during the night, but tasks like checking in on people during breakfast and making recommendations for restaurants and activities.

As hospitality manager, her mother's job had been one part kitchen and housekeeping supervisor, one part wedding coordinator, and one part concierge. Little Taylor had wanted nothing to do with that. She'd thought her mother spent too much time being bossed around by the guests, and she'd wanted to be the one who did the bossing. Now that she was older and wiser, she'd realized someone was always going to be telling her what to do. At least this way, her job was making people happy, not selling them crap or making some faceless corporation more money.

And it was good to be around her family. When it wasn't also terrible to be around her family, anyway—in other words, when the feud interfered.

And then there was Josh. Every time she thought about leaving, she felt sick. The fierce way she'd missed him last weekend was not something she wanted to experience again. But staying here, daring to think she could be with Josh for any true length of time if she did—that was foolish. Wasn't it?

She drank more wine and cast a glance at the stuffed husky he'd given her, sitting on her pillow. "This is good, but I want food."

"You want your man. I see the way you're staring at that stuffed animal."

Taylor sighed. She did want him, but she also wanted to figure out what had bugged her the last time she'd seen him.

Rather than respond, Taylor began assembling a feast from the sparse contents of Lydia's kitchen. Smoked salmon, some surprisingly good cheddar, garlic and herb spread, crackers, and the stash of her favorite chocolate she'd brought back from L.A. Tomorrow she'd have to do a grocery run. Her sister had adopted her parents' habit of cooking only out of necessity, but eating takeout or prepackaged food most nights was not to Taylor's taste.

Outside, the light rain continued to tap on the windows, making it appear far darker than it should be. No wonder she was tired. Her years down south had taught her body to take darkness as a cue to sleep.

Merlot wandered into the kitchen and meowed pitifully at Lydia, who was apparently negligent in feeding him quickly enough. As was becoming his habit, he'd swatted Taylor with his tail but otherwise ignored her.

"Ungrateful wretch," she called after him.

"You do have a facsimile of a dog sitting on the bed. You should be glad he hasn't tried tearing it to shreds."

"Don't you dare." She pointed a finger at the cat.

Lydia laughed and helped herself to the cheese. "So you want to tell me what was bothering you all day? Usually I'd expect a woman who spends the night with her forbidden love to be annoyingly sappy, but you were distracted and snippy until about an hour ago when you had to put on a happy face for potential clients. So?"

Taylor carefully layered smoked salmon on top of her herb spread, considering. "The fact that you're calling our relationship forbidden might have something to do with it. Do I need anything besides that?"

"Yes. Because that's nothing new."

She ate a bite while she stalled, and cracker crumbled onto her plate. Lydia, like anyone in her family, was not the best person to discuss Josh with. But there wasn't anyone here she could discuss him with, period. Taylor had thought about calling Stacy, but ultimately she'd decided against it. She'd attempted—again—to explain the weirdness of Helen to her friend, but the more she told her about the feud, the more confused Stacy had become. To be fair to Stacy, that was a logical reaction. The situation was so absurd that outsiders with normal families should be confused.

Lydia cleared her throat. "Well? What do I have to do to get in on your sisterly secrets?"

"Share some of yours?"

"I have no secrets. I'm thirty years old, I run the family business, I'm single, and I'm considering adopting a second cat. I figure it's never too early to start my eccentric old cat lady collection. What secrets could I possibly have?"

Taylor blinked and cheese fell off her cracker. Lydia's view of her own situation was so contradictory to everything Taylor considered true that she would normally assume Lydia was only saying it to goad her. Except her sister sounded serious. Serious and depressed, and both emotions shocked Taylor.

Her whole life, she'd envied the way perfection came so easily to her older sister. Not only was Lydia classically beautiful, she'd excelled in school, had never gotten into trouble, and had been completely fine with taking over the running of the Bay Song. She was the perfect child, dangled in front of Taylor to torment her. The idea that Lydia could possibly be unhappy with her ideal life made no sense.

Scraping her food back together, Taylor tried to gather these thoughts into words. But sisterly bonding wasn't something they'd done in a decade or more, and Taylor faltered in her delivery, too tongue-tied to be eloquent. "You run a successful businesses. You have tons of friends. And our family isn't furious with you all the time."

"But my closest male companion buries his poop in a tray in the kitchen. For some people, that's enough. I wish I was one of them."

"Have you tried looking farther away than Helen?"

Lydia absently broke off a piece of chocolate. "I haven't had a choice. Grandmother is determined I'm the key to our family's future good fortune and has been scouring the state for me, throwing anyone who meets her arbitrarily high standards my way, regardless of what I want."

"What do you want?"

Her sister blinked like no one had ever asked that before, and her features pinched. She clearly had an answer, and for a moment, Taylor thought she was going to share a secret after all. Then Lydia waved off the entire conversation with a flick of her wrist. "Stop making this about me. You are not derailing the conversation. If you want to help me feel better, tell our grandmother to stop mentioning the state of my ovaries the next time you see her. Now back to you. What's wrong?"

Taylor forced herself to push aside the cheese, feeling slightly ill. "I'm not sure, to be honest. Something felt off the last time I was with Josh, but I can't decide if it's my imagination, the fact that our families have both gone on the offensive, or something else."

"You think Josh is hiding something? He is a Porter."

"Damn it. This is why I didn't want to talk about it." Taylor gritted her teeth and got up. Apparently, their bonding time was over already.

Lydia grabbed her wrist. "All right, calm down. You can't even take a joke these days."

"That didn't sound like a joke." But she sat, proof that she truly did need to talk to someone. Anyone.

"It was, although it was possibly a bad one. Poorly timed." Lydia slid the chocolate bar closer to Taylor. "I assumed it's what you expected I'd say."

"It's what I expect everyone to say."

"Not without reasons, Tay. But if he's such a good guy, why are you worried?"

That was the crux of it, wasn't it? Josh was supposed to have been a good mistake—an accidentally rebellious date that had turned into something amazing. Instead, Taylor feared he'd become another regular mistake. With her dating history, assuming the worst was usually the wisest choice.

"Are you scared to confront him?" Lydia asked.

"No!" Taylor flopped back in her chair. She could see out the large living room window from where she sat, and the rain clouds had turned the sky a mottled gray. Around the inn, the lamps used to light the paths between the buildings would be turning on, cued by the early dimness, and the strings of twinkling lights hung around the patio would glow like brilliant cobwebs. Pretty and peaceful—it was the Helen that belonged to the tourists, not her.

"Then why not ask him directly?" Lydia said.

Luckily she still had wine left, and Taylor took a long drink. "I don't want to? That sounds pathetic, but when I'm with him, I just want to concentrate on the happy stuff. There's a shit storm kicking up around us, and he's the rock I'm clutching in the middle of it. When you're holding on for survival like that, the last thing you want to do is question the rock."

Lydia reached down and attempted to pet her cat as he slipped past, her expression thoughtful. "Ignoring the fact that you two clutching each other is what's caused the storm in the first place, I think you need to figure out what you want from your relationship with him. If it's just to have a fun, then put any worries out of your head and enjoy your time together. If it's more, though, you need to be able to talk to him. Communication is key, or so all the relationship advice columns I read keep telling me. And look at Mom and Dad—I don't think they talked in years, and that worked out great."

Taylor pulled her feet up onto the chair, curling into a ball. Funny that Lydia was making a similar point to the one she'd made to Josh about why they needed to come clean to their families. Less funny was the fact that it felt so much harder to take this advice than her own.

It was supposed to have just been fun between her and Josh, a fling to keep her happy for the short duration of her stay. She wasn't sure how that plan had gone so awry, but it had slipped away like sunshine on a winter's day. Which meant Lydia was right. She and Josh needed to talk, not only about what was bothering her, but in general. About the state of their relationship. About how they handled their families' crap going forward. It would not be fun, but they'd long passed the just-for-fun phase.

Taylor groaned and lowered her head to her knees. "I suppose you have a point. We should talk."

"Good girl."

"Don't patronize me."

"Okay, fine. Bad girl." Lydia shrugged and went to refill their wine. "You are dating a Porter."

20

⟡⎯⎯⎯⎯⎯⎯⎯⟡

LYDIA HAD INSISTED Taylor didn't need to buy her groceries, but her sister was wrong. As far as Taylor knew,
her sister had eaten one decent meal a day before she'd
moved in—breakfast. That was because Marie had insisted on cooking it for her on the days when she worked.
Otherwise, her sister seemed to live off of bagged salads,
food bars, and takeout.

Taylor wasn't having it. Not while she was staying in
her sister's apartment. Although she was planning to
meet Josh tonight, she'd emailed Lydia a simple recipe
earlier, and she was currently meandering through the
grocery store, buying all the ingredients Lydia would
need to prepare it.

As she tossed food into her cart to replenish Lydia's
fridge, she also bought everything she'd need for dinner
with Josh. The cooking would relax her during what
could be a tense conversation, or so she hoped.

Taylor paused her shopping cart in the bakery section,
debating whether she and Josh truly needed crusty bread
with their meal, then decided the hell with it. Life was

short. Their families were acting irrationally. She wanted carbs.

"Excuse me, Taylor?"

She didn't recognize the voice, and Taylor turned around with trepidation. "Yeah?"

A petite blond woman carrying a basket stood behind her. Without her dogs, it took Taylor a second to realize it was Kelsey Porter.

Taylor steeled herself for whatever was to come. "Kelsey." She left it at that. Saying anything more, even hi, felt too friendly.

Kelsey glanced around, but no one else paid them any attention. Taylor wondered if Josh's cousin was going to take a swing at her, but Kelsey didn't come closer. "You need to stay away from Josh. I'm not asking you to. I'm telling you."

Lovely. Wasn't it enough that she had to put up with this crap from her own family? Did she have to get hounded by Josh's too? It seemed only fair that the Porters kept their harassment limited to their own blood.

Still, if she didn't take demands from her family, she sure as hell wasn't taking them from a Porter. Josh's cousin had a lot of nerve. "My relationship with Josh is none of your business, and I'm assuming he told you the same thing. So leave me alone." She spun around, but Kelsey darted in front of her, blocking the bread.

"It is my business when your family threatens him."

"What?"

Some of the fury drained from Kelsey's face, perhaps in acknowledgment of the surprise rippling through her. "I'm guessing he declined to mention that to you too. Someone in your family broke into his house Monday, trashed the place, and left a note threatening to hurt him if he didn't stay away from you."

Taylor's mouth went dry, and for a moment, she could do nothing but let Kelsey's accusation sink in. When the shock subsided, her immediate reaction was to deny it. Luckily, that passed quickly before she could say anything so stupid.

Because it would have been stupid to deny it. God, it made sense. The online negative reviews were pitiful, childish stuff, probably done by actual Lipin children and their friends. An honest-to-God threat? That, unfortunately, was more like what she should have expected to happen. And the breaking into Josh's house to do it was a calculated move, proof of how easy the threat would be to carry out. How he wasn't safe.

It was no surprise at all that Josh had neglected to mention this, but she'd been right that something had been off with him. While she had no clue what had tripped her instincts, she'd known. Josh was so good at reading her moods, and apparently she could read his as well.

She should hate Kelsey for getting in her face this way, and she should definitely not trust her, because Josh's family had their own motivations for causing trouble. Yet Taylor's gut knew what her heart begged to deny. Kelsey was telling the truth.

"Did he tell you that?" Taylor asked once she regained her voice. She was hurt that he might have confided in his cousin before her, but with so many emotions swirling through her, it was tough to give that one breathing room.

"Eventually." Kelsey took a step aside, allowing her space to walk, but Taylor couldn't move. "If you actually care about him, then break it off. Do it before your deranged family truly hurts him."

Without another word, Kelsey disappeared into the frozen food section, leaving Taylor to stare at a basket of cellophane-wrapped French bread. Her hands curled into fists. Somewhere inside, anger was slowly replacing her horror. But not anger at Kelsey for the verbal slapping, nor even anger at Josh for hiding the truth from her. Anger at her family.

That they would threaten Josh made perfect sense. If they couldn't convince Taylor to end things, why not try him? They probably thought he'd be easier to convince anyway—faithless, no-good Porter that he was.

Taylor took a deep breath, her heart aching. More than ever, she wanted to find Josh and apologize for her "deranged" family. And then? She didn't know what then. Awful and unfair as it was, Kelsey had a point.

Taylor snatched one of the long, skinny loaves of bread, briefly imagining it as a sword. No, a cudgel. She wanted to smash something. But it was neither, and she wasn't particularly violent. The urge would pass. The anger, the betrayal—she was less sure of that.

Regardless, she and Josh definitely needed to have a talk tonight.

JOSH HASTILY WASHED down a handful of almonds with a gulp of water before heading off to see his last patient of the day. He was tired and hungry, but at least this appointment should be easy, and he had Taylor to look forward to afterward.

Unfortunately, seeing Taylor would be its own source of stress. Yesterday's rain hadn't let up, but she'd demurred on the idea of him picking her up, asking what if people saw him? When Josh had reminded her that their secret was out, she'd mentioned it wasn't wise to continue flaunting their defiance of their families. They'd already agreed to keep a low profile, but picking her up at the inn hardly struck Josh as flaunting their relationship. Her insistence had therefore left him uneasy. Was her family increasing the pressure on her? Had they threatened her too? He needed to know.

Pushing these thoughts aside, he knocked once on the exam room door and entered. "Good afternoon, Mr. Buteau."

"I told you—it's George." The seventy-one-year-old shook his hand.

Josh read over the information on his vitals that the nurse had collected, and refrained from mentioning the smell of cigarette smoke his patient had carried into the room. Despite the man's age, George Buteau's only ailment was high blood pressure, and Josh's repeated suggestions that he quit smoking had amounted to nothing. George was determined that a life spent captaining a fishing boat had kept him in top health even though he'd started smoking in his teens. Josh was determined it was lucky genetics and that quitting might improve his blood pressure.

Josh had also determined, however, that this was not an argument he would win. As with the rest of his life, he opted to choose his battles carefully.

"George, yes, sorry." Josh grinned as he brought up the man's file on the computer. "How is retirement doing by you and Susan?" His wife was also one of Josh's patients.

"Boring." George barked a laugh. "Avoid it if you can. Too much time together."

"That's a bad thing?"

George's laugh turned into a cough that he tried to cover up. "Nah, I'm just being funny. Never marry a person you don't want to spend most of your time around, yeah? Choose wisely."

"Sounds like good advice."

"You should take it if what I hear is true."

Josh blinked. He'd only been half listening to his patient's comments while he reviewed his notes, but that one snapped him out of his thoughts. "Sorry?"

Although the door was closed, George lowered his voice. "Is it true you're dating a Lipin?"

Josh's jaw dropped. It wasn't uncommon for some of his patients—the ones who'd known his mother, for example—to ask after personal matters. But this was different, and he was completely unprepared for it. "I'm sorry. What?"

George shrugged. "I heard it, that's all. You can do better. After what those people have done to your family, well, it's a damn shame."

Too stunned to speak, Josh tried desperately to remember what he'd been about to do when George's comment had caught him off guard. A shroud of awkward silence fell over the exam room before he managed to adjust his face into the fakest of fake smiles. He'd always received positive feedback on his bedside manner, but medical school had not prepared him for this sort of encounter.

"Anyway." Josh cleared his throat. "Anything new since your last visit? Any concerns?"

"Your face." George waved a finger in Josh's direction. "They do that to you?"

"We're here to talk about you," Josh reminded him. "I'm fine. Nothing you need to worry about."

Somehow, he kept his voice steady and firm, but it was a damn good thing George was his last patient today. Bad enough the Lipins had sent someone to threaten him. Worse that he'd been forced to endure his uncle and cousin lecturing him. But knowing his relationship with

Taylor had become town gossip? That might be the straw that drove him to utter and hysterical despair.

Josh wasn't sure whether to laugh or scream, but it was becoming ever more apparent that something was going to have to give. He just hoped that when it did, it didn't rip him and Taylor apart.

21

⟜——————⟞

IN THE END, Taylor got her way. Rather than Josh picking her up, she'd ridden her bike to his house. Josh's entire body sighed in relief as he saw her bringing her bike around to his backyard. He'd unlocked his shed so she could store it out of the weather, but it was probably pointless. The rain had let up, but a pervasive mist hung in the air. Not quite rain, and not quite not rain either. Everything felt damp.

Josh held open the door for her, and she darted inside. The ride over had been long enough to soak her, and her shirt clung to her frame, accentuating her mouthwatering curves. Her hair was down, too, just the way he liked it, and Taylor pushed wet strands from her face as she kicked off her shoes and set down the backpack that presumably had the groceries she'd insisted upon buying. He wanted to carry her straight into the bedroom.

"Your face is looking better." The concern in her voice was palpable, and she gently touched a finger to his jaw.

His face was much better, although his skin remained

discolored on one side. He didn't want to talk about his face though.

Josh slid his arms around Taylor's hips, enjoying the swell of her ass under his hands as he pulled her closer. "You don't look so bad yourself."

"I bet you say that to all the soggy women."

He grinned. "Only if they're wearing tight shirts. I do think I like you best this way. It reminds me of what you were wearing when we met."

Taylor draped her finger down his jaw and onto his neck. Nerves ignited under her touch, shooting sparks straight to his groin. He was positive she could sense his growing arousal as she slid her hands around him. "You remember what I was wearing when we met?"

"Not precisely. Just that it was very tight running clothes. I think there was a butterfly on your shirt?"

Her laugh was silent as she rested her head against his chest. "I think you're right. So all of this could have been avoided if I'd just gone running in a baggy sweatshirt?"

Josh decided not to press for what *all of this* meant. "No, that makes fate too capricious. I like to believe it wouldn't have mattered what you were wearing. I still would have been wildly attracted to you."

"But would you have talked to me if my boobs hadn't gotten your attention?"

Pleased for the excuse, he cupped one of them. They really were perfect, and the desire to pull off her shirt and suck on those delicious nipples was overwhelming, especially as he could feel the one beneath his thumb getting hard. Was it strange to think he wanted to let his mouth make love to her breasts all evening? He could spend hours licking and sucking and admiring the view, and oh shit—what had she asked?

"Actually." Josh cleared his throat, which did nothing

to ease his desires or stop his tongue from aching for the chance to taste her. "It was your smile that had me. You lit up everything within miles. So yes, you could have been wearing the baggiest of shirts, and I would have thrown myself at you. I'd have done it literally if I knew it would earn me a smile."

That did earn him a bright smile, yet there was something sad about it all the same. "I would love to see a grown man literally throw himself at me."

He pressed Taylor closer, as if he could squeeze that hint of sadness out of her. "I would love to see if you're as wet as your clothes are. I think both could be arranged."

"How—"

He cut her off with his mouth, kissing her with a desire to make them both forget whatever weirdness had been going on the past several days. Taylor wanted to forget it, too, that much was clear, and she wove her fingers through his hair and attacked his mouth like she was starving. Some part of his brain yelled at him to figure out what was wrong before he indulged in her like this, but Josh wanted to concentrate on what was right. And this was right—the way her body fit against his, the way her lips tasted and her skin smelled like the rain. The way her touch drove all the unpleasantness of his day straight out of his brain. These were the things that mattered.

TAYLOR KNEW SHE was supposed to be talking to Josh, not kissing him or abandoning plans to make dinner in order to get naked with him. But suddenly, all of that could wait. What was kissing Josh if not also communication? And she needed to communicate this way with him too. It was so much easier to express what she was feeling this way and so much harder to hide.

"Josh . . ." Taylor wasn't sure what she wanted to ask, but he answered anyway. He let go of her breast and slid his hand back to her ass. Then Josh picked her up and carried her toward the stairs.

A moan slid up her throat as he set her on the bed a moment later and yanked up her shirt, and her hands fluttered against his cheeks with the lightest of pressure. "Sorry."

"It's all right. Although . . ." Josh gazed down at her. She was wearing the blue bra with the lace, the one she knew he liked so much, and he skimmed his fingers along the fabric's edge. Taylor's breath hitched, and Josh swallowed. "Maybe, to be safe, you shouldn't touch me this time. You should let me do all the work."

Taylor's hands had already slipped beneath his shirt. "Oh, no."

"Oh, yes. If you want to see me throw myself at you."

She couldn't tell if he was joking, but more importantly, she had a bunch of things she needed to tell him. She'd planned on doing it nonverbally. "You're wounded. You shouldn't have to work."

"You took care of me on Tuesday. It's my turn." He released her hands, and stepped between her legs. His thumbs dipped beneath the fabric of her bra, gliding along her skin, seeking out her aching nipples. The retort that had been dancing on her lips dissolved in the tidal wave of sensation. "I'll take that as a yes. So first, let's remove these damp jeans."

Taylor hesitated, her brain not as convinced as her body about this change of plans. But fine. If he wanted to do it this way, she was going to make him pay for it.

Taylor reached down and unzipped her pants, and Josh tugged them off, urging her to scoot back on the bed. So she did, watching him watch her. Watching him struggle with his self-control. She could ask him right now about the threat, and she knew he'd have no choice but to tell her. As sure as she'd stripped off her clothes, they were stripping the boundaries between them. Every time she kissed him, they fell a little more.

On that thought, Taylor slipped a finger beneath her panties. "You said no touching you. Nothing about myself."

"That's not fair." He swallowed but didn't seem capable of averting his eyes.

So she spread her legs wider. "You'd better throw yourself over here quickly, but take your clothes off first."

Josh's shirt went flying before she'd finished the sentence. "I'm going to make you pay for this."

"I thought that's what I was doing to you." Although, to be fair, he was turning the tables on her as he stepped out of the rest of his clothes, and Taylor bit her lip. Her fascination with his forearms had been a warning shot—if she'd found them so attractive, his naked body might be too much for her, and it almost was. She still hadn't grown accustomed to it. The powerful muscles in his legs, the sleek lines of his chest as it tapered to his waist. He didn't spend hours sculpting himself in a gym like so many of the guys she met in L.A., and she appreciated that. Appreciated that Josh claimed his only exercise came from walking his dogs. There was something adorable about that, and it made him all the hotter.

"Ready?" he asked.

She was more than ready, but not for what Josh apparently had in mind. He jumped on the bed next to her, and Taylor squealed, first with confusion, then with laughter.

"I did promise I'd throw myself at you. I hope it was worth it because I'm not sure my bedsprings agree."

She reached out for him, joyful warmth temporarily overriding her arousal. "You're too cute for words."

He turned slightly red. "I'll just do anything to see you smile like that. But . . ." He grabbed hold of her arms and raised them above her head, his grin fading away into something heavier. "Nope. Remember our deal. It's my turn."

"Josh."

"No." He held her arms in place until she stopped resisting, and then lowered his face to her neck.

Taylor sucked in a breath, her head filling with his familiar lemongrass and musky scent. That alone could undo her. His mouth working its way along her collarbone, his delicately kissing the skin down her chest and the spot between her breasts—it was wonderful agony.

Josh unhooked her bra and tossed it to the floor. He took his time with her, kissing and sucking and nipping at each breast, driving her wild until she was squirming beneath him, begging him in barely audible whispers for more.

"What was that again?" he asked innocently as he nuzzled her below the belly button. His stubble was the perfect mix of sharp and soft against her skin.

"Please." Taylor thrust her hips up at him. As lost as she was in her own need, she wasn't unaware of his body. Josh was trembling along with her.

He defied her, though, kissing her lower until his tongue spread apart her most sensitive skin. "Ask nicer."

She couldn't because she didn't have any ability to form new words as he continued to torment her with his mouth. All too quickly, the orgasm tore through her.

Josh raised his head slowly as her shuddering died down. "I'm not sure that was English, but it was nicer."

She couldn't decide whether to smack him or kiss him, but he took the decision away from her by reaching for the condoms he kept in his nightstand. Kissing him it was. "Are you done torturing me?"

"Not as long as you like it."

She couldn't retort because he sank into her, and her words vanished.

If you actually care about him, then break it off. Do it before your deranged family truly hurts him, Kelsey's voice growled in her head.

Shit. While Josh was on top of her, the only thing she wanted to think about less than Kelsey was her own family's attempt to break them apart. But what if she was being selfish? What if she did cause Josh to get hurt? What right did she have to put him in danger when she'd be leaving eventually anyway?

But what if she didn't leave? Would Josh even want that?

She did. Denying it was pointless. She wanted to stay here and be with him.

Taylor wrapped her legs around him, forcing him even deeper inside, and Josh gripped her tighter in return as he kissed her throat, her chin, her mouth. She devoured him, and he devoured her. If they pulled each other close enough, no troubles could split them apart.

"Tell me you're mine." His breath was hot, tickling her ear.

Taylor couldn't look at him, afraid all the thoughts that had been rushing through her head would be too obvious. So she pressed her face first against the crook of his neck, against the warm patch of skin there that smelled of musk and lemongrass, then reached up and flicked her tongue over the softness of his earlobe. He shuddered, so she did it again, then took it in her mouth and sucked. The moan he let out was surprising, as was how much she liked tasting him while he was buried inside her. It shouldn't have been though. She already knew she couldn't get enough.

"Taylor."

Belatedly, she remembered he'd said something a moment ago, but she couldn't remember what. Sensation had overruled thought. Her body had control, and the rest was along for the ride.

"Yes." Whatever he'd said, that was the answer. Yes, kiss her harder. Yes, hold her tighter. Yes, thrust deeper.

Josh rested his forehead on hers. "Say it. I need to hear it. I need to know you're willing to fight with me."

Yes to that too. "I'm with you. I'm not going anywhere."

"No, you're not." He kissed her, fiercely, protectively, stealing her breath. Her emotions overloaded, and Taylor cried out, overtaken by another orgasm.

Josh followed in an instant, and he didn't let go once they stopped shuddering. He just held her closer. It should have left her content, feeling wrapped in a cocoon of warmth and peace. But with the burst of pleasure receding, she couldn't shake the feeling that he was determined to assuage any doubts or worries in either of their heads, and so his arms had the opposite effect. She feared he was holding as tightly to her as she was to him because they were both too aware of the forces trying to pull them apart.

It was time they addressed those fears, and perhaps her fearsome thoughts about leaving.

Taylor shifted and traced a gentle finger over his bruises. "I'm so sorry."

"You have nothing to be sorry about."

"But I do. I know what my family did."

* * *

JOSH CLOSED HIS eyes, wanting to nuzzle Taylor closer and make this entire conversation go away, but that wouldn't be a good idea. So he sat up, trying to sort through familiar refrains and the hodgepodge of emotions clouding his mind. Anger simmered in his veins, not because someone had broken into his house, but because that someone was making Taylor feel bad about actions beyond her control. Guilt also gnawed at him. She hadn't accused him of it, but he'd been hiding stuff from her and she obviously knew it.

"I'm the one who should be sorry," he said at last. He owed her an apology even if he'd do it again.

Fury of her own flashed over Taylor's face and she punched his bed, no doubt in lieu of a person. Who, exactly, he wasn't certain, but there were plenty to choose from.

Her movements weren't intended to be seductive, but the glimpses of her skin, the sinuous way the sheet slipped off her back—it had that effect on him anyway. Never mind his emotional turmoil.

Josh turned away so he couldn't focus on her breasts or the graceful curve of her spine, and a warm hand brushed his side. Her touch wasn't helping him focus.

"I understand why you didn't want to tell me," Taylor said. "I'm not mad about that."

He sighed, forcing himself to look at her. "I didn't want you to be . . ."

"Afraid?" Taylor sat up, too, and pressed herself against him. Her head rested against his shoulder, and her breath caressed his skin.

"Maybe we should get dressed before we continue this conversation." But he made no move to do so, and

Taylor's response was to wrap her arms around his waist from behind. He could feel every glorious inch of her, and his cock wasn't getting the message that they had real issues to discuss. That this was about more than just sex, no matter what his cousin thought.

"I am afraid, Josh. For you. I knew what our families were capable of, and yet I still became delusional with hope. God, I no longer know what I was thinking, believing we could make people see reason."

This was exactly what he'd been afraid of. "Hey, remember, we were found out by accident. Never blame yourself for wanting to believe the best of people."

Of course, they'd been found out by accident in part because he'd delayed telling the truth to his family. While he was annoyed at himself for that, he couldn't be too annoyed under the circumstances. He had room in his heart for only so much self-reproach and anger, and he felt worse about hiding things from Taylor than he did about dragging his feet.

Taylor tensed in obvious frustration. "That's not the point. Your cousin's right. My family's deranged, and I can't—"

"My cousin? Did Kelsey tell you what happened?" He'd been under the assumption that Taylor's family had clued her in, hoping to make her do and say exactly what she was saying now.

If Kelsey was the one to blab though, damn it, he might kill her.

Taylor confirmed it by nodding against his back. "I knew something was off, but I hadn't figured out what or whether I was just upset about everything I did know about. I ran into Kelsey today and she told me."

Kelsey might have the best of intentions—or not—but either way Josh couldn't let her actions stand. He twisted around to face Taylor in his agitation. "That's why you didn't want me swinging by the inn to pick you up. In case someone alerted your family."

Taylor dropped her gaze to his bed sheepishly, and he lifted her chin.

"I can deal with your family, Taylor. I'm not afraid of them, and I'm not losing you because they make you afraid. You understand?"

"I don't want to lose you, either, but I couldn't deal if they hurt you." She swallowed. "Believe me, I suspect I know who was behind this, and we are going to have words. Very unpleasant words. The sort of words that might result in them not wanting me in town anymore. And that's its own set of problems."

Josh took her hands and squeezed them. "You don't have to leave early because your family is angry at you."

"That's the thing—I'm not sure I want to leave at all anymore. I've been fighting it, telling myself I am leaving no matter what, but I'm no longer sure why." She gazed at him questioningly, as though she wasn't sure how he'd take such an announcement.

Josh's breath caught, and he realized he'd started squeezing her hands a little too hard in his excitement. He had to be rational. She wasn't referring to not leaving him, but to the town. But whereas he'd once assumed her leaving would make things simpler, the idea of her staying was the best news he'd heard in a long time.

He would just have to make sure that if she stayed in town, she stayed with him too. Anything else had become unthinkable. She was his, damn it. She'd said so.

Taylor was waiting for him to respond, and Josh pulled her close. "Then stay if you want. Don't let your feelings about your family or mine dictate what you do." Or his own feelings, although he was half a breath from promising her that if her sister kicked her out for fighting with the family, Taylor was welcome to stay at his place.

But perhaps that was putting too much pressure on her.

"Do it for my dogs," he said as he kissed her. "You'll make them happy."

Taylor laughed, and Josh hoped that meant he'd hit the fine line between begging her to stay and trying not to influence her.

"The dogs are very persuasive. I need to think this through."

"Understood. Let's go make dinner, and I can let the dogs work their magic on you."

22

❦⸻⸻❦

TAYLOR WAS BLEARY-EYED with exhaustion as she wandered into the inn's kitchen. She'd stayed up far too late with Josh last night, snuggling with him and the dogs on the sofa while they watched TV and fed each other bites of the chocolate peanut butter pie he'd bought her. She'd forgotten mentioning how much she'd loved it as a kid, but Josh had remembered. He'd braved the crowds on his way home from work yesterday to procure one for her at the bakery in town.

He kept doing these little things—buying the pie, stopping by the inn with her favorite coffee on the way to work, sending the plushie when she'd returned to L.A. It was amazing how such tiny actions could make her feel so good. It was also amazing that she'd never noticed how other men hadn't done them. No fancy restaurant dates came close to the way a hand-delivered double espresso tasted. And yet Josh still demurred when she tried to cook for him—the one thing she could do well in return—as though his thoughtfulness wasn't a big deal.

Possibly to him it wasn't. It was just how a decent person behaved. But that was all the more reason to hold on to him and accept that falling for him had been inevitable.

"I take it you and Josh worked out your issues?" Lydia glanced up from her laptop as Taylor took a seat across the table with the breakfast quiche Marie had made her. Her insistence that she could make her own breakfast had been lost on the cook.

"Why do you say that?"

"Because of that goofy smile on your face. I'm happy for you, even though it's him."

Taylor attempted to make her face less goofy as she ate.

Focusing on the heavy decision ahead of her helped. Josh's reaction to her desire to stay in Helen had been a relief on one hand, but it didn't help her make up her mind. He was happy about the possibility, of that much she was certain, but he wasn't going to pressure her in one direction or another. He seemed to understand just how much factored into it. Yes, he was a part, possibly a bigger part than Taylor wanted to admit to either of them, but she had a lot of parts to consider. How the conversation with her family would go was a big one.

"Tay, can you do me a favor and check on the bikes when you're done?" Her sister shut her laptop. "They should be fine, but it's been a few days since anyone last borrowed them, and I want to make sure the tires don't need more air before they're used today."

"Yeah, sure." That was the sort of task that should fall under her purview anyway, although it was likely the sort of responsibility she should delegate. For the moment, though, Taylor preferred being hands-on. She'd fallen naturally into the routine of the job and was enjoying making it her own, and there was something to be said for gaining firsthand knowledge of all the daily and weekly tasks. The inn was large enough to have a dedicated full-time staff plus weekend help, but also small enough that occasionally covering multiple roles was necessary if someone called in sick.

Taylor finished her breakfast and took the remains of her coffee outside with her as she headed to the shed. The inn maintained ten bikes that were available for guests to sign out on a first-come, first-served basis. Due to the crappy weather over the last few days, she wasn't surprised they'd languished unused.

The day was overcast, but that wasn't so odd. Temperatures were supposed to rise into the upper seventies, though, and that was. She quietly chuckled to herself, preparing for the onslaught of complaints about what constituted an atrocious heat wave around here.

Those chuckles subsided in a flash as Taylor approached the large wooden building. The door looked to be hanging slightly open. Muttering a curse, she set her coffee down on a nearby stone ledge and hurried over, trying to recall who was supposed to have locked up last.

As it turned out, it didn't matter. The padlock hadn't been opened properly; someone had cut it. It hung by a sliver of metal from the door, useless and broken. Braced for the worst, Taylor opened the door wide, letting sunlight flood the space. Had they been robbed? She searched, but nothing appeared missing. Not the bikes, not the leaf blower or the snow thrower, and not the garden tools or the shovels. Everything was exactly where it was supposed to be.

Confused, Taylor pulled one of the bikes forward, figuring she'd check them before alerting Lydia to what happened, and that's when she discovered what was missing—the air in the tires. They'd been slashed. Not just the tires on the bike she'd grabbed, but the tires on every single bike.

"Shit." Theft could have meant anyone was behind it. This was a special type of crime, one that pointed to only a single, logical culprit.

Taylor's grip on the bike handles turned white. How were she and Josh supposed to deescalate a situation that everyone else was determined to blow up? At what point did Lydia raise her hands into the air and declare she was done trying to help? It wasn't like Taylor could blame her if she did. Replanting all the flower beds in time for last week's wedding hadn't been cheap. Replacing ten bikes' worth of tires wouldn't be, either, and they had to explain to the guests that the bikes that had been promised were unavailable. That was a hit to the inn's reputation just as much as it was a hit to their profit margins, and all of that screwed over her sister, who counted on the income.

And that infuriated Taylor. As much as she wanted to deescalate, she also wanted to lash out. Strike back. Josh's family was screwing with her family, and while he didn't deserve the fallout, the rest of them did. He was the only reason she could contain her rage.

Taking a deep breath, Taylor stuck the useless bike back into the shed. Property damage was nothing compared to direct threats, but how much worse were things going to get? Josh didn't think his cousin was going to tell the rest of his family about the break-in, but if he was wrong, Taylor had no delusions that the Porters would stick to petty vandalism.

She retrieved her coffee mug and went in search of Lydia.

* * *

HER SISTER HAD blackmailed her. Taylor couldn't believe it.

Without prompting, Lydia had promised yesterday to not say a word about the bikes to their father. In return, Taylor simply had to lie about Lydia's whereabouts and why she couldn't attend Sunday night dinner with her father and grandmother.

Taylor didn't blame Lydia for wanting to skip the family meal, and if she hadn't needed to speak her mind to the two others present, she wouldn't have gone either. But as she'd told Josh, there were words to be said, and it was simplest to say them simultaneously to both people who most likely deserved them.

"Lydia is sorry she couldn't make it," Taylor said. "She had a date."

As expected, her grandmother seemed pleased as she shooed the cats out of her kitchen. "With anyone we know?"

"Some guy she met through an app." Actually, Lydia had left for Anchorage earlier in the day with friends to go to the movies and do some shopping. That wouldn't have been an acceptable reason to miss a family dinner though. A date was the lie she'd settled on since it served the dual purposes of being an acceptable excuse and would get her grandmother off her case for a while.

"An app." Her grandmother's nose twitched.

That reaction was exactly as Taylor had expected. Her grandmother disapproved because she couldn't vet the alleged guy this way, but she didn't have enough knowledge of dating apps to bother Taylor with questions.

She removed one plate from the stack of four sitting on the counter and slid the rest toward Taylor. "Set these out?"

Taylor gladly obliged because it got her out of the kitchen. Holding her tongue until her father arrived was so painful it felt like she was literally clamping it between her teeth.

"I was hoping your sister would be here, because I thought she might be able to get through to you while the rest of us can't," her grandmother continued. "Once your father arrives, we need to have another conversation."

Yes, they did, but it was not going to go the way her grandmother anticipated.

While her grandmother finished putting together the salad, Taylor turned her attention to the photographs and knickknacks decorating the living room—a dried rose pressed between glass, a photograph of her and Lydia taken when Taylor was about four and they were dressed in identical ugly Christmas dresses. There was another photo of her grandparents on their wedding day, looking surreally young, and one of the whole family that had been taken not long before her grandfather's Parkinson's disease had rendered him mostly immobile.

He'd been the warm to her grandmother's cool. Quick with a joke while she'd always been quick with criticism. But her grandmother had been softer around him, too, or so Taylor recalled. She'd played with her and Lydia and taken them on special "girls' days" to Anchorage to go shopping. Those times had been fun but stressful all the same.

Since her father was one of four boys, if Taylor wanted to be charitable, she might believe that her grandmother put so much pressure on her and Lydia because they were the daughters she'd never had. But that was no excuse for her current actions, and besides—memories were fuzzy and prone to self-manipulation. It was nice to think her gruff but kindly grandfather wouldn't tolerate

Josh being threatened, but Taylor suspected she was lying to herself.

She really needed to disabuse herself of all this wishful thinking about her relatives. Her grandmother could call the Porters mercenaries and thieves, and probably pirates while she was at it, but she'd proved her own family was no better.

Speaking of her kin, the front door opened and her father arrived carrying a large takeout bag from which the aroma of fish and crabs carried through the house.

"I wasn't sure what everyone wanted, so I brought a variety." He set the bag on the dining room table. "Where's Lydia?"

"A date," Taylor said, taking the salad bowl from her grandmother. She wondered if she'd be able to snag a haddock burger when she left. Hanging around to eat after she'd screamed at the people with her didn't seem probable.

Her father grunted and scowled at the bowl of leafy greens. He was not as concerned about the state of Lydia's ovaries as his mother, but he was clearly suspicious of vegetables with his burgers.

Hungry, Taylor popped a fry into her mouth while her grandmother grilled her father and they finished setting the table.

"How did negotiations go?" her grandmother asked.

"Everything's fine. Denise is divesting from the inn as we'd discussed. There's only one sticking point we have to work out still." He plucked at a piece of lettuce with great dissatisfaction, as though it were the cause of his marital woes.

Despite her determination not to get sucked into the conversation and pretend all was well among the three of them, Taylor licked grease from her fingers, feeling uneasy. She was still bothered by the way her mother had run off, but her father's behavior leading up to that decision didn't sit well with her either. How much of her anger at her father was due to her dilemma with Josh, Taylor wasn't sure. It would have been nice, though, if her father had admitted his culpability in the divorce.

"What's sticking?" she asked.

Her father cast his gaze down at his plate, seemingly reluctant to bring it up in front of her. "The cats," he said at last. "We can't agree on custody. Your mother thinks she should take them both because she's the one who adopted them originally, but she's living in a tiny place. Cats need space to move about. They're as much mine as they are hers now, and it makes more sense to keep them here."

"The cats." Taylor picked a burger from the bag and considered tossing it at him. She'd throw one at her mother, too, if she were here. They could settle their finances, the house, the family business, but they couldn't settle the damn cats. All the stress she and Lydia had dealt with, and this is what it came down to.

"Your mother's being ridiculous." He stuffed a fry in his mouth.

"Just her? You had no part in this?"

"Taylor!" Her grandmother's sharp tone reminded her that she wasn't alone with her father.

He held up a hand. "No, she has a point, and so did Denise. I'm not denying I made mistakes, Taylor. I didn't pay enough attention to realize your mother was unhappy. But what's done is done."

How convenient he got that as an excuse. Taylor doubted she'd get away with it if she tried the same tactic about her situation with Josh.

Which reminded her, she'd come here to speak her

mind, not eat. It was time to speak and deal with the consequences. "You care more about the welfare of your cats than you do about people."

Her father and grandmother exchanged glances, and she could see them practically sharing some prearranged signal to attack. Well, she was not standing around and listening to whatever bullshit they intended to deliver.

"If you make another move against Josh, I swear I will prove to you what being labeled the family trouble-maker really means."

Her grandmother didn't so much as startle as she opened her burger wrapper. "I didn't do anything to that man."

For goodness' sake. That was the route she was taking? "Don't play word games with me. I'm not in the mood. You may not have personally broken into his house, but you're the one who arranged for it. Do you know what that makes you legally?"

Her grandmother finally paused. She set the burger down and nudged the salad bowl in Taylor's direction, but Taylor refused to sit. "Legalities don't interest me. What I did makes me a grandmother who cares about her grandchildren. I might not knit you sweaters or bake you cookies, but I will look out for your interests whether you like it or not. And, to be clear, it was your father who arranged for Ralph to take care of it."

They must be referring to the head of maintenance at the inn. Wonderful. She hadn't realized her family's business was cultivating burglars along with a five-star reputation.

She also hadn't realized her father had played such a direct role, although she wasn't surprised. Once Taylor knew her family had arranged for a break-in, her suspicions had jumped to her grandmother, her father, or her uncle Marcus, her least favorite of her father's brothers. But for some reason, she'd always assumed her grandmother was the true mastermind, probably because her grandmother had always been so aloof and demanding while her father had taken more after her grandfather. The man cooed over his cats for crying out loud. How did someone who did that also stoop to acting like a member of the Lipin mafia?

For that matter, how could she be related to these people? They made her sick. The only knowledge that might sting more would be discovering her uncle Dex had been involved.

"You're a bunch of criminals!" She slammed her hands down on the table so hard the glasses rattled.

That got her father's attention, and he set down his burger, the jovial lines on his face turning hard. "Something had to be done. I knew we could trust Ralph not to do anything other than send a message, but a message had to be conveyed."

"I can't believe you. No, wait." Taylor raised her hands. "I can believe you, and that's worse."

She had to get her head on straight. Her father's cooing over his cats aside, she'd always known there had to be two versions of the man. There was the warm one who ruffled her hair like she was still a kid when she visited and sent her cheesy "dad joke" text messages when she was in L.A. That was the one who had enough emotional range to rue the mistakes he'd made in his marriage, but not enough to have prevented them. And then there was the other one, who used his political power to throw legal obstacles at the Porters for sport, the one who—allegedly—had broken Chuck Porter's throwing arm on purpose back in high school during a football game, thus ruining his chance to play in college.

Try as she might, it hurt Taylor's brain to reconcile these men. The closest she could come was the time her father had grabbed his shotgun and chased a rabid bear away from the library on his own. He'd considered it his responsibility as mayor but hadn't felt like waiting for backup to arrive. That man was equal parts ballsy and caring.

Also incredibly reckless.

"I can't believe you would disappoint this family so," her grandmother said, snapping her back to the present. "I take it the message wasn't received then?"

Taylor's hands closed into fists, and she focused on the pain of her nails digging into her palms. "Oh, we heard you loud and clear. Now hear me. I'm not going to bail on Lydia since she had nothing to do with it, but if anything else happens to Josh, I'm gone. Threats, vandalism, online harassment—I will cut all of you out of my life for good. Forever. Is that clear?"

Her father made a muffled noise, the sort he used to make when she got in trouble as a kid. He'd been too indulgent to want to punish her or Lydia then, leaving the discipline mostly to their mother, and it looked like he still struggled with taking a firmer role when it came to her. That was a relief, especially because her grandmother had no such qualms. She stared Taylor down with thin, disapproving lips. The scent of warm fish, so appealing a few minutes ago, turned Taylor's stomach, but she ignored it. She would win this staring contest, so help her. Words and empty threats were the only weapons she had to fight, and she could only pray her family never decided to call her on them.

A full minute seemed to drag on, and the air hummed with tension like an unseen swarm of bumblebees lurked in the curtains. Then her grandmother shrugged and, nonchalantly, piled salad onto her plate. "You'll leave your Porter behind, will you? Is that a threat or an offer?"

"When I said I was gone, I meant as far as you were concerned, not this town or my sister. Go ahead, test me if you want. I've been doing fine on my own for years." Spinning on her heel, Taylor left the room.

"You might not appreciate it yet," her grandmother called after her, "but you will grow up one day. You'll see we're trying to help you. Those people will hurt you in the end, Taylor. They're no good."

Taylor shook her head and kept walking. The woman was unbelievable.

"Taylor." Her father caught up to her at the door and placed a hand on her arm. His face was still hard, but his voice was warm. "I know you're angry, but everything we work for, right down to the reason I stepped up and ran for mayor, was to make a better life in this town for your generation and our future ones. You think I'm being unfair or cruel, but the Porters have left us no choice. I just want the best for you, and I will do what's necessary to get it."

The most horrible part of all this was she believed he meant it. So did her grandmother. Of course, when her father said *generations*, he was referring to Lipins only, and you couldn't make life better for Lipins without crushing some Porters.

Channeling the rage in her veins to keep the pain away, Taylor removed his hand. "If you mean that, then let me figure out what's best for me, and don't hurt the people I care about."

Then, before she screamed with frustration, she stepped outside and shut the door.

23

TAYLOR WAS NOT going to be happy with him, but Josh parked his Jeep in front of the Bay Song anyway. He was concerned about her and dying to know what had happened at her dinner last night. The plan had been for her to come see him afterward, but a medical emergency with one of his patients who had a sudden and severe drug reaction had forestalled it. Josh had ended up in the ER until after midnight, coordinating care with an oncologist in Anchorage until it was determined that his patient should be transferred up there as a precaution.

Taylor wasn't half as clingy as his dogs, so when he'd tell her things like "medical emergency," she didn't bug him. He appreciated the hands-off approach when he had to concentrate, but he would also have appreciated a few texts explaining what had gone down even if he couldn't read them for a while. But since that wasn't her style, he'd never gotten an update, and by the time he'd finally climbed into bed, it was too late to call her.

"Be right back." Yawning, Josh ruffled Jay's head and popped inside the inn to look for her.

Perhaps if he'd had more than five hours of sleep, he would have reconsidered this plan or his patience would be more abundant, but he had not and it was not. And perhaps if his brain hadn't been so tired and consumed with concern, he'd have realized that Taylor wasn't the only Lipin up at such an early hour of the morning.

A desk clerk, who looked far more alert than Josh felt, pointed him to the far side of the lobby when he asked after Taylor, indicating he needed to head past the guests who were loitering around a breakfast setup. Josh thanked the guy and wondered why there was breakfast in the lobby when he'd have sworn Taylor said they had a dining room. Shrugging it off, he followed the clerk's directions.

Although he'd never been through the main entrance before, Josh was too tired to notice much other than the inn giving off a warm, rustic vibe, which was at odds with the draft of cold air coming from somewhere. More alarming than the chill, however, was the terrible yet familiar stench.

He turned the corner into an informal dining area—he knew it—and came face-to-face not with Taylor, but with her sister. As he'd once told Kelsey, he and Lydia had never met, but it had occurred to Josh since the break-in that recognizing the faces of various Lipins might be handy, so he'd started searching for photos online. At the moment, from the expression on her face, Lydia looked like she'd just stepped in dog shit, and she might have, because that was definitely what was reeking in the room, despite the windows having been thrown wide open.

"Breakfast is in the lobby today," Lydia said, barely glancing at him.

Apparently her foul expression wasn't personal if she didn't realize who he was. Something awkward—perhaps it was his common sense kicking in—poked at Josh's brain. "Actually I was looking for Taylor."

Lydia straightened and turned back around. Suspicion replaced her irritable expression as she dropped her gaze to the Helen Regional Hospital insignia on his jacket. "Are you Josh?"

"I am."

"Ah." With a heavy exhale, she placed her hands on her hips and shouted into the next room. "Tay!"

Lydia went back to doing whatever she'd been doing before he arrived, which appeared to be flipping over all the chairs. There were quite a few of them. If Josh had to guess, the room would hold about thirty people at the various tables. There was a sideboard on the far wall, currently not in use, and two hefty wingback chairs on either side, both also overturned. The stench of dog excrement appeared to be coming from that direction.

"Is everything okay?" he asked. It was a supremely stupid question, but he was too tired to come up with a better one, and his sense of not belonging was growing stronger by watching Lydia work.

"Someone in your family thought it would be a great idea to smear dog shit over our furniture, so not exactly. No."

Josh swore and ran his hands through his hair. He should have guessed. "I'm sorry."

"No doubt, but these incidents are increasing in frequency."

Taylor popped into the dining room at that moment, sparing him from the need to find appropriate words. "If it's only those two chairs, we can take them outside for now and use the upholstery cleaner on them, and . . ." She spotted him and blinked comically.

Josh waved.

"It is just those two," Lydia said, setting another wooden chair upright. "Whoever did this might not have had enough dog crap for all of them, so they only targeted the ones that are hardest to clean."

It was nice to know whoever in his family was behind this stunt wasn't a complete idiot, but Josh opted to keep that thought to himself. "Can I help you carry the chairs?"

They were big and looked like they might be challenging to move, and he felt the need to do something since he was indirectly responsible.

Lydia started to decline the offer, but Taylor cut her off. "Thanks."

"We have it under control," her sister said.

"We do, but you need to leave in forty-five minutes to meet with Ian and finish hacking out the promo plan. You need to wash up again and change your clothes, and you said you had numbers you wanted to review before the meeting. You should go, and I can't maneuver these chairs on my own."

Lydia pushed her hair out of her face and glanced between him and Taylor. "Fine. Thanks." She kind of grumbled the word in his direction, and Josh nodded.

He kissed Taylor's cheek after her sister left, enjoying for the moment the simple familiarity between them and the way it made Taylor smile. "I brought you your coffee."

"I thought I smelled cinnamon. Thank you." She kissed his lips sweetly, but it was still enough to stir a reaction from his overtired brain, despite the stench. "Are you on your way to work or home from work at last?"

"To, unfortunately. I got home about six hours ago."

They both went silent for a moment as they hauled the foul-smelling furniture onto the inn's patio. Given how tired he was, Josh was thankful he didn't walk into a wall in the process.

"I wanted to stop by," he continued as they headed inside, "to see how it went with your family."

"No clue. I said my piece, but what my father or grandmother will do . . . ?" Taylor shrugged. She gave him a brief rundown of the events but didn't sound hopeful.

Josh wanted to reassure her that he wasn't worried for himself, but it was an odd thing to do while standing in the middle of evidence of his family's ill intentions. "Lydia said something about the vandalism incidents increasing in frequency. Did something else happen besides this and the garden?"

"Oh, jeez. Yeah." Taylor pulled out the band around her ponytail and redid her hair. It was chilly in the room because of airing it out, but she and her sister had clearly been working hard before he arrived, and her face was shiny. Josh enjoyed seeing her like that, but he doubted she'd feel the same. "Someone broke into our shed and slashed all the guest bikes' tires."

Josh groaned. "First your gardens, then breaking into the shed, and now sneaking into the inn. I don't like this. Whoever it is, they're getting more brazen."

Knowing his family like he was starting to, anything could be next. Unlike Taylor and her situation, he doubted threats would work on them. He couldn't even narrow down who was likely to be behind it. His uncle had been the first to confront him, but he hadn't been the last. He would need to try a different tactic to deal with this—one that played to his strengths.

He wasn't a rebel like Taylor and he hated confrontation. But as Kelsey had pointed out, he was a healer and he knew how to make people feel good. Possibly he could use that.

Taylor leaned against him. "If they're trying to make me leave you, it's not working. But if they're trying to piss me off, mission accomplished. This kind of garbage was so much easier to deal with when I was California. It was so distant then. I could roll my eyes and forget about it. Now I want to kick the ass of whoever is behind it."

"That makes two of us."

She smiled up at him, but it wasn't one of her sunny smiles. "There's this bitter, ugly anger that I've been carrying around for over a week. I guess that's how my family feels all the time. It's not healthy. I don't want to become like the rest of them."

He squeezed her tighter, knowing exactly where she was coming from. He hadn't put it in quite those words, but the tension he'd been carrying around—it was a lot like that. And yet there was a rather large difference. Taylor had the inn she could take pride in and a sister who supported her. She had reasons to be loyal even if she was furious with her own family. He didn't have that, so his anger was more diffuse.

"You won't become like the rest of them." He kissed the top of her head. "The rest of them would not be here with me. But you're loyal to your sister and to your family's work, and that's not a bad thing. Loyalty is good. It makes you a dog person at heart."

She laughed into his chest and poked him in the stomach. "That explains a lot. You really need to go?" She raised an eyebrow suggestively and tugged on his waistband. "If I recall, we have some unfinished business in my office."

He hadn't remembered until this moment, and his cock stirred, pleased to be reminded. It wasn't fair, her playing dirty like that when he should have gone five minutes ago. With great regret, Josh removed her hand and twined his fingers with hers. "Unfortunately, I'm going to have to put that off a while longer. I'll talk to you later. I might have an idea about dealing with my family." *Idea* might be too ambitious a word, but it was as close as he could get.

Taylor's sultry pout turned to an expression of interest. "I'm intrigued."

"I'll let you know once I feel out whether it could work."

"Do that." Taylor shook her head at the state of the disarray. "I should go find Lydia and run over the plan for Ian. You remember him from the brewery, right?"

"I do." The last time he'd seen him was when Kelsey was writing him off as rude at the concert. "What kind of plan?"

"The kind that involves negotiating a deal for the inn to promote his brewery by offering special pricing for guests and possibly other perks. Since winter's such a dead season, I'm trying to help Lydia find ways to increase business year-round."

"You're very clever."

"You're very charming."

Josh grinned. "And it has nothing to do with the dogs, right? I knew you'd eventually wise up to it."

He left Taylor to get back to work and so he could get to the office before his first patient. After that, he'd see if he could be clever too.

24

JAY, PEPPER, AND Bella led the way as Josh crossed the street into the park where Kelsey was waiting, and unexpected relief surged through him. He hadn't realized how worried he was that his cousin might not meet him. Their relationship was already strained because of Taylor, and yelling at Kelsey for telling Taylor about the break-in hadn't improved it.

The way their dogs greeted each other was a lot friendlier than the way she eyed him. "You haven't broken up with her yet, have you?"

He seriously hoped this line of inquiry was not the sole reason she was here. "No."

She whined in a very doglike way. "Didn't think so. You don't look miserable enough." Kelsey jerked on her dogs' leashes, trying to detangle them from his dogs'. "Come on. Let's move."

Slowly, they freed their own and began their usual circuit around the grass. Six of the eight of them bounded forward in good moods. The two-legged members of the pack were weighed down by their thoughts. At least Josh was, and Kelsey seemed pensive too.

"So if you didn't break up with Taylor," his cousin asked, "what was it you wanted to discuss?"

"Two things. First, do you know anything about whoever's been vandalizing the Bay Song?" He didn't think Kelsey would lie to him. It wasn't her style. Hell, if anything, she'd proudly admit it. But Josh watched her carefully for clues anyway. Trust in his family was at an all-time low. Actually, his trust in anything that only had two legs was, except for Taylor.

"I don't," Kelsey said, and Josh believed her, which was perversely disappointing. He'd been hoping to confront the culprit much like Taylor had confronted her family. "I heard about the garden. Has something else happened?"

"A couple other things."

"Like what?"

"I'm not telling you so you can salivate over the details."

"Oh, please. If it was anything worth cackling over, I'm sure I'd have heard. That tells me whoever it is lacks a spine or imagination. Or both." She made a noise of disgust.

Josh felt a half smile tug on his lips in spite of himself. "I guess that means it really wasn't you."

"Damn straight. I wouldn't mess around pulling out some flowers. If I was going to send a warning to your girlfriend, I'd do something with more flair. More menace. Like what the Lipins did to you, or maybe kill one of their cats."

"You would never kill a cat." There weren't many things he'd put past his cousin, but violence against animals, even cats, was one of them.

Kelsey glared at him. "Fine. You know me too well. But you don't need to go spreading that around. I have a hard-won reputation in this town."

His half smile cracked into a real one. "The fact that you're secretly a marshmallow is safe with me."

"Says the gushy one."

"Takes one to know one." He laughed at her sour expression, glad that regardless of any damage to their friendship, he could still get away with teasing her. Maybe Kelsey had always been more marshmallow than he'd believed.

He hoped she was. His idea depended on it.

"Honestly," Kelsey said as they approached the water, "the Lipins should be grateful that a little vandalism is all that's done after they directly threatened you."

"No one's supposed to know what they did to me."

"And they don't." She ground her teeth, clearly still pissed off at him for extracting a promise of secrecy from her. "But you really think they aren't going to do something else since their first plan failed?"

"Taylor made her feelings on the matter clear to them."

Kelsey snorted. "For your sake, I wish her luck, but I don't have that kind of faith in anyone's innate humanity, especially not the Lipins'. What was the second thing you wanted to talk about?"

The second thing. His idea. Josh took a deep breath of air that was laden with the salty scent of the bay. "You know how your dad's had a change of heart lately about Kevin's engagement?"

"Yeah." Kelsey's voice was filled with suspicion. They both knew the reason why his uncle was suddenly much more on board with the wedding.

"Well, I figure Kevin owes me one for taking all the

family heat off him, and by extension, so do you." Sure, he hadn't intended to make his uncle realize he was flipping out over the wrong things, and his uncle was still an ass for flipping out in the first place, but Josh wasn't sorry about making Kevin's and Peter's lives easier.

Kelsey hurried in front of him and barred his ability to walk farther down the dirt path. "What are you getting at exactly?"

"Dinner. You, me, Kevin and Peter, and Taylor."

To his surprise, Kelsey tossed her head back and laughed. "What—you want me to break bread with a Lipin?"

"Nothing so medieval. I want you to meet her. That's all."

"You're serious." When he didn't deign to respond immediately, she swore. "Does Taylor want this?"

It was a good question, since he hadn't asked her, but Josh figured she'd go along with his plan if his cousins did. He'd wanted to secure Kelsey's agreement before bringing it up.

"Taylor's a rational person who agrees that the feud is ridiculous." He hoped that was still true anyway. Taylor's confession that she was being drawn into the drama weighed on him. He didn't blame her for it one bit, but that made it all the more necessary that he run an intervention, and this was the only plan he could think of that played to his strengths.

Taylor talked about the feud in terms of war, but Josh was starting to think of it in terms of a sickness. The feud was a plague that infected both their families. The ones who'd been living with it for so long might be beyond help, but those like Kelsey and Kevin—and himself and Taylor—were not. Like the immune system, if he could teach Kelsey and Kevin to recognize the feud for what it was, they would be able to influence others to do the same until the disease was wiped out or died out.

"Fine," Kelsey said.

Josh resisted the urge to sink to the ground in his relief. "You'll do it?"

"Yes, but . . ." She smiled wickedly. "I'm bringing my dogs."

"Okay." He'd counted on it.

YOU REALLY THINK this is going to help?" Taylor popped the caps off two beers and set one down on the table by Josh's grill.

Josh didn't have to see her face to know she looked as skeptical as she sounded. She'd easily agreed to his plan, but that hadn't stopped her from expressing her doubts, and she'd expressed them plenty in the last twenty-four hours. Josh had his own, but he was plowing ahead anyway.

Satisfied that the hardwood charcoal would soon be hot enough to dump from the chimney into the grill, Josh picked up the beer she'd brought out from the kitchen. His cousins and Peter should be arriving any minute.

"I think it might help," Josh said for the third or fourth, possibly fifth, time. Most of his pep talks had been to himself, not Taylor, but that didn't stop the words from being old and worn. "Just remember what I told you about Kelsey's dogs."

Those dogs—skittish Romeo in particular—were key to his plan. Kelsey judged the character of people by how much they liked her babies. Josh had known that before, but seeing the way Kelsey reacted to Ian keeping his distance a few weeks ago drove the knowledge home. In truth, Josh strongly suspected Kelsey's willingness to meet with Taylor tonight was because Taylor had cooed over her dogs that one evening in the park.

As for the dogs, Juliet and Puck were typical of most huskies—they loved people in general. But Romeo was even more wary of strangers than Jay had ever been. If Taylor could earn Romeo's trust, it would go a long way to influencing Kelsey.

Luckily, Josh knew how to do that, and he'd filled in Taylor as soon as the plans were set.

Josh couldn't help but feel like he was cheating by warning Taylor about how to act around Romeo, but it was cheating for a good cause. And besides, Taylor was bound to love Kelsey's dogs. He was just easing the introduction. That was all.

He took a swig of beer, determined not to think too deeply about dog ethics when he stood upon the precipice of achieving something more elusive than world peace. Hell, if he could pull this evening off without bloodshed, he'd deserve a Nobel Prize.

"I remember." Taylor sipped her beer. "But it's not the dogs that worry me."

Josh considered telling Taylor that Kelsey's bark was worse than her bite, but that would be breaking his promise to his cousin, and he only had it in him to be so underhanded.

It was Josh's own dogs that alerted him and Taylor to his family's arrival. Three sets of ears perked up at once, and their excited barking was answered by more excited barking. A couple of seconds later, Kelsey, Kevin, and Peter came through the gate into Josh's backyard, led by Kelsey's huskies.

Josh squeezed Taylor's hand, and together they crossed

his deck. Taylor wore her perkiest smile, but her grip on his fingers gave away her true feelings.

While she and his cousins eyed each other, Peter seized the opening and held out his hand. "You must be Taylor. Nice to meet you. Funny—I was led to expect you might have horns and some scales. Possibly a forked tongue."

Kevin jabbed him in the ribs. "You think you're funny."

"I know I'm hilarious."

Taylor's fake smile relaxed into something that looked more real. "I only break out the forked tongue when Josh is on his best behavior."

Josh rolled his eyes, glad those two seemed like they could get along. "I didn't think we'd get that personal so quickly. Beer?" Both Kevin and Peter accepted, and Josh raised a hand in Kelsey's direction before she could object. "I got something sweet and pink-colored for you."

His cousin wrinkled her nose. "I suppose that's okay then."

Josh worried about leaving Taylor alone with his cousins, but only for a moment. She'd already dropped into a crouch and was lavishing attention on Juliet and Puck. Romeo held back between Kelsey's legs, and Taylor held out a hand toward him.

"He's shy," Kelsey said. Though not much, it was a surprisingly helpful comment from his cousin. Josh assumed it was for the husky's sake.

Gingerly, Romeo crept forward and sniffed Taylor's hand while Kelsey let all the dogs off their leashes. Josh kept an eye on them as he darted into the house and grabbed the drinks. By the time he returned, Romeo had stuck his nose toward Taylor's neck, and she was slowly petting the fur on his back, like he'd instructed her to. It would take some time—and a few treats—before the husky would let her go closer to his face, but he was warming up to her.

"I thought you weren't dog people," Kelsey said, accepting her glowing pink concoction from Josh. She kept her gaze on Taylor and Romeo, seemingly disconcerted that her most suspicious dog was allowing her enemy to pet him.

Taylor snorted and stood back up, and Romeo ran off to join the others. "I wanted dogs since I was kid. We weren't allowed, so I lived vicariously through friends who had them."

"It's possible to like dogs and cats," Josh said, and Kelsey sighed heavily.

"Doc, leave the metaphors to us former English majors. That was too heavy-handed to be effective."

Josh shrugged. "Fine. I tried." Let Kelsey think he was being heavy-handed and clunky so she missed his subtlety. His real plan was working perfectly so far.

"I'm surprised you didn't bring Neptune," Peter said to Kevin.

Kevin shook his head. "He's not ready. New puppy," he explained, seeing Taylor's confused expression. "Still working on socializing him. He'd be overwhelmed here."

"I think we're all overwhelmed with the socializing going on here," Peter said.

Josh grinned, and even Kelsey shot her cousin's fiancé a sardonic look. He was damn glad he'd insisted Kevin bring Peter. Not only did his nonfamily status allow him to say whatever he wanted, he tilted the numbers in Josh's favor. This was precisely the sort of situation that was so hard to find in Helen. Everyone who grew up here had picked a side, and most had inherited one.

Josh stepped aside to go dump the charcoal into the grill, and everyone followed. Without the dogs underfoot to keep them occupied, it appeared he was the life-line they were all clinging to. Either that or he was the drain they were all circling in a terrible idea. Josh was optimistic but not entirely convinced yet.

"I'm surprised Romeo let you pet him," Kelsey said to Taylor. Although she wasn't being openly hostile, she continued to eye the other woman like she might be a witch.

"I'm very likable."

That finally got Kelsey to turn her attention from Taylor to Josh. He smiled at his cousin. "So it would appear. Give him a bite of your steak at dinner, and you'll go from okay to friend for life," Kelsey said.

Josh fought down another grin. He'd already told Taylor the same thing. In fact, he was making a little extra steak to feed the dogs a treat. But Kelsey sharing that tidbit with Taylor felt earth-shatteringly significant. Maybe he could actually pull off this long-game plan after all.

"Will do," Taylor said. She turned to Kevin. "Is the puppy also a husky?"

"I'd risk being disowned if I adopted anything else, and I'm already the family black sheep." Kevin punched Josh in the arm. "Or wait, I was. Thanks for that."

Josh shrugged. "I do what I can."

"You're all killing me, you know that?" Kelsey raised her face to the sky as if to ask why. "You all have death wishes."

First, Kelsey helping Taylor make friends with Romeo, and now this. It looked like he'd been right to be optimistic. His cousin had just clearly placed him and Taylor on the same side as her brother and Peter. It was as good as he'd get in way of acknowledgment that she was accepting their situation.

Josh held up his beer bottle. "Here's to death wishes then."

Kevin seemed to have the same realization as Josh. He hesitated a second, then laughed and joined him. "Shit."

"I'll stick to dogs," Kelsey said with a sigh. "You'd better all leave me yours in your wills."

25

⋄————⋄

I HEAR YOU had dinner with some Porters last night."
Marie looked up as Taylor entered the kitchen. The cook
had been checking the food delivery against the inn's
invoice while her assistant was on a break. Crates of
milk and eggs and boxes of dry goods covered the cen-
tral island.

"Don't tell me you have spies in town too."

Apparently satisfied that all was correct, Marie set the
invoice aside and began loading the industrial-size fridge.
"No, but my son was doing maintenance on one of Kevin
Porter's boats yesterday, and he overhead some conversation. The words 'that unruly Lipin woman' came up, and
he assumed it referred to you."

Taylor mockingly glowered at her as she tackled one
of the boxes. "Such nerve. I'm not unruly."

Marie wisely made a noise that was neither agreement nor disagreement. "But you did have dinner with
them?"

Coming from anyone else, these nosy questions would

have had Taylor turning tail and leaving the room in a huff, but it was hard to be annoyed with a woman who had sneaked her pastries behind her parents' backs and had never once raised her voice when little Taylor had sloshed the eggs she was supposed to be beating all over the counter. "You know I've been seeing Josh."

"I think the whole town knows you've been seeing Josh."

While that confirmed everything Taylor suspected, it wasn't exactly welcome news. She lowered her head to a convenient cabinet door and groaned. "I hate this place."

"Do you?" Marie sounded serious, so Taylor turned. The cook was holding the last bundle of egg cartons and gazing thoughtfully at her. "You don't act like someone who hates it."

"I hate the feud."

"The feud is not the same as the town."

She knew that. Logically, she understood, but her emotions were another matter. The town and the feud were so wrapped up in each other that the longer she was here, the harder it was to separate them, and yet the more she wished she could, especially since she'd reached a major decision this morning.

"I got the job I interviewed for," Taylor said, placing the last twenty-pound bag of flour in the cabinet. She'd gotten the phone call only a couple of hours ago, and her decision was fresh enough that it hadn't entirely settled yet. Like one of Marie's cookies hot out of the oven, it needed time to solidify and thus could still be ruined if she tried to eat it before it was ready.

That said, she needed to test out the words on someone, and Marie was a natural choice. She wasn't family with all their complications, and Taylor trusted her judgment. Mostly, though, she needed to hear herself speak the decision out loud. It was the right one; she was positive. But that didn't stop it from feeling surreal.

With the order fully unpacked, Marie wiped her hands on her apron. "You leaving us then?"

"No. I'm not taking it." Odd how a decision that felt right also felt scary. Since the interview, she'd known that she didn't truly want the job, but she'd never ruled out the possibility of taking it if offered.

Holding on to the possibly had enabled her to put off the hard choice. As a result, it had been hanging over her head for a while, tormenting her sleep, making her question everything she'd learned to believe about herself. And yet, the choice to remain in Helen had come so easily when Taylor had gotten off the call. She'd known that instant because she hadn't been thrilled by the news. She'd been disappointed.

No, more than disappointed. Dread had settled in her stomach. Taking the job would require leaving town, and leaving town meant leaving Josh, probably forever. It also meant leaving behind her sister, whose company she was finally learning to enjoy, and giving up her responsibilities at the inn. That working at the Bay Song had dropped entirely off her Worse Than Losing a Kidney list was a shock, but then what about this unexpected visit home hadn't been? She'd known at the time that meeting Josh was oddly momentous. She'd just certainly never expected it to be in this way.

Marie's face lit up with the same sort of elation that Taylor knew she felt, even if the emotion itself was being elusive. She was happy with her decision, but too much weighed on her mind for her mood to be as light as it deserved.

Possibly, a similar weight flattened Marie's mood as well because her smile wobbled as easily as it had formed. "I'm so glad, but are you sure that's what you want?"

"I am." Her dread had vanished the moment she'd reached the decision. It was the fear of such a big change, the hassle it would bring, and the losses it entailed—like regularly hanging out with Stacy—that remained. "I am. It's just that moving back means constantly dealing with the feud again and living with the uncertainty that any day someone in my family or Josh's family might decide to lash out more than they already have."

"But he's worth it?"

More than, but it wasn't only Josh she couldn't bear to leave. "You're all worth it."

Marie wrapped her arms around her, enveloping Taylor in a perfectly squishy hug. "Then stop worrying about the bad and focus on the happy. After all, you had dinner with Porters last night and no one died. Right?"

The hug's effect on Taylor's mood was immediate. Maybe she'd been wrong to delay telling Lydia and Josh. Marie's enthusiasm was infectious, and it chased away the darkest of her worries.

Taylor laughed. "The only thing that was stabbed last night was a steak."

"See? That's progress."

She supposed that was, but progress was going to be slow. Although Taylor had to admit that dinner with Josh's cousins had gone better than she'd expected.

Josh deserved credit for teaching her that the way to Kelsey's alleged heart was through her dogs, but Taylor opted to take some credit for herself too. Her former career had given her an excellent education in how to talk to fussy people, and her time spent appeasing guests at the inn, answering their questions, and being the social face of the business had further honed her people-reading skills over the past few weeks. If she could placate the domineering tourist who hadn't packed for the weather, was suffering from severe jet lag, and demanded a gluten-free and vegan breakfast, she could handle one dinner with Josh's allegedly friendliest relatives.

Kelsey hadn't exactly been warm and friendly by the end of the evening, but she'd never had that reputation with anyone as far back as high school. She'd been civil at least and had shown distinct signs of an underlying pleasant personality as long as Taylor kept the conversation focused on her dogs. Kevin had been easy enough to figure out, too, after a while—all she had to do was talk about boats and his wedding plans.

Josh was convinced the dinner had gone splendidly and he was on the verge of a feud break-through. Taylor's bar had been set lower, and she'd take the lack of bloodshed as a sign of success.

Although she wasn't sure Kelsey would ever approve of her petting her dogs.

Still, it might work. Taylor had hope again, and that had probably influenced her decision even if she wasn't consciously aware of it.

"You sound as optimistic as Josh," Taylor teased the other woman. "He thinks we can outmaneuver the haters."

"Nothing wrong with a little optimism. It's optimists who change the world because they're the ones who believe something better is possible."

"Meanwhile I'll hang out in the pessimist corner, enjoying the fact that I'm never disappointed like the rest of you."

Marie tsked and got out the sugar for the afternoon cookies. "I don't think that's true."

"No, it's not true." If it were, she'd be booking her return flight to L.A. this moment.

"Have you told your sister yet?"

Taylor shook her head and smoothed out the bag of chocolate chips that she'd set on the counter. "Not yet."

"I didn't think so. I haven't heard her screaming from across the inn yet. Go on, get out of here and share the happy news, and put those chips away. It's oatmeal raisin cookie day. You know that."

"Yes, but in the spirit of optimism, I was hoping we could celebrate with chocolate chip cookie day instead."

JOSH POKED HIS head into the billing office and signaled for the dogs to come over. It had been one of those mornings where he hadn't been able to catch more than a couple of minutes to gather his thoughts, and he had the most exciting appointment of the day coming up—Taylor had asked to stop by over his lunch break because she had news to share. He didn't want to get his hopes up, but his hopes were definitely up.

Christian, who worked the front office, was eating lunch while talking to Elise, and he paused his conversation as Josh put the leashes on. "The phone has been ringing off the hook for you today."

"No emergencies I take it, or you'd have put them through?" If something wasn't an emergency, he was taking his damn half hour to eat and to hear what Taylor had to say.

"Mostly it was the usual—prescription refills, you-know-who is asking for sleeping pills again, and one consult call from a nurse at Fairbanks Memorial who said it wasn't urgent. Also calls from Karen Young, Walter Fishman, and Beverly Clark, who are very concerned about you and think you need to break things off with your girlfriend." Christian snickered into his wrap, and Elise tried—and mostly failed—to hide her smirk.

Josh sighed. These were not the first calls he'd received to that effect. George Buteau's life advice had started a trend that was kind of funny and yet not at all funny. "Helen is too big a town for people to be this nosy."

"Not when you're related to the Porters," Elise said. "That's like being Helen royalty."

"Swell." He turned back to Christian. "Tell me you didn't put any of those calls through to my voice mail."

"Hell no. But I did promise I'd relay the message."

"Consider it relayed." He tugged on the huskies' leashes. "Come on, let's go for a walk before anyone else wants to offer me dating advice." He then proceeded to hightail it out of the office before he could hear any laughing.

Luckily, just the cure he needed to combat his long morning and his busybody patients was waiting behind the hospital. There were a couple of picnic tables by the back of the employee lot, and Josh and Taylor walked over to them together.

Josh kissed Taylor's cheek as she unpacked the sandwiches she'd brought for them. "If you're wearing sunglasses because you want to hide, be aware you're not fooling anyone. I've received three calls this morning telling me to dump you."

"Well that makes this conversation awkward since I didn't just swing by to bring you lunch. I've decided I'm staying." She bit her lip in that adorable way of hers, waiting for him to respond.

Josh had to make Taylor repeat the news to ensure he'd heard correctly and his wishful thinking hadn't overtaken his brain.

"I haven't officially turned down the job. It all happened too fast, but I'm going to." She twirled her bracelet around her wrist as she watched him, as though she feared he'd be anything other than ecstatic about this news.

Was she kidding? His pulse was pounding and he suddenly felt like he had the energy to do a couple of laps around the neighborhood. Maybe while breaking into song.

Down, he instructed himself in much the same voice he used with the dogs. He could flatter himself that he had something to do with Taylor's decision, but she'd been mulling over a career switch for weeks. There were lots of reasons for her to stay.

Those reasons hardly mattered though. What did matter was that she wasn't going anywhere. And so they weren't going anywhere. This whole accidentally-falling-into-a-serious-relationship mistake wasn't going to end badly. And by end badly, he was thinking end period.

Yes, their families had to be dealt with, but Josh felt like that was getting under control. The Lipins had left him alone since Taylor had spoken to her grandmother, and as for his family, he had a plan. Kelsey and Kevin might never be true allies, but it looked like it might work, and now Taylor would be around to find out with him.

With him. Just the words made him want to grin.

"What are you thinking?" Taylor asked, and Josh realized he had, in fact, been grinning at her. His metaphorical tail was wagging as hard as when they'd met.

Josh grabbed her hands and yanked her close. "I'm thinking we need to celebrate."

"We do, but—"

He had no time for buts and cut her off with a kiss. He was almost too excited about this news to care that anyone could see them. The hospital didn't have that many windows on the back of the building, after all.

Taylor hesitated for an instant, then seemed to decide that if he didn't care, she wouldn't care either. Her mouth yielded to his even as her body melted against him. He could kiss her for hours, breathing in the sweet scent of her hair and tasting the softness of her lips. Her touch revitalized him as much as her decision had. With her pressed against him, there was nothing they couldn't do, no obstacles they couldn't conquer.

Except, possibly, the lack of privacy. That was a frustrating one at the moment because although kissing her was nice, Josh wanted more. And the options for that here were nonexistent.

He pulled back before he got too carried away, and ran his fingers up her cheeks to remove her sunglasses.

Taylor's cheeks were flushed as she took them from him. "What will your patients say?"

"I guess they'll have to deal." Josh kissed her again, but didn't let himself linger this time. Happiness pulsed through his veins, but other thoughts were occurring to him. "This hiding stuff has got to stop."

"I know." Taylor rubbed her eyes and began unwrapping the sandwiches. "Sneaking around made sense before, but it's no way to live."

"And you're going to live here." He grinned some more because apparently no serious thoughts were enough to dampen his enthusiasm.

Taylor matched his grin and, as usual, outshone it with her internal brightness. Now he was the one who needed sunglasses. "I'm going to live here."

26

❦━━━━━━━━━❦

IT WAS UNDOUBTEDLY a coincidence, but on the first full day since Taylor made up her mind to stay in Helen, she had a dog.

It felt like a sign. A new life. A new life-form. A new her, one resolutely determined to build a bridge between two families and stake her claim on her hometown.

Okay, so the dog wasn't hers exactly. He was Josh's, but that could also be seen as a sign. Once she chose to stay, Josh chose to trust her with Jay. It wasn't the same as joint dog custody, but it was a step in the right direction. As she was moving forward, so was their relationship. They no longer had to worry about holding back, because there was no longer a guaranteed expiration date on what they had.

She should have confessed to Josh that she loved him last night, but coming off her momentous decision, she hadn't wanted to conflate the two. As much as her reasoning to stay had to do with Josh, she feared he'd feel pressured by that knowledge. Just because they no longer should hold back didn't mean she should go around spewing her innermost thoughts without concern for how they might be taken.

Still, being entrusted with Jay felt a bit like Josh's own confession. Jay had severe vet anxiety, but Josh didn't need her to dog-sit while Pepper and Bella had their appointments. Jay could have stayed home alone or gone to his cousin's or even waited in the car. But Josh had asked Taylor if she wanted to watch him in that sweetly cautious way of his, and she'd known his asking was a big deal.

She might have squealed a little and agreed before coming to the realization that she should have consulted Lydia about it first. Fortunately her sister was so pleased that Taylor was planning to move back permanently that her only demand had been to keep Jay away from Merlot.

So far that hadn't been difficult. Josh had dropped Jay off in the morning before heading to work with the other dogs, and the husky had spent most of the time in the room Taylor now considered her office. They'd gone for walks, he'd basked in affection from the guests, and he was currently hanging out with her in the kitchen.

"Which wine do you think?" Taylor asked him. They had not quite half a bottle of yesterday's red left to put out first, but that wouldn't be enough. She held up a Shiraz in one hand and a red blend in the other.

Jay's ears perked up, and his head swiveled between the bottles. When it became evident she wasn't offering him food, however, he whined his annoyance.

"You're not a very good conversationalist," Taylor told him, setting the red bottles down next to the whites she'd already selected. "But you are a much better listener than my sister's cat. I think we'll go with the blend. Thanks for your help."

She locked the Shiraz away in the wine cupboard and

then got out the cheese she'd planned to serve. Marie's assistant had already sliced it, so Taylor took her time artfully arranging it on the tray. Although she wondered if any of the guests noticed, she'd taken to trying a new design each day.

Funny how these tasks she'd once considered dull and beneath her had come to be ones she looked forward to. Something as simple as pairing wine and cheese and perfecting the presentation both entertained and soothed her. Even if there were parts of this job that were stressful, there was something extremely satisfying about making others happy. Something that her former career hadn't been able to provide.

"You know what the best part of this job is?" Taylor asked. Jay likely didn't appreciate her monologue any more than the guests noticed her cheese art, but she was discovering she liked having an unargumentative listener. If she didn't watch out, she'd turn into Josh. He'd copped to a similar habit after she caught him asking his dogs' opinion about his shirts one morning.

"The best part," Taylor continued, getting out a glass, "is that I need to taste yesterday's leftover wine to make sure it didn't go bad overnight."

For some reason, Jay didn't seem to care about that benefit nearly as much as she did. The husky barked, a sharper, less friendly kind of bark than the sort she'd grown accustomed to.

Startled, Taylor managed not to spill the wine she'd been pouring, and she glanced down at Jay. His ears were cocked but his tail wasn't wagging. Taylor hadn't seen him like this before, but it didn't take a canine expert to realize something was bothering him.

"What's wrong?" She squatted down to his level and glanced around the kitchen.

Her human senses didn't detect anything amiss, but Jay's behavior was so out of character that her own hackles—whatever those were—were raised.

Jay barked again, and Taylor held still. The inn sounded quiet to her, though there were voices in the distance. A breeze blew in from the open window, tickling her neck with the hairs on the back of her head. Through the cracked open door into the dining room, she saw nothing.

"Is it the cat?" That was the only thing she could think of. Josh had said Jay was the twitchiest and least trustful of his dogs, but Taylor had only ever seen any of them adore people. A cat, on the other hand—that could be different. Merlot had darted out of the apartment occasionally before, and it wasn't impossible he'd done it to her sister again.

Taylor clipped Jay's leash to his harness in case he became too excitable, and urged him forward. If Merlot had gotten out, she needed to find him before another creature decided he'd make a tasty snack.

"Come on." She nudged Jay forward.

A quick circle around the kitchen revealed no cat, but Jay had yet to calm down, so Taylor took him into the dining room. Feeling increasingly silly, she searched under the tables and the sideboard, but there was no cat and no humans either.

Jay whined some more as Taylor walked him into the lounge, peeked into her office, then doubled back toward the kitchen. In the dining room entryway, he barked again and a low growl rumbled from the back of his throat.

Taylor's feelings of silliness were starting to be replaced by frustration. She'd seen no signs of Merlot and had no clue what had riled up Jay, but she was concerned.

Maybe it was time to text Josh. He should have been back from the vet a while ago, but he wasn't done with work for another hour. In the meantime, she'd set out the wine and cheese a little early and take Jay for another walk. Running always helped when something was bothering her.

She'd left the kitchen door slightly ajar, and Jay yanked on his leash as Taylor pushed it open. She almost lost control of him and with good reason.

There was a stranger in her kitchen. A stranger who was dumping something into her opened bottle of red wine.

"Hey!" The word exploded from Taylor's mouth due to shock, and only too late did it dawn on her that yelling at the guy might not have been the safest choice. After what her family had done to Josh, she should have turned tail and run in case he was armed. But the deed was done, and even if she hadn't yelled, odds were he'd heard her open the door. Jay was barking like mad.

The intruder moved so quickly his face barely registered in Taylor's vision. He stuffed the rest of whatever he'd been adding to the wine into his pocket as he darted for the kitchen's back door.

Jay strained at his leash, barking furiously and dragging Taylor with him. It was as though Jay made the rash decision for her. Together, they ran after the intruder.

Taylor slammed open the door, and she and Jay gave chase down the delivery driveway. Jay could clearly have caught up to the guy if she'd let him go, but there was no way Taylor was doing that. She might not be thinking entirely rationally, but she hadn't lost complete control of her mind. Unfortunately, as a result, she lost sight of the guy as they sprinted through the trees toward the Tavern.

Breathing far harder than she should have for such a

short run, Taylor dropped to a crouch about fifty feet from the restaurant and held Jay close. An engine started on the far side of the building. Likely, the guy had gotten into his vehicle. Even if she kept racing after him, he'd be long gone before she got there, and it would be just as impossible to identify the car as it had been the guy's face. The best she could say was he was about average build and white. His face was a total blur.

Swallowing, Taylor stayed in place, waiting for her heartbeat to slow. Jay whimpered and licked her face. The husky seemed in need of some calming himself.

"Good boy." She scratched the back of his head in his favorite spot, and repeated the phrase several more times. "Did you realize that guy wasn't supposed to be there?"

God, how close had he been to her? Although her adrenaline surge retreated, Taylor's pulse picked up again as she was able to consider the situation more clearly. Had he been lurking at the door or in another room? Wherever he was, he must have been watching her and close enough to alert Jay. What if the husky hadn't been there? This incident aside, all of Josh's dogs were friendly, but perhaps the intruder hadn't known that and so didn't take more drastic action because of Jay's presence?

Taylor couldn't help but cast a glance around the woods as she got up on shaky legs and made her way back to the inn.

Josh had supplied her with a few dog treats when he dropped off Jay, and Taylor gave them to him now. Jay seemed to have recovered far more quickly than she did, but then, he didn't have to look at the bottle of red wine sitting on the center island.

What had that guy put in it? Was that what Jay had

reacted to? Had he smelled something foul? And was it just something to make the wine taste bad, or was it something more sinister?

Whether poisoned or simply tainted, it had to go. Before she could consider the consequences, Taylor dumped her glass and the open bottle down the drain. For good measure, she tossed the cheese in the trash too. She wouldn't trust anything sitting out that wasn't factory sealed.

God, even if the guy hadn't planned to directly attack her, she might have drunk whatever was in that glass. Their guests could have gotten ill. The Porters had just escalated the feud from petty vandalism to who knew what.

It was only after that thought that Taylor questioned her judgment in dumping the wine. Lydia was unlikely to want her taking it to the police, but Taylor didn't see another choice this time. Potentially going after the inn's guests took this outside the family. That wasn't done. Ever. Taylor had never considered it before, but there had always been an unspoken code. Lipins and Porters never went after people who weren't family. Nonfamily might be recruited to the cause or lend their support, but even the nastiest incidents created no unintended victims.

Until now.

So regardless of what the families or the police preferred, a legal response was required. Someone out there needed to have some sense slapped into them even if the police couldn't determine the culprit, which Taylor assumed would be the case.

Holding the wine bottle up to the light, she could see dregs sloshing around in the bottom, and Taylor hoped that would be enough. Her hands shook as she texted Lydia to come find her in the kitchen ASAP. The least she could do was give her sister a heads-up about what she was going to do.

"Do I need to tell Josh too?" she asked Jay while she waited, but it was a rhetorical question, so it didn't matter that the husky couldn't respond. Yes, she had to tell him. She couldn't get upset with him withholding information and then do the same, even if he was going to take it badly. Which was pretty much a guarantee. "Maybe he'll let me keep you around more often, huh?"

She'd focus on that upside. She had to focus on something positive. The optimism Josh and Marie had tried to instill in her had taken a serious blow. But damn it—she wasn't going to be cowed. She was stirred and shaken, and she could go for a drink, but that was it. In the future, she would be more cautious, and she'd work with Lydia to increase the inn's security, which was on her sister's to-do list anyway after the first couple of incidents.

But she wouldn't let the Porters destroy her plans.

Taylor curled her trembling fingers into fists, took a deep breath, and then picked up a cheese knife and got back to work.

JOSH COULD HAVE swung by the inn to pick up Jay and Taylor, but it was walking time for the dogs, and she'd offered to take Jay down to the park to meet him. Such a public display of togetherness was brazen, but since Taylor was officially staying, their routine had to change. As they'd discussed, they were not going to spend the rest of their time together sneaking around.

The aroma of frying fish from one of the nearby restaurants intermingled with the less pleasing scent of brine coming off the bay. Josh could smell something else beneath it, too, like a crispness in the air that defied the humidity, a hint that winter was never as far away as everyone thought it was. He'd be glad for winter by the time it came, and he looked forward to the excuse to stay indoors, drink hot chocolate, and wrap himself and Taylor in blankets. But not yet. Like everyone else around here, he'd greedily hold on to whatever summer he could get.

Josh finally caught sight of Taylor crossing the street as he and the dogs finished their first lap past the ice cream stand, and he changed direction. He couldn't rid himself of the sensation that everyone was watching them and that as soon as his back was turned myriad spies whipped out their phones and sent the damning information to his family. Granted, his suspicions weren't exactly unfounded, but surely not everybody could be a spy. Possibly just one or two of these people. In that case, they'd get something juicy to report.

Jay barked excitedly as Josh neared, and Taylor let him lead her in a jog until they were reunited. The husky didn't give him the chance to greet Taylor until Josh had apologized for leaving him all day. But once Jay relaxed, he leaned over and kissed Taylor on the cheek.

He hoped the spies enjoyed that.

"Everything go okay?" He wasn't used to leaving his dogs with anyone other than Kelsey—hospital staff didn't count since they were in the same building—but Taylor had shown herself to be more than capable of watching them, and Jay adored her. Handing his leash over to Taylor for a day had seemed like a no-brainer and possibly a little symbolic. Was it weird that he liked watching her walk his dogs? It definitely gave off a she's-part-of-the-pack vibe that made him ridiculously happy.

Taylor hadn't sent him any panicky texts, so Josh assumed all had gone fabulously, but as he stepped back he reconsidered that assumption. Something was not right, and it was etched into the lines around Taylor's mouth. She was trying to smile and seem normal, but he knew her well enough to see the tightness.

"We had another incident at the inn," she said at last. A low, rocky wall encircled a paved area near the bandstand, and she took a seat.

Josh's stomach sank. More vandalism was not a good sign. His plan required taking a long-game approach, but long games necessitated accepting short-term hits. He'd counted on those hits decreasing over time. "What kind of incident?"

A bad one, obviously. Taylor was pissed off, as she'd understandably been the last couple of times, but she was also rattled. That was new.

"Someone put something into the evening wine." Taylor twisted her fingers together.

Josh swore. "Did anyone get sick?"

"No, I caught them. Thanks mostly to this guy." She smiled down at Jay and ruffled his fur. "So, it's all fine, but it was close, and under the circumstances I thought I'd better notify the police even though it would piss everyone off."

This did not sound "all fine" to Josh. While he was relieved that Jay was around, someone sneaking into the inn and tampering with the food took things to a new level. And it did not explain why Taylor was acting so spooked.

Josh had a feeling, though, that Taylor didn't want to alarm him, and that was too bad. He was already alarmed, and the less he knew, the more alarmed he was. "What did the police say?"

"Not a lot. They took my statement and what was left of the wine, but I doubt much will come of it. They seemed mostly concerned that things were escalating, but since no one got hurt this time, I don't expect them to dig too deeply."

That sounded right. The cops were content to let Lipins and Porters toss rocks at each other as long as they didn't target anyone else. They might poke around a bit after this incident and say a few words to the known instigators, like his uncle Wallace, to make it clear that they'd best not do something like this again. But without an actual non-Lipin victim, they wouldn't spend any additional resources.

"Good boy." Josh petted Jay, and phrased his next question carefully, and to the dog. "What did you do to help out Taylor?"

As he'd predicted, Taylor was eager to praise Jay, and she filled him in on the events with more detail. Josh got the sense she was holding back, but he could easily fill in those pieces himself.

Too easily. The more he thought about what had happened, the more panicked he became. Someone had been lurking around Taylor, unseen, for who knew how long. What if Jay hadn't been there to alert her? What if she'd drunk whatever that person had put into the wine?

What if he'd been an idiot to think they could weather this storm relatively unscathed?

Not only were the incidents increasing in frequency, they were increasing in intensity too. Taylor could be in danger. No, clearly Taylor was already in danger. He'd just been too blind to see what was right in front of his face. Her family hadn't thought twice about breaking into his house to threaten him. Surely it had only been a matter of time until his family decided to directly threaten Taylor in a similar fashion. Josh did not doubt for an instant that they'd do whatever they thought they could get away with.

His mouth went dry, and his entire body was numb with a new realization. He'd been willing to risk himself for their sake. He would not, could not, risk her.

"I hate this." Taylor's voice broke Josh out of his stupor. "I hate that these people ruin everything that's good about this place. Your family, my family—I'm so done. This crossed a line. They were targeting outsiders to get to us."

Another good point. One that he should take more seriously, but all he could think about was protecting Taylor.

I'm so done. He didn't blame her, and it was for the best if she couldn't tolerate this situation any longer. In his determination to make things work between them, he hadn't been thinking clearly. He'd wanted to believe they could be together in spite of the feud, and in doing so, he'd ignored the threats to her. Taking the short-term hits for the long-term gain was acceptable if he was the potential target. Not her. It had been his idea, and therefore his to shoulder the risk.

He loved her too much to let that happen, and that was why he needed to let go of his false hope. And let her go too.

He loved her. He'd known it for a while but hadn't wanted to admit it to himself. For so long, it had seemed inevitable that one day she'd leave. Even yesterday, when she told him she'd decided to stay, he'd kept the truth buried in his heart. On some level, maybe he'd known it was too good to be true. That all the love and determination in the world wouldn't be enough to overcome a century of irrational hate trying to force them apart.

Josh wet his dry lips, feeling ill. Even the dogs seemed to have realized something was wrong and had quit playing around by his feet.

"Sorry." Taylor hung her head and sighed. "I'm just so furious."

"Don't be sorry. You're not the one who's done anything wrong." Besides, he was sorry enough for both of them. Sorry he'd encouraged her to have hope when it would only make them both more miserable in the end.

They fell into silence, and Josh ran his thumb over Taylor's hand. He wanted to touch more of her, all of her, to pull her close and consume her, never letting go. But family spies aside, he had to resist the temptation. His head knew the right thing to do, and he couldn't let his heart interfere.

For a moment, it was peaceful watching the seagulls fight over scraps of bread and listening to the waves rhythmically crash onto the rocks. Josh's will almost broke before he ever spoke his decision out loud. But those waves were eternal, and so were the problems that defined Helen and that would torment them if they stayed together.

He found his voice before his will crumbled entirely. "You haven't turned down the job yet, have you?"

"No. I have to call them back, but I was too busy this morning, and then this afternoon . . ." She grimaced.

Then this afternoon she had too much occupying her mind, and from the sound of it, making her question her choice. It was a good thing, the latter. Knowing she was having second thoughts made encouraging her to take the job marginally easier. He was already positive it was the right call, and eventually she'd see that too.

No matter how much it hurt. Better emotional pain than one day seeing her show up in his ER in real pain as well.

"Good. I think it's for the best if you take it, and I think . . ." Damn it, this was harder than he'd imagined it would be, even with her second thoughts helping him along. "I think we should let things end between us when you go, at least temporarily. When it was only me at risk, I didn't care. But I can't do this now that I know what my family is capable of doing to you. I should have known it would get to this point, but I wanted to hope too much. A slow plan is a dangerous plan, and nothing is worth the risk of you being hurt."

Saying the words turned his stomach, but he had to do whatever he could to keep Taylor safe, even if it meant ruining the best thing in his life.

Josh watched her closely, memorizing every eyelash, the curve of her lips, the faint pink of her cheeks, knowing this was the last time he'd see them so close up. The need to run his thumb over those cheeks, to bring those lips to his own, to take back everything he'd just said was killing him. But somehow his will held. He loved her enough to keep from breaking down. And still he waited for her reaction.

Taylor said nothing. She didn't even blink. She just stared at her hand clasped in his.

Her silence, her stillness, unnerved him. Josh hadn't been sure how she'd take his words, but he'd braced for some reaction. He hadn't been sure which would be worse—making her cry or arguing with her. Now he knew. This nonreaction was worse.

She should argue with him, damn it. He'd argued with her when she tried pulling the same noble shit and leaving him. And though he'd vowed he wouldn't back down, doing anything to hurt her was like having barbed wire dragged along his insides. He'd been prepared for agony. So why wasn't she arguing? Why wasn't she doing anything?

"Taylor?"

She jerked her hand from his grasp. There. Something. But her eyes didn't flash like they had a minute ago, and no color rose to her cheeks. "Is that really what you think is best?"

The weakest trace of anger underlay her question. It was some emotion at last, a sign that he'd hurt her. But of course he had. "Yes."

Her lip trembled, and for a second, it seemed like the explosion he'd braced for was coming. Then the fight—as small as it was—left her features. It was as if he could actually see her retreating inward, her body growing smaller next to his. "Okay then. It all works out very conveniently, I guess."

Okay then? Every word she spoke that wasn't about putting up a fight became a barb, a tooth on that wire tearing him to pieces inside. Josh hadn't realized how much he needed her to fight, until she refused. It would make this more painful and messy, but it would let him know she was alive, that their relationship had been real. It would let him know he was doing the right thing, even if it felt awful. For her to give up at his say-so suggested she'd been shaken today beyond caring.

And could he blame her? After everything, after the threat she'd encountered today, he was glad Taylor was willing to say enough was enough. Glad—he told himself that again. Glad that she wasn't being reckless. Glad she was willing to take care of herself. Maybe she was even secretly relieved for the excuse to return to L.A. The feud had colored his opinion of Helen, and Taylor had lived with it far longer than he had. She'd left, in part, because of it. He couldn't blame her if she wanted to leave again for the same reason.

But he could sure feel like shit. He needed a drink, a bottle he could crawl into for a couple of days.

"Taylor?"

Saying her name provoked her, but rather than lashing out, she simply drew a deep breath. Josh recognized the expression. She was doing what he'd been doing—drawing deep down within herself for the strength to do what every cell in her body rebelled against.

Taylor tucked her hair behind her ears. "I guess it was nice while it lasted. Take care of yourself, Josh. We probably won't run into each other again since I don't intend to return to Helen."

"Taylor—" But she was up and hurrying away before he could get out the words, not even pausing to say good-bye to the dogs, and the *I love you* died on his tongue. Something warm and good inside him died along with it. He had no ability to move, to chase after her and make her listen. In fact, he wasn't sure he'd ever get up. He'd sit on this wall until the salty breeze eroded the shell he'd become.

She hadn't said *I love you* either.

27

◦────◦

TAYLOR OPENED THE door to Lydia's apartment cautiously, braced for her sister's reaction, but Lydia was nowhere in sight. She must still be working. That was good. Taylor wasn't ready to deal with another human face-to-face. Or a cat, for that matter, but Merlot merely looked up from his lazy perch on the windowsill and then went back to ignoring her.

In the bathroom, she splashed some cold water on her stinging eyes. They were red, as was her nose. She'd tried not to cry on the walk back to the inn, and failed. Luckily she'd been able to pull the hood up on her sweatshirt, put on her sunglasses, and avoid eye contact with the people she'd passed. She didn't want to make eye contact with herself, either, though, and she dropped her gaze and stared at her fingers grasping the porcelain sink. The water hadn't helped because water couldn't wash away what she was feeling, and those emotions were plainly visible.

A text arrived as she wandered back to the living

room, and Taylor fumbled with her phone in her haste to read it. But it wasn't Josh lamenting his words.

Well, she hadn't expected it to be, had she?

No, but she'd hoped. Somehow that was worse. Hope hadn't been her friend lately.

The message was from her mother, whom Taylor had texted on her walk. She wasn't sure why she'd chosen her over Lydia or Stacy, or any of the other more stable people in her life, but perhaps that instability was exactly the reason when she felt so unsettled. Or perhaps sometimes a girl just needed a mother's comfort.

Yes, please come up! I'm going to start a batch of your favorite peanut butter brownies right now. Get here tonight and they'll still be warm.

A smile brushed Taylor's lips like a ghost and vanished like one too. She had half a mind to consider whether her phone was bugged for her mother to have guessed she needed chocolate. Those brownies were her favorite. Denise Lipin didn't cook much, but she'd always made them for Taylor's birthday and other special occasions, whether good or bad.

Get here tonight . . . Taylor hesitated for a second, then dragged her suitcase onto the sofa bed. That sounded like a brilliant idea. What was the sense in hanging around when she'd have to fly out of Anchorage to get home anyway?

Home meaning L.A. She'd been delusional to believe Helen could ever be her home again. Delusional to think she could start over here.

Merlot meowed at her as Taylor dumped a pile of laundry next to the suitcase.

"You know nothing about it," she told the cat through a sniffle, and she cringed at the defensiveness in her voice.

She'd sworn she wouldn't let the Porters destroy her plans, but apparently that proclamation had come with a caveat—all declarations were off if that Porter was technically a Krane whose first name was Josh. Her plan hadn't depended on him alone, but while pondering it on her lonely walk back to the inn, she'd realized it had depended on three pillars. Her family. Her career. And yes, Josh. Take away any one of them, and like a three-legged stool, the whole thing collapsed.

Perhaps that was for the best. If her dramatic attempt to restructure her life had been so heavily dependent on one person, it was better to learn now that that one person wasn't as invested in their relationship as she'd been. Josh's former determination to push on when faced with challenges had led her to believe he was. But she'd been wrong about men before. What was one more time?

Nothing. Absolutely nothing. Just her heart breaking.

She didn't blame him. For all his assurances that they could outlast everything their families threw at them, she should have known it couldn't be. Oh, it made perfect sense that he was trying to protect her. She didn't doubt that was part of his reasoning. But if he'd only been trying to protect her, he could have just encouraged her to leave Helen. He could have suggested she take the job in L.A. and they could try a long-distance relationship. It would have sucked if she'd done it, and she'd have refused to leave, but in theory they could have carried on in secret in their separate states. Their families wouldn't have known they were still together. Breaking up with her hadn't been necessary.

But he'd done it anyway, and it left her with an inescapable conclusion—there was more to Josh's decision than trying to protect her. As for that, the only thing that made sense was that he didn't feel as strongly about their relationship as she did. It was why she hadn't protested his decision. There was nothing to protest. She was not about to plead her case, to beg from a guy who didn't feel the same way about her as she did about him. She deserved better.

It was simply too bad that she didn't want better.

Suppressed tears stung her eyes as Taylor folded another shirt. She hated this town. Hated it. The sad part was that she'd started letting it fool her into thinking it wasn't so bad. She'd spent too many hours strolling the park, watching the boats. Too many evenings playing with Josh's dogs or sharing a glass of wine with Lydia. Too much time enjoying the breeze, the familiarity, and everything she wished she didn't like but that was as much a part of her as her family's legacy.

And she'd spent too much damn time with a Porter, something else she wished she hadn't liked. No, make that loved. She might as well be honest with herself. Pretending she didn't love Josh didn't make the situation hurt any less.

Taylor drew a deep breath and realized the tears she'd been holding in had gotten past her defenses and were leaking down her cheeks. She had to stop thinking about Josh and start thinking about plans again. New ones. Thinking about him and his reasons for dumping her hurt too much, but thinking about the long drive ahead and everything she had to do once she got home would let her be numb. Better to be numb than to notice the horrific pain in her chest and the emptiness in her gut.

Hastily, Taylor wiped the tears away before Lydia could get home and see them. She wasn't about to lie to her sister about what had happened or why she was leaving, but she would not look like the mess she was.

On cue, the door opened and Taylor braced herself. Lydia was one of the only people she wanted to say goodbye to in person. Her father, her grandmother, the gaggle of aunts and uncles and cousins—they were all complicit in the feud, one way or another. While those actions weren't what directly led to her present situation, they'd no doubt contributed to the Porters' retaliation.

Although, on that thought, maybe she should thank them from saving her from making a mistake and exposing the weaknesses in her and Josh's relationship.

Maybe, when she was a few breaths farther from a raging, crying breakdown.

"Taylor?" Lydia dropped her keys in the dish by the door.

Taylor grabbed an empty shopping bag and tossed her shoes in it. Why wasn't everything fitting into her suitcase anymore? "Yeah?"

"You're packing. Why?"

Since the suitcase could no longer contain the rest of her crap, she zipped it. She could always repack before getting on a plane, when her head was clearer. "I need to leave. I changed my mind about staying. I'm sorry."

Taylor actually thought those sentences came out rather well considering her throat kept closing up on her, but she couldn't fool her sister. Lydia pulled her into a hug, which was almost enough to give birth to a fresh round of tears. When did her sister stop being the cold, disapproving girl Taylor remembered and become this warm, friendly woman?

"Something happened with Josh, didn't it?" Lydia released her, and her dark eyes defied Taylor to lie.

There was no point in denying it. She was clearly a wreck. "He dumped me."

"Oh, Tay." Lydia pulled her close again. "I'm sorry. I'm sorry, and what the fuck? Why?"

Taylor filled Lydia in on Josh's official reason as well her theory while she shoved her remaining items in the shopping bag. She had to keep moving or the pain would bring her down for the count, and she did not want to be too upset to drive. Besides, she was getting really damn sick of crying.

"That's such bullshit." Her usually unflappable sister looked ready to hit someone, and that was enough to keep Taylor from bawling. "I tried to give him the benefit of the doubt, but that's such a Porter thing to do, so stupid and self-centered and assholish. His family tries to kill our guests, and so he hurts you?" She let out a scream of frustration. "I'm so pissed off on your behalf."

"Thank you." Taylor forced a small smile and sniffed. "I probably should be, too, but I'm too upset for anger. Please go on and rage for both of us."

"I will. Don't worry about that." Lydia's voice was grim enough to send warning signals down Taylor's spine.

She grabbed her suitcase from the bed. "Don't go doing anything rash, and don't tell Grandmother. Please. I don't want Josh to get hurt."

"Even after he dumped you for a bullshit reason?"

"I love him. I don't want to, but I do."

"You're better off without him, and I don't mean that because he's a Porter. I mean it because he's treating you like dirt."

Was he though? If he no longer felt strongly enough about their relationship to fight for it, then that was just a cold, unpleasant fact. The reason she was angry—or should be angry—was only because he wasn't being completely honest about why he'd broken up with her.

Lydia picked up the shopping bag and paused. "Wait, where are you going and how are you getting there?"

Taylor's suitcase hit the floor with a thud that sent Merlot scampering out of the room. She blinked, then laughed somewhat hysterically, forcing more tears down her cheeks. In her need to get out of town before she broke down completely, she'd missed that minor detail. "I don't suppose you'd mind driving me to the rental company so I can get a car?"

Lydia sucked on her lip. "I can if that's what you want, or you could stay another night and take the train or the bus tomorrow."

Taylor shook her head. She was in no mood to linger and in less of one to have to be polite to strangers.

"Eat dinner before you go?" Lydia tried again.

"I'll steal one of your energy bars. This place is suffocating me. I want to get on the highway and leave it all behind."

Lydia sighed with resignation. "Text me when you get to Mom's. I don't care how late it is. Okay?"

"Okay." She hugged her sister, feeling a whole new wound open in her chest.

She was leaving so much more behind this time—a better relationship with Lydia, plus a deeper appreciation for her hometown. It made a difference experiencing it in all its summer glory while the trees were heavy with leaves and the water sparkling, when the buildings were bright and colorful and not buried under slush and stained with salt. When all the shops and restaurants were open and bustling, and she could walk through the woods without the wind feeling like it was peeling off her skin. Maybe she hadn't enjoyed the crowds of tourists so much, but she could almost see why they came for the northern charm.

But she'd made her choice years ago to stay away and work in a profession she'd grown to dislike. And Josh had made the choice for her to keep it that way. It would be a long time before she could return without her heart breaking.

28

JOSH WASN'T SURE whether it was his dogs that woke him or the person pounding on the door, but he wasn't feeling particularly charitable to either. That likely had to do with the pounding in his head. He'd swear he could feel it inside his skull every time the mystery person's fist collided with the wood, a vicious drumbeat accented by enthusiastic barking.

Glancing at the time, he groaned. He'd let the dogs out about four hours ago and then crawled back into bed, and it felt more like four minutes ago. Whatever was going on, he wanted no part of it. It was Saturday. Couldn't he sleep off his hangover in peace?

"Josh! Open the goddamn door!"

Clearly not.

Swearing, he shuffled down the stairs half-blind as he squinted into the light pouring through his windows. It wasn't even sunny out. A light rain fell, but it was bright enough to add to his already high levels of misery.

A damp and dour Kelsey hustled inside when Josh

opened the door, and she pulled off her hood. "Were you sleeping?"

"Yes, actually I was."

She frowned up at him as she greeted his dogs. "You smell like vodka."

"It was bourbon." To be sure, he sniffed his arm. Yes, bourbon. He vaguely remembered spilling some on his shirt, but that didn't explain why he was also certain it was seeping out of his pores.

He'd been drinking two nights in a row. That was bad. Very bad. At least on Thursday, he'd gone out with friends to keep him sane, but last night he'd had no such excuse. Somehow he'd made it through the day, stumbled through the door exhausted, and then been unable to sleep. His mind had fixated on Taylor's hollow expression, her stillness, the way she'd slipped away like a warm summer's day. Like she'd never been there. It had been too much.

It killed him that he'd needed a bad idea to get through a good decision. But if he started wondering whether his decision hadn't been good, then where did that leave him? Putting Taylor at risk? He couldn't do that. Even with her in L.A., he didn't trust his family to stop trying more and more desperate ways to tear them apart. The next time Taylor returned to Helen, who knew what they would attempt?

No, he'd made the right decision. No one ever claimed that what was right was easy. If history was any guide, what was right was usually hard. Easy decisions were selfish ones, and this was further proof.

That was where the bourbon had come in.

"Whatever. It all tastes gross," Kelsey said, returning his thoughts to the bleak, drizzling present. "Taylor left, you know. She's on her way to L.A. You broke up with her?"

His cousin's words were a boot to the gut. How did Kelsey know what he'd done? He hadn't told anyone. Oh, wait—her spies. Of course. Kelsey had refined the skill of kicking people when they were down to an art form. She wasn't just a secret mother hen. She was a damn homing pigeon, seeking out his squishy spots.

Kelsey raised her arms in mock surrender before he could get a word in. "Well done. You came close to warming my cold, cynical heart, but I'm relieved to not be proven wrong after all. Men suck and love is a lie."

He should kick her out. "I was trying to protect her, and no offense, but you're one of the last people I want to talk to about this."

"Fine, we don't have time to deal with your issues anyway. You have ten minutes to shower off your booze stink and put some real clothes on. I hope you wrapped your present already."

"What?" He fumbled with the coffee maker, spilling grounds on the counter.

"Emily? You know, our niece? Her party starts at noon."

Shit. He had bought her a present, but the idea of being surrounded by family today was intolerable. These people who'd fucked up the best thing that had happened to him. "I can't go."

"Not an option."

"Kels, no."

"Your four-year-old niece has nothing to do with your hangover. We're family, Josh, like it or not. Even when some members make us want to scream, we have each other's backs. So be there for your niece and act like it. I'm sure there'll be more alcohol. Besides . . ." She took the coffeepot from him and finished filling it since he'd been doing a terrible job. "I need the moral support."

"Where's Kevin?"

"He'll be there, but late. Conveniently, Peter needed to do some data collection this morning, which meant he conveniently needed someone to take him out onto the bay. Naturally, my brother is going to give him a ride so he doesn't have to pay for a charter."

"Is Peter going?"

Kelsey grunted and turned the coffee maker on. "He's not family yet."

"What do you need moral support for?"

"Stop stalling!" She began pushing him toward the bathroom. "Who do you think I need support to deal with? My father wants to base his political campaign on trying to bring a Walmart or a Costco or any similar store into town. That's the latest issue we're having."

Josh half fell into the bathroom and rubbed his eyes. He wasn't entirely sure why he was letting Kelsey drag him into company he'd rather avoid, but she was right that their niece didn't deserve his wrath. He also had a feeling that if he didn't let Kelsey force him out of the house, he'd mope around all day and be miserable. Surely it was preferable to be miserable in company where lunchtime drinking was considered socially acceptable.

"That's one area where I don't disagree with your father," Josh said, shutting the bathroom door. "I wouldn't mind not having to drive five hours round-trip the next time my toaster dies."

Kelsey clicked her tongue. "Honestly, I'm disappointed in you. I'm still pissed off that the coffee-shop-that-shall-not-be-named opened up here a few years ago. One of the best parts about living here is that we don't look like a strip mall."

She wasn't entirely wrong, so instead of responding, Josh turned on the shower. He'd wanted to stay in Alaska near his family, and he could have chosen Anchorage or Fairbanks or a few other cities, any of which was more urban than Helen. But in the struggle between convenience and small-town charm, he'd chosen charm.

That charm had lost a lot of its luster.

IN RETROSPECT, JOSH decided he should not have let Kelsey drag him out. Moping alone with his dogs and a beer might have sounded like a country song cliché, but at the moment, he'd take being a cliché over this.

The rain had let up while he was showering, so the birthday party had not been crammed inside a too-small space, which was about the only positive thing Josh could say for it. That, and the cheap hot dogs went pretty well with a hangover.

Approximately thirty adults, twenty children, and a couple dozen dogs—including his own—wandered about on the damp grass. Kelsey had called Emily his niece, but Josh's quick internet search suggested she was more like a second cousin.

Or not. Despite his coffee and a couple of ibuprofen, his head continued to ache, and he had a hard time concentrating on anything, even something as simple as genealogy. It was taking significant effort to simply keep a scowl off his face. People kept wanting to talk to him. Cheerful people. People who would probably rejoice if they knew he'd broken up with Taylor. He couldn't help resenting them all for their role in that.

He also couldn't stop himself from watching each one and wondering. Who had broken into the Lipins' inn? Whose idea had it been to taint the wine? Who had thought it was okay to hurt Taylor and innocent guests? What else had those people been planning?

Jay parked himself by Josh's feet and made a pathetic and all-too-relatable noise. His dual-colored eyes never left the hot dog as Josh took another bite. That pitiful expression elicited the first real chuckle he'd managed in two days.

"Oh, buddy. I know. Life is unfair." Josh broke off the end of his hot dog and held it out for the husky, who gratefully snatched it with an expression that seemed to ask, *Is that all?*

Kelsey trudged up to him, sipping from a plastic cup filled with the bright red nonalcoholic fruit punch that Josh would have passed on even if he hadn't wanted to drown his sorrows in a bottle. Just the thought of the amount of sugar in that punch bowl made his teeth hurt. "Save me. The other reason I needed you here is coming."

Josh sighed. "What reason is that?"

"Interference."

He caught on a second later. Parker waved as he approached the section of fence Josh had staked out. "Hey, Josh. Man, you look like shit."

Josh cast about for an appropriate retort, but his brain was too addled to find one. In a surprising show of understanding, however, Jay barked at Parker in a shockingly unfriendly fashion.

Good dog, is what Josh wanted to say. Instead he once more forced himself to be polite. "What's your problem, Jay?" He rubbed the husky's head in confusion.

Jay scooted backward and continued to glare at Parker, ears and ruff up, which was weird enough to fully capture Josh's attention. Sure, Jay could be skittish, but this was bordering on hostile, which was not a reaction Josh had ever seen in the dog. It wasn't like Jay had never met Parker before either. They weren't total strangers. Even Kelsey looked as surprised as he was.

Parker just laughed. "Everyone grumpy this morning?"

"Apparently." Josh squatted next to Jay, attempting to soothe him.

"This about your girl? Word is she left."

Josh cast a glace at Kelsey, but the truth was, his cousin didn't have to be the one spreading the news around. Kelsey's spies were family spies. He knew better than to assume she'd voluntarily talk to Parker.

Josh hoped that holding Jay close was calming his dog because he was getting riled up himself.

"I hope she was worth the hassle she caused us all," Parker continued, oblivious to the fact that he was pissing off beast and man both.

Josh hand faltered on Jay's back. *Worth the hassle*? He was so sick of this nonsense. Rage awakened beneath his grief and self-pity, and it cracked a bloodshot eye out at the world.

"I fail to see why my relationship had to be a hassle for anyone." His voice held steady, but Josh tightened his grip on Jay. The husky was normally a comforting presence, enough to keep him calm. Except this time Jay wasn't calm for some reason, and Josh's own mood was probably going to start rubbing off on the dog, making this situation worse as they fed off each other's negativity.

Parker shrugged. "People were agitated, man. She was a Lipin. We had to look out for you."

First of all, Parker wasn't technically part of the family, and therefore had no business inserting himself into it for kicks. Second of all—*we*? Overtired and addled his brain may be, but Josh skipped right over all the other absurdities about how people needed to look out for him and focused on that one word.

We. As in Parker had been a part of the plan?

Suddenly, Jay's behavior presented itself in a new light. Taylor had been badly shaken up by the intruder at the inn, and she and Jay had given chase. Had that intruder been Parker? Had Jay known that Taylor felt threatened by him? All the huskies were usually too friendly for Josh to have ever considered such a possibility, but Jay had loved Taylor from the very beginning. If he was going to defend anyone, she'd likely be the only other person besides Josh.

He swallowed and stood. There was only one way to find out. "You're the one who's been vandalizing the Bay Song."

It was supposed to have been a question. Part of him must have known it was an accusation.

Parker finally had the good sense to look uneasy, and he scratched his neck. "I did a few errands, yeah."

"A few errands?" He fought to keep his voice down. He might be furious, but he was unlikely to have any support around him, and he knew it. None of these people cared what he was feeling. And by extension, none of them cared about him. All they cared about was their damn feud. "Like trying to poison everyone at the inn?"

Parker held up his hands. "Hey, it wasn't poison. No one would have died."

"You don't know that."

"It was salt, to make the wine taste foul. That's all. Shit, I'm not trying to kill people. Calm down."

Sensing Josh's rising fury, Jay barked again.

"Calm down?" Josh laughed unsteadily through the haze of his headache and anger. He was half a breath from taking a swing at Parker. This asshole wasn't even part of the family, and yet he was responsible for freaking out Taylor so much she'd questioned her decision to stay. For freaking him out so much that he didn't want her to. Punching Parker wouldn't even feel good because no amount of pain he could inflict would come close to what he'd been carrying around inside his chest since Thursday.

"Hold on." Kelsey took a step between Josh and Parker. "Am I understanding this correctly? You put something in the wine that was going to be served to guests at the Bay Song? People who aren't Lipins?"

"Nothing that was going to seriously hurt anyone. Jesus." Parker cast a glance around the yard, clearly searching for backup, but most of the guests were either inside the house or on the opposite side, watching Emily open her presents.

Kelsey gritted her teeth together. "We don't target people who aren't family. What the hell were you thinking?"

"If you've got a problem with the plan, talk to your father." Parker sounded pissed off now too. "It was his idea."

Kelsey's jaw dropped open but she seemed too stunned to speak. Muttering to himself, Parker stalked away and headed toward the kids, probably assuming he'd be safe there.

Josh watched him go without a word. Of course it was his uncle Wallace. The de facto patriarch had likely been behind everything, and Josh had been wasting his fury on the man's lackey. No, maybe not wasting. Now that the initial anger had run its course, Josh's head felt clearer than it had all morning.

He hated conflict. Despised it. And Taylor was gone, so he had no reason to court it. Practicality therefore demanded he make peace with the decisions that had led him here, at least until he could find a new job and move to a new town if that's what he chose. But practicality and peace be damned. All his pain had founds its target.

"Come on, Jay." Josh patted the husky's back. "Bella! Pepper!" He signaled for his other dogs to follow him, glad he and Kelsey had come in separate cars.

"Where are you going?" his cousin demanded, trailing along with the animals.

Josh opened the Jeep's back door and the dogs climbed in, but he turned back to the house instead of joining them. He wanted to be able to make a hasty getaway if things got ugly. "I'm going to have a word with your father. You might not want to come."

"Like hell I don't."

Josh grimaced but there was nothing he could do about that. He was liable to infuriate her, but he supposed she might as well be there to witness it. Word would get around soon enough, and his friendliest relative in town would have no qualms expressing her displeasure.

The sound of male voices and laughter made it easy for Josh to track down his uncle once he opened the house's back door. He was right where Josh would have expected, in the kitchen, surrounded by several other male relatives and sharing a more potent drink than the beers that were being served outside.

Josh's hands curled into fists, and it finally dawned on him that he wasn't sure what to say. He wanted to hit something, to call the man all the foul names running through his head. But he wouldn't condescend to his level.

Wallace noticed him as soon as Josh stepped into the room, and the bastard's lips turned up slightly at the expression on his face. "Josh. I'm glad you chose to be a part of this family, after all."

"What you did at the inn—involving strangers in your pathetic fight? Having Parker scare Taylor? That's revolting."

Kelsey ducked past Josh into the room, but said nothing.

His uncle sighed and swished his drink around in his glass. "Those were necessary steps. No one would have gotten ill from what Parker put into the inn's wine. We had to send a message, though, and it was obviously received."

There was the excuse again, as though that made it acceptable. "Yeah, a message was received—that you're a far sicker group of people than I wanted to believe."

"Collateral damage is a part of war." His uncle downed the rest of his drink and set the glass on the counter. "I was doing you both a favor, spreading out the hits rather than allowing them to be more concentrated on your girlfriend. No one was physically harmed."

"You mean no one has been harmed yet."

Wallace shrugged. "I don't like hurting women. Luckily, it sounds like you both got the point before things reached that level."

"Lucky for you I don't like hurting my elders."

That finally seemed to surprise the smugness out of his uncle's tone. "Like I told you before, you have a choice. I welcomed you here. We all did. We want you to be part of this family, but to do that, you have to choose us."

Josh forced his fists to open. That was all, huh? Well, that was easy. It didn't matter that he was killing any hope for peace and a quiet life. It didn't even matter, in this instant, that Taylor was gone and he'd lost her for good. He would choose her. Always her. There was no contest when it came to love or blood, especially not in this case.

Four pairs of eyes burned holes in him, but Josh

calmly shook his head. It was odd to find some kind of peace at last in this conflict, but maybe that came about from being confident in his decision. In knowing in his heart and his bones that he was making the right call, regardless of the hell it would bring down. "Sharing DNA with someone doesn't make them family. It just makes you related. Family are the people who love you for who you are and no matter what you do. Taylor was family. You're not. That's my choice."

He half expected someone to call out after him as he left, but he must have stunned them—or pissed them off—into silence. No one said a word. No one followed. Josh's pulse was still pounding when he climbed into the Jeep, his heart still aching. But at least that was done.

Three furry heads fought to poke through the gap between the seats and lick him, as though sensing his mood, and Josh smiled as he pulled out onto the street. He might have lost the Porters, but he wasn't completely devoid of family in town, was he?

29

━━━━◦━━━━━━━━━━◦━━━━

TAYLOR TURNED THE corner and slowed her pace as she approached her mother's apartment building. Although farther north, Anchorage was warmer in the mornings than Helen, but the temperature was still a vast improvement over L.A. There, most of the year Taylor resigned herself to an air-conditioned gym. While some dedicated folks managed to exercise year-round outside, she had too much Alaska in her blood.

She'd been running a lot these last few days before she flew back to California. It was symbolic, she told herself. She was running toward her future where a new job and fresh start would be waiting for her. But any idiot could tell that was a lie. The company would be new, but the job would be the same, and there was nothing fresh about returning to her old routine. A new job and a fresh start were what she'd planned to create for herself in Helen. She wasn't running to, but from. Yet no matter how far or fast she ran, she couldn't leave the pain that chased her in the dust.

Catching her breath, she stood outside the building's

main doors and completed her stretching, trying to ignore the man walking his chocolate Labs across the street. Even though they weren't huskies—three in particular— the scene was enough to set off the ache in her chest.

Taylor turned away and wiped the sweat from her neck. She had to get a grip. Men everywhere had dogs. She could not allow herself to feel sad every time she saw them walking together. In fact, maybe she should adopt a dog of her own and form her own little pack. A dog wouldn't replace the affection she felt for Jay, Pepper, and Bella, but maybe it would help plug the husky-size holes in her heart.

It was worth a shot. She couldn't outrun her emotions, she couldn't shower them off, and she couldn't even bury them under a pile of her mother's peanut butter brownies. So here was to hoping a canine friend and several thousand miles between her and the source of her pain provided some relief. Her flight left tomorrow. She could pretend everything was fine until then.

By the time Taylor emerged from the bathroom, clean and resigned to her fate, her mother had returned from church. "You should have come with me," she said, preparing a pot of coffee. "The sermon this morning was all about being willing to take leaps of faith. You might have gotten something out of it."

Taylor made a noncommittal noise and stuck a couple of English muffins in the toaster. It was possible, she supposed, but likely the run had been more beneficial. It had cleared her head for a half hour, forcing her to think of nothing but her feet and her breathing, and for a while, she'd had the benefit of all those endorphins flooding her bloodstream, making her believe that maybe all would work out for the best. Religion might be able to provide that same sort of relief for some people, but she'd never been one of them. Even the pageantry at Christmas—the only time she attended services with her parents these days—had never been more than a mildly pleasant distraction. And that was mostly because she enjoyed the music.

"I'm glad you're settling in," Taylor said, "and it sounds like the sort of thing you'd have gotten something out of."

Her mother set the butter out on the counter. "I already made my leap of faith, but yes, it was nice to hear words affirming my decision."

True, her mother had leaped, and she seemed to be landing on her feet. So was her father, despite not having much say in the decision.

Taylor's shock had worn off along with a bunch of feelings she'd come to recognize as betrayal and fear. Perhaps the fear had been justified; she hadn't known what the divorce would mean for her family, the people she cared about most. But the betrayal had made her angry, and that wasn't entirely fair. She understood better now where her mother had been coming from, and although she wished her mother had handled things differently for Lydia's sake, she couldn't begrudge her the need to follow her own dreams for a change.

Over the past couple of days, Taylor had learned that her parents spoke somewhat regularly. Ostensibly the conversation about who got custody of the cats was still being hotly debated, but from what Taylor had overheard, the calls were just as much about checking in on each other as they were about where Ginger and Tortellini would live. Her mother might have felt stifled in Helen, and her father might seem mostly indifferent, but she suspected they were still fond of each other. The cat custody might never be fully settled, which made a convenient excuse to keep in touch.

The coffee maker chortled away while Taylor buttered the English muffins. It was a comforting, familiar sound, enhanced by the always appealing aroma, but this morning it did little to improve Taylor's sense of well-being. Her endorphin high had long worn off, and simple pleasures weren't much good at replacing it.

If her parents were still figuring out their paths in life, what hope had there ever been for her to do so at such a relatively young age? Or poor Lydia? Taylor would have dragged Lydia with her, but her sister was settled in a couple of important ways—she liked where she lived and liked her job. Relationships, well, Taylor couldn't help her sister if she refused to expand her horizons, but that was Lydia's choice. And besides, expanding one's horizons didn't necessarily work out so well. She was a case study in that particular failure.

"You're flying out tomorrow?" her mother asked.

"Yup."

"I can't convince you to change your mind and stay longer?"

Taylor forced a smile every bit as thin as the skim milk her mother had for the coffee. "I already stayed way longer than I ever intended to stay. I have a new job starting in nine days and a termite-free apartment waiting for me."

"I just don't like seeing you go when it feels so wrong."

"It's not wrong. It's what has to happen."

"Exactly what I said almost my entire life." Denise Lipin sat down at the very modern wooden table in the apartment's tiny kitchen. All of the furniture in the apartment was modern, and Taylor wasn't sure if it had come with the place or if her mother had bought it, exposing yet another side of her personality Taylor had been previously unaware of.

"I don't resent any of it for a second," her mother continued, cupping her coffee mug. "Raising you and your sister is one of the things I'm most proud of. But I only ever did what I had to, and I'm not proud of that. I put my own wants aside until I was suffocating under their burden. And that's not you, Tay. Nor would I want it to be. Remember our conversation from a few weeks ago—I meant it when I said I was glad you left for California for college if that's what you needed to do."

Taylor swallowed. She hadn't quite believed her mother about that at the time, but she'd been wrong about a lot lately, and her frustrations had been clouding her judgment. "I appreciate that. A lot. You might have been the only person who supported me leaving. Well, except maybe Grandmother, but I don't know if she supported it or if she was simply relieved to see me go. But leaving is still what I need."

"Is it? Or are you running away because the pressure got to be too much?"

Taylor scowled. She was running away, but that didn't change anything. "It wasn't pressure, and you're hardly in a position to judge me." She instantly regretted the words, which came out bitter and which she didn't really mean. She was back to feeling defensive. Her mother was making her question her choices, and she couldn't do that. There was no other choice. No other direction to move in except back south.

Fortunately, her mother seemed to understand all of that intuitively, and she placed a hand on Taylor's wrist. "Judge you, no. Advise you, yes. First because I'm your mother. You're obligated to hear me out. Second because I don't want you making the mistakes I did. We owe it to our children to prevent them from following in our footsteps."

"I'm not making a mistake."

"So you're telling me you're more interested in your new job than you are in working with your sister."

Taylor responded by sipping her coffee.

"I see." Denise drummed her fingers on the table. "Was it the feud that made it all too much?"

"I could handle the feud. I hate it, but I could handle it."

"I'm sure you could."

"Josh couldn't. Or at least, he didn't feel strongly enough about me to try." She'd spilled everything the moment she'd arrived while her mother had fed her the peanut butter brownies. Unlike Lydia, her mother hadn't fumed. She'd merely listened and, when Taylor had finished emptying her insides, reminded her that she deserved the best and would one day find it. Taylor questioned the last part, but at the time, she'd been too stuffed with chocolate to contest it.

"So you're leaving your family and the job you want because of a man? That doesn't sound like the daughter I remember."

No, phrased that way, it sounded pathetic. "I was considering relocating and rethinking my entire life. That's a lot of upheaval, even for me."

"Mmm."

"It's about support." Taylor sighed, thinking back to her analogy. "I had three reasons why I might have stayed—family, job, and Josh. I needed all three to feel supported in my decision. Take one of those away, and there's not enough reason to go through with it. A stool can't support you on two legs."

"Nonsense. You're not a stool, Taylor. You're a woman. You only need two legs to stand on, and in a pinch you can balance on one if you want it enough. And if you lost them both, that's why we have chairs, and your family and friends would be there to push you if needed because we love you."

"If I go back, they win!" Taylor slammed her hands on the table hard enough to jostle the coffee, and she stood, surprised at the words coming out of her own mouth. "Our family, Josh's family—they both succeeded in driving us apart. If I stay, they get the satisfaction of knowing we couldn't beat them and he didn't care enough to try."

God, was that really part of it? Was she running away so she didn't have to face everyone? She didn't like that at all.

"And if you leave," her mother said, "they have the satisfaction of having driven you away."

"Last time, leaving was the ultimate act of rebellion." Josh had pointed that out to her, hadn't he? If she thought too much about it, she'd get teary again.

She plopped back down in her chair and reached for her coffee.

"Last time it was, yes. Because last time you did it for yourself." When Taylor didn't have a good response to that, her mother leaned forward. "Look, if you really want to leave, then leave. I will support you. But it's stupid to rebel by doing something you hate. You should rebel by following your heart. You already won this battle, Tay. No matter what Josh does or doesn't feel. You won because you alone were brave enough to love when others chose to hate. Now you need to keep being brave enough to stay true to your goals."

"I have goals other than causing trouble?" The smile that cracked over her lips this time felt small but genuine. Which seemed strange when she was so confused. Her plan—the second in one week—was crumbling.

Hell, her world was crumbling. She hadn't the first clue what she should do next.

"Maybe you should consider that causing trouble is sometimes a worthy goal itself," her mother said, sliding the plate of English muffins over to her. "Trust your instincts. You've always been pretty good at trouble."

30

⟡⎯⎯⎯⎯⎯⎯⎯⟡

THE RAIN WAS back, coming down in a steady drizzle outside Josh's windows. That was nothing unusual for Helen in the summer, but it did seem like it had rained an awful lot since Taylor left.

Restless and dangerously bored, he paced around the living room, ignoring the concerned looks his dogs were giving him. He was on call so he couldn't drink, and frankly, he shouldn't be drinking regardless. One night of drowning his sorrows was okay. Even two nights was acceptable as a sleep aid. But this was evening number four, and he had to find a healthier coping mechanism.

Unfortunately, taking the dogs for a hike was out of the question in this weather, which didn't leave him with much. Adrian was stuck working, and his other friends had families they no doubt wanted to spend their Sunday evenings with. As for people like Kelsey, he was just hoping she didn't try setting his house on fire for what he'd said to her father. He hadn't heard from her since he'd stormed out of the party yesterday, and her silence was unnerving him more than a Molotov cocktail would have.

If he got called in to work . . . Josh glanced at his phone but it stayed silent. For the best. He really shouldn't be hoping for an emergency to take his mind off his own problems.

"All right, who wants dinner?"

Three pairs of ears perked up. The dogs followed Josh into the kitchen, as eager as if they hadn't been fed all day. If only the promise of food could fill him with that much joy too. He wasn't even particularly hungry, but cooking something for himself would keep him occupied, and a man could not live on beer and other people's hot dogs alone. At least he shouldn't if he didn't have a death wish.

He was putting away the dogs' food when someone knocked on the door. Warily, Josh peeked through the window and discovered Kelsey. Inviting her in would definitely keep him occupied, though likely not in the most pleasant of ways. On the other hand, hearing from her was inevitable, and he might as well get it over with.

"Kels." He opened the door but didn't immediately step aside.

"Would you move? It's raining and dinner's getting wet."

Josh backed aside on autopilot, surprised to see his cousin barge in carrying a brown takeout bag. "Dinner?"

After shrugging off her jacket and wet shoes, Kelsey set the bag on the kitchen table. "I hadn't eaten yet, and I had a hunch you'd need food too. So yeah, dinner."

"Is it poisoned?"

She rolled her eyes. "Jeez, Parker gets caught putting a mysterious substance into somebody's wine, and now you're assuming we're all Mrs. White in the kitchen with the cyanide."

"I'm glad you find it funny."

"I don't find it funny. That's why I'm here."

Confused, but curious enough to see where this was headed, Josh produced two cans of soda from the fridge while Kelsey unpacked the bag. "Thanks for the food."

"No problem. I asked Kevin if he and Peter wanted to join us, but they were already eating. Eating! At a reasonable time on a Sunday." Kelsey waved an onion ring around. "My brother's getting responsible. It's odd."

Josh took a bite of the burger. It didn't taste poisoned, and Kelsey knew him well enough to know what toppings he liked. Still, he couldn't help but be wary. "Were you looking to make this a party, or did you want Kevin here to yell at me too?"

"I'm not here to yell. Relax. I'm here because I'm concerned. You were in a bad place yesterday, and I wanted to see how you were holding up." She grimaced. "Because I guess I am a mother hen. Damn you."

"If you think I'm going to change my mind about what I said to your father and apologize, you're going to be disappointed. I meant it. It wasn't just because I was in a bad mood."

Remembering the scene made his current mood worse. He'd gone from believing he could influence the family for good to alienating himself from it completely. Not only had his immune system plan failed before it started, he'd gone ahead and sabotaged it for good measure.

"My father's not ready to hear an apology anyway, which makes my life kind of awkward because I don't think you were wrong to say what you did. Honestly, it's what either Kevin or I should have said to him when he gave my brother shit about marrying Peter. It's just . . . harder for us, I guess. We grew up with him."

Josh blinked. "Are you sure you didn't put drugs in my food? I think I'm having auditory hallucinations."

Kelsey kicked him under the table. "Don't be more of an ass than you already are. Kevin and I talked, and we agreed that we stand with you on this issue. We even looped Nate into the conversation, and my elder brother is on your side too. Honestly, that was kind of surprising, but that's low-drama Nate for you. Anyway, I just don't know what this means since you were an idiot and dumped Taylor, but I'm not going to firebomb your house or anything."

No, really, were there drugs in his food? Even after the words he'd had with his uncle Wallace, Kevin and Kelsey were siding with him? They were okay with his relationship with Taylor?

Maybe his plan hadn't failed at all. If Kelsey was standing on his side after everything, that was a monumental victory. No doubt it helped that, in many people's eyes, his uncle would have gone too far in his attack on the Lipins, but regardless—lines were being drawn. Assumptions were being challenged. Given time and his cousins' influence . . .

It didn't matter. Taylor was gone. Maybe things would have changed, but the risk would have remained. She was better off where she was safe.

"I was afraid you'd toss a Molotov cocktail through my window," Josh said, collecting his thoughts.

"I'd never do anything that might hurt your dogs."

"True." He chewed on another bite of his burger, attempting to process what had just happened. The relief and gratitude that washed over him were profound and almost enough to overpower the constant emptiness in his chest. "Thanks, Kels. It means a lot to me."

His cousin shrugged like it was no big deal to defy the rest of their family, and Josh left it at that. She wouldn't want it any other way.

"You need more company in your life than your dogs," Kelsey said after another moment of eating. "And I'm still annoyed with you, so don't think this negates anything."

"Annoyed with me about what?"

Her expression was exasperated. "Annoyed because you didn't give Taylor a choice, you sexist, hypocritical bastard."

"What?" Why was everything Kelsey saying to him tonight forcing him to wonder about the state of the food she'd brought? "A choice?"

Kelsey made a noise of disgust. "When the Lipins broke into your house, and she tried to end things to protect you, you refused. So when she was the victim, why didn't she get a say in whether to end things?"

"It's different."

"How?"

"It just is." Because, clearly, he was being sexist and hypocritical, as Kelsey pointed out. But he didn't care. He loved Taylor too much, even if she didn't love him enough to fight him on it like he'd done with her. "She had a chance to argue with me, and she didn't take it. So, obviously, she doesn't care to risk as much for us as I was willing to. I hope that means she realizes she's better off this way."

"Did you ever consider that maybe dumping her shocked her? If I understand the timeline for how your breakup went down, she was probably still shook up from Parker. Then you went and broke up with her on top of that. She's human, Josh. It might have been more than she could deal with in the moment."

He swallowed, suddenly wishing he hadn't eaten anything and pushing the remnants of his burger away. "So I'm a hypocrite. I love her. I can't risk anything happening to her."

"If you love her, how can you not let her make that choice?"

"I don't know." Because he should have. He hadn't been fair, and he'd known it all along. It was why he'd worked so hard to tell himself that Taylor hadn't wanted to stay. He had to believe he'd made the right call, that he was making the decision easier for her.

Josh closed his eyes. "I hate risks. I hate knowing something could happen to her here."

"Lots of people hate risk. That doesn't mean you don't take them. You took one when you chose to date Taylor in the first place. You took one when you told off my father. This one—this one wasn't your risk to take."

Jay came over and sat at Josh's feet, followed by Pepper and Bella. Great, he had an audience. They probably recognized Taylor's name and wondered where she was.

So did he. Had she arrived back in L.A. yet? Had she gotten over him already?

Absently, Josh reached down and scratched a furry head for comfort. "What if she tells me I'm wrong when I tell her I screwed up? What if I made life easier for her by telling her to leave? I could make her unhappy all over again."

Kelsey looked ready to toss her soda can at him. "Then, in that case, I can go back to hating the Lipins in peace. But if that's what worries you—why? Seems like that's minor compared to what you were willing to risk by being with Taylor here."

Josh gritted his teeth. Kelsey was right, and he hated it. Hated that he'd been a fool. From the beginning, he'd known Taylor was a risk worth taking. But she'd become so much more. She'd become the person he was willing to risk everything for.

Fool didn't even begin to cut it. He'd never even told her he loved her. It had all happened too quickly, and he'd just let her walk away without saying the words. Without letting her know how much it was killing him inside to let her go. He'd told himself she hadn't fought, but he hadn't shown her a reason to fight.

Josh shoved his chair away from the table before stumbling into the next dilemma. How did he fix this? Never mind how did he explain everything to her; it would take a miracle to do his emotions justice, and there was no excuse for his actions. But how did he go about finding her to try?

"Where are you going?" Kelsey asked. She stood as well, looking mildly alarmed.

"I don't know. But I need to find Taylor."

"So you're saying I was right?"

"Yes." He picked up his phone. Calling would work no matter where she was, but calling was wildly inadequate when he'd screwed up so badly.

"You're going to apologize?"

"Yes." He was going to kick Kelsey out in a second, too, so he could track down Lydia. Taylor's sister would know where she was, and she might be persuaded to share. Lydia had also never stood in the way of their being together. She was another hopeful sign that he'd ignored in his panic. Although whether she was more likely to hear him out or deck him was yet to be determined.

"You love her and are going to stop being so stupid going forward?"

"Yes!" He spun around so quickly the dogs scattered.

"What is your point, Kels? I have to figure out how to do this."

His cousin raised an eyebrow and gave him a once-over. "My point is that I had to be sure. I'm going to give you something now, but you had to earn it."

31

IT WAS AN unhealthily early hour of the morning when Taylor's ride pulled up to her departure terminal at the airport. Her mother had offered to drive her, but Taylor hadn't wanted to make her get out of bed. She hated weepy airport scenes and had experienced her share of them over the years, so it was for the best that they'd said their goodbyes the night before.

All she had to do now was find the energy to remove herself from the Uber, check in, and prepare to sit for a while. Before she knew it, she'd be in Seattle for her layover, and from there, she'd eventually get home while it was still light out. Home in a place where it didn't stay light in the summer.

Not that it was exactly bright and sunshiny in Anchorage at this time of day. The sky was more of a milky patchwork behind the blinding airport lights. To Taylor, it looked sleepy, the cloud patterns reminiscent of a quilt or a sea of tiny pillows. Or maybe she just needed more sleep herself.

Actually, there was no question she needed more sleep, but here she was anyway with a flight to catch and a million things to accomplish in the next forty-eight hours.

With a yawn, she lugged her suitcase onto the terminal sidewalk as the car sped away. Down the length of the building, several dogs barked. Taylor smiled sadly to herself, adjusting her carry-on strap. Someone was leaving and their dogs weren't happy. She wondered if Josh's dogs missed her. She missed them, almost as much as she missed their owner, but she'd been too upset to think clearly when she left, and had done so without a pet goodbye. Stupid of her. But if she'd been thinking clearly during that conversation, she might have handled it differently, regardless of whether it changed anything. Which was unlikely and no doubt for the best.

She was fine.

Fine.

Exhaustion made people mopey. This was nothing a strong cup of coffee couldn't cure.

The barking sounded familiar, and it was getting closer. Taylor turned and stumbled backward into her luggage. Three huskies—one with dichromatic eyes— were dragging their owner her way.

And he was letting them.

Well, maybe not exactly letting them. Josh looked as tired as she felt, and he was precariously holding on to the leashes with one hand and an insulated cup with the other.

There was nothing to do but succumb to the furry hurricane as Jay and his sisters launched themselves at her. Greeting the dogs was easier than dealing with

Josh's presence, and her allergies were the perfect excuse for why her eyes were getting teary and her throat was getting rough.

But why was he here, damn it? When the dogs calmed down and she couldn't put it off any longer, Taylor stood back up to face their owner.

Josh's greeting was less enthusiastic than nervous. "Hi."

"What are you doing here?"

He held out the cup, which she now recognized as being from the Espresso Express. "I brought you coffee. Double shot, extra froth, touch of cinnamon. It might have gotten cold on the drive, but you can't get this particular roast in L.A., so hopefully it's worth it."

She took it instinctively and her fingers brushed his, sending a jolt more potent than any caffeine straight through her nervous system. The coffee was cool, but that hardly mattered. Josh had brought her favorite coffee one more time. She was so confused and on the verge of tears.

"You came here to bring me coffee?" Her heart was suddenly beating in her throat, making speech perilous. That would be completely ridiculous, and yet she was horribly afraid there couldn't be any other reason for his showing up.

He didn't care enough to fight for us. Why would he care enough to drive two and a half hours overnight to bring me coffee? It made no sense.

"No. The coffee was so you'd hear me out." He laughed nervously. "So are the dogs, honestly. I figured if you were too upset to talk to me, you'd want to see them. They are my most charming asset."

"Smart. I can see why you made it through med

school." Taylor took a sip of the tepid coffee, hoping to clear her throat. "Josh . . ." Regardless of her throat's state, words were elusive.

It was just as well; he held up a hand. "Wait. Your sister gave me your flight information. After she yelled at me, that is. So if you want to yell at her for telling me, you can. But I drove up, hoping to find you before you left because I have things to say that shouldn't be said over the phone. I'm here because I messed up, Taylor. I was trying to protect you, and I did it the wrong way. I didn't give you a say, and I didn't think it through. But the thing is, I love you, and I want to marry you and spend the rest of my life with you. I knew that then, and I know it a whole lot more now, but I didn't know what to do, so I fucked everything up because I was terrified something bad would happen to you. But I would risk everything to be with you, and you deserve to make that same choice. So whatever you decide—and maybe you've already decided and I'm making an ass out of myself—you should have your say."

He let out an enormous breath. "I think that was everything, although it was a lot more eloquent when I planned it out on the drive."

She must have been holding her breath the whole time, too, because she was getting lightheaded. Taylor almost dropped the coffee cup on the poor dogs as she clasped her hand over her lips, struggling for emotional control. She didn't even know if she was laughing or crying, but something was coming out of her mouth. Her eyes too. God, she was leaking her emotions everywhere.

Josh rubbed his neck. "Just so we're clear, I want you back if you still want me. I'm not actually asking you to marry me—yet. Please don't panic."

There, that noise was definitely a laugh. A somewhat hysterical one, but a laugh. "Okay."

"I'm just saying I'd put a bit more effort into it if I was officially asking you to marry me. More than bringing you a double espresso."

Had she really believed she could avoid a messy airport scene? She was a disaster—sniffling, and crying, and she was positive that half-asleep people had taken out their phones and were recording them.

And she didn't care. She didn't care one damn bit.

Her hands shook so badly Taylor had to set the coffee cup down. "Well, you wouldn't have to bring me more than a coffee for me to say yes, just so you know. If you ever do feel like asking, I mean."

"Really?" The relief that swept over Josh's face was the last thing Taylor saw before she threw her arms around him.

Dog leashes tangled around her legs as he pulled her closer, until she was confined in a knot of arms and huskies and everything wonderful. Taylor squeezed her eyes shut, trying futilely to stanch the tears flowing over Josh's shirt. With her ear pressed against him, she could hear his heart beating, and it raced like her own. She could smell his skin, the lemongrass scent that was all him, one that never failed to liquefy her insides. She was a gooey mess, certain only his grip and the desperate way she clung to him were keeping her upright.

Somewhere nearby, people applauded.

Obviously, the people spying on them weren't from Helen.

WITH THE RELIEF that shuddered through him, Josh could have collapsed to the concrete, but somehow he managed to remain on his feet. The look Taylor had initially given him when he finished his speech had him bracing for the worst, which was quite a feat considering he'd been running on nothing but wild hope since last night when he realized what he had to do. When he mentally replayed his verbal onslaught, though, her response was no wonder. Had he really told her he wanted to marry her? Idiot. It was true, but first he was trying to get her back, not scare her off. If the idea of it hadn't been so pathetic, he would have written down his speech.

But it didn't matter. It didn't matter at all because she was in his arms, and he couldn't think of anything beyond her. He was sure she was crying into his chest, and he threaded his fingers through her hair, pressed her so tightly against him that he feared he might break her ribs. The familiar scent of her shampoo, the slope of her hip beneath his hand—everything about her filled him with so much warmth it was like he hadn't realized how cold he'd been before. Cold and empty, and he never wanted to feel that way again, so he would never let go.

"I need you back, Taylor. Permanently." He was vaguely aware that people had started watching them, but there was nothing he could do about it. He couldn't even follow her into the terminal because he had the dogs with him. The best he could manage for privacy was to whisper in her ear, and that wasn't so bad at all because he didn't have to release her then. "I'd hate not having a winter, but I'll move to L.A. with you if that's what you want. Just tell me where you want to go, and I'll go with you."

Sniffling, Taylor raised her head from his shoulder. "I thought you loved Helen."

"Parts of it." The town had definitely lost some of its appeal in recent weeks. "But I love you more than I love any place. And believe me, I've lived in a lot of places. None of them can compare. Wherever you go, that will be my home if you let me come with you."

There was no question anymore that she was crying. Fat drops rolled down her cheeks as Taylor raised her head, and Josh realized his own eyes were misty as well.

Taylor took an unsteady breath. "It's convenient then that I've decided I'm not leaving Helen. My mother pointed out something to me over the weekend. She told me I needed to stop rebelling by doing things I don't want to do, that rebelling should be about doing what you want to do. Well, this is what I want. I want you. I want my hometown. And I want to rub my presence and our relationship in our families' faces until they have no recourse but to drown their agony in cheap liquor every night just like I drowned mine in chocolate after they broke us up. I'm not running away, and I won't let your family chase you out. I need to return to L.A. to take care of some things, but I turned down the job. I'm moving back to Helen."

Now he understood exactly why Taylor had gaped at him after his meandering speech. Josh was positive he wore the same expression on his face that she had. He'd heard her words but it was taking his heart a few seconds to let them sink in. He wanted to believe too badly to trust his ears.

So while the rest of him caught up to the best news he'd ever heard, he kissed her, unable to care that people were watching. Kissed her like he'd just succeeded at the scariest dare of his entire life, and possibly he had. She tasted of coffee and cinnamon and sunlight in the middle of December. It was going to be hell letting her get on the plane, even if only temporarily, and he still hadn't told her what Kelsey had done for them.

"You have no idea how much I love you, Taylor Lipin," Josh whispered to quiet applause from the terminal.

"Hopefully as much as I love you, Josh Krane who is technically a Porter."

32

⚬——————⚬

THREE WEEKS LATER, Taylor stepped out into the Anchorage air, dragging her suitcase behind her. It had been
a busy and sad trip back to L.A. Busy because she'd had
to pack up her life and arrange for movers to transport the
past ten years three thousand miles to her new-old home.
And sad because she was leaving friends like Stacy behind. But now that Stacy knew she had internet access
and cell phone service in her quirky hometown, they
could stay in touch. One day she might even convince her
friend to visit if she got over her fear of bears.

Taylor had texted her ride that she'd arrived once the
plane touched down, and she heard the greeting committee
before she saw the familiar Jeep waiting for her. A trio of
huskies clamored for her attention at the window as she
approached. Then she lost sight of the dogs as their owner
was in front of her, and she pressed her face into his neck
as he wrapped his arms around her. Taylor wasn't sure who
held who tighter, but it was the happiest she'd felt in weeks.

"You didn't have to take a day off to come pick me
up," she said.

"Like hell I didn't. It's been twenty-three days since I last saw you. One more hour might have done me in." Josh kissed her, first with a tender wonder, like he couldn't believe she was back. Then hungrier, as though determined to make up for lost time. Taylor's travel stress melted away, replaced by a burning need that wouldn't be satisfied until she could hold him and kiss with far fewer clothes on.

Until they were home.

And she was home. Never mind the two-and-a-half-hour drive that awaited. Home smelled like lemongrass soap. It was perfect.

Apparently recalling they were in public, Josh finally pulled away. Flushed and giddy, Taylor kissed his cheek and let him load her luggage into the Jeep. "I think you could have survived."

"Okay, fine. Maybe I could have, but those guys couldn't." He motioned to the dogs. "Every time I said your name, they went nuts. No one likes having a member of their pack missing."

She grinned. "I'm a part of the pack, huh?"

"Like you didn't know that."

She did, but she wouldn't get tired of hearing it. Just like she wouldn't get tired of Josh's kisses or the enthusiastic greetings she got from the furrier pack members when she climbed into the vehicle.

"All right, guys." Josh made soothing gestures at the dogs. "Calm down. She's back."

The dogs settled down, although their tails suggested that calm might have been too much to ask for, and Josh pulled out of the airport.

Taylor stuck her sunglasses on, relaxing into the seat. "Any need to drop the bomb since we last checked in five hours ago?"

She couldn't believe it, but Kelsey had given Josh a

video of his uncle confessing to vandalizing the Bay Song. Apparently when Josh had confronted his uncle, his cousin had recorded it. According to Josh, Kelsey had given it to him only after he came to his senses and realized he'd made a mistake by suggesting Taylor leave town. Kelsey had figured Josh didn't deserve the ammunition if he wasn't willing to risk everything without it.

Taylor suspected she and Kelsey would never be close, but it was a good step forward, even if she'd only done it because she cared about Josh.

The best part was that Josh hadn't needed to use the video as a threat yet. His uncle didn't know he had it.

And, of course, the video would help keep only one side of the feud in line, but Taylor had reason to hope her family would be on their best behavior initially, as thrilled as they were about her returning. Her grandmother, perhaps, aside.

"All's been quiet on the hometown front," Josh said. "But we're about two hours from finding out if it'll stay that way."

"It probably won't. Not forever."

Josh reached across the Jeep and took her left hand in his right. "It doesn't have to be forever."

"And we have a pack." Not just them and his dogs, but Kelsey and her dogs, and Kevin and his fiancé, and her sister and a cat.

Well, maybe the cat.

Josh gave her fingers a squeeze. "True. No feud can beat that. I love you too much to let it happen."

"And I love you." Taylor gripped his hand tighter, for the first time able to relax and smile as they headed toward the battleground she called home.

ACKNOWLEDGMENTS

Although I might have written the words in this story, the book owes its existence to an awful lot of people. It's practically guaranteed that I'm going to forget some of them, and for that I apologize. I first started playing with the bones of this story several years ago, and I don't always keep the most organized notes. I appreciate everyone who helped me get to the point where I'm writing these acknowledgements, whether their help was with the writing itself or with emotional support.

First and foremost, I need to thank my agent, Rebecca Strauss, who championed Taylor and Josh from their very different beginning, and whose fantastic editorial eye, ceaseless cheerleading, patient guidance, and hand-holding got me here. I truly could not have done this without her. I'm forever grateful to Sarah Blumenstock at Berkley for giving me a chance and for helping me take this story and make it so much better than it was—not to mention sharing adorable husky photos! Also thank you to all the Berkley staff working behind the scenes who were instrumental in making my little husky romance into an actual book.

Thank you to Jennifer Walkup and Jezz De Silva for their notes on an earlier version of this story. This version might be virtually unrecognizable from the one they read, but it wouldn't be here without them. And thank you to Kell Andrews, R. M. Clark, Bryn Greenwood, Colby Marshall, Jenna Nelson, and Jennifer Walkup (again) for their feedback and/or brainstorming when I needed it the most. And thank you to all the Y-Nots for their advice, assistance, and general camaraderie that helps keep me sane in this business. On the note of writing groups and writer friends, I also have to send out a bootay shake to all the members of Purgatory. Sometimes I can't believe how many of us are still hanging in there, but I'd have quit years ago without them.

I owe so much to my parents, who instilled a love of books in me, even though I think they often wished I was as interested in real people as I was in imaginary ones. I still don't understand why when imaginary ones are so much better.

And finally, thank you to my husband for his willingness to be ignored in the evenings so I can write, and for his ability to humor me when I go off on a tangent about something I'm researching. One day, I will write the sprawling sci-fi epic he longs for. Until then, I just promise not to bring home any surprise puppies in the name of research.

Don't miss Kelsey and Ian's story in

PAWS AND PREJUDICE

coming Summer 2021 from Jove!

IAN RESTED HIS head against the doorframe, his pulse racing. He'd just slammed a door on Wallace Porter's daughter. That was, he was 90 percent certain the woman on the other side of the door was Wallace's daughter. He hadn't gotten a good enough look at her to notice a family resemblance, but no other women were supposed to be stopping by today.

No, he'd barely glanced at the woman because his attention had immediately been drawn to the three dogs around her legs. Big dogs. Not huge dogs, but dogs that looked like they were the size that could jump on you and tear out your throat.

Logic informed Ian that those dogs were unlikely to do any such thing, but his brain paid little heed to logic in the face of three large dogs. They had a wolfish look to them too. That probably meant they were huskies or part huskies, but it really didn't make a difference. He simply did not like large dogs of any breed.

Actually, Ian did not like any dogs, and to be fair, it was the dogs that had started it. He'd been three when one had jumped on him, and that was all he remembered—a large furry object zooming in for the kill and knocking him to the ground to feast. The dog had probably not been trying to kill him, but in reality it made no difference to the irrational part of his brain, which from that day forward considered all dogs to be furry killing machines. Even those little fluffy ones with the loud barks that everyone else thought were so cute.

Ian refused to be intimidated by those ankle biters, but the dogs this woman had were definitely potential throat biters. And they were not entering his brewery.

Shit. *Shit.* This was embarrassing on a personal level, not to mention problematic on a business one if that was in fact Wallace Porter's daughter outside. He'd never have asked for writing help, but Wallace had assured him that his daughter did stuff like this all the time and wasn't busy right now, and Ian could really use the assistance.

The woman with the dogs banged once on the door, hard enough for it to vibrate and make Ian raise his head. "Um, hello?"

He thought he heard her add "What the hell?" under her breath, and he supposed he couldn't blame her. He'd acted like a first-class schmuck.

An excuse—that's what he needed. Ian's pulse had started lowering, but it rose again in desperation as he swept his gaze over the brewery's still-under-construction tasting room. He'd been installing shelves behind where the bar would eventually be, and a variety of tools—a drill, screws, a level, and more—were scattered about the area. If experience had taught him anything, it was that dogs could not contain the need to chase things. They smelled fear and charged it down. He would try to keep his distance, and they would home in on him like four-legged heat-seeking missiles. That meant a dirty floor was a dangerous floor. Excuse found.

Ian cleared his throat. "Sorry. Are you Kelsey Porter?" That was the name of Wallace's daughter, right? He didn't need to do anything else embarrassing like get it wrong.

"Yeah."

"Right, sorry again." Bracing himself, Ian cracked the door an inch. By keeping his focus on Kelsey's face, he could avoid seeing the dogs. It wasn't ideal—his nerves were still quite aware of their presence—but it helped.

So did focusing on her face because—wow—Kelsey was cute. Her blond hair was pulled back, making it impossible to miss her big blue eyes and the couple freckles that dotted her nose. She had the sort of face that sang of sunshine and innocence, but whispered that its owner was capable of much dirtier things in the bedroom.

That sort of perky-cheerleader pretty had never been Ian's thing, but something about Kelsey told him he'd make an exception in her case. Possibly it was her lips, which made it clear that the perky-cheerleader look was a lie. They were twisted in obvious annoyance with him.

Unfortunately, that was understandable and the reminder kicked Ian out of his temporarily lustful state of mind. "You're welcome to come in, but you shouldn't bring the dogs. It's a construction zone in here."

Those big blue eyes narrowed at him, but they never quite met the threshold for being called icy. "Seriously?"

"Sorry." He was a broken record with this apologizing, but if he got rid of the dogs, it would be worth it.

Kelsey sighed in a far more dramatic fashion than Ian felt the situation deserved. "Fine. I'll go take them back to the car."

Ian watched her turn away long enough to make sure

she really was heading toward the unfamiliar SUV—and okay, also long enough to appreciate the way her ass looked in those jeans—then he ducked back inside. Time to make good on his not-quite lie.

Quickly, he scattered a few screws around the floor and took a broom to the pile of sawdust he'd so meticulously swept up a couple hours ago. For good measure, he also carried the circular saw from the back room into the main room, and set it on top of the sawhorses sitting in the corner. In a few seconds, he'd uncleaned the room and made it hazardous to energetic animals.

Two steps forward, one step backward. That seemed typical for how getting the brewery off the ground was going. He and Micah had run into more roadblocks than any reasonable person could have expected. Sure, there were the normal *It takes how long to ship that to Alaska?* kind of delays. But there were also delays that Ian could ascribe no other reasoning to than malice.

He'd just finished wiping his dusty hands off on his jeans when he heard Kelsey's footsteps on the stairs. Crisis averted. Barely.

"You can come on in."

"Thanks." For someone who looked so sweet she could pack an impressive amount of bitter in one syllable. Kelsey reminded Ian of that coffee stout he'd once made that was too cloying on the initial taste and a bit like drinking diesel fuel in the aftertaste. Not every recipe that was good in theory worked in practice. Not on the first try anyway.

On the note of second tries, Ian introduced himself. Kelsey's skin was pleasingly cool, and he had to fight the urge to clasp her hand more tightly. If he had to guess, she was nearly a foot shorter than him, and that difference in size made her hand fit perfectly in his. He rather liked the thought of that too much, so he pushed it as far into the back of his mind as he could. It wasn't too difficult when Kelsey continued to scowl at him.

"Sorry about slamming the door on you," Ian said, trying once more to smooth away her expression. "I was worried the dogs might dart inside and hurt their paws."

If anything, Kelsey's scowl deepened. "My dogs are very well behaved. They don't dart. If I told them to stay, they would."

Okay then. Given the way she glared, Ian was doubly glad he'd made her keep the dogs outside. She'd probably have told them to go for his jugular.

He'd make one more attempt since he didn't like getting off on the wrong foot with someone. "Good to know for the future. Can I get you a drink?"

"I'd rather you get to the point. I don't like leaving my dogs in the car for too long."

Fine. That seemed fair, and besides, he could take a hint.

Ian started to ask another—to the point—question, and that's when he saw the pin attached to Kelsey's purse. Before her dogs and before her face (or ass)—that's what he should have noticed. That pin likely explained so much about her attitude. Although the Save Helen Society had been a thorn in his side for months, it was only recently that Ian had discovered the group had a name as well as a mission.

Ironically, he didn't even disagree with their mission. But like dogs, the Save Helen Society was fine in theory, but in practice it was a massive pain in his ass. Part of what Ian loved about this town was its size and unique charms, and he didn't want it overrun with chain stores and restaurants or bland housing developments either. But while that might be the SHS's ostensible goal, it seemed like they'd taken their ire beyond it and were aiming it at any and all outsiders—him and the brewery included.

For no reason, Ian had had perfectly-put-together permits denied or simply held up at city hall until contractors became unavailable. Zoning issues that should have been completely straightforward had been questioned, forcing him and Micah to petition for them. And they'd been outright told by people on the town council that Helen was no place for a brewery.

The first time a permit had been "misplaced" Ian had assumed it was a mistake. The fourth time, he assumed it was one person with an anti-alcohol agenda. It was only after meeting the mayor's mother herself that Ian learned she'd been spearheading a group—the SHS—to protest any and all new development.

Well, screw that. Everything he and Micah had done was entirely legal, and no matter what a small band of xenophobic townspeople thought, most of Helen was clearly excited about the brewery. And Ian was excited to open it.

Excited and determined to make it a success. Also far past the point of believing he could make this process go more easily by being nice to the zealots. Even if the zealot in front of him was supposed to be helping him and happened to look damn good in a pair of tight jeans. Kelsey Porter had made her feelings abundantly clear in one pouty-lipped scowl.

Ian motioned to the pin. "You a member?"

Kelsey seemed confused for a second as her eyes dropped to her purse. "Oh, that. I'm not much of a joiner, but I appreciate the sentiment. This town is getting too big, too many new people moving in. No offense."

Oy. Her tone clearly intended offense. How was he

supposed to trust her to do a write-up of the brewery? What had Wallace been thinking?

God, he wished Micah was here to deal with this crap. All Ian wanted to do was brew and sell some beer. Micah was the people person, the sales guy. He could fake a smile and sincerity like no one's business. Ian usually had no trouble getting along with people so he didn't need to try. Everything about Kelsey, however, was putting him on edge. Blame it on her dogs maybe. That had made him twitchy to begin with. Toss in that her sweet face was having an unwelcome impact on his lower body, while at the same time he wanted to kick her pert ass out the door for interfering with the one goal he had in life, and yeah, he was on edge.

Since he didn't feel like lying and pretending that no offense had been taken, Ian didn't bother to fake a smile. Small talk was over if it had ever begun. He had to get Kelsey out of here so he could get back to work. Neither she nor the SHS were going to get in his way.

"So what do I need to do for you? Besides get out of town, that is?"

Kelsey raised an eyebrow. "I didn't suggest it."

"Your pin did the talking."

"You sound defensive."

"When one side goes on the offensive, being defensive is smart."

Kelsey's face lit up in an expression that Ian might have considered cute under other circumstances. "You know, usually I have to open my mouth before people call me offensive. What a good little pin this is." She stroked it. "I've leveled up if I can hurt someone's feelings without saying a word."

Ian grabbed one of the screws sitting on his makeshift plywood table, and spun it around to keep his hands busy. It was either that or start futzing with the drill, and that seemed kind of violent. "I don't recall suggesting my feelings were hurt. I promise you, they're not. The brewery is open for business even if the tasting room isn't completed and the website is unfinished. I feel very good about that actually, and we're not going anywhere."

That froze Kelsey's cruel smile in place. "I'm sure. So about the website?"

"Never mind. I'll handle it." Writing something as short as a five-paragraph *About* section would cost him hours of stress, but he'd do it. Too bad Micah hated writing even more than he did.

"I can do it." Kelsey crossed her arms. "I told my father I would. I just need you to give me information, and to tell me what exactly you want it to say."

He wondered if he could actually trust her, but Ian supposed nothing would be posted without him reading it, so it wasn't much of a risk. "My family's brewery has a short *History*-slash-*About* section on their site. I wanted to include something like that on ours."

"Your family down in Florida?"

Wallace must have told her where he was from. "Yeah. My aunt and uncle started it. I worked for them."

"Explain to me why anyone who lived in Florida would want to move here?"

Ian sighed. It was a fair question and certainly not the first time he'd heard it, though maybe the first time he'd heard it asked so disdainfully. But the answer was complicated, and there was no way he was about to share it with Kelsey.

Before he could decide what sort of nonanswer to give her, she kept going, "Tell me it's not because you have some obsession with a book or something."

He could have choked on the bland answer he'd been

settling on. The dogs, the SHS pin, and now this. It was like she knew exactly what pressure points to poke to cause him pain.

Yes, he did love *The Call of the Wild*, or at least the illustrated children's version of it his mother used to read to him before she died. Was it ironic because of his dog issues? Sure. But Ian associated the story with warmth and love and everything exciting. It had been instrumental in him begging his grandparents to take him to Alaska when he was younger, and that trip had cemented his love of the untamed, snowy north.

Knowing Kelsey would scoff at him for it increased Ian's frustration with her a thousandfold.

The screw's sharp edges dug into his fingers, but hopefully the pain kept these thoughts off his face. "I'd visited Helen before, and when my family discussed opening another brewery, some place as far from Florida as possible sounded perfect."

There was some truth to that, more than Kelsey deserved, but he'd have to explain for the website regardless, so this didn't feel like he was giving up any secrets. The fact that his aunt and uncle had been skeptical of letting him open the brewery in Helen wasn't something that would be going in any PR materials. They'd been thinking of a location in Florida, or at the very farthest, Boston, which was at least still on the East Coast. Ian was certain their reasoning had been that it would be easier for them to help out that way if needed. His brewery and their brewery had different names, and he was fully in charge of this brewery's recipes and production, but financially, the two businesses were linked. If he screwed up and couldn't pay off the loans, he'd cost his aunt and uncle a lot of money and possibly hurt their brewery's reputation.

"I grew up in Massachusetts," Ian added. "I'm familiar with the concept of cold, so don't worry about finding me frozen like a Popsicle one day."

Kelsey's lips twitched in a manner Ian couldn't decipher. "I wasn't worried."

"I'm shocked." He glared at her, daring her to toss another punch.

She glared back.

The staring contest that followed probably only lasted a second, but it felt to Ian like an eternity as he debated whether it was worth being the one to break it so he could get back to work. It should have been an easy call. Who got into staring contests as an adult anyway? But Kelsey was absolutely infuriating, and the fact that she looked hot while being so was doubly infuriating.

Ian had no clue what malicious thoughts were running through her faux-perky head, but Kelsey broke out of the moment at the same time he did, and they talked over each other.

"Is there anything—"

"I need to go."

Relief swept through Ian. "Okay. How will I send you the brewery information?"

She shrugged. "I'll look at what's on your family brewery's site and email you questions."

Email sounded good to him. The less time spent with Kelsey and her dogs, the better.

Ready to find
your next great read?

Let us help.

Visit prh.com/nextread